To Have
— AND TO —
HARLEY

regina cole

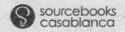

sourcebooks
casablanca

Published by Sourcebooks Casablanca, an imprint of Sourcebooks, Inc.
P.O. Box 4410, Naperville, Illinois 60567-4410
(630) 961-3900
Fax: (630) 961-2168
sourcebooks.com

Printed and bound in the United States of America.
OPM 10 9 8 7 6 5 4 3 2 1

To Mary. You pulled my cookies out of the fire time and time again. Can't wait for the next one!

chapter
ONE

THERE MIGHT HAVE BEEN A BETTER WAY FOR TREY Harding to get his client's backdated child support. But pounding the hell out of Vinnie was so, so satisfying.

"Sorry," Vinnie mumbled against the dirty floor of the motel room where they'd found him. "Didn't know she—"

"You didn't know she what?" Trey grabbed the bastard by his collar and slammed him against the wall.

"Easy, Boss," Wolf, his right hand, grunted. "You'll shove him straight through if you're not careful."

"They can put it on his bill. He's got all kinds of cash, don't you, Vinnie?" Trey jerked his head toward the pile of Baggies on the flimsy TV table. Vinnie had been packaging to sell.

"I don't have anything!"

"Lie." Trey squeezed the guy's throat a little, just to get the point across. "Want to try again?"

Vinnie clawed at the hand holding him up, his legs flailing in midair.

Trey's vision went red. This waste of space was

holding out on them. He'd seen Vinnie down on Trade Street, seen the bankroll he'd flashed at Cherry Ice, the strip club downtown. When Lynn had begged them to hunt Vinnie down, Trey and the rest of the Shadows had agreed that this job was pro bono, though they usually were paid handsomely for this type of shakedown.

But Lynn was a mother trying to support her family. As the kid of a mom who'd dumped her baby in a gas station bathroom, Trey was all about helping Lynn out.

Enjoying the gig was just a bonus.

"Boss? Boss, he's turning blue." A big, meaty hand landed on his shoulder, and Trey bared his teeth in irritation but let the useless meat sack hit the gritty carpet.

Vinnie coughed, moaning as he clutched at his throat.

Trey crossed his arms over his chest, his leather jacket pulling tight over his shoulders with the movement. "Go through his bags. Check his pockets."

Wolf, Jameson, and the other two Shadows who'd ridden along for this mission complied. Trey didn't move from that spot, standing there and staring down at the bastard who'd left a young single mother high and dry.

She'd been saving up to get her and her kids out of this North Carolina backwater town. But now she needed every dime she could bring home just to feed her kids.

"Got it," Wolf said, returning to Trey's side.

"Now," Trey said, squatting beside Vinnie, whose cheeks were splotchy and red, "you're going to listen to me, and you're going to listen good. I'm not going to kill you."

"Oh, thank you," Vinnie said, his voice thin as he clutched at Trey's sleeve. "I—"

"For now," Trey interrupted, shaking the hand off. He stood again, forcing Vinnie to look up and up and up.

Glaring at the gutless worm, whose features had gone suitably pale at the threat, Trey smiled a not-very-nice smile. "If you ever screw over Lynn or those kids again? I will personally see to it that your ass is carved into seventeen pieces and force-fed to those lowlifes you call friends. We clear?"

Vinnie nodded, pressing himself back against the stained wallpaper.

Trey glanced back at his allies. "We're out."

Heavy footfalls indicated they followed as he shoved his way out of the hotel room, but he didn't look around. He didn't need to.

Wolf would be right behind him. If he'd had such a thing as a best friend, it was dark, sinister, and utterly dangerous Wolf. Jameson would be next. He was a military hard-ass with haunted eyes and a helluva dark side. Nobody messed with Jameson unless they wanted to go home in a body bag. All of the Iron Shadows were that way. They were together because they all had something society found unappealing. They worked well together. Trey could count on them.

They were the only family he had, and he was damn proud of the fact that they'd chosen him to lead them.

A thin girl with greasy hair and baggy clothes started into the hallway. She looked their way and backed the hell up.

Five dudes in bike leathers with tattoos and pissed-off attitudes apparently weren't the type she wanted to hang with tonight.

Trey shoved through the doors from the stinking, run-down lobby, glad to be in the cold of the fresh air. He slung his leg over his Ducati ST. Wolf paused by Trey's handlebars.

"Ruby's?"

Trey nodded.

Bike engines roared, and Trey led the way out of the motel's postage-stamp-size lot and down the rural highway, his gang of brothers behind him.

North Carolina winters could be cold as balls, but at least they weren't the bitter freeze that he'd endured as a kid back in Michigan. The February wind buffeted his leathers, cutting his cheeks like a fistful of knives as he opened up the accelerator.

The speed felt good. No, the *hurt* felt good. Distracted him from the thoughts that were threatening to eat him alive.

Lynn was a good woman, and she'd been trying to do her best for her kids. Trey envied them, in a way. Sure, it was a tough life. That single-wide trailer had definitely seen better days, and there wasn't a lot of room for fun in their threadbare budget.

But she and the kids had each other. And until the Shadows, that was something Trey'd never had.

Almost half an hour later, Trey's headlights swung around the corner into the parking lot at Ruby's. The rickety old honky-tonk was made for the blue-collar set. Ask for anything other than beer, straight-up whiskey, or Jack and Coke, and you'd get a hairy eyeball.

It belonged to the Shadows. At least, as much as any establishment could belong to anyone who didn't actually pay the mortgage.

Trey cut his engine on the small concrete pad by the back door, and four other bikes filed in. One by one, engines silenced.

"I thought that loser was going to piss himself," Ace

said, laughing as he swung his leg over the bike saddle. "I haven't had that much fun since we tailed that asswipe who was dating the porn star, you remember?"

Dean rolled his eyes. "How could we forget? You hooked up with her after the fact and wouldn't stop talking about it for months."

Ace rolled his hips as Trey and the rest of the crew walked by on the way to the door. "Who wouldn't want this?"

"Can it, Ace. I'm not in the mood."

Ace fell silent at Trey's words and hustled to the door with the rest of them.

Trey's skin was too tight and his muscles twitchy as he pushed through the heavy wooden doors into the darkness of Ruby's. A few people were in there — construction workers, truckers, a working girl or two. The crowd was pretty light; after all, it was a Tuesday. But of course, some new clueless wonder had set up camp at the Shadows' corner table, a blond twentysomething sitting on his lap.

"Hey, y'all." Ginger had a tray on the flat of her palm, a pitcher of beer in the other. "Oh, shoot. I'll clear your table."

Before Trey could tell her not to worry about it, she'd hurried away to deliver her drinks.

"That woman's going to work herself into an early grave," Jameson muttered, and Trey couldn't help but agree. With her sister, Lynn, having delivered a baby only four weeks ago, and Ginger the only paycheck going into the household, she'd been making double time for months now. The strain was beginning to show on her face.

She'd been hoping to drop back to shorter hours to help Lynn with the new baby and the older kids, but Vinnie's disappearing act had forced her to change her plans to make financial ends meet.

The waitress bent down, and with a smile and an efficient manner, had the interlopers out of the Shadows' table and the surface clean and waiting for them. She pulled out Trey's chair as he approached.

"Here." Trey reached into his jacket and retrieved the money they'd found in the motel room. He hadn't counted it, but there was obviously more there than she'd been missing.

He didn't give a rat's ass. Vinnie had put the family through hell, and they deserved every dime.

"Oh my God," she said, eyes widening as she took in the sight of the money. "That's too... How did you—"

"Take it home to Lynn and the kids," Trey said, pressing the money into her hand. "He won't be late again."

Ginger bit her lip. "Thank—"

"Don't. Just...don't."

She tucked the money into her apron and hurried off toward the bar.

"Damn, Boss," Ace said as he sank into his usual chair at their big, round table. "You could have at least let her thank you."

"No need." Trey sat down as Jameson headed to the bar to get their drinks.

The tabletop was mottled and scarred from years of abuse. Who knew how many games of cards, drinks, and pissed-drunk assholes had beaten the hell out of this surface?

His insides felt like that. Pockmarked and scarred and

too chewed-up to be useful. His twenty-nine years of life had more than left their mark.

"You okay?"

Trey hiked an eyebrow at Wolf, who then looked away with a sniff.

"Sorry, Boss."

Accepting the beer that Jameson dropped at the table, Trey sighed. He was being a dick, and it wasn't Wolf's fault.

It was his own.

"What's that guy doing in here?"

At Ace's question, Trey looked up.

There, silhouetted in the doorway, was a man wearing dark cargo pants and a form-fitting gray sweater. His haircut was short, almost military. He didn't look familiar.

"Who is it?"

Ace curled his hand around his beer mug, frowning hard. "He's a private investigator. Came knocking on my door last year when we roughed up that asshole bookie who cheated Flash."

Trey's hackles rose. Why was this PI on his turf, and who was he looking for?

He stood, intending to head over there and figure out what was doing, when the guy looked his way. Their gazes locked, and the PI nodded, walking toward him.

Trey just folded his arms and waited.

"You Trey Harding?" the PI asked. His gaze raked Trey up and down.

Not flicking an eyelash, Trey responded, "Who wants to know?"

The PI slapped a paper down in front of him. Trey didn't look down, just waited for the question to be answered. "That'll tell you all you need."

"You can't answer the question?"

"You can't read?"

Trey's hand shot out and grabbed the smart-ass by the throat. "You want to play around a little, or you want me to take you outside and show you why you need to watch your mouth?"

The PI just smiled. "Your mother's going to love you."

Trey's blood ran cold, and his fingers went numb. He dropped the PI, hardly daring to breathe.

"My...who?"

HH

Bethany Jernigan's smile was as brittle as a ninety-five-year-old's bones, but it didn't crack.

"I'm sorry, what did you say?"

The teenager flipped her hair over her shoulder and rolled her eyes. "I said I'm leaving early today. I've got stuff to do."

Bethany could actually feel her blood pressure rising in the thudding of her pulse in her ears. Mindful of the shoppers who were milling around the women's shoes just a few yards away, Bethany kept her voice pitched low.

"Tiffany, you can't just leave early whenever you want. We've had this discussion multiple times before. In fact, your last two write-ups were for exactly this."

The girl shrugged. "Uncle Ernest doesn't care."

Bethany's teeth ground audibly. "I know you got this job because of your family connection, but I'm the manager. It's my responsibility to ensure all our employees—"

"Blow it out your ass," Tiffany snapped and then flounced away.

"Wow."

The unfamiliar voice made Bethany turn, and she was mortified to realize that a customer had heard Tiffany's outburst.

"I'm so sorry. Did you need help finding anything?"

"No thanks," the woman said with a smirk and walked away.

Un-freaking-believable. Bethany had had it. She marched past displays with vibrant red and pink hearts declaring their last-minute Valentine's Day sales. Her office was at the back of the store, just past the security station where a uniformed guard was seated in front of a bank of monitors. She nodded to him and shut the door.

Her desk was littered with sales reports, employee schedules, and time cards from the archaic system corporate refused to replace with anything more modern. Rounding the desk, she slumped in the relic that passed for her office chair.

Fingers stabbing the phone's keypad like it owed her money, Bethany dialed Ernest Junes, the district manager…and Tiffany's uncle.

"Junes," the voice on the other end of the line snapped.

"Mr. Junes, this is Bethany Jernigan."

"Yeah, the top shelf. Don't give me any of that cheap stuff."

Bethany's nails stabbed into her palm, and she drew a deep breath in through her nose as she grabbed the nearest pen and started doodling giant, emphatic *X*s on the scrap of paper in front of her.

"Mr. Junes, this is Bethany Jernigan," she started again. "Store manager of—"

"Yeah, yeah, I know who you are."

The background noise got even louder, music and laughter forcing Bethany to turn down the volume on her handset. "Is this a bad time?"

"No, no, just a business lunch. What can I do for you?"

"I need to talk to you about an employee termination."

The frown was easy to hear in his voice. "Jernigan, why do I care about that? It's supposed to be your responsibility. I've got much more important things to be doing. You handle—"

"It's your niece Tiffany."

"What?"

Suddenly the background noise faded. Bethany couldn't relax though. She was pretty sure she knew where this conversation was going.

"What do you mean, my niece is being terminated?"

So she told him. She outlined the many written warnings Tiffany had gotten, the attitude she'd thrown, and the final insult in front of a customer. Any other employee would have been out months ago. But Bethany had held off because of the family relationship.

She was good at her job. She'd started at the store when she was just a teenager, stocking at first, and then making her way up to department manager. She'd had to work hard to earn her degree in business while juggling her job at Hudson's, but she'd done it.

It wasn't that she'd always wanted to manage a department store. Far from it. But she'd wanted stability. And Hudson's had offered that. But with every passing day, she wondered if she'd made the right decision. The creeping dread every time she walked through the doors was becoming impossible to ignore.

And now…

"You can't fire her."

"But Mr. Junes, she's—"

"Did I stutter? I said you can't fire her."

"Sir, you're completely undermining my authority. How am I supposed to manage my employees when they see Tiffany getting special treatment? It's already caused a lot of grumbling, and—"

"I don't care. This is your responsibility, and if you go against my word here, you'll be replaced. Understand?"

Bethany's blood ran cold. "So you're saying if I fire Tiffany, even knowing her attendance problems and issues with authority, you'll fire me."

"That's it."

"Well, then get my pink slip ready, sir. I'm submitting her termination right now."

Bethany cut the call. The relief that cascaded over her was palpable.

She'd just effectively quit her job. And for some reason, it felt fabulous.

The upbeat song made Bethany hum along as she entered the restaurant. The rest of her day had been spent cleaning out her desk. As she'd expected, Mr. Junes had called back to bluster and yell and threaten. But Bethany had already checked out.

She'd put up with enough. It was time to figure out what she really wanted to do with her life.

"Bethy!"

At the sound of her nickname, Bethany turned. Sarah Yelverton, her best friend since seventh grade and almost-sister for nearly as long, waved vehemently. Her long, honey-gold curls bounced with the movement. Bethany smiled and walked over to the table in the corner where Sarah already had a bottle of wine waiting.

Sarah, who was attending pharmacy school up in Virginia, had fortunately come home in time for Bethany to unload her drama in person.

"So tell me all about it," Sarah said, pouring a glass of red for each of them.

"I quit. Well, I got fired. Well, it's a little of both." Bethany took a long sip of the rich wine while Sarah gasped.

"I thought you'd be there forever. They really didn't appreciate you enough. You poured your heart and soul into that place." Sarah shook her head mournfully.

Bethany bit her lip in consternation. "Well, that's not the reaction I was hoping for."

Sarah grinned. "I'm so proud of you." She lifted her glass. "Cheers."

With a soft clink, their glasses met, and they both drank to Bethany's new beginning.

As their wineglasses descended back to the tabletop, a glint caught Bethany's eye.

Sarah's left hand was adorned with…with…

"Holy crap," she gasped, grabbing Sarah's hand and turning it this way and that. The big, honking diamond on her ring finger was insanely gorgeous. "When did this happen?"

Sarah's cheeks pinkened, and she glanced away with a shy smile. "This morning. That's why I wanted to meet you out for dinner tonight. Bethany, I'm getting married!"

The mutual squeal of excitement earned them a couple of glances from nearby tables, but neither of them paid any attention.

Looking at her best friend's face as she excitedly told the story of her longtime boyfriend Mark's proposal, Bethany couldn't help but be swamped by emotion.

Mark was finishing his doctoral degree in Asheville, but they'd agreed to meet over Valentine's Day weekend back in their hometown. And at the lake where they'd met, back when they were both in high school, he'd taken her out for a romantic boat ride on icy waters and popped the question.

The way Sarah told it, it was perfect.

Of course Bethany was happy for her friend. Sarah had been more like a sister than a friend for far too many years, even convincing her parents to take Bethany in when her father passed away suddenly. Bethany would always be grateful for that. She had known more love and acceptance in their home than she could ever have dreamed possible.

But she couldn't help but be a little jealous. Sarah's fiancé, Mark, was sexy, kind, and head over heels for her. And Bethany—well, Bethany was perpetually single. After about a dozen Tinder dates gone wrong, she'd resigned herself to her singledom.

No matter what she did, she couldn't shake the notion that she was somehow being left behind.

"…hoping you'd help plan the wedding."

Bethany shook her head. "What?"

Sarah laughed. "I could tell by your glassy expression that you were getting overwhelmed. I know, I go overboard when I'm excited. But you know how Mom is. She's already bought out the wedding magazine section at the bookstore. She's been texting me pictures of flowers and dresses and hair all afternoon. I've got finals coming up, both Mark and I are so far away at school, and you're so much better than me at organizing events. After all, you did it for the store for years."

"But sales events aren't weddings." Bethany scratched her inner arm, desperate for any sensation to bring her back to reality. She couldn't be hearing this.

"Besides, you're at loose ends, right? I'll hire you as a wedding liaison. That way, there's no gap on your résumé while you search for a new position. Plus, you'll have some money to live off without messing up your savings, and you can run interference while Mom goes wedding bananas. I trust your judgment completely."

"You don't want to pick anything out?"

"Nope. Not the first flower, not the first dress. I want to run to the courthouse, but it'd break Mom's heart. Mark totally agrees. Come on, Bethy, will you plan our wedding? Please?"

Sarah fluttered her dusky eyelashes.

Bethany shook her head and gave a heavy sigh. "You're insane."

"So you'll do it?"

Bethany grabbed her wineglass and drained it, then snagged the bottle and poured another glassful. "Better get another bottle. I'm going to need alcoholic fortification if I'm planning a wedding with Mama Yelverton."

Sarah's whoop of joy and Bethany's groan of despair sounded at the same moment.

Bethany had somehow found herself planning her best friend's wedding.

Well…crap.

chapter
TWO

THE POUNDING OF HIS HEAD AND THE CHURNING OF his stomach had less to do with the mass quantities of alcohol he'd consumed than he would've presumed.

Even if he'd been drinking pure water, the hangover of discovering that his whole past was a lie would have been sickening enough.

Trey shook his head as he sat on the deck behind the house he'd bought when he became leader of the Shadows. His under-the-table private security gig—and Lars's flair with investments—had gained them enough capital to need a home base.

It was simple. An old stick-built shack, really, in a rural area of Durham County. But it was surrounded by woods. Solitude. And with Wolf's construction background, it was now in much better shape.

The coffee in his hand and the sun high overhead competed for control of Trey's headache. He squinted as he leaned his head back against the Adirondack chair.

His mother. *Mom*. For so long that person had been a demon in his head.

But now? Now?

The memory of just two nights ago sucked him in, and he replayed it in his head as he'd done almost incessantly ever since.

~HH~

Trey thumped his fist on the table, the loud sound drawing more than a few sets of eyes his way.

"Ginger," he barked, and the waitress immediately came over. "I need somewhere private."

"Sure. You can use the office," she said, her gaze darting from Trey to the stranger and back. "Let me know if you need anything else."

Trey gave her a terse nod and beckoned to Wolf and the stranger. The trio walked through the beat-up door marked "Office—Employees Only."

Trey didn't pay a lick of attention to the junk strewn around, the boxes of liquor, the tacky decor that Ruby had placed about the room like a tchotchke-obsessed Martha Stewart. He rounded the desk and sat down, Wolf sticking to his side like a huge, bearded guard dog.

"Say your piece," Trey growled. "And no bullshit."

The investigator smoothed his wrinkled pants with a quick motion. "Yeah. No problem."

He looked around for somewhere to sit, but Trey was in the only available chair. With a shrug, the PI pulled over a stack of empty plastic egg crates and plopped down. "I was hired to find you."

"How do you know it's me you're looking for?" Trey wasted no time.

"Because you were a suspect in a violent crime four years ago."

Trey sat bolt upright. "I had nothing to do with that murder. I was in the same club that night, but I was nowhere near that fight when it went down. The evidence didn't lie."

The guy held up his hands. "Not saying it did. Even though you weren't charged with anything, your DNA was taken and put into a state database. You came up as a match when we did our search."

Sagging back into the chair, Trey felt curiously light-headed.

"Why does she want to see me now?" Suddenly the fight seeped back into his veins. He launched out of the chair, bracing his palms on the desk and sending a cup of pens flying to the floor. Gritting his teeth, he stared the investigator down. "She abandoned me. She left me in a gas station bathroom stall, with nothing but a ragged blanket, a dirty shirt, and a spare diaper. Why does she suddenly give a damn now?"

"Because you were kidnapped."

Trey's elbows were locked, which was the only reason he didn't fall back into the chair again. Wolf had moved closer to the desk, and his right hand's presence reminded Trey that this was reality, not just another of those stupid dreams he'd had over and over. The ones where Mommy Dearest wasn't a drug addict who'd abandon him without a second thought.

"Your mother is Dolores Yelverton. When you were born, you had some problems. Difficulties with feeding, gaining weight, that kind of thing. Your parents hired a nurse to help cope with your special needs.

Unbeknownst to them, that nurse had her own issues. And one night she took off with you."

Wolf's hand appeared on Trey's shoulder, guiding him back into the chair. Trey was grateful, but he was too stunned to do more than shake his head slightly as the investigator continued.

"For months, there was a manhunt for the two of you. The Yelvertons were desperate. But then the nurse's car was found by the authorities in a lake in Roanoke County. Her body was recovered after dragging the lake, and there was a car seat in her vehicle. It was presumed she'd freed you from the car seat before you both drowned."

The investigator smiled. The expression was so at odds with the emotions swamping Trey that he nearly launched himself at the guy.

Control. He had to get control of himself.

"I was found in Michigan. Where is my..." Trey cleared his throat. "Where are the Yelvertons from?"

"Wake County. Southwater City. Steven moved away after the divorce, and unfortunately passed away about three years ago, but Dolores still lives there."

Trey's whole body turned to stone. He couldn't even draw breath.

All this time, his mother, his family, was a single county away from him. A town that was only a fifteen-minute drive from his front door.

Fate could be so incredibly cruel.

"If they're from around here, how'd I end up in Michigan?"

The PI looked down at his hands. "The nurse was suspected to have participated in human trafficking. She was posthumously connected to several other mysterious disappearances of infants and young children. You were presumed dead then. I think she passed you off to another middleman who was being investigated by the cops. He was tipped off and dumped the evidence."

"Me," Trey said without a hint of emotion.

The PI nodded.

"So why'd Dolores keep looking for me?" Trey's voice was the barest whisper.

The investigator's expression turned wry. "Because she never believed you were truly lost to her."

Those words had haunted him for the last forty-eight hours.

She never believed you were truly lost to her.

There'd been a funeral for little Samuel Yelverton, which had been his birth name. But his mother hadn't attended. She'd been too busy fighting to continue the search.

"Boss."

The deep voice broke through Trey's thoughts, and he glanced over his shoulder.

Wolf was mounting the steps to the deck, his big, copper Doberman, Pistol, at his heels. At odds with her name, Pistol was the biggest mush of a dog Trey had ever met. It wasn't unusual to see the pair of them this early—they lived on the other side of the property. Trey reached down and scratched Pistol's ears as Wolf dragged over a chair and sat beside him.

"So. You gonna call her?"

Trey shot Wolf a look. His second's dark hair was still wet from the shower, the tattoos just peeking above his plain black shirt's collar, adding to his dangerous appearance. The screen of the cell phone on the side table between them reflected the midday sun's light, almost as if taunting Trey.

"Here," the investigator had said, pushing a piece of paper toward Trey. "She wanted me to give you this. Now that you know what happened, it's your call if you want to make contact or not. But she never stopped believing you were alive, Samuel."

"That's not my name," Trey barked before he could stop himself, and then he'd stormed out of the room, leaving the folded paper where the investigator had set it on the desk.

"Can't call her," Trey said, remembering the shape and dusky-blue color of the folded note. "Didn't take her number."

Just then, Wolf stood and reached into the pocket of his well-worn jeans. He tossed a small, pale-blue folded note atop the blank screen of Trey's cell.

"Now you do."

Patting his hip for Pistol, Wolf walked away without another word.

Once the jingle of dog tags and the sound of footfalls faded into the distance, Trey looked over at the piece of paper.

Should he?

Could he?

A lot of who he was had been tied up in the fact that nobody wanted him. Hell, it was the reason he'd basically built the Iron Shadows in the first place.

Fuck blood. Blood was who you chose, not who genetics determined.

But then again—

"This is crazy," Trey muttered and paced along the edge of the deck.

Uncertainty was eating him up. This wasn't like him. He chose a path and stuck to it. He had to. Indecision got people killed, or worse.

"Damn," he spat out, then turned and faced the side table.

The edge of the folded paper stirred slightly in the breeze.

His mind made up, he grabbed the paper and the phone in a single movement.

Without any trace of a tremble, he unfolded the page and tapped out the number that had been written in a neat, feminine hand. Then the handset was at his ear, and the call connected.

He swallowed hard before he spoke.

"Hello, Mo—Mrs. Yelverton."

His bike rumbled beneath him, his thighs tense as steel girders as he drove down the long, curving, paved driveway. Sunlight scattered beams through branches just spouting early buds, the flickering of light irritating to his already stretched-taut nerves.

He rounded a sharper bend in the drive, and suddenly a run-down Victorian house came into view. Chipped paint and falling-down boards marred the appearance of what once would have been a true showpiece of architecture.

His mother—Mrs. Yelverton, he corrected himself—had told him about it. An old man lived there, with three times as much stubbornness as he had money. As a result, the home was in pitiful disrepair. Trey's destination was farther down the drive, on the next property.

Past the Victorian, down another quarter of a mile, the drive bent the other way, and the trees opened up to reveal a huge brick home. Three stories, classically beautiful, it had obviously been given all the care and attention that the Victorian lacked.

And in that home, at that very moment, was the woman who had given birth to him.

Waiting for him.

He cut his bike's engine a good distance from the house, close to the three-car garage. Without getting off his bike, he looked down at the hands that still gripped the handlebars.

Scarred. One of his knuckles was misshapen from a break that hadn't healed quite right. Tattoos spread across his knuckles, reading "Iron Life." Further ink disappeared into the long sleeves of his leather jacket.

His jeans were dark, his boots were heavy, and he looked more like he should be there to rob the joint than to meet the lady of the house.

Trey raked his hand through his hair and looked at the puffy-cloud-dotted blue sky.

What was he doing there? He didn't belong. He belonged back at Ruby's, or riding the highways looking for trouble.

This wasn't him.

And then he closed his eyes and remembered her voice.

The soft catch as she drew in a shaky breath at realizing who she was talking to. The sound of her tears as relief spilled through her words, cascading in a rush of love long suppressed.

"My son. My son."

His throat had felt curiously thick too, as she'd said it. She hadn't called him Samuel, and he was grateful for that. He could pretend that it was really him she was longing for, really Trey she cared about.

He looked at that house again. In another lifetime, maybe, this could have been his home, where he had grown up with a family that loved him.

What was the harm in pretending for just a moment? He'd go in, meet her, show her that he was the farthest thing from the perfect son she was imagining, and then beat feet for the door.

He owed her that much, he supposed. Since she'd spent nearly thirty years looking for him.

His footfalls were extra heavy on the brick front steps. His shoulders lifted with tension as he raised his finger to the doorbell.

Before he could push the button, the heavy wooden door opened. There, on the threshold, stood an absolute angel. An angel with his own eyes, soft, curling brown hair with just a hint of gray at the temples, and a smile on her curved lips that belied the shine of tears in her eyes.

"Trey, my son," she whispered and opened her arms.

And without even realizing it was happening, Trey stepped into her embrace.

Her fingers dug into the muscles of his back; her face buried into the leather of his jacket as tears racked her.

Steady, he told himself as adrenaline and emotion overtook him in a rush.

He wasn't sure what to do. She hadn't gotten a good look at him before hugging him, he supposed. She'd probably be disappointed when she pulled back and really took him in, but for the moment, he let himself pretend that this was his first hug from his mother. The first of many. He closed his eyes and rubbed her back, relishing the feeling, foreign as it was, of being home.

Much too soon, and far too late for comfort, she pulled back with a shuddering breath and smiled up at him.

Her cheeks were blotchy and red, but her smiling green eyes, so like his own, were shining with happiness this time.

"Trey, please come in."

She laced her fingers through his and led him into her home.

She still hasn't really looked at me, he thought as he followed her through a large living room and formal dining room into a modern, tastefully decorated kitchen. *In just a minute, she'll realize that I'm not what she expected.*

"Please sit down," she said, pulling out the chair at the head of the small table in the breakfast nook. "I've made a fresh pot of coffee, if you'd like? Or some soda, or juice, or—"

She stopped, and his chest filled with air, but the breath refused to release. She was looking at him. Really looking at him.

He knew what she was seeing.

A huge man with more tattoos than exposed skin, a bump on his nose from multiple breaks, and a pissed-off resting expression that he could no more change than he could his love of fighting.

A walking, breathing disappointment.

But her expression never wavered. In fact, she broke into a laugh, the sound shooting shocked adrenaline into his heart and making it jump.

"I'm sorry," she said, wiping her cheeks as she chuckled. "You just haven't changed a bit."

"What?" His voice was gravel over concrete, as if he hadn't spoken in years.

"When you were a baby, you had that same expression. So serious, so studious, as if you were figuring out the mysteries of the universe and weren't quite happy with the results. Oh God, I have missed you."

She pressed a quick kiss to his forehead and turned and hustled away before he could react.

His knuckles went white on his knees as she busied herself with clinking mugs and the trickle of pouring coffee.

This wasn't how he'd pictured this meeting. He was… Well, he was completely befuddled. How the hell was he supposed to manage this?

He couldn't hit things. He couldn't threaten. He couldn't bluster. Navigating this emotional minefield was at more than his pay grade, and while part of him longed to relax into the welcoming, loving atmosphere this lady was offering, another part of him—the part that had been hardened by the worst foster homes and a childhood belief that he'd been abandoned—cautioned him to get out while he still had a chance.

"I guess you're wondering about me, about all this," she said as she brought two mugs to the table. "Oh, I should have asked if you wanted milk and sugar."

"I take it black," he said, accepting the rustic mug.

She smiled, an expression he was realizing hadn't really left her face in one form or another since she'd clapped eyes on him on her front stoop. "I do too."

They sipped in silence for a while. Trey tried to be surreptitious, but he couldn't help staring at her.

She was tall for a woman. Of course, it stood to reason, since he was close to six foot five himself. Her hair had the same sort of loose curl to it that his did. The way she moved was even similar.

God. He was falling into this without even meaning to.

"I want to ask you so many things," she said. At her words, he tensed, but she continued. "I know it's not fair though. I only wish your father could have been here to see this."

Her expression changed, sadness hiding behind her eyes.

Trey cleared his throat. "I was sorry to hear... The PI told me..." He trailed off, unable to voice the words.

She nodded. "Cancer. About three years ago." Shaking her head, she wiped her cheeks. "I only wish he could have been here to meet you too. Is there anything that you'd like to know? About your father, your sister? Our family?"

His teeth hurt, he'd clamped them together so hard. His knee bounced beneath the table, little rings spreading in his coffee cup from the movement.

Sister. He had a whole family he didn't know. A world was opening up in front of him, a world that felt more like a chasm that he was poised on the edge of.

He clung to the only solid thing in front of him.

"You. I want to hear about you."

Her stare was direct and warm as she nodded at him. "When you were born—"

"No," he interrupted. "I want to hear about you now."

She paused for a moment, her head tilting to the side a bit. He didn't move, not a muscle betraying the turmoil inside him. His poker face was something he'd perfected long ago, but he couldn't shake the feeling that she was somehow seeing through it.

"Well," she said, "I run a community help center downtown. We cater to the homeless, to runaways, provide counseling and job-readiness courses. We teach art classes, provide child care, and try to help people get back on their feet." She looked down at her cup, her fingers curling around the ceramic body of the mug. "When I started it, I was trying to think of it as a place that you might be able to go to for help. That's why I named it what I did."

"What's it called?" The question came before he realized it.

"Sam's Place."

chapter
THREE

IT ALWAYS TOOK A WHILE FOR BETHANY TO GET accustomed to the scent of her grandmother's home. Well, *scent* wasn't exactly the right word. *Odor* was too nice a term too. *Stench* might cover it, but her grandmother's temper would never have accepted it if Bethany were to dare to utter that aloud.

In any case, being surrounded by the clutter, junk, and general filth of her grandmother's home was a chore that she avoided if at all possible. Sadly, today, it was unavoidable.

Breathing as shallowly as she dared, Bethany nodded as Grandmother Trudy continued.

"I was going through some things, and I just can't sort all these pictures on my own. I got some scrapbooks from the craft store, and I want to put my Marine's pictures in them, but I can't figure out what order to put 'em in. And since you've finally come to help me, I thought maybe we could get it figured out at last."

My Marine. Bethany forced the curl out of her fingers.

Grandmother Trudy never referred to her son, Bethany's father, by his name. It was always "her Marine." Never her son, never Bethany's father. It was as if the only identity Hugh Jernigan had had was in uniform.

There were many reasons Bethany despised being in her grandmother's company, but that one in particular was tough to deal with. The only reason she was there at all was the promise she'd made to her father when she was young, to look out for her grandmother.

It was a promise she'd regretted a million times over since her father had passed away.

"Okay. I'll try to help, but I've got a lot to do today, so we need to get started."

Bethany gestured toward the pile of boxes in the corner of the room. Her grandmother's hard life had manifested in several types of issues, hoarding chief among them. Any foray into the myriad bags and boxes that littered the space was a dodgy proposition at best, downright dangerous at worst. It wasn't the first time, and Bethany was on high alert.

Her grandmother's mood could turn on a dime, especially if she caught someone mishandling her possessions.

"Here, I'll get the first box down."

Grandmother stood on a half-crushed Amazon box to reach a full plastic grocery sack. Once she'd grabbed it, she set it on the only empty corner of the table. Bethany took the bag as Grandmother went for the next one.

"These aren't pictures," Bethany said, frowning as she started searching through the bag. The knot on the top had been tied so tightly that she'd had to tear the plastic handle slightly to get to the contents. "It's Dad's stuff though. Here's some paperwork and some boxes—"

"Give me that." Grandmother's voice cracked through the air like a whip as she reached out and snatched the bag away from Bethany.

But Bethany had already retrieved a slim, black case from the bag. Her throat went curiously thick as she lifted the lid. "How…how did you get this?"

Her father's Purple Heart was nestled against the dark velvet.

It shouldn't be there. It was Bethany's. Given to her by her father when his brain tumor had been diagnosed, Bethany had kept it close to her always. It hurt to look at it, actually. For that reason, she'd kept it hidden in her apartment, atop the mantel and behind a picture of her father in uniform. It was always there, always reminding her that even though he was gone, his heart would remain with her.

She hadn't looked for it lately. Hadn't known that she needed to.

The evidence in her hands couldn't be denied. Her grandmother had stolen Hugh Jernigan's Purple Heart. It must have happened a few months ago when she'd invited her grandmother over for dinner. It was a mistake that she wouldn't be making again.

"He's my Marine," Grandmother Trudy snarled, reaching for the case that Bethany still held in her trembling hands. "Mine. I deserve that!"

"In what universe do you deserve it?" Bethany couldn't stop the words once they'd started. "This belonged to my father. He gave it to me. What right do you have to take it from me? You took everything of his! Everything! Every last dime he had, our home, his clothes, even our freaking dog!"

"I suffered so much. I had to take those things,

because they belonged to my Marine." Grandmother's hands had curled into claws as she reached for the slender black box, her voice pitched shrill enough for the neighborhood's dogs to hear.

"You suffered?" Memories assaulted Bethany, and she could no more stop them than she could stop the words falling from her lips. "What about him? He supported you. He was in so much pain, but he still had to dance to your tune. He was on his deathbed, and you kept everyone away from him!" The pain lanced through her. "You put his nurses through hell, you ran up his credit card bills, and you even tried to keep me out of the hospital room!"

"He needed his mother! I was the only one who could keep him safe, and I am the only one who can keep that medal safe now. So give it to me!"

"Safe?" Bethany's own voice was a shriek now, and tears were streaming down her face. "You call this firetrap safe?"

The sharp crack of palm on cheek rent the air, and Bethany's breath left her on a sharp gasp. Pain ricocheted from her face to her brain and back again, and her free hand covered the stinging place where her grandmother had struck her.

The old woman's face was puckered and purple with rage, and she snatched the medal from Bethany's hand.

Right then, it was as if she'd lost him all over again. Hands and heart empty and aching, she swayed on her feet, stunned.

Dad, I'm sorry.

"Get out of my house. You don't deserve anything of his. You're a shame to our name."

The evil words Grandmother Trudy spat out pierced through the pain and fog that had surrounded Bethany. Steel shot up her spine, filling her with a determination unlike any she'd felt before.

"I'll go," Bethany said, proud that her voice was steady even though tears still trickled down her cheeks, "but I'm taking Daddy's medal with me. I couldn't save him from you then, but I can now."

For a moment, Bethany thought her grandmother would attack her as she grabbed the medal and wrestled it free of the older woman's grip. A cry racked from Grandmother Trudy's chest as she began to wail, throwing boxes and bags at Bethany as she gripped the medal's case and made her way toward the door.

Closing the portal on the angry yells behind her, Bethany got into her car and drove away as fast as she could.

Away from the pain of her disintegrated family. Away from the betrayal of her closest living relative. Away from the fact that she was alone in missing her father the way she did.

Toward the one place that had given her haven when Hugh Jernigan had left her.

Toward the Yelvertons', where she'd been assured she had a home for life.

Her tears had stopped during the drive, and when she pulled around the curve toward the house, she was glad that her face wasn't quite so splotchy.

Of course, she fully expected Mama Yelverton to notice that she'd been crying. It was impossible to put anything past that woman.

Bethany shouldered the strap of her purse and held

her father's medal tight to her chest as she walked to the garage, using her button to open the door and passing an unfamiliar motorcycle on the way in.

That was weird. She didn't think they knew anyone who rode a bike.

Closing the garage door between her and the motorcycle, Bethany let herself into the house with her key. Kicking off her shoes, she wiggled her toes in her socks with a sigh of relief. Leaning against the washing machine, she closed her eyes and took in the fresh scent.

Home.

Then, she heard the voices coming from the kitchen.

"You named it…" A deep, gravelly voice stopped to clear its throat. "You named it after me?"

"I did." Mama Yelverton's tone was the one Bethany remembered from many times across the years. It was the one she used when someone was sick, or hurt, or scared. A soothing tone, the kind of voice Bethany had always imagined had special calming powers.

"I don't know what to say."

"You don't have to say anything, Trey. I'm just glad you're home."

Silence fell between them, and Bethany eyed the door back to the garage nervously.

She should go. This seemed like a private conversation, and she shouldn't interrupt. She'd have to pass through the kitchen to get anywhere else in the house, so there was no way she could get in undetected.

Her apartment wasn't very appealing at the moment, since her grandmother had violated the space by stealing her most precious possession, but where else could she go?

While she fretted, the conversation kept going.

"— would love to hear about you," Mama Yelverton was saying to the stranger. "What is it that you do?"

"Well, it's nothing as noble as what you do. I mean, it's not… It's really…"

Bethany chewed her lip as she eyed the door. She couldn't go home. Not now. She needed to be here. Maybe she should just scoot through the kitchen with a quick wave and an apology and dash upstairs to the room that had been hers since she'd been welcomed there years ago.

With a deep breath, Bethany reached for the handle of the kitchen door.

He was in way over his head.

Mrs. Yelverton was a freaking saint. All his life he'd been imagining her as an evil, heartless, empty stranger who had abandoned him, and now? Now?

How could he tell her what he'd turned into?

"I, well, I'm in charge of a kind of group." He paused to clear his throat, his hand rubbing the back of his neck to ease the tensing of the muscles there. "Yeah."

"A group? Like a business group?"

He coughed, then took a sip of coffee. "Yeah, you could call it that."

"What kind of business are you in?"

Damn it.

Her stare was too clear, too honest, much too direct. He was struck by a feeling he hadn't been expecting. Somehow, someway, he was afraid of disappointing her.

Well, if that wasn't a kick in the teeth.

There wasn't a way around it. Was there?

Nerves pinging, he glanced around while he took another long sip of coffee.

What to say? Because the truth—the shakedowns, the Robin Hood–style robberies, the bodyguarding—none of it was exactly on the up and up. There were definite legal and moral gray areas to what he did. And while he had no problem with it personally, he didn't want to run the risk of disappointing her.

Who was he turning into?

Desperate, his gaze flew about the kitchen.

"Well, we do a little…" Hell, she'd never believe he cooked. *Something else. Quick, you dumbass. Keep it vague. Stall.* "A little organizing, you might say."

She nodded, an interested look on her face inviting him to continue. *Ah, dammit.*

Keep looking. A container of herbs sat on the windowsill above the sink. Gardening? Screw that. He scanned the rest of the kitchen. Nothing. No ideas whatsoever.

"What kind of events do you organize?"

Dammit. Dammit, dammit, dammit.

He rested his elbow on the tabletop, knocking a magazine to the floor.

"Whoops. Sorry." He bent down to get it.

A woman in a beautiful white gown was spread across the back of the magazine. The tagline for a bridal boutique advertisement read *We help you tie the knot in style.*

"Not a problem. So, you were saying?"

His mind was blank. Totally, completely blank. His mouth opened, but nothing came out.

Mrs. Yelverton furrowed her brow in obvious concern. "Are you okay?"

He had to say something. He looked down in

desperation. The magazine was still there, facedown beside him, the laughing woman in the white gown like an angel of salvation.

"Weddings," he blurted out as he straightened in his seat. "We organize weddings."

What. The. Actual. Fuck. Had. Just. Come. Out. Of. His. Mouth?

"Weddings. Wow, I hadn't expected that."

He coughed. "Yeah, me neither."

Mrs. Yelverton laughed. "I can imagine. How did you get into it?"

Wanting nothing more than to jump up and leave the county at a dead run, Trey shrugged, trying to play it off. "I got a chance to do some, enjoyed it, made my own business."

"That's really impressive! What's the business called?"

His hand was lying atop the magazine beside him, his knuckles lining up with the ad copy perfectly. He read the words out together.

"The Iron Knot."

Mrs. Yelverton laughed, clapping her hands delightedly. "That's absolutely perfect. Trey, I'm so proud of you."

Those words should have made him feel amazing. Instead, he felt like a scum-sucking bastard for lying to her.

Just then, the door behind her opened, and Trey's chest went vise-tight, his heart flinging itself against his ribs in triple time.

She was long, lean, with bone-straight blond hair and elfin features complementing porcelain skin. Her blue eyes were a bit red, as if she'd been crying recently. But despite the obviously brimming emotion beneath the surface, she wore a bright smile. It was the kind of expression he'd adopted many times over the years. Pretending things were all right when everything had turned to ashes around him was the only option he'd had at times, and seeing the same kind of defense mechanism in her touched him in a way he wasn't expecting. Physically, she was just his type, and the way she moved into the room, both cautious and confident—strong as hell despite whatever was trying to bring her down—sparked immediate interest and admiration in his gut.

This was...unexpected.

"Oh, Bethy, I didn't expect you until late this afternoon." Mrs. Yelverton rose and pulled the girl into her arms.

A wave of nausea overtook Trey. Was this girl... Was she...

Well, so much for that short-lived spark of attraction.

"Trey, I'd like you to meet Bethany."

"Hi," the blond said, and Trey stood. She looked a little intimidated as he stood to his full height.

He'd been about to step toward her for the introduction, but he stopped. No need to make her more uncomfortable. But the idea that she found him scary was oddly disappointing.

"I'm Bethany Jernigan," she said, sticking her hand out for him to shake.

"Trey Harding," he said, gripping her much smaller hand in his, trying to ignore the softness of her skin, the faint tremble of her touch.

"Bethany, I hope you won't mind keeping this quiet from Sarah for now. I haven't had a chance to tell her about it. But this…" Mrs. Yelverton drew Trey's arm through hers. "This is Samuel."

Bethany gasped, her hand over her mouth, and Trey looked away. "Samuel? *That* Samuel?"

Mrs. Yelverton nodded delightedly. "My son. He's finally home."

"Oh…oh my God."

Trey hated this. He felt awkward, like a sideshow freak. His spine prickled, his feet nearly bouncing with the urge to get the hell out of there.

"Trey, Bethany has been part of our family for years now. She's your sister Sarah's best friend and lived with us until she went to college. Of course, she's still got a room here. She'll always be welcome to come back home." Mrs. Yelverton's smile was gentle as she looked at Bethany.

"Wait. So we're not related?" Trey gestured between himself and Bethany.

Mrs. Yelverton laughed. "No, not by blood. But I hope you'll be close."

Something uncurled in his belly then, a knot of anxiety releasing as he looked at Bethany Jernigan—no relation—with new eyes.

"I hope so too," he said. She blushed a little and glanced away.

"I didn't mean to interrupt," Bethany said, adjusting the strap of her purse on her shoulder. Something he hadn't noticed before slipped in her hand with the movement, nearly crashing to the floor before she snagged it and stuffed it in her bag.

Weird. The way she clutched the purse closer after putting that little rectangular box inside declared it to be something really important to her. For a moment he wondered if that might have been the reason for her obviously tangled nerves.

"I just thought I'd do a little preliminary work on the wedding before we met this afternoon."

Wedding? Ah, hell.

"Oh, Trey was just telling me he runs a wedding planning service! We have to hire him for Sarah's wedding, don't you think?"

Trey's mouth fell open. Air wouldn't leave his lungs. He was never lost for words, but just then, he couldn't have uttered a syllable if he tried.

Bethany looked from him to Mrs. Yelverton and back again. "Well, Sarah's paying me to plan the wedding. It seems like a waste to hire two people for the same job."

He could have kissed her right then. *An out. Perfect.*

"I don't want to step on anyone's toes," Trey said hastily. "You were hired first, so it's only right you have the job."

"I was thinking the two of you could collaborate. And besides, it will be a great way to get to know each other. Working together as a family." She smiled at them, and the expression sapped the fight right out of Trey. "Don't you think?"

Bethany's shoulders sagged almost imperceptibly, but she nodded. "Of course, well, whatever you think is best."

Mrs. Yelverton looked at him, gripping his nerveless fingers in hers, drawing him in with that clear, honest, kind gaze of hers.

"Trey, I would be honored if the Iron Knot could help Bethany plan Sarah and Mark's wedding. I'll pay all your normal fees. It would be so nice to see what you've built, to meet your associates. What do you say?"

Suddenly he was a little boy again, the kid who'd wanted so badly to have a real mom to please. He'd hated every Mother's Day, every time he'd been reminded there was nobody who cared if he made them happy or not.

And for that moment, that one single moment, he wanted to please her, and damn the consequences.

"I'd be happy to."

chapter

FOUR

IT HAD BEEN THE STRANGEST MORNING THAT BETHANY could remember.

Mama Yelverton had insisted she stay. Bethany had agreed on the condition that she cook lunch. At least then she could busy her hands and give her brain some room to think.

She didn't trust the guy. It wasn't the dark clothes or the tattoos. She didn't care about that kind of stuff. It was the menacing air around him, the completely outrageous story that he'd tried to feed Mama Yelverton.

A wedding planner? Really? How stupid did he think they were?

The pot lid slammed down a bit too hard, and Bethany jumped.

"Everything okay in there?" Mama Yelverton called.

"Just fine," Bethany said, her voice thin as she yanked open the drawer where the kitchen knives were kept. "Lost my grip."

"Let me know if you need anything," Mama Yelverton said.

"I've got this… You two just catch up."

The buzz of voices from the living room indicated that they'd taken Bethany's advice, and she relaxed a little.

Money. It had to be about money. This guy was taking advantage of the fact that the Yelvertons' child had died as a baby and was pretending to be Samuel in order to get his hands on some cash. *Scum-sucking jerk. To prey on a family's pain that way—*

Honestly, it reminded her of her grandmother. Bethany sliced tomatoes with a vengeance. She'd be damned if she'd watch this lowlife take advantage of the Yelvertons that way. Mama Yelverton was too kind, too generous. Sarah was much the same way, but she was busy with pharmacy school, and it wasn't like she was close enough to keep an eye on things.

If anyone was going to protect Mama Yelverton from this money-grubbing fake, it would have to be Bethany.

"Can I give you a hand?"

She jumped and gave a little cry as that deep, sexy voice was suddenly right behind her. A broad hand steadied her, the touch sending electrical impulses from her elbow throughout her body.

"Didn't mean to startle you," he said as she jerked away. "No need to get violent."

She looked down and saw that she was still holding the chef's knife she'd been using to chop vegetables— pointed straight at him.

"Oh God, I'm sorry."

"No harm done," he said with a smile that was part

mischief, part evil, and all kinds of hot. "I shouldn't sneak up on a lady like that."

"Where'd Mama Yelverton go?"

"She got a phone call." He nodded toward the front of the house. "Thought I'd give her some privacy and see if you needed a hand."

His proximity was doing deliciously decadent things to Bethany's insides. He was just so damn... big. Imagining him tossing her around like she weighed nothing was causing her heart to do loop-de-loops.

No. Focus. This guy isn't trustworthy, and he's trying to take advantage of people you love.

Tamping down the desire that had curled warmly in the pit of her belly, Bethany turned back to the veggies for her pasta salad.

"Nope. I'm good. Thanks anyway."

"What's in the box?"

She froze, her insides suddenly going cold. "What?"

He nodded toward her purse where it sat on the edge of the counter. The corner of her father's Purple Heart case was sticking out of the top, plainly visible. The knife she'd been using clattered to the cutting board, and she reached for the purse, stuffing the box as deeply as she could to the bottom.

"It's nothing."

"Must be a big nothing if it made a strong girl like you cry."

She rounded on him. "Why do you care? I'm a stranger."

"I guess I just don't like seeing people hurt."

The defensive anger that had been building inside her disappeared in a cloud of confusion. She leaned against the counter, looking at him. Really looking at him this time. Past the tattoos, the muscles, the dangerous air that surrounded him.

His deep-green eyes spoke volumes. There was a steely strength in his expression, in the set of his jaw, the carriage of his shoulders, but those eyes told her he knew what it was to have a soul-deep, searing, painful loss, just like she did.

He cared. Despite the fact he'd never clapped eyes on her before, he'd noticed her pain and cared enough to check on her.

And despite herself, despite her better judgment, she found that incredibly attractive.

"Thank you," she whispered. "For asking, I mean."

There was a moment of silence, and then there was a big, hard body leaning up against the counter, lessening the difference in their height. She tried to look away, but his eyes were so magnetic.

God, he's going to kiss me.

And, insanely, she didn't mind. Instinctively tilting her chin up for his kiss, she waited.

And waited.

When it didn't happen, she opened her eyes. Trey was popping a slice of cucumber into his mouth, stepping away. As he chewed, she shook her head to clear the insanity.

It didn't work.

He grinned, reaching for another cucumber slice. "Fishing for a kiss, huh?"

"What?" Bethany squeaked. "No, I wasn't—"

"We just met. Give me a chance to get to know you. I'm not that kind of girl." He winked.

His confidence was maddening and a little charming

at the same time. Despite herself, she laughed. *Damn him.*

He leaned close, and his whisper blew across her ear, sending shivers up and down her spine. "If you want a kiss, just ask."

She leaned closer, tipping her chin upward until mere centimeters separated their mouths.

For a second, she wondered what it would be like to give in to the screaming temptation of her body and to kiss him. A voice from the other room snapped her back into the moment.

This was a con man. And he was trying to con her as well as her surrogate family.

Not on her watch.

"You should know," she said, not lessening the distance between them. "If you hurt the Yelvertons, I will come after you."

"I'm going to like you, Strong Girl," he said, then winked as he sauntered away as if nothing had happened.

Bethany stared after him.

What the? Who the hell did he think he was? *Really?*

She turned back to attack her vegetables. Her reaction to the man was as maddening as him being there in the first place.

Just then, Mama Yelverton's voice floated in from the living room, grinding Bethany's thoughts to a halt.

"Bethany? I've talked to Sarah. She's still in town, and she's coming for lunch. Will there be enough?"

Bethany did a couple calculations in her head. "Yup, I can make it work."

"You're a star." Mama Yelverton smiled. "Sure you don't need any help?"

The question reminded her of Trey's offer of assistance, and Bethany had to fight the blood that rushed into her cheeks. "Nope, I'm good. It'll be done in about ten minutes."

"I'll get the table set. Trey, would you mind helping me?"

As Mama Yelverton opened the cupboard, Bethany looked in Trey's direction. The teasing laughter was gone from his expression, replaced by a carefully crafted blankness.

She looked harder. His shoulders were tense, a slight tremor in his hands the only giveaway. Was he...nervous? And why did she have the sudden urge to comfort him?

He looked over at her, and their eyes met. He looked away quickly, as if afraid to give away too much of what he was feeling.

Con artist. Swindler. Crook. Don't let yourself fall into his trap. Her self-motivational speech broke the spell, and she curled her hands into fists.

She didn't know what to make of him. But she did know she'd watch every move he made. One misstep, and she'd be all over him.

Semper fi, as her father had constantly reminded her. Always faithful. She wouldn't let the Yelvertons down. Not even for a man that set her nerves on fire.

When the sound of the garage door met her ears, Bethany was swamped with a strange mixture of gratitude and dread.

On the one hand, the fact that her best friend was there was amazing. Never having been as drawn to a man as she was to Trey, Bethany could really use the extra support.

On the other hand, that man was Sarah's long-lost brother.

It looked like Bethany's frustration and unexpected attraction was her own problem for now.

"Hey, hey," Sarah chirped as she came through the door that led to the laundry room and garage entrance. "Mom said you were cooking lunch. What's the occasion?"

Bethany bit the inside of her lip as she finished cutting the sandwiches on the diagonal. "I'll let her tell you."

"Hi there, baby." Mama Yelverton came into the kitchen, a nervous smile on her face. "I'm so glad you could come."

"Mark had something come up, so he's headed back to Asheville." Sarah plopped onto the barstool opposite the counter where Bethany was arranging food on a large serving plate. "What's with the impromptu family gathering?"

"I've got something to tell you," Mama Yelverton said, reaching over and taking Sarah's hand.

"I'll give you guys some privacy," Bethany said, grabbing the platter of sandwiches and scooting from the kitchen before anyone could protest.

Anxiety climbed her spine with every soft murmur of voices from the kitchen behind her.

This was an unknown. Sarah had confided in Bethany many times over the years about her mixed feelings regarding her older brother's disappearance. Due to Papa Yelverton's feelings on the matter, Mama Yelverton hadn't really kicked the search into high gear until about a year after Papa's death. Of course Sarah wanted her mother's search to be successful, but Bethany couldn't forget the hurt in Sarah's eyes when she'd wondered aloud if she just wasn't enough for Mama Yelverton to be happy.

In any case, Bethany was on Sarah's side. She sighed as she set the plate in the center of the table, in between the pasta salad and the deviled eggs.

Footsteps behind her made her tense, but she didn't turn around.

"Looks good."

That voice was still doing things to her. *Damn him*.

"Thank you," she said coolly, pouring herself a glass of water, keenly aware of his gaze raking her up and down.

Jesus, she had to get things under control.

"Can I get some of that?"

"I'm sure you can," she said, setting the pitcher in front of him and creating some much-needed distance between them.

"It's okay, Strong Girl. Wasn't asking you for any favors."

The urge to snap back at him was huge, but Bethany just took a sip of her water and ignored him.

"Trey?"

They both turned and looked at the kitchen doorway, where Mama Yelverton and a somber-looking Sarah stood. Mama held Sarah's hand, looking from her to Trey as she said, "This is your younger sister, Sarah."

"Hi," Trey said, and for the first time, Bethany thought she saw a crack in that hard-ass facade he'd been presenting.

It was almost imperceptible, really. But the way his weight shifted before coming back to center, the way his shoulders moved, all seemed to indicate that he'd been knocked off his axis and wasn't sure how to handle what was coming at him.

Good. Gold-digging, scum-sucking cheat had it coming. Maybe he did have a conscience and would stop this charade before it went any further.

"Hello," Sarah said, her smile a little brittle.

Silence fell, an awkward, thick quiet that Bethany wasn't sure she should break. Fortunately, Mama Yelverton stepped into the gap.

"Well, Bethany, this looks excellent. Should we sit down?"

"Sure," Bethany said, pulling out Sarah's chair before sinking into her own. It looked like her best friend could use the help. Sarah's expression was a mask of politeness over a darkly confused mix of anger and sadness.

Bethany wished she could drag her friend from the room and give her some space to process this news before being forced to spend time with this stranger in their midst.

But in actuality, she was the outlier. The only one who wasn't—rightly or wrongly—claiming the Yelverton name.

For a few moments, there was only the clinking of silverware as food was passed and plates were loaded. Bethany kept as close an eye on Trey as she reasonably could.

He carried himself well enough, she guessed. He didn't make a giant mess, kept his elbows off the table. Said "thank you" when Sarah passed him the pasta salad. He even kept the olives he picked out of it in a neat little pile on the corner of his plate.

Hmm. She bit down harder than necessary on her turkey and cheese. He was just a good actor. Had to put on a good show to pull the wool over their eyes.

"So, Sarah's about to be a doctor of pharmacy," Mama Yelverton said, smiling over at her daughter as if oblivious to the brewing storm in that direction. "She graduates this May."

"Mom, he doesn't want to hear about that."

"That's really interesting," Trey said with a polite nod. Bethany couldn't help but notice how the tattooed snake climbing up his neck twitched with the movement. It was intimidating and sensuous at the same time.

Down, girl.

"And Trey runs a wedding planning company," Mama Yelverton continued. "It's such great timing, really. We couldn't have asked for him to come into our lives again at a better moment. He's already agreed to help Bethany with the ceremony plans. I thought if Sarah's still here then, we could all get together tomorrow afternoon and—"

Sarah's chair scraped back suddenly. "Hey, Bethany, I think this pasta salad could use more tomato."

Mama Yelverton frowned down at her plate. "I think it's fine, Sarah."

"No, it definitely could," Sarah said, grabbing the bowl. "Beth, can you come and help me?"

"Absolutely," Bethany said, tossing her napkin down beside her plate and hustling toward the kitchen after her best friend.

She glanced over her shoulder before shutting the dining-room door. Trey's face had gone stony, his strong jaw tight.

Good. Let him notice how his sudden appearance has rocked things. Let him realize that Easy Street isn't a real place.

Once they were alone, she turned her full attention to her best friend. "Are you okay?" Bethany rubbed Sarah's back. Sarah's palms were splayed on the countertop, her hair hanging down as she faced the floor.

"I just don't know how to process this," Sarah said, her voice a little thick. "Mom is so freaking happy. I just… I'm happy too. But he's so…different than I'd pictured him."

"I know," Bethany said, rubbing small circles on Sarah's back.

"Honestly, I'd felt like Dad was right. That he was dead, and searching for him was just a way for Mom to put off processing the grief. And for him to show up like this? Right before the wedding? Mom said that the DNA test proved it, but…I don't know."

Sarah turned, and Bethany was stunned to see the sheen of tears in Sarah's eyes.

Her best friend never cried. Ever.

"Bethy, I'm so sorry to ask you this. But right now I can't afford to be distracted. With finals and then the NAPLEX licensing exam, it's too much. I have to focus. I know things are different since you agreed to make decisions for my wedding, but with him"—Sarah nodded toward the dining room—"it's even tougher. Can you please work with him? For me? For Mom?"

Of course the answer would be yes, but Bethany's thoughts went deeper than that.

She knew he was lying about the wedding planning business. No way in heck did that huge, muscle-bound, tattooed biker plan weddings for a living. If she worked with him, maybe she could get some proof and show it to Mama Yelverton before Trey got his hooks even farther into her. DNA or no DNA, this guy was lying about his job if nothing else.

It was a good plan. Noble, even. She felt sure that her dad would have approved.

"Of course I will," Beth said and hugged Sarah hard. "Everything's going to be fine. Trust me."

"I do," Sarah whispered.

Bethany closed her eyes and held her best friend. Her family.

This bastard wasn't going to hurt them. Not even over Bethany's dead body.

chapter
FIVE

WHEN TREY'S BIKE RUMBLED INTO THE LOT AT RUBY'S that night, he had a helluva lot on his mind.

The family he'd just found. The welcome his mother had given him. The loss of a father he'd never known. The standoffishness of his new sister. And the sexy surprise who was the best friend.

Not to mention the freaking polka-dotted elephant in the room. The one that was wearing a poufy white dress in a church full of flowers.

This was not gonna be fun. He jammed his hands in his pockets as he pushed through the doors.

"Hey there, Boss," Ace called from the corner where Jameson was racking up a new game of pool. "Want to join?"

"Not now," Trey said, drawing himself up to his full height. "We need to circle up. I've got something to tell you all."

"Big job?" Ace's voice was full of curiosity. It wasn't like Trey to call a meeting of everyone at one time.

"Something like that," Trey rumbled before glowering at them. "Get the rest of the boys and come outside."

Ace and Jameson nodded as Trey turned on his heel and walked back out into the night.

Pacing in the parking lot, Trey tried to plan his words. Nope. There was nothing he could couch this in that would make it sound any less ridiculous.

Maybe he should just come clean with his mother at the meeting tomorrow. Tell her he'd lied straight out of his ass to impress her.

But the image of her face as she'd talked about how proud she was haunted him, and he knew he couldn't break her heart already. Not when things were so new, so fragile.

He'd never known that a mother like her existed, and he didn't want to lose her now.

"We're here, Boss."

Wolf's voice snapped Trey out of his reverie, and he walked back to the concrete pad where twelve bikes sat, looking like shiny jungle cats leaning to the side, ready to pounce.

Eleven hard-eyed killers looked back at him, ready to go anywhere and do anything he asked of them.

They were loyal. They'd sworn the same oath Trey had. To keep their brotherhood strong, to protect their turf, to look out for their own.

He'd never imagined that he'd be asking them to do something like this.

"Okay," he said, reaching into his jacket pocket for his smartphone. He opened the notes app where he'd jotted down ideas earlier. "Wolf, you're on venue, with Lars and Rocco for backup."

Wolf nodded, and the two others moved behind him. Trey cleared his throat and continued.

"Jameson, you and Hawk are down for flowers. Ace, Dean, and Flash, I want you on fashion. Dresses, tuxes, all that crap. Mac—"

"Wait a minute, Boss. Flowers? Tuxes? What the hell kind of job is this?"

Ace was the one that spoke up, but when Trey looked, every single one of his bikers was giving him an eyeball hairier than Pistol's ass.

He opened his mouth, but nothing came out. Clearing his throat, he tried again.

"We'... Uh-hum. We're going to be planning a wedding."

You could have plopped a Harley Cosmic Starship down in front of that crew and seen less shock on their faces.

"Do...do what now?" Ace stuttered.

"You heard me, assholes. Wedding. Now, Mac, Doc, and Stone, you three are on the food. The booze, the cake, the whole shebang. I'll be overseeing everything and organizing everything else."

Wolf was suddenly beside him. "Boss, we need to talk."

"Not now, Wolf. We don't have much time. Go do some research. I need some information by noon tomorrow."

"How?" Dean asked, his normally furrowed brow narrowing even farther. "I don't know anything about wedding dresses."

"Why do I give a damn how you do it? Get on the internet, go to the fucking library, get a book. Get out of here. You're wasting time."

Trey realized it probably wasn't fair to take out his

worry and frustration on the Shadows, but damn it, he didn't know what else to do.

One by one, the bikers disappeared. Some of them back into Ruby's, others onto their bikes with some questioning glances back toward Trey and Wolf, who was still standing beside Trey.

Once they were alone, Trey took a deep breath and let some of the starch out of his spine. "I know. Go ahead. Let me have it." He sank onto the curb that ran the length of the building.

"What is going on, Boss?" Wolf's voice held no judgment, just a major dose of curiosity. "You being blackmailed or something?"

"She's an angel." Trey groaned, covering his face with his hand. Scrubbing down his chin, the bristles of his stubble scratching against his palm, he sighed. "My mother. She started a community center for homeless kids and runaways and named it after me. She's like a real-life saint. How could I tell her that my day job is chasing drug dealers and shaking down cheating bookies?"

Wolf sank onto the curb beside Trey, saying nothing. He didn't have to. His presence was the kind that invited confidence.

"She asked me what I did, and I panicked. There was a wedding magazine, and the lie just came out." Trey shook his head. "The Iron Knot. What kind of name is that for a wedding planning service?"

There wasn't much warning. A little movement in the corner of Trey's eye. The soft intake of breath.

And then Wolf was down on the concrete, legs drawn up as he howled with laughter.

Anger sparked in Trey's chest and had his fists clenching.

"You...you told her...the Shadows were wedding... pla...planners? Oh Jesus," Wolf gasped between fits, clutching his ribs and rolling.

"You questioning my authority?" Trey snapped at his second, whose legs were in the air like a dog with an itchy back.

"I can't..." Wolf gasped, tears trickling down his cheeks. "I can't..."

Trey took the two steps that separated them, intending to grab the front of Wolf's shirt, haul him to his feet, and beat the hell out of him.

But then he met his second's eyes.

The ridiculousness of the situation hit him like a baseball square between the eyes. Trey's hands fell, the corners of his lips lifted, and then he was laughing as hard as Wolf.

"Jameson out picking daisies for bouquets." Wolf's face was bright red.

"Ace modeling bridesmaid dresses." Trey's shoulders shook.

"Mac scattering flower petals over a big, white cake." Wolf's voice was a wheeze.

"Rocco with a little pillow for the rings." Trey's ribs hurt.

"Lars and Flash can sing a duet."

"'Endless Love'?"

"Which one's Diana Ross?"

"It'd have to be Lars. But we'll have to remove his nuts to get him to hit those high notes."

"Rocco can just keep them in the pillow."

They both laughed until they couldn't laugh anymore.

Wiping tears from his eyes, Wolf sat up, propping his arms atop his knees. "Boss, you've asked us to do some crazy things, but never anything like this."

Trey sighed. "I know. Think the guys will ever forgive me?"

Wolf quirked a half smile. "Doesn't matter. You're the boss. We'll do anything you ask. Even if it's stupid as hell." He stood. "I'm going home. Pistol needs her dinner, and I've got to figure out what a wedding venue looks like."

Trey lifted his fist. Wolf pounded it, and then he slung his leg over his bike and rode away.

As the sound of Wolf's engine faded into the night, Trey looked up at the stars.

He'd needed that laugh. That release. The tension of the day had been incredible, and not knowing how the Shadows would react to his scheme had made it all worse.

He'd known this would be a tough sell. But he needed it to work.

Maybe, just maybe, he could show his mother that he was worth the kindness she'd already shown him. Giving him a reason to hope was worth the aggravation.

Bethany's morning was spent preparing her arsenal.

First, her armor. Her hair took ages to curl, and her makeup was more carefully applied than her usual application of a little BB cream and some mascara. Her clothes were selected with care: a sleek-looking pair of slacks paired with a high-necked silky top. Stockings. Heels. She was dressed to get business done.

No mistake, she was as polished and professional as she'd ever been.

Looking good and feeling confident, she turned her attention to the meeting to come.

Her list of questions took almost as long to prepare as her appearance had, but that was worth it too. She didn't expect this to take that long. Exposing Trey's lie would be laughably easy, she presumed.

No way in hell would the guy know anything about dresses and flowers and photographers. Get him out of the way, and then she and Mama Yelverton could focus on making Sarah's wedding day as perfect and stress-free as possible. Sarah had hightailed it back to school, and Bethany couldn't blame her.

She could handle this.

With her list of questions tucked into her leather folio, Bethany climbed into her car and made the short drive to Mama Yelverton's, singing with the radio all the way.

It was good to feel useful.

Happy to see that the motorcycle from yesterday wasn't there yet, Bethany hurried into the house to set up camp.

"Afternoon," Mama Yelverton sang out from the study. "I'll be right there."

"It's just me," Bethany said, setting her folio on the coffee table. "Want me to get some snacks ready?"

"No, thank you, dear. I've already done that. My, don't you look extra pretty today." Mama Yelverton dropped a kiss on Bethany's cheek as she smiled a welcome. "What's the occasion?"

Bethany patted Mama Yelverton's arm. "Just felt like looking nice today is all."

As Mama Yelverton disappeared into the kitchen, Bethany eyed the seats in the living room. No, too casual. She wanted Trey to feel under scrutiny, as if she was putting him in the hot seat—which she was.

"Can we set up in the dining room? I think it would be good to use the table."

"If you think so, that's fine with me," Mama Yelverton called from the kitchen.

Nodding, Bethany scooped up her folio and the pile of pictures and magazines Mama Yelverton had left on the coffee table.

She took all but three chairs away from the big oak dining table. Two of them on one side, one sitting right by its lonesome on the other.

There. Like a job interview, which was how Bethany fully intended to treat it.

Trey had to prove himself, and she and Mama Yelverton were the jury. Her father had always told her to trust her gut, and her gut did not trust that smooth-talking, too-handsome roughneck bastard.

But he did notice how upset you were and cared enough to ask… that traitorous part of her whispered.

The doorbell rang.

"Bethany, I've got soapy hands. Can you get that?"

"No problem."

Bethany cracked her knuckles on the way to the front door, anticipation quickening her step.

This was it. She was ready.

The door swung open, and she swayed on her Ferragamos, purchased with her now-defunct Hudson's employee discount. "Sweet Jesus," she said breathlessly.

He'd transformed. Well, not totally.

His hair was still too long, but it was styled in a carefully tousled way. Instead of a black T-shirt, he wore a dark-gray button-down, open enough at the throat for her to see more of his impressive tattoos. His dark jeans were neat, his boots looked clean, and his leather jacket was slung over one shoulder, giving him the look of a J.Crew model on steroids.

"Hello," he said and leaned forward.

Without thinking, she tilted her head up to accept his kiss.

Her lids fluttered closed just as the lightest brush of his lips touched her...cheek.

"Still too soon for a real kiss," he said teasingly as he drew back. "Buy me a drink first."

Her mouth fell open, but a retort was nowhere to be found.

"Can I come in?"

Wordlessly, she stepped back to allow him entry. He strode into the foyer as if he owned the place.

Her insides in an uproar, Bethany took a deep breath.

Okay, so the initial meeting didn't quite go as planned. Focus. Don't look at his tightly muscled ass as he walks in front of you. Pay no attention to those thighs that are thick as tree trunks, those arms that could pick you up, those hips that your legs could wrap—

"Where are we setting up?"

Bethany cleared her throat. "Erm, the dining room."

Under one arm, he had a plain white binder, the kind you could pick up at Staples for a couple of bucks. He set it down on the table as Bethany gathered her mental defenses.

"Trey! Oh, it's so good to see you," Mama Yelverton

said. She reached forward, but Trey didn't move to accept her hug. Her hands fell away, her expression faltering just a bit. "Sorry."

"It's all right," he said, while Bethany gritted her teeth.

Wait a minute. Why was she upset that he had rebuffed Mama Yelverton's affectionate greeting? Shouldn't she be happy that he wasn't using that to further manipulate her?

Bethany pulled her chair out and sat down, frowning as she decided, yes, she was glad, but either way, Mama Yelverton was going to be hurt. And that really, really sucked.

"So, let me get some information from you before we get started," Trey said, opening his notebook. He clicked open a pen and began to write on a blank sheet of paper. Left-handed, Bethany noted idly. Just like Sarah.

"When's the wedding date?"

"June sixteenth," Mama Yelverton said, sinking into the chair beside Bethany.

"And do you have any ideas for venues?"

"Well," Mama Yelverton began and then rattled off several ideas while Bethany scrutinized Trey's every move.

He made notes as Mama Yelverton talked, nodding and asking questions during pauses. Underneath the table, Bethany's leg shook nervously.

He was a good actor. That was all. He'd been trying to disarm her by pretending to care about her feelings. And it had worked.

It wouldn't work again.

"So we'll need a close backup in case it rains," Trey was saying. "What would be your first choice for an indoor ceremony?" He flipped through his notebook. "There are some nice churches close by, or—"

"We'd love to hear some places you've held ceremonies before," Bethany interjected, hiking her eyebrows in his direction. "We're looking for that special touch. You know, not your typical traditional wedding. That is your specialty, right?"

He met her gaze, and she took great delight in taking a leisurely look up and down his torso, lingering obviously on his exposed tattoos.

"Of course," he said, hiking one brow in her direction. "If nontraditional is how you want it." His attention swung over to Mama Yelverton.

She looked from Bethany to Trey and back again.

"I'd love to see what ideas the two of you come up with." The oven timer dinged, and Mama Yelverton stood. "Oh, that's the cookies. I'll be right back."

She left the room, and Bethany wasted no time in leaning forward. "I'm on to you," she hissed. "You won't get away with this."

"With what?" He asked the question coolly, his tone at odds with the warm twinkle in his eye. "Kissing you? Sorry it disappointed you, but I told you, I'm not that kind of guy. We need to take things slow."

"Here we go," Mama Yelverton said, pushing the door open with her back and spinning into the room. "Hot chocolate chip cookies. They're Bethany's favorite."

"Mine too," Trey said and reached over to snag a cookie before returning to his notebook like nothing had happened.

Numbly, Bethany reached over and took one herself. It was official. She was in way over her head.

chapter
SIX

TREY WASN'T SURE WHICH HE ENJOYED MORE—THE cookie or the fact that Bethany looked torn between kicking his ass and kissing him senseless.

He knew which one he'd vote for.

Mrs. Yelverton and Bethany were discussing the alternative venue while Trey finished his cookie. It was damn good. Being there was good.

Except for the little matter of Bethany trying to undermine him. Her whispered warning was like a rough spot on his leathers—irritating without a true reason for it.

Yeah, he'd known the wedding gig would be a tough story to sell. But his mothe—Mrs. Yelverton—seemed to buy it. What was this girl's deal? She wasn't even related to them. Being friends with Sarah, of course she'd want to make sure that nothing untoward happened, but her threats went beyond mere friendship.

Trey smiled to himself. He could almost imagine her as one of the Shadows. She was showing the type of camaraderie he'd come to expect from his biking brothers.

"Don't you agree, Trey?"

"What now?" He started, crumbs falling into his lap.

"I was just telling Mama Yelverton that it would be a good idea to keep the guest list fairly small. Sarah and Mark aren't really into the idea of a big spectacle, and it'll keep costs lower."

Mrs. Yelverton frowned. "I understand that, but are you sure she won't want to invite her classmates, her friends from her pharmacy rotation, her old teammates from the tennis club—"

"Of course the number of guests is totally up to you," Trey said smoothly and then fell silent.

If this was really his job, he'd come up with some snappy remark about how having fewer chairs at a wedding meant good luck for the happy couple, or some such BS. As it was, he leafed through the notebook Wolf had helped him assemble that morning with the research his surly, grumbling Shadows had handed in like so many homework assignments.

"Keeping it at a hundred people will be more than large enough." Bethany smiled, having finally gotten through to Mrs. Yelverton. "So, if you get the guest list started, I can look over it, add to it, and then we can finalize it together. Now," she said, turning her eagle eye toward Trey, "invitations. Of course you have some samples we can look over?"

Dammit. He hadn't thought of that. *Bluff. Keep her guessing.*

He cleared his throat, straightening his shoulders as he shifted in his chair and affected a thoughtful look.

"Normally my clients trust me to come up with the design on my own. You know, talk over the look they want, that kind of thing."

Bethany's perfectly arched brows rose. "You do graphic design work too?"

"Of course." *Lie*.

"What about printing? Do you do it in-house?"

"Wouldn't have it any other way. Best thing for keeping costs down." *Another lie*.

"Hand-addressed?"

"Yup." *Bullshit*.

"Calligraphy?"

"That's the best way, isn't it?" *Damned if he knew*.

Bethany sank back into her chair as if some of the wind had left her sails, and Trey felt his chest swell with victory.

But it was a short-lived sensation.

"I can't wait to see what you come up with." Mrs. Yelverton smiled. "When can we expect the proofs?"

Trey cleared his throat. *Think*. "Two weeks?" Surely he could find some computer geek to design a wedding invitation in that time.

Bethany snorted. "You don't move very quickly, do you?"

He shot her a thunderous glare. "A week. I'll have the proofs ready in a week."

"But Trey's right," Mrs. Yelverton countered. "We have to make sure the venue is available before we can finalize the invitations."

Whew. Bullet dodged.

"Of course," Bethany said, then smiled at him sweetly. "You can manage booking the venues, right?"

"Me?" Trey blinked.

"That is part of your job, isn't it? Mr. Wedding Planner?"

And with that question, he knew.

Bethany had every intention of proving him to be a fraud in front of the Yelvertons. Her cooperation would only extend as far as exposing his lie. She was that determined to protect the people she loved.

And damn if that didn't make him like her even more.

He leaned forward, his biceps straining against the fabric of the dress shirt he'd borrowed from Dean. Good thing that brother was a clotheshorse, because Trey didn't own anything that could pass for business casual. He noticed the slight darkening of her eyes, the way her nostrils flared at the sight.

She was anything but indifferent toward him, her mistrust notwithstanding. And he'd use every bit of that to his advantage. He'd never had a problem with flirting his way into and out of trouble when he had to.

"Of course I'll handle it, if it's what Mrs. Yelverton wants."

"I don't mind calling the venue—"

Bethany cut Mrs. Yelverton off with a quick shake of her head. "No way. That's why you hired a wedding planner. If you're not going to use his services, then why's he even here?"

In the first emotion other than agreeable delight he'd seen from her, Mrs. Yelverton rounded on Bethany.

"I know you're trying to protect Sarah, but I won't tolerate you being rude to Trey for no reason, Bethany. Trey is here not only because I hired him, but also because he's my son. Mind your manners."

Her scolding held no venom, just the tinge of stern

disappointment that made a person want to curl up into a hole in abject apology. Trey wasn't the target, and he still wanted to immediately say *sorry*.

"I didn't mean to be rude," Bethany said, tilting her chin in just a hint of defiance. "But I don't want to see anyone taking advantage of you. Even him." She jerked her head in Trey's direction.

"I'm not being taken advantage of, trust me. If anything, I'm taking advantage of his services in order to spend more time with him."

Mrs. Yelverton looked at him, and the expression on her face was one of tenderness.

Awkwardness settled around his shoulders like a too-warm, itchy blanket. Trey had to look away. He didn't know what else to do.

"I apologize," Bethany said shortly.

"No need," Trey said with a tight smile, closing his notebook. "So, I'll get back with you about…" What the hell was he supposed to be doing again? He had no clue. All he wanted was to get as far away from this house as possible while his hide was still intact. Mrs. Yelverton's defense of him, and that look she had given him, were too much for him to handle. "I'll get back with you on everything soon."

Mrs. Yelverton walked him to the door, talking lightly as if the last few minutes hadn't happened. As he followed her out of the dining room, his spine prickled as if he was being watched. He looked over his shoulder.

Bethany's expression was dark, her full lips pursed as she looked directly at him.

His stomach ached as if he'd been punched all the way to Wolf's.

"Hey, Pistol," Trey said as he mounted the steps to the front porch that Jameson, Wolf, and Doc shared. The old farmhouse would have been drafty and miserable for one person, but with three of them to split the space, plus the big Doberman, the farmhouse had always felt kind of homey. Well, as homey as a triple bachelor pad could feel.

"Hey, Boss." Jameson was sprawled in a big leather recliner front of the large-screen TV, a can of soda in his hand and a bag of chips on the side table beside him. A wrestling match was happening on-screen.

"Still watching that crap," Trey grunted as he swiped a handful of chips.

"This is high-quality entertainment. It's real to me, dammit." Jameson pulled the bag out of Trey's reach and continued munching, losing himself in the high drama of flying bodies and scripted rivalries.

Like all the rest of the Shadows, Jameson had a past that he'd rather forget. Trey sometimes wondered—if there was an award for suffering, would Jameson come in first?

While he was deployed to Afghanistan, a car wreck had taken both his parents and his baby girl. His wife had left him after emptying his bank accounts and blowing the pitiful inheritance his parents had left after paying for the funerals. Jameson had ended up broken-hearted, flat broke, and totally alone. When Trey'd run across him, Jameson had been neck-deep in the bottle, doing his damnedest to ride his bike straight into the mouth of hell itself.

Trey had strong-armed him into joining the Shadows. He'd improved dramatically since then, but there was still a darkness that hung around him—a cloud that never fully dissipated.

Trey could empathize. Their losses had been so different. Jameson had had it all; Trey'd never had anything.

Until now.

The reminder of his current predicament sent him sinking to the couch, his head in his hands. How was he supposed to pull this off? This was so far out of his comfort zone it might as well be in another universe.

A sound at one end of the room brought his gaze up. Doc was entering the room, a bowl in his huge hands. The scar that ran down one cheek, a startling streak of light pink against his dark complexion, was wrinkled in a smile.

"Try this," he said, handing a spoon to Trey.

"What the hell is it?"

Doc's smile didn't falter. "Just try it."

Trey hiked his eyebrow, but shoved the spoon into the weird greenish fluff inside the bowl.

He tasted it gingerly.

"This... Well, it looks like Pistol got sick on the kitchen floor and you scooped it into the bowl, but it doesn't taste half bad. What is it?"

Doc grinned, flashing white teeth. "Watergate salad. Called my mama, and she gave me the recipe. Thought it would be good for the reception."

Trey's fingers curled tighter around the spoon.

A knock on the door came then. Jameson didn't have time to get to his feet before the portal swung open.

"Help me out here," Dean grunted around his burden of binders and books. "I'm about to lose the whole pile."

Jameson grabbed the top half, and together they set the books on the floor in front of the couch.

"What is all this?"

Dean shot Trey a glare. "What does it look like? It's research. I spent all morning at the library. This is everything they had on wedding clothes."

Dean's last word was half drowned out by the sound of power tools from outside.

What was going on now?

Trey moved to the sliding glass doors at the end of the room. Wolf was building…something.

Trey stood and watched for a moment as his second confidently put together a structure right before his eyes.

"He's building an arch," Jameson said in answer to Trey's unvoiced question. "Thought it would be nice at the end of the aisle."

Shaking his head, Trey looked down at the toes of his boots.

He'd doubted them. How could he have doubted them? These were his brothers—his family. They'd never let him down before. And they weren't about to start, even though he'd dived straight off the edge into a swimming pool full of crazy.

"Let's go to Ruby's," Trey said, clapping Jameson on the back. "You boys could use a break. I'm buying."

"Fine by me," Dean said, slamming a book shut. "If I see one more damn wedding dress today, I might just punch someone."

Doc frowned down at his bowl as the rest of them trooped toward the door. "Doesn't anyone want any more of this?"

"Bring it," Trey said, shrugging into his leather jacket. "Somebody will eat it."

Doc stood, but he still didn't look happy. Trey stopped him with a hand on the arm.

"Hey, man. Thanks. It really was delicious."

Doc flashed that grin again. "Thanks, Boss."

They all headed to Ruby's after even Wolf was convinced to put down his power tools for the evening. The sun was sinking low in the west as they pulled into the pitted gravel lot.

A handful of bikes were already there, their riders having received Dean's text. The whole crew was present, and Trey couldn't be prouder. At the end of the day, if this thing with the Yelvertons didn't work out, these were the guys who had his back.

He'd forgotten about that for a while, but he didn't intend to again.

"Hi, boys!"

Trey blinked twice as Ginger's cheerful greeting sailed to them. She was smiling—no, beaming—as she wiped down an empty table near the door.

"What can I get y'all?"

"Some more of that sweet smile will do for me," Ace said, leaning toward the waitress with a suggestive grin. "I like the sunshine you're giving off tonight."

"Sorry to break your heart, Prince Charming, but none of that sunshine is because of you."

Dean snorted as Ace weaved on his feet. "You're killing me, baby."

"Gonna have to let you die. My fiancé doesn't want me making time with strangers." Ginger straightened, waggling her ring finger toward Ace.

"Congratulations," Trey said, straightening as Ace

checked out the little sparkler on her ring finger. "Who's the lucky bastard?"

"Well," Ginger said, blushing a little as she looked toward the bar. Brian, the bartender, was over there, and if Trey didn't know any better, that was a little bit of jealousy on the dude's face as Ace held Ginger's hand to get a good look at her ring.

"Oh, I see."

Trey caught Dean's eye, then gave a head jerk toward Ace. Dean gave Ace a swift kick in the shin in response.

"Ow, what the hell, man?"

Ace was still bitching about his sore leg while Ginger happily continued.

"He proposed last night. I couldn't believe it. I've been so busy with Lynn and the kids that I haven't even been thinking about—" She gave a shake of her head, then her smile returned full force. "Anyway, we're eloping this weekend."

"What, no wedding?" Ace said. "No church, no white dress? I didn't think people could get by without that stuff nowadays."

Making a mental note to kick Ace's ass later, Trey spoke. "Is that what you want?"

Ginger glanced back at Brian and then toward the bikers again. "Well, a real wedding would be nice, but we can't really afford it. We decided it'd be better just to go to the courthouse and get it taken care of sooner rather than later."

An idea sparked then. The glimmer of a notion that, once it had taken hold, built into a towering blaze of a thought that couldn't be denied.

Part of the problem with this Iron Knot Wedding

Planners idea was that they'd never done anything like this before. Jameson had been barely more than a kid when he'd gotten married, and his ex-wife's mother had done the whole thing. Ginger wanted a wedding but couldn't afford it. These roughneck bastards needed experience planning a wedding, and Trey could definitely afford a small event to give them the practice.

"Hey," he said, stepping close to Ginger, "let me talk to you alone a moment."

"Sure," Ginger said, and Trey steered her toward the empty end of the bar. Brian shot him a glare that clearly was a warning, but Trey only nodded politely at the bartender before leaning close to Ginger and pitching his voice low.

"What if I told you I could give you a small wedding? Would you be down with that?"

Ginger's eyes went wide. "What? Trey, why would you do that?"

"Long story. Think you can trust me?"

chapter

SEVEN

SARAH'S APARTMENT WAS DECORATED IN THE MOST calming shades of blue, gray, and white, and it always made Bethany feel as if she'd just taken a deep breath. But today, that cool and calming atmosphere wasn't doing as much to keep her chilled out as normal. She'd made the two-hour drive up to Virginia to see her best friend on a whim, and at the moment, it looked like a good thing she'd done so. Bethany had needed the break from the so-far-fruitless online job search, and Sarah… Well, Sarah wasn't handling things well.

"I just don't understand it," she said as she paced in front of the balcony doors. Bethany was sitting on the little slip chair in the corner, a glass of iced tea on the modern round table between the chair and its partner. "He just comes from out of nowhere, and now Mom wants him to plan the wedding. This is… I don't know what to think."

"She said she was using it as time to get to know him," Bethany said, leaning forward. "On one hand, I get that. But on the other, how does it make sense that a guy like him does wedding planning?"

"Ugh," Sarah said, sinking into the other chair. "I don't need this. My residency is almost over, I've got to prep for the NAPLEX, and Mark is worried that our wedding will turn into Sturgis Bike Week." Sarah looked over at Bethany. "You're my favorite person, you know. If not for you running interference, my life would be a total mess right now."

"I'm at a loose end, and you're going in seven different directions. It makes sense that I step in to help. Besides, right now the only places that are hiring are fast-food joints and nursing homes, neither of which really fits what I'm looking for." Bethany reached over and hugged her friend. "Tell Mark not to worry. I'm going to make sure that your wedding is the best, without a single Harley in sight."

"I know. You're awesome." Sarah took a sip of her water, and Bethany followed her gaze out the sliding glass doors.

It was a gray day, slightly drizzly and cool. The spring winds were whipping the young foliage of the trees back and forth like tiny flags. All too soon, the weather would turn hot, the flowers would open, and spring winds would turn into summer breezes.

Wedding season.

"It's not…" Sarah started, then set her water down and tried again. "It's not that I don't want to get to know him. I do. I mean, I've spent my whole life hearing about this baby that was born and disappeared a full four years before I was even conceived. I used to imagine what it would be like to have my big brother here. But Dad always told me that he died, and that Mom was just not willing to face the loss. I'd figured Dad was right. And now?" Sarah shook her head.

"My mom is fawning all over a person that I have no relationship with, and I don't know how to reconcile that with what I've always believed, DNA or not. Dad isn't… Dad isn't here anymore. I can't ask him. I'm not sure what I should do, if I should see Trey or whatever. Talk to him. But I—I kind of want to. You know, on my own. Without Mom."

"Hey," Bethany said, taking her best friend's hand. God, she hated to see Sarah—bubbly, confident Sarah, who always had an answer for everything, who was never at a loss for anything ever—feel like this. "This affects you on a personal level. It's not just about your mom. It's about you too."

"So you don't think I'm crazy?"

Bethany drew a brow up in a credulous smile. "I never said that."

They both laughed, and Bethany drew her cell from her pocket.

"I've got his number. I grabbed it from Mama Yelverton so I could contact him about the invitations. Do you want me to call him and see if you guys can set up a phone call? Get to know each other?"

"Would you?" Sarah bit her lip. "Oh God. Really, I just don't know. Do I even have enough mental energy to deal with this right now?"

"That's up to you," Bethany said gently, her phone screen still dark in her hand. "I won't push you either way. But if you want me to, I'll call."

Closing her eyes, Sarah took a deep breath. Bethany

wished so hard she could take this burden too. This was something Sarah had to face on her own. But Bethany would be there, as close as she could, every step of the way.

"Call him. Please."

The phone was at Bethany's ear a split second later.

Three rings. Four. Bethany was afraid that voicemail would kick in, but then the call connected.

There was a crackling and rustling sound in the background, as if paper was being crumpled up. Gruff male voices were arguing—shouting, actually.

"—get some damn scissors that are big enough for my hands! Where did you get these, kindergarten?"

"They're safety scissors, you idiot. You want Lynn's kids to have gashes from hedge clippers? Bring your own next time. Now cut out that flower before I rip your—"

"Shut your flapping pieholes, I've got a phone call!"

Bethany had to bite her lip to keep the stunned laughter from escaping.

"Harding," Trey bit out as the arguing continued, fading into the background as if he'd stepped away.

"Trey? It's Bethany Jernigan."

"Well, hello there," he said, his voice low and rumbly like his bike's engine. God, it shouldn't do things to her, but it did. "What can I do for you?"

Sarah shifted in her seat, and Bethany snapped back to the present.

"I was calling for Sarah. Your…" She coughed. "Your sister. She wanted to know if you had some time to talk sometime soon. Kind of get to know each other."

"Boss! You need to yank your boy's leash. He's screwing up my invites. I told him I was using—"

"Ace, I swear to God, I will end you if you don't shut

up right now." Trey's voice was suddenly muffled as if he'd tried to cover the mouthpiece and hadn't quite managed it. A snort escaped Bethany, and Sarah gave her a look. She shook her head and kept listening.

"That would be nice, but I don't really have time over the next few days. We've got a wedding we're doing this weekend. So maybe next week."

"Oh," Bethany said, blinking. "Really? You've got another client?"

"Sure do," Trey said shortly, as if her question had gotten beneath his skin. "The Dutmers-Carlisle wedding. Give Sarah my number, and we can text about setting up a call."

"Sure," Bethany said. "Will do."

The call ended, and as Bethany's hand fell to her lap, Sarah tilted her head in question.

"Well?"

Bethany's forehead furrowed as she looked at the dark phone screen.

"He's got another wedding. I don't believe it. Man, I have got to see that."

By the time Ginger's wedding day had rolled around, Trey was stunned that he hadn't landed himself in jail. Or the rest of the Shadows in the hospital.

"Where the hell is the bride?" Flash was saying, red-faced and blustering as he waved around a veil. "I've been gluing flowers to this thing all morning, and she's going to wear it come hell or high water."

"I told you, the bride is the boss, and this is her day. She said no veil. Now put that piece of crap in the garbage

where it belongs and help me with this bow tie." Dean
was towering above Brian in the back room of Ruby's,
the bartender looking nervous as Dean's hands worked at
Brian's throat. Trey wasn't sure whether the expression
was because of the impending nuptials or because Dean
could quite easily snap Brian's neck if he chose to.

Probably the matrimonial noose.

Flash moaned and complained, but he tossed the veil
aside and took over from Dean.

"What's our status?" Trey asked as Dean accompanied him from the room.

"Bride is dressed, maid of honor's helping with
makeup. Kids are under control. Groom's almost done.
Best man showed up in a goddamn Bud Light tee. Ace
has got him handled."

"Good," Trey said, smoothing his damp palms down
his darkest jeans. He was going to have to get some better
clothes before Sarah's wedding. Couldn't keep borrow-
ing Dean's threads. Besides, his shirts weren't quite large
enough. Dean was already whining about the popped
threads across the shoulders of the gray button-down.

"What the hell are those?" Trey glared down at the
raggedy bundle of flowers atop the bar.

"It's a bouquet," Hawk said, tying a lopsided bow in
the piece of yellow ribbon he'd wrapped around them.

"It looks like you picked them from a ditch."

"I did," Hawk said, and Trey had to grit his teeth to
keep from biting the idiot's head off.

"Where is Jameson? He's in charge of flowers.
Jameson!"

"Don't worry, Boss," Jameson said as he entered
the bar. He held a big cardboard box full of bright

yellow and pink flowers. "I stopped at the grocery store. Stargazer lilies and daisies."

"Much better," Trey said, then pinned Hawk with a point and a death glare. "Don't even think about trying to give anyone those."

Trey moved through the space. Despite the hiccups, they were fairly on schedule. Guests would be arriving soon, and—

The door to Ruby's opened. A figure appeared, silhouetted by late-afternoon sunlight. Trey blinked, and blinked again. It was hard to see who it was until the door swung shut.

Slim. Female. Long, blond hair styled into beautiful, loose waves. Elfin features, blue eyes. *Ah, hell.*

"Bethany," he said, smiling tightly even as his insides shouted to get her the hell out of there. "What are you doing here? It's a long way from Southwater."

"Wanted to give my congratulations to the happy couple." Bethany held a gift bag aloft. "I know it's bad manners to crash a wedding, but I brought a gift. I just couldn't stop myself from seeing what kind of event you were capable of putting on. Is that okay?"

Nope. Nuh-uh. Not even a little bit.

"Sure," he said through gritted teeth, then held a hand out to where the wooden chairs had been set up in rows facing the bar, each with a fluffy, white bow on the end. Lynn had tied those after shaking her head at Rocco's efforts. "Please, have a seat."

Bethany smiled at him, an expression that made his insides roar and sit up in expectation at the same time. God, that girl turned him inside out. But for her to show up here? Now?

Her timing was shit. Or much too good. Either way, he was almost definitely screwed.

"Boss, the cake's got a problem."

Mac had appeared from the small kitchen at the back of the place, his clothes covered in flour and smears of pale green. Probably more of Doc's Watergate salad.

A pounding began behind Trey's temples as he turned to walk toward the kitchen and address the latest disaster. Before he could leave, Bethany raised her hand and gave a little wave.

He couldn't worry about her right now. He had a long line of disasters to handle.

The cake wasn't too bad, but the appetizers were a total nightmare. Trey'd had to threaten to take Stone out back and pound the life out of him before he'd give up on the Ritz crackers, peanut butter, and pickle idea. Once Trey had established—again—that Doc was in charge of catering, and that his word was as good as Trey's, he'd had to calm down a six-year-old who'd gotten dirt on her fancy dress. Once he'd passed her off to Hawk, who was much better with little kids than he was with picking flowers, Trey was able to hunt down the preacher. Who'd gone to the wrong bar, nearly twenty minutes away.

Disaster after disaster was piling up at Trey's feet, and he wanted to torch the place to the ground, especially because Bethany was witnessing these spectacular failures. Mrs. Yelverton was sure to hear about all this. He was not the kind of son she'd want. He couldn't even put together a twenty-guest wedding in a dive bar, for God's sake.

"Do you, Brian, take Ginger to be your lawful wedded wife?"

Trey looked toward the front of the room. Somehow, while he'd been so preoccupied with everything, the wedding had started. Ginger was beautiful, radiant in a short, white dress with a pale-pink bow at the base of her spine, her strawberry hair in loose curls secured at the base of her neck. Brian looked terrified and proud as a peacock at the same time as he nodded and said, "I do."

Lynn and her two older girls were dressed in the same pink as the bride's bow, the little ones standing proudly with the tiny bouquets that Jameson had made them. He hadn't been able to give them to them, though. He'd bailed as soon as the kids appeared. Being near them was too painful for him with the memory of his daughter's death. Especially with the new baby being cuddled and shushed by Ruby in the back of the room.

"I now pronounce you husband and wife. You may kiss the bride."

The guests erupted into cheers as Brian kissed Ginger, a long, deep embrace that added the cherry to the top of the ceremony. Trey's quick glance at Bethany revealed that she was smiling, even though she didn't know the happy couple from Adam.

There, Trey thought, a little smug. There had been bumps in the road, but things had gone off well in the end. Maybe now she'd believe that he really was a good wedding pla—

"Baby Got Back" rocked through the room, loud enough to shake the windows in their frames. The music thumping through the bar's speakers startled a laugh from the crowd but shot a bolt of pure rage from

Trey. He vaulted the corner of the table that served as a DJ booth in the back of the room, but he wasn't close enough to catch Ace.

"Sorry, Boss, couldn't resist!"

By the time Trey'd found the right buttons to cut the music, it was too late. Ginger and Brian had boogied back down the aisle to Sir Mix-A-Lot, and Ace had hopped on his bike to take a few laps while Trey cooled off.

Bethany was laughing, her blue eyes sparkling as she joined the rest of the guests milling around and congratulating the happy couple.

God, he was going to murder Ace. But damn if Bethany wasn't beautiful when she smiled.

chapter
EIGHT

Showing up uninvited to a wedding was definitely up there as one of the rudest things she'd ever done, but Bethany couldn't help but be glad she'd done it.

Trey's operation was obviously a fly-by-night proposition. A wedding at a bar? With the weirdest hors d'oeuvres she'd ever seen. The drinks were good, thankfully. She'd needed a stiff one to wash down the shrimp and orange slice on a mini bagel that had been pressed into her hand by a huge, tattooed guy who'd introduced himself as Stone.

And then there were Wolf and Doc and Flash. Every one of them huge, mean, tattooed, and working there. She'd thought she might have stumbled into some kind of comic book.

But Trey was there, standing in the back, huge arms crossed over his barrel chest, surveying the proceedings like a king looking over his lands. He barked orders like a general, ordering those burly dudes around like they were kids. And when he said jump, every one of them did.

If she hadn't been so convinced he was out to screw over her favorite people in the world, she would have been impressed. As it was, the reception was winding down, and she intended to have a very serious conversation with Mr. Harding.

"Excuse me," she said, stepping up to him. "I was hoping I could have a word with you if you're not busy."

"It's not really the best time," he said, his jaw working as he watched a guy slink in through the back door. "Ace, I see you."

She recognized the newcomer. He was the one who'd played "Baby Got Back" at the end of the ceremony and then disappeared. With the way Trey was eyeing him now, it looked like that was the last prank Ace might ever pull.

"Sorry, Boss. I've promised the bride this dance." Ace snagged the bride, who'd been laughing with a guest, and twirled her out into the middle of the floor, which had been cleared of chairs to make room for dancing.

Trey glowered, then shook his head. "I'll kill him later. Come on."

Bethany followed him out into the night. This far out in the country, the stars twinkled brightly. Crickets chirped, the low thump of music from inside muffled by the closing door.

Gravel crunched under Bethany's shoes as she followed Trey a short distance from the building, around the corner to a concrete pad that held a good dozen-plus motorcycles.

"What can I do for you?"

Bethany shivered.

It wasn't the night air. It was the way he stood, feet braced apart, shoulders square, arms loose and ready, body big and strong and near enough for her to sink into.

If she wanted. Which she didn't. Really, she didn't. She cleared her throat. *Focus, Beth.*

"That was…an interesting event." She chose her words carefully. Though she'd clearly won, she didn't want to make him feel bad. Weird, that. She didn't want to make a liar feel bad for lying? What was wrong with her?

"Thank you," he said shortly, his stare direct. She fought the urge to squirm. She hadn't done anything wrong. A little rude, maybe, but not wrong.

"Now will you agree that you can't handle Sarah's wedding?"

"No."

His short answer took her aback, and she blinked. "I'm sorry?"

"I said no."

Her temper rose, blood heating as her pulse quickened. "That's my best friend you're talking about. You think you can get away with something like this for her? A wedding at a bar with shrimp and orange bagels and peanut-butter pickle boats?"

Trey's glare shot toward the bar. "Damn it, Stone, I told you to drop the pickles."

"You can't do this to them. To Sarah, to Mama Yelverton. They're trusting you, and you're lying to them!"

"I know!" he roared, and the sound was so loud and close that her heart jumped into her throat. "I know they're trusting me! That's why I'm trying to do the best job I can. And you're always in the way and trying to ruin it! Why aren't you letting me help them?"

"Because I don't trust you!" She went toe-to-toe with

him, shoulders heaving as she stared straight into his glowering eyes. "You're too—"

"Too what? Too rough? Too mean? Too *bad* to plan a wedding?"

"Yes! All of that! You don't know what you're doing, and you're going to ruin things for them and take their money and break their hearts, and I won't let you do it! I love them, and you're not going to take advantage of them like this!"

Trey stopped, his expression blanking. "You think I'm trying to take advantage of them? For money?"

Bethany's insides stuttered, uncertainty creeping into her voice. "Well, aren't you?"

He looked away from her, an unnamed emotion rolling off him in waves.

"No. I'm not. I don't want anything from them but a relationship. And I hope you understand that you're doing your best to ruin any chance of that."

For the first time, the certainty that she'd held about Trey began to crumble. Standing there in front of her, with his strong, broad shoulders silhouetted against the parking lot lights, he looked—human. Angry and hurt and lonely, as if her words had peeled away the outer shell he presented to the world. His gaze swung back to her, and she saw in that moment just how shallow she'd been. How wrong. How prejudice had blinded her, how the exterior of the man in front of her had shielded her eyes from the true heart of him.

"You were lonely. Weren't you?"

Her whispered question rocked him on his heels as if it were a gunshot.

"Yeah. Yeah, I was. I thought I'd been dumped by

the woman who'd given birth to me in a gas-station bathroom."

Her hand covered her mouth, and she just stared. As if a tourniquet had been released, words flew from him.

"I had nobody. The system yanked me back and forth so many times, I had whiplash by the time I was eight. Nobody wanted me. Nobody—"

He gritted his teeth and stared straight out at the horizon, as if by simply looking at it, he could stem the tide of emotions she'd unwittingly released.

But they hung there, unspoken, and Bethany's heart ached for him.

She'd known love. She'd had the most amazing father for fifteen years. And after that? She'd had the Yelvertons to rescue her from her grandmother. Without them...

Without them, she might know a little more of his pain.

God, how wrong she'd been. Because he looked like a roughneck, she'd judged him as unfit for the Yelvertons. But now...now she could see a glimpse of the little boy he'd been once. Lonely, afraid, abandoned. She longed to comfort him, to heal him, to take away the pain her thoughtlessness had inflicted.

Her father would be ashamed of her.

"I'm sorry," she said, and without thinking, she stepped forward and wrapped her arms around him. He was warm and hard, his body unmoving, like a living rock. "I'm so, so sorry."

For a moment he didn't yield, didn't budge, didn't return her embrace. And then his big, broad hands swept up her back, and he relaxed into her embrace, taking the physical comfort she offered.

With each heartbeat, she tried to communicate her

true feelings to him. To return the kindness he'd shown her in the kitchen. To apologize for ripping open his decades-old emotional wound. To make amends for the fact she'd stood in his way when all he'd wanted was to get to know his family.

But it wasn't enough. She needed to do more.

Of its own accord, her hand wandered up and cupped his cheek. As she looked into his eyes, twin mossy pools of pain and sadness, she did the only thing she could think of.

She kissed him.

"I'm sorry. I've hurt you, and I know what that feels like, and I'm so damn sorry."

The words went unspoken, but she prayed he could feel them in the brush of her mouth against his.

As their lips touched, her heartbeat quickened. Though the kiss had started as a simple comforting measure, she couldn't stop her body's response to his nearness. The sweet cage of his arms around her quickened her pulse, and the scent of him made her blood rush. Her mouth opened to his, her body pressing against him. He took what she so willingly offered, his tongue sweeping deeply into her mouth as his hands cupped her ass and brought her hips in sharp contact with his own.

With every movement of his mouth on hers, he possessed her, took over the body that had betrayed her at the first sight of him. Her body molded to his hard planes, her mouth and tongue tangling wildly with his as her hips and breasts pushed against him, seeking greater, deeper contact.

"Boss?"

A voice behind them made Bethany jump, but Trey didn't release her, lifting his head only long enough to growl at the intruder, "Get lost."

"But the bride and groom are ready to—"

"I said get lost, Dean."

The sound of a door shutting in the distance finished breaking the spell, and with a sigh, Trey released Bethany. She swayed on her feet, but he steadied her.

She bit her lip, looking into his eyes, not knowing what to say. The parking lot that surrounded them had disappeared while he was kissing her, but now she realized just how exposed they'd been, there beneath the light of the parking lot, where anyone could walk by and see them.

What had she been thinking? Easy. She hadn't.

"I've got to go," Trey said, stepping away with obvious reluctance. "Are you coming back in?"

"I need to get going," Bethany said, reaching into the pocket of her dress for her car keys. "I've got some stuff to think about. And…I'm sorry. Really."

Trey nodded, and without another word, he strode toward the door of the bar, leaving her alone.

She looked after him, her insides curiously cold and warm at the same time.

What was she supposed to do now?

She couldn't get him off her mind. Not that night when she went to bed. Not the next day when she cleaned her apartment like some kind of possessed Merry Maid. Not when she slammed her laptop shut after another fruitless job search. And especially not Monday, when she was on her way to dinner with Mama Yelverton.

Her teeth caught her lower lip as she pulled into the parking space at the restaurant.

He'd basically confessed that he wasn't a wedding planner. But at the same time, he'd shown a glimpse of vulnerability that she hadn't expected.

She cut the engine and let her forehead rest against the steering wheel.

She'd been so hell-bent on exposing him. So determined that he was out to screw the Yelvertons over. If not for that little glimpse of something else in him, she'd be walking in there right now to ruin his charade.

So what was stopping her?

With a deep breath, she reached over and grabbed her purse and exited the car.

She still didn't know what to do. Not when she walked to the door, not when she pushed it open, not when she smiled and waved back at Mama Yelverton, who was sitting in a cozy booth toward the back of the restaurant.

"Hello, dear," Mama Yelverton said as Bethany sank onto the bench opposite her. "You feeling okay? You look a little pale."

"Oh, I'm totally fine," Bethany said with a quick smile as she tucked her purse beside her.

"Good. I was worried that I might have been over-burdening you with wedding planning on top of your job search."

Bethany thought she'd hidden her wince fairly well, but apparently not well enough to conceal it from Mama Yelverton. She reached over to pat the back of Bethany's hand.

"Sweetheart, if it's too much, Trey and I can take over ourselves. I'm sure he can help me with everything."

Bethany shook her head. "No, no, I'm enjoying the wedding planning…really. The job market is pretty dismal at the moment, and I've got enough to live on for a good while, so it's a nice distraction." She glanced away for a second, drawing a deep breath in through her nose. "I'm glad you brought the wedding planning up actually, because I wanted to talk with you about that."

Mama Yelverton poured Bethany a glass of wine, looking at her curiously as Bethany searched for the right words.

Your son is a fraud. The Iron Knot doesn't really exist. I want to see Trey romantically.

God, all of it was so wrong to say out loud. And where had the last part come from?

"Beth?"

"I just wanted to say that I think it's going to be wonderful. I talked with Trey this weekend, and he's got some unique ideas that I think will really work well."

Mama Yelverton's smile lit up the whole restaurant. "That's so great," she said. "I'm so happy that you think you can work with Trey. I have to admit, I was a little worried that you didn't like him."

Bethany gave a nervous laugh as she took a big swig of her wine.

It wasn't that she didn't like him—quite the opposite. She wanted to strip him naked and let him do increasingly decadent things to her.

Even though he'd shown her a glimpse of his true self out in that parking lot, she still couldn't shake the worry in her gut that things weren't right. But was she such a monster that she would rob a man who'd been stolen from his family the chance to get to know them?

The sympathy and doubt warred within her, causing her hand to shake a little as she took a sip of her wine.

Whatever else she was feeling, her mistrust didn't justify wrecking what Trey and the Yelvertons were trying to build together.

As Mama Yelverton began talking to the server who'd just appeared beside their table, Bethany pretended to be really interested in the menu. But her mind's eye was filled with a tall, broad, sexy-as-hell biker who'd shown her a glimpse of something she couldn't resist.

For the good of the family—for him—she'd work with him. Her crusade to prove him to be a fraud was definitely over.

She didn't know why, exactly, but she was convinced that helping him succeed was the right thing to do.

Hopefully, he and that crew of tattooed bodybuilders could get organized enough to not screw up Sarah's wedding. And hopefully she could keep her libido under control enough to keep her hands to herself.

Maybe not that last one. If there was ever a resolution she hoped to fail to keep, it was that one.

The week wore on uneventfully. Honestly, by the time Thursday rolled around, Bethany was climbing the walls of her apartment.

She wasn't used to all this free time. At least today she had to go by Hudson's to pick up her final paycheck. Helping with Sarah's wedding was a decent distraction, but there was only so much she could do. It certainly wasn't a full-time job, especially with two other people in on the planning. She'd sent her résumé out for positions at six different companies, none of which had called her back. Disappointing, but it was early days yet. She'd just have to make the best of her unplanned sabbatical.

She was walking toward the front entrance of Hudson's when her cell phone rang.

Trey's name was flashing across the screen. Bethany looked around, glad there were no employees or customers outside the doors at that point.

Gosh, she was acting like a twitterpated teenager.

"Hello?"

"Hi, Bethany." Her name rumbled through the phone like velvet over gravel, sending shivers down her spine.

"Trey," she said, tucking her hair behind her ear. She leaned against one of the concrete pillars near the main entrance of the department store. "What's up?"

"I told you I'd contact you when I had some updates on the wedding."

"Ah, yeah. You did." A little disappointment crept into her voice, damn it all. For some reason she'd been hoping he'd call because he wanted to talk to her.

Idiot.

"Are you free now? I've got some things to show you."

She glanced toward the door, noting the way the store name on the glass was starting to peel slightly. She should—

No, it was somebody else's problem now.

"I'm running an errand at Hudson's. Maybe we could meet at the Starbucks that's nearby when I'm done. I'll only be a minute. Do you know where that is?"

"Yeah. I'm not far. I'll see you there."

The call disconnected, and Bethany let her cell fall into her bag.

Phew. Okay. Seeing Trey today wasn't something

she'd mentally prepared for, but she could handle it. She just had to remember to treat him like a brother, and everything would be fine.

Of course, stopping herself from wanting to kiss him was an impossibility. Wanting to kiss him wasn't the problem, though. Actually following through was the mistake.

Probably a mistake. Yeah. Definitely a mistake.

"Hey, Kate," Bethany said as she passed the customer-service counter. "I'm just here to pick up my paycheck."

"Oh!" Kate looked surprised, then a little panicked as her cheeks flushed, and she picked up the phone. "Hi, Bethany. It'll be just a few minutes, okay? Mr. Junes wanted to talk to you."

Bethany stifled the urge to roll her eyes. "I don't really have anything else to say to Mr. Junes."

Kate's next words were directed into the phone. "Yes, sir, she's here. Okay. I'll ask her to wait."

The handset clicked into the base as Kate looked at her, a bit of sympathy in her brown eyes. "He wants you to wait in your office. Well, *the* office."

Bethany stiffened her spine. "Can't you just give me my check? I really don't want to have to hear him go on and on about this anymore."

Kate shook her head. "Sorry. I would if I could, but it's not with the others. He's got it."

A heavy sigh escaped Bethany, and she adjusted the strap of her purse on her shoulder. "Okay. I'll wait."

Not like she had a choice. But he needed to hurry.

There was a big, burly, sexy man waiting to talk wedding plans with her.

chapter
NINE

TREY WAS MOST OF THE WAY THROUGH AN OVERPRICED coffee when he looked at the time on his phone for the sixth time.

Where was she? She'd said a quick errand, but it had been over half an hour. He'd texted her, but she hadn't responded.

Damn it.

Draining the rest of his coffee, Trey stood, ignoring the nervous looks that the two old ladies at the table across the way gave him.

He tossed his paper cup in the trash on his way by and stalked through the parking lot toward his pickup. The threatening rain had kept him off his bike today, and now he wished he'd just taken it anyway. His frustrations blew away much faster when he could ride into the wind and forget them all.

Nothing like being stuffed into the cab of the old Ford that Doc kept running for him.

The door creaked as Trey slammed it behind him.

The department store she'd mentioned was just across the street and down a block or two. He'd have walked there, but he didn't want to take the chance of passing her on the way.

He wanted to get this over with.

Their encounter at Ginger's wedding had left him feeling shaken—a sensation that he didn't care for in the slightest.

He hadn't meant to show his hand that way. Certainly not to Bethany, who hadn't exactly made a secret of thinking that he was full of it. But God help him, she did things to him that no other woman had. She made him stupid, and stupid men did stupid things. Like basically admit that he was a lying asshole.

By the time he cut the engine in front of Hudson's, he was good and pissed off at himself.

What was he doing? He should have just texted her a picture of the invitations. But his dumb ass wanted to see her, and so here he was, waltzing through this store like he was looking for a long-lost girlfriend.

Idiot.

The store was quiet, the weekday morning not exactly the height of shopping frenzy. The entrance he'd chosen wound right past the empty customer-service desk, with a door behind it marked "Employees Only." And from behind there he heard raised voices, one of which was familiar. Bethany's.

His blood heated instantly, adrenaline pumping through his veins as he stepped closer to the counter, trying to make out what they were saying.

"…just here to get my paycheck. That's all. I'm not

interested in coming back after you fired me for no good reason."

"There was a good reason! But that doesn't matter now. Tiffany quit. It's over, and I can't find another manager on what we paid yo... I mean, we can't find another manager that's as capable as you. You've got to come back."

"I told you, I'm not interested. Now give me my paycheck before I call the cops."

"We aren't done here. I'm not giving you anything until you agree to hear me out."

And then Trey was around the counter. Forget waiting for the cops. This asshole wasn't going to keep Bethany's money hostage so he could try to manipulate her into taking back a job that she clearly wasn't interested in. *Screw that*.

Trey opened the office door, and two sets of eyes swung in his direction, both of them widening as they took him in.

He drew in a breath to make sure he was as filled out as his six-foot-five frame could be. He knew the sight he presented, and even if he didn't, the look on the balding manager's face would have given him a clue. Dude looked ready to wet his pants.

"Is there a problem here?" Trey let a good amount of pissed-off bleed into his tone, glowering down at the man for good effect.

"N-no," the guy stuttered. "I mean, no, sir, thank you. Just a small employee matter. Did you need help with anything?"

Trey looked at Bethany. The exasperation in her expression was clearly not directed at him, but it was enough to encourage him to get this matter over with as quickly as possible.

"You giving my girl grief?"

Out of the corner of his eye, Trey saw Bethany jerk at his choice of words. He didn't give a good damn.

"You two are together?" The man looked from Trey to Bethany and back again.

Trey's fist landed on the desk, causing the objects atop it to shake. "I asked a question. Are you giving my girl a hard time? I'd think real hard about what your answer is, if I were you."

"Trey..." Bethany shook her head, but she didn't deny their supposed relationship. Good. She was as smart as she was beautiful.

"Give her what she came for." Trey leaned closer, watching as beads of sweat popped out along the man's much-too-high hairline. "Do it now, while I'm still playing nice."

"My paycheck, Mr. Junes. Now."

Trey didn't look back at her, but damn was he proud of the strength in Bethany's voice. He'd been right when he called her *strong girl*. That was definitely a key aspect of her personality.

Trey might have sped this process along, but he had no doubt she'd have handled Junes on her own just fine, eventually.

Junes's hand shook as he reached for the drawer in the center of the desk and withdrew a white envelope. He wet his lips nervously as he looked back and forth between the two of them.

"One more time, Bethany. I'm begging. Come back—"

Trey's hand shot out to grab Junes by the collar, but slim, pale fingers circled his wrist, stopping him.

He looked at her in stunned surprise. She shook her head slightly.

"No, thank you." She let go of Trey long enough to take her paycheck and then laced her fingers through his. "We're done here."

Trey's head buzzed as if he'd been struck by lightning as she led him from the office.

Never had anyone stopped him that way. She'd shown no fear, no worry. Just a simple control of the situation that stunned him.

"Thank you," she said once they'd reached the outside. She looked up at the overcast sky, squinting a little. "He wasn't giving up. You certainly intimidated him."

Trey didn't say anything in response. He was too interested in the delicious feeling of her fingers laced through his. It was a comfortable feeling, a safe one. Her hand was so slight in his; it felt so much smaller. But it was strong.

Eventually she'd realize she was still touching him and pull away. But for now, he just enjoyed it.

Bethany drew in a deep breath, and then his hand was empty.

"You had him," Trey said, jamming his hand in his pocket as if he could keep that feeling closer to his skin by doing so.

"I'm sorry I grabbed you like that. I just didn't want you to do anything that might cause him to press charges."

Trey shook his head. "You were right. As much as I would have enjoyed pounding the smug out of that jackass, he's not worth a night in lockup."

Bethany smiled, and there weren't enough gray skies in the world to cloud his day right then. "Thanks for coming to my rescue. I kind of like having a white knight, even if his horse is a motorcycle."

Nothing she could have said would make his chest swell further.

Back at the coffee shop, Trey got another overpriced drink—hard as hell to order a plain, black coffee in that joint, but Bethany insisted she was buying—and sat down with Bethany and her latte in the corner.

"Thanks again," she said as she stirred another pack of sugar into her drink. "Sorry that whole thing made me late and you had to come looking for me."

"Not a problem," Trey said smoothly, leaning back in the seat and keeping his eyes trained on her profile as she looked out on the now-rainy day. Her eyes looked stormy, like the clouds. He liked it. He liked her.

He took a long draw on his coffee, burning his tongue in the process.

"So, I'd love to know your progress."

He blinked. *Oh yeah, the wedding crap*.

Fairly pleased with his progress, Trey reached into the black leather saddlebag he'd brought with him. "I got the venue reserved for the ceremony, and they have an indoor space if it rains. The reception will be held in the restaurant on-site, like we discussed. Here's the confirmation number."

He passed over a sheet of paper that had Wolf's messy contractor's scrawl all over it.

Bethany frowned at the page.

"This says the rental is from 10:00 a.m. to 10:00 p.m."

Trey looked up from the notebook that was precariously balanced on the edge of the bistro table. "Yeah? So?"

"The wedding's at seven. You think people will be done drinking and dancing and cleaned up and out of there by ten?"

Damn it. She was right.

"I'll call them and change the times."

"You'll have to get the contract updated too before Mama Yelverton can sign it."

As Bethany schooled him in the many ways he'd screwed up so far, his sense of accomplishment went up in smoke.

He should have known that things were coming together too well. His mood got darker and darker as their conversation wore on. Finally, Bethany tucked her hair behind her ear and looked straight at him.

"So, the invitations. Do you have anything there?"

Oh yeah. Maybe he could rescue this fiasco after all. Reaching into his bag, his fingers closed on the edge of the large manila envelope he'd stuck in there.

"There are twelve to choose from," he said and handed her the envelope. He was pretty proud of himself there. Holding a contest might have been a junior high concept, but those hairy bastards worked a lot harder for the promise of a five-hundred-dollar bounty than they would have otherwise.

"These…" Bethany's eyes were wide as saucers. "These are… Wow."

"Handmade touches on these things make all the difference." He'd read that on the internet.

"Well, that's true," Bethany said, gingerly flipping through the stack, "but that's not the problem here."

Trey frowned, his irritation flaring to life again. "What's the problem now?"

"These look like they were made by an elementary-school art class." Shaking her head, Bethany tucked the construction-paper invitations back into the envelope. "Trey, listen. I know you're doing your best here, but maybe it's time to throw in the towel. You're just not cut out for this kind of thing."

His hand curled into a fist in his lap, and he didn't meet her eyes.

She wasn't telling him anything he didn't already know. But what choice did he have? It was too late to come up with another lie about his occupation. And telling the Yelvertons—and Bethany—that he headed up a motorcycle gang was out of the question.

Bethany leaned closer to him, her blond hair falling in a curtain over one shoulder.

"Why are you doing this? Who are you, really?"

And just like that, the steel filled his spine again, and ice hid everything behind his eyes. Bethany was just another person. In Trey's life, there were two kinds of people—the Shadows and everyone else. And Bethany? She wasn't a Shadow.

"My business is none of your damn business," he said coldly. "I'm doing a job, and that's all you have to be concerned about. I'll fix the problem with the venue and get better invitations. But my personal life and my past are off-limits. We clear?"

Bethany drew back as if he'd slapped her.

"I... Sorry, I didn't mean to pry, I—"

"Save it," he said, shoving the papers back into the bag. "If it's not about the wedding, there's nothing for me and you to discuss."

"Oh. Okay."

The rest of the conversation was stilted, businesslike, and awkward. Bethany was polite, but much warier than he'd ever seen her. And with each passing minute, he was more and more pissed off with himself.

He'd been the one that started all this. She had more than enough information to expose him to Mrs. Yelverton and Sarah, but she'd chosen not to for whatever reason. So why was he being such a dick? She was helping him cover up his ineptitude, for Christ's sake. And he rewarded her for that by acting like a raging cock-nugget?

"I guess that's everything," Bethany said, capping her pen.

Trey sighed. His rage had cooled enough that he was beginning to see how right she was. Maybe…maybe he could try to climb out of this hole, just a little.

"Do…" He cleared his throat. "Do you have any ideas for making the invitations better?"

She bit her lip, narrowing her brows for a moment. "You sure you want feedback?"

"Yeah. I want them to look good. And it's clear that we're not on the right track. So, if you wouldn't mind…"

Bethany nodded. "Okay. Can I see that envelope again?"

He handed it over, and she reached inside.

"This one is actually not too bad as a concept. But you need much better paper, and there are paper cutters that could do a much more precise job. So, if you go to a craft store—"

"A what now?"

Bethany laughed. "Why don't we head over to Mitchell's Crafts? It's down the road, and I can show you the stuff I mean."

Trey looked at Beth. Hard.

"You want me"—he drew out the word, gesturing down to his tattoos, leather jacket, and steel-toed boots—"to go to a craft store?"

chapter
TEN

WHAT A WEIRD DAY IT HAD BEEN. BUT, AS ODD AS IT had been to have to keep Trey from murdering—justifiably, but still—her ex-boss, it had to be six times more bizarre to walk a six-foot-five tattooed biker through his first craft store.

"What the hell is this for?" He held a Styrofoam ring in his hands, his tattooed knuckle running down the curve of the green foam.

"It's for wreaths. You know, like flowers?"

"It's fricking seven dollars."

Bethany shrugged. "Craft stuff is expensive." She wheeled the cart toward the wedding section, laughing to herself as she heard him muttering about Styrofoam cups being cheap and just as useful as a damn seven-dollar ring.

He was quick though. Once she showed him the type of paper she meant, and they went through the different options for cutouts and embossing and all that, they'd finally come up with a plan.

Since Bethany had a die-cutting machine at home—
Mama Yelverton had gotten on a scrapbooking kick several years ago, and both Bethany and Sarah had received
one for Christmas—she and Trey would work on the
invitations there.

As they checked out and Trey paid for their selec-
tions, Bethany thought about how it would feel to have
a man in her apartment. Not just any man either.

Trey Harding.

With his cold expression, his lethal movements, and
his completely endearing determination to see this wedding through.

God, she was in trouble. At least she'd been bored
enough to clean everything four times that week. No
need to worry about stray laundry or a ring around
the tub.

"You sure you've got time this afternoon?"

"Sure," she said, giving him a smile as he put their
purchases in the passenger seat of his old, black Ford
pickup. His truck was as beat-up as his bike was nice.
"I don't have any plans until tomorrow when we're supposed to finalize the guest list."

"Great." He palmed his keys and stood there, waiting.

God, he was so hot. Even when he'd been questioning why anyone would need a set of picture frames
shaped like seashells, she'd had to keep her eyes glued
on something to keep them from wandering over the
muscular planes of his body again.

What would it be like to be with a man like that?
All of her previous boyfriends seemed so…colorless in
comparison to him. Trey was big all over, tough, and
larger than life. He'd be in control in the bedroom, she

was certain. She'd never thought of herself as a sexual submissive, but damn if the idea of Trey ordering her to her knees didn't make her stomach tighten with want.

"So, what's your address?"

Blood rushed to her cheeks as she realized she'd been stripping him naked in her mind's eye while he waited for directions.

Jesus, she needed to focus.

"Sorry. I... Sorry. Moorcliffe Apartments, over on Parker Road. Apartment 3-A."

"See you there," he said with a nod. He stood and waited while she climbed into her Corolla, which was parked only a few spaces away from his truck.

She waited for a moment, but he motioned her out first. *Oh duh*. He was going to follow her.

The whole drive back home, she told herself to keep it professional. She wasn't taking him home to unwrap like a big, old piece of man-candy. This was about Sarah and Mark's wedding. Not about her starving, malnourished libido.

She managed to last ten minutes before mentally undressing him again.

"You sure it's up here?"

"Yeah," Bethany said, trying and failing to keep her eyes off his glutes. Good God, she'd seen less attractive asses on male models. "I put it in the top of the closet. It was one of those gifts that I thought about returning, but I was too busy to get around to it."

He was standing on the lowest step of the step stool and reaching all the way to the back of her spare room's closet shelf. She would have needed to put a box atop the step stool to achieve the same reach.

"Here," he said, unearthing a box from the far back corner. "Got it."

"My hero," Bethany said with a smile as he stepped to the floor. "Thanks."

"You've got to stop with this white knight, hero crap," Trey said without venom as he set the die-cut machine on the table by the window. "I'm not that kind of guy."

"So far, you haven't done anything to convince me otherwise."

She thought back to the moment he'd burst into her old office, looking like the world's most badass avenging angel as he stared down her ex-boss. Yup, he wasn't doing a good job of pretending not to care.

As she busied herself unboxing the die-cut machine, she watched him out of the corner of her eye. He wandered around the room, taking it all in.

"Nice color," he said, nodding at the pale-blue walls.

"Thanks," she said. "I like calming shades."

He stopped at her dresser and picked up a framed photo. She and Sarah smiled out from the frame, their graduation tassels hanging at jaunty angles as they mugged for the camera.

"You must have been popular in high school."

Bethany barked out a laugh. "Not hardly. If not for Sarah, I'd have been a complete loner all through school."

Trey hiked a brow at her as he put the picture back atop the dresser. "No way that's possible."

"It is. I was awkward, too thin, with a bad acne problem when I moved here. But Sarah somehow saw through my social anxiety, and we became best friends. Then, when my dad died, they took me in."

Bethany bent down to plug the machine into the wall, glad for the motion that hid her face from him. She didn't know what it was about this man that made her want to spill her guts to him.

"This is him?"

She turned. Trey had answered his own question, picking up her dad's last service portrait.

"Yeah. That's him."

"He looks like you."

"Yeah." Bethany kept the answer short, trying to stifle the old pain.

Clearing her throat, she leafed through the instruction booklet, and for a few moments the only sound in the room was the soft rustle of paper and the occasional honk from traffic outside.

"I wondered…" he started, breaking the silence, then coughing. "I wondered what it would be like. Living with them…as a kid, I mean."

"The Yelvertons?" Bethany lowered the instruction booklet. "They were amazing. They treated me as if I were their own flesh and blood. Still do," she said, smiling ruefully down at her toes. "You couldn't find a more giving and loving family than them."

"You must love them a lot."

"I do."

Trey turned his back to her, and she studied him in silence for a long moment as he perused her bookshelves.

What he was doing was both sweetly touching and heart-wrenching. Not only was he trying to get to know her by exploring her space, but he also seemed to be imagining what he'd have been like if he'd been who he was born to be.

But the boy who'd been Samuel Yelverton was gone forever, and Trey Harding stood in his place. Hurt, lonely, and desperate to find his place in the world.

Bethany stood and let the booklet fall to the tabletop. Crossing the distance between them, she wrapped her arms around his waist and pressed her cheek to his back.

She didn't say anything, just closed her eyes and enjoyed being close to him. And, after a moment, his hands covered hers on his rock-hard abdomen.

"You keep acting like this, and I'll forget I'm a gentleman," he said in a husky voice. She shivered a little as the deep rumble went through her.

"I already bought you a drink," she said, loosening her grip so he could turn to face her.

"I guess you did," he said with a crooked smile and a twinkle in his eye.

"Doesn't that mean I get another kiss?"

"Whatever Strong Girl wants," he said, leaning down, then lowering his voice to a whisper, "Strong Girl gets."

Mouth descending to hers, he kissed her. Softly at first, gently, as if the emotion in the room had driven them together, their mouths tangled sweetly in a dance of getting-to-know-you. Bethany sank into him, her heart threatening to escape her ribs if it beat much faster.

But the hunger that had been growing between them couldn't be held at arm's length forever. Bethany opened her mouth to him, and then he lost control. Kissing her wildly, deeply, passionately, he moved against her as if this was his last day, and she was his last hope.

His hands were everywhere—rubbing down her

back, across her waist, down to cup her ass and lift her straight off the floor and hard against him. She gasped against his mouth at the feeling of his erection pressing into her belly.

He clearly wanted her as badly as she wanted him.

Whirling, he took the three steps to the bed that was pressed against the wall opposite the closet. Down onto the mattress they went, his big body covering her, holding her down, imprisoning her with the passion she'd imagined over and over again since their first meeting.

"Beth," he growled against her neck, and she arched her back to encourage him.

His teeth grazed her pulse point, and her blood rushed through her veins at triple speed. Her nipples were so hard they were aching inside her bra, her core getting wetter with every touch, every caress, every kiss.

His hand was broad enough that, when he brought it from her waist upward, he covered her whole breast with a palm. She gasped, the fabric of her bra and shirt not enough to keep the feeling of his hand from her sensitive nipple.

"I can't wait to see these," he said, rubbing his hand over her breast in a gentle but demanding circle. She moaned, her legs shifting against each other in a fruitless bid to ease the ache he was stoking there. "You are so beautiful. I want to see and touch every part of you."

"Then do it," she whispered, tangling her fingers in his hair to bring his head down to her again. "I want you too."

His fingers went low, to the hem of her shirt, and her breath caught in her throat as his touch skirted across her bare belly. His fingers were a little rough, and the foreign sensation heightened her anticipation and excitement as they bumped over her lower ribs.

"If you've got any ideas about changing your mind, this is the moment to do it. Once I see you—"

She grabbed his hand and looked deep into his beautiful, sea-green eyes. "I want you, Trey."

A hungry smile spread across his face, and his fingers had just crept beneath the edge of her bra when—

The doorbell rang.

With a little shriek, Bethany jumped. Trey clapped a hand over her mouth.

"If you want to keep this quiet, screaming isn't the best way to do that," he whispered.

Shaking her head, she scooted out from under him. "Crap. I… Crap. Where's my… Okay. Stay here."

Weaving her way out of the room, Bethany skidded toward the front door as if her ass were on fire. In a way, it was. Trey had been so willing to help her stoke that flame. And now she had to pretend to be normal for whoever was on her front doorstep.

Hopefully, it was a salesman, or a religious invitation, or a new phone book that would land straight in the recycling bin.

Bethany peeped through the hole and winced. No such luck. She twisted the lock with a jerk and opened the door, just a bit.

Her neighbor, a sweet—but incredibly nosy—older woman, was trying to peer through the crack in the door.

"Hi, Mrs. Sanders! How are you?"

"Just fine, dear. I'm sorry to bother you, but I need some help. The light bulb in my bathroom blew, and I'm not too steady on the stepladder. Would you mind?"

Crap.

"Oh no, no problem," Bethany said with a tight smile.

"I just… Well, I'm in the middle of something, is all. I was—"

"Oh dear," Mrs. Sanders said, her eyes brightening with interest. "Is your boyfriend here? I didn't know you were dating someone. Oh, do let me meet him."

"What?" Bethany's denial was half breath, half squeak. "No, no, of course I don't have a guy here. Why would you say that?"

Mrs. Sanders laughed, almost a cackle. "I'm not so old that I don't remember that look. I'll ask Matthew across the way to help me with the light bulb. You have fun." She patted Bethany's hand with a wink. "Bye now."

The door closed behind her.

"Jesus," Bethany moaned and collapsed onto the couch.

She had to get this under control. Who the hell knew what would happen if the Yelvertons found out that Bethany wanted their long-lost Samuel?

She didn't want to know. She really, really didn't.

Leaving Bethany had been difficult, but she'd asked him for time, and he wouldn't say no.

Still gave him a raging case of blue balls and a pissed-off attitude though. And two days later, it wasn't fading. He'd texted, but she hadn't responded. Knowing it was a bad idea just to go to her apartment, he settled for sitting at home, or at Ruby's and glowering into a glass of Jack.

"Hey, Boss." Evidently, Ace hadn't gotten the message that Trey didn't want to be bothered. The blond-haired biker sank down beside him with a grin. "We going out tonight?"

"No."

Ace leaned forward on crossed arms as Trey downed the rest of his drink. "But it's Thursday. We always go looking for dealers on Thursday."

Several of the Shadows had had problems with addiction in the past, and none of them wanted anyone dealing hard drugs in their territory. Their weekly ride-through ensured that anyone who got the bright idea to start would be fully aware of who'd be handing them their own asses once they got word.

"Wolf's handling it." Trey grabbed the bottle and poured himself another, thankful that Ginger had left it.

"But it's your favorite night of the week."

Trey bared his teeth at Ace just as Jameson walked up.

"Ace, Wolf wants you outside."

Grumbling, Ace shoved his chair back and headed outside.

Any hopes Trey had of solitude were short-lived when Jameson sat down in Ace's recently vacated chair.

"You mind?" Jameson nodded toward the bottle.

Trey pushed it over to him wordlessly.

For several moments, they drank in silence, Trey from his glass, Jameson straight out of the bottle. The low buzz of voices from other tables acted like a barrier between them, each man alone with his own thoughts. After a few minutes though, Trey eyed the other man with a sidelong glance.

Jameson was a couple inches shorter than Trey, still topping out at just over six feet. His tattoos were all black and gray, most of them from his time in the military. The glaring exception was on the back of the hand that was wrapped around the bottle of Jack—a set of angel wings around the initials CM done in a purple, feminine script.

Trey looked down at the glass in his hand again. He really was a bastard. He was so up in his damn head about Bethany that he'd completely turned his back on the rest of the Shadows.

"Boss."

Jameson broke the silence. Trey looked at him.

"What's up?"

"I don't know if I can keep doing this wedding shit. It's—" Jameson rubbed a hand over the back of his military-style haircut. "All the families around. The kids. I... It got to me at Ginger's."

Jameson lifted the bottle and took a long, hard pull.

Trey didn't say a word. Jameson continued.

"It will—it would have been—her birthday in June. It's always worse then. You know I'd do any damn thing you asked. I'm just asking—no, I'm begging—you to let me do something else."

Feeling lower than dog shit, Trey pounded the rest of his drink and pushed the glass away. "You're off the hook. I need someone to keep up with our regular jobs anyway. You can take point on that. The Thursday night rides, the usual security details, any calls that come in."

Jameson's eyes widened slightly. "You want me to do all that? What about Wolf?"

"Wolf does what I ask him to. Same as the rest of you assholes."

The relief was clear on Jameson's face, but that didn't make Trey feel any less like a dick. "You got it, Boss."

"Good. Now go get me a bottle of water. Ginger's up to her ears in alligators right now."

Jameson nodded and took the empty bottle and glass up to Brian at the bar.

Alone again, Trey laced his hands atop his head and looked at the low, exposed beams of the ceiling.

He really was a selfish jerk. That wasn't really a surprise though. What was a little out of the ordinary was the fact that it was bothering him.

He couldn't pretend that it wasn't because of recent events. Now that he had a frame of reference for where his genetic material had begun, it felt as though he should be doing better. Caring more. Hell, his mother's influence even had him wondering if he should step down as head of the Shadows.

He was that serious about fitting into her life. And how stupid was that? He could change his wardrobe, he could sell his bike, but he'd always be a tattooed loser from the wrong side of the tracks. No amount of new clothes and fancy talk could cover up the stink that was his early life.

And that was the asshole who was doing his best to worm his way into the Yelverton family and to get into Bethany's panties. A woman his mother had made clear was basically a second daughter to her.

"Damn it," Trey said, shoving his chair back and stalking outside.

He was a rotten bastard.

Wolf, Ace, and several of the other guys were outside, talking about the route they were about to ride.

"Wolf." Trey beckoned his second with a nod. Wolf came over to the shadowed side of the building where Trey waited.

"We're ready to ride."

"Let Jameson take point."

Wolf frowned, an expression that was made plainer by the wrinkle in his forehead than the corners of his mouth, which were obscured by his impeccably groomed dark beard.

"He needs this." Trey tapped the back of his right hand. Wolf's eyes lit with recognition, and he nodded immediately.

"Give him an hour or so to sober up, and then circle back so he can take over."

"What about you?" Wolf tightened his glove as he asked. "You've been hitting the bottle quite a bit lately yourself."

The question made Trey's fists tighten, but he forced them to relax. "Just had a lot on my mind. I'm working it out."

Wolf nodded. "Just make sure you work it out before your liver craps the bed."

"Drop dead," Trey said without venom and nodded toward the group of men who were trying to look casual as they clearly attempted to overhear the conversation from the shadows. "They're waiting for you."

He clapped Wolf on the shoulder, and then his second walked back to the concrete pad where their bikes all sat.

With a heavy breath, Trey sank down on the curb.

He'd kissed Bethany out here after Ginger's wedding. What he wouldn't give to have her in his arms again. But that was a bad idea, and he knew it. Especially since she'd pushed him away.

He needed to focus. Keep this charade going long enough for Sarah to get married and his mother to believe that her son was the kind of man she could be proud of.

Then he could back off. It's not like Mrs. Yelverton and he moved in the same circles. He could tell her he'd moved and see her from time to time, but not so often he had to *keep* lying.

It could work, if he kept his brain on the task and his cock in his pants.

Which was easier said than done, especially when he remembered how incredible Bethany felt beneath him.

Ah, damn it.

chapter
ELEVEN

BETHANY SHIVERED AS THE COLD AIR OF THE BATHROOM hit her wet skin. She'd needed a shower less for her body than for her mind.

Grandmother Trudy was at it again.

After the Purple Heart incident, Bethany had toyed with the idea of never speaking to the woman again. But her promise to her father kept ringing in her head, a constant reminder that he'd loved the woman—difficult though she was.

Bethany snorted as she briskly rubbed the green-striped towel down her body. *Difficult* wasn't the word for Grandmother Trudy. *Terrible? Impossible? Pure evil?*

In any case, the phone call she'd gotten that morning had definitely left Bethany feeling off.

"I need to talk to you."

"There's nothing that needs to be said," Bethany had said curtly, tossing the covers back and swinging her feet over the edge of the bed.

At six on a Saturday morning, the only phone calls

that should be happening were for bodily injury or garage-sale early birds. This was neither. Well, the bodily injury was a thought…

"Your misunderstanding about my Marine's medal has nothing to do with this."

"My misunder—" Bethany shook her head and paced back and forth in front of her closet. "Never mind. Not discussing that with you. What is it?"

And then Grandmother Trudy had dropped the bomb.

"The family is coming into town this afternoon."

Bethany's stomach dropped, and her knees almost buckled, but she grabbed onto the knob of the closet door just in time to stop herself.

"What?"

"The family is coming in. Your uncle, aunt, and cousins. They want to see you."

Even the memory of her grandmother's words made Bethany want to hop straight back into the shower and stay there for the rest of the day. But she couldn't. She had to go meet with her grandmother's side of the family and pretend that everything was peachy keen, jelly bean.

She hated everything about that.

Jerking a brush through her wet hair, she avoided looking directly at the mirror. She knew what Sarah and Mama Yelverton would say if they knew what she was planning to do that afternoon.

"Are you insane? Why would you put yourself in that situation again?" Sarah would yell and rail, threatening to shake sense into her.

Mama Yelverton would shake her head sadly. "Bethany, I don't think it's a good idea. You remember what happened last time."

She did. She remembered all too well how her grand-mother's brother, her great-uncle Reuben, had nearly set her grandmother's house on fire. He'd gotten drunk while grilling, and an overreaction to a flare-up had sent flaming burger patties straight into a pile of cardboard boxes on the porch. His wife, Great-Aunt Wendy, had screamed at him the whole time, as if that would help to calm the flames that were licking their way toward the house. Bethany, ever the problem-solver, had immediately worked to put out the flames, but Uncle Reuben had stumbled into her, shoving her hands-first into the fire. She'd ended up in the ER all night with blistered palms and a deep-seated desire to never see those people again.

No wonder Grandmother hadn't warned her in advance.

"So why are you even going?" Her question to herself was voiced aloud, but her answer was silent.

Because of that freaking promise. *Dad, if you knew what this was going to cost me, would you have put me in this situation?*

She wasn't sure. But in any case, she'd do what she had to do to protect that horrible old woman.

For her father's sake. *Semper fi*.

She took her time getting dressed. After all, it wasn't like she wanted to be in her grandmother's company any more than she had to be. Especially after the most recent violation she'd so cavalierly tossed Bethany's way.

Clothes. Makeup. Hair. Bethany sighed as she turned off her curling iron. At least if the whole group of them was arrested for a public WWE-style brawl, her mug shot would look pretty good.

If she still had all her teeth. Aunt Wendy had a mean right hook. She'd witnessed it being aimed at Uncle Reuben plenty of times.

A soft trilling from her bedroom wrenched a groan from her.

Phone ringing again.

For a moment she was tempted to let voicemail have it. That way, if the caller had the last name of Yelverton, she'd be saved from having to lie about her plans for the day. And if it was Grandmother? Well, she'd be seeing her soon enough anyway.

But ignoring problems wasn't inside Bethany's comfort zone. With a curse, she sprinted toward the bedroom, skidding to a stop in front of the bedside table.

Her heart did a little turn and skip when she saw the name flashing on the screen. With a quick breath to compose herself, she swiped the answer button.

"Trey?"

That deep, rough voice never failed to warm her from the inside out. "Beth. How are you?"

"Okay," she said, wrapping her free arm over her stomach in an effort to calm the butterflies.

Hadn't she told herself that she was going to keep her distance from Trey? That she'd treat him like a brother from now on? Why hadn't her body gotten the hint?

"Sorry to bother you so early on a Saturday, but I wondered if you would have some time to help me with those invitations this afternoon. I need to get the proofs to Mrs. Yelverton soon."

Bethany bit her lip and looked toward the spare bedroom, where her die-cut machine sat in the same place that Trey had left it.

"Oh, I wish I could. Believe me, I do. I would much rather be doing that than going where I've got to go today."

"It's okay. We can work on them some other time. Just thought you might have a free day. Don't want to interrupt your plans."

The wheels in Bethany's head started turning then. A smile broke out across her face as the notion formed.

"Hey, Trey. You're pretty good at keeping people straight, right?"

Trey snorted. "I've made a career out of it."

Incredulity crept into Bethany's tone with a good bit of mirth. "I guess wedding planning *is* kind of an exercise in crowd control."

Trey cleared his throat. "Yeah. Um, yes. Right. Why do you ask?"

"If you're free this afternoon, think you could give me a hand? It'll take a little acting on your part, but you'd be making my life a lot easier."

She could almost imagine him crossing his arms over that broad, muscled chest as he said, "Details. And don't skimp."

As much as she could without talking about her father, Bethany gave him the scoop. She finished up with "…and if you're with me, I think they'd be much more inclined to behave. I mean this in the nicest way possible, but you're a little, erm, physically intimidating."

His laugh brought the blood rushing to her cheeks.

"I'll take that as a compliment. But what's the excuse for bringing me to a family function? Won't they wonder who I am?"

Her cheeks got hotter. "Well, if you were to pose as

someone important to me, that'd explain it pretty well, I think."

"I could do worse than act like the boyfriend to a perfect blond princess like you."

Her hackles rose. "I'm not a perfect blond princess."

"You're right, Strong Girl. My mistake. I'm in. No charge. Where should I meet you?"

Relief soaked her as she rattled off the address to the restaurant her grandmother had chosen.

As the call ended, Bethany looked down at the phone in her hand.

Well, it was a Hail Mary pass for sure. Here's hoping it worked out. And if not? Worst case?

She got to pretend to be Trey's girlfriend for an afternoon.

That was a guilty fantasy almost worth facing her family for.

HH

Trey cut the engine of his bike at the back corner of a crowded parking lot. His nostrils twitched as he took in the sight of all the SUVs, minivans, and hybrid sedans crowded around the Olive Garden like suburbanite piglets rooting for a spot at the faux-Italian teats.

Of all the places Bethany's family could have picked…

He gritted his teeth and swung his leg over the bike. He could put up with the place for her. At least they had good breadsticks.

Frankie Blue Eyes crooned through the tinny speakers aimed at the poor jokers stuck outside in the chilly breeze. Trey strode past them toward the entrance. Bethany had already texted him that she was inside.

The hostess shrank back a bit at the sight of Trey—or it could have been the dark look that probably crossed his face when he took in the pungent scent of garlic that clung to the place like cheap perfume. But in any case, she ushered him back to the corner of the restaurant where Bethany was sitting alone at a table for ten.

"Hi," she said, smiling up at him. And with that one expression, ninety percent of his pissed-off drifted away on the vampire-repellent breeze.

"Hey," he said, sinking into the chair beside her. Despite the crowded restaurant, there was a good amount of space around their mostly empty table. "How long have you been here?"

"Since they opened," Bethany admitted, circling her glass of water with both hands. Drops of condensation puddled in the tender spot between her thumb and palm. Trey wanted to reach over and brush it away, but he didn't. "It's better if we're back here. Disturb fewer people that way."

"It's only one. You really think he'll get that drunk?"

Bethany bit the side of her lip as she looked up at him. *Damn.* She really shouldn't do that. It reminded him how soft her mouth was, how it had felt as he kissed her—

"He starts early. And he doesn't really need to be drunk to be an asshole. He's a lot like Grandmother Trudy in that respect."

"I see."

And Trey did. In the way her hand shook a little as she lifted her glass to her lips. In the wary way her eyes darted toward the room's entrance over and over. In the waves of frustration that were almost visibly rising from her.

His strong girl was rattled, and if that didn't make

him want to throttle whatever was bugging her, almost nothing would.

"You've got this," he said, reaching over and catching her hand. Her skin was cold and damp from the glass, and he rubbed it with his warmer one. "I'm here with you. Everything's going to be fine."

"Thanks," she whispered, looking up into his eyes with those baby blues of hers. God, she was so beautiful. "I'm sorry for dragging you into this, but I can't help but be really happy you're here."

He didn't respond. He couldn't. There weren't words for the weird feeling taking over his chest, the swelling mixture of pride and he didn't know what else inside him. But it was a good feeling. A big feeling.

She was shaking him up in ways he'd never expected.

"Oh God," she said, looking out the window. "They're here."

She started to jerk her hand away. He gripped it tighter. "We're supposed to be together, right? Let me help."

She nodded and squeezed back. "You're right. Oh God, this is going to be a nightmare."

Trey sank back into the chair's cushioned backrest, smiling a little to himself.

Bethany didn't know who she'd chosen for her backup. She had no clue that Trey regularly handled addicts, prisoners, the dregs of society. There was no way for her to understand that there wasn't anything her drunk uncle Reuben could throw at him that he wasn't prepared for.

This, Trey thought, rubbing his thumb across the rapidly jumping pulse at Bethany's wrist, *is going to be fun*.

But, then again…

"Bethany!"

Trey blinked twice. The man was probably 150 pounds soaking wet. His face was flushed, his walk unsteady, as if he'd already been hitting the bottle before walking in.

Behind him was a pinched-faced, thin woman with dyed-black wispy hair. His wife, Trey presumed. Behind them was a stooped-backed, gray-haired woman whose sweatshirt had entirely too many fake gems hot-glued to it. The way her faded blue eyes darted around the room, her fingers curling into her palms, Trey guessed this was the hoarding grandma that Bethany was not fond of.

A group of teenagers followed behind them, staring down into their phones and pretending not to be there. Trey couldn't blame them as Bethany and he rose to greet the newcomers.

"Hi, Uncle Reuben," Bethany said weakly as the man gathered her into his arms for a hug. He lingered too long, and Trey's protective instincts kicked into gear as the guy's bony fingers wandered a little too far down Bethany's back for a friendly uncle's hug. He reached over and grabbed Bethany's arm, pulling her free of Uncle Handsy's embrace. She shot him a grateful look as he slung his arm possessively over her shoulder.

"Who's this?" Aunt Wendy sniffed as she sank into a seat in the center of the long table.

"This is my...my boyfriend." Bethany didn't meet his eyes as she said it, but Trey gave her an encouraging squeeze. "Trey Harding. This is my aunt..."

As Bethany made the introductions, Trey started cataloging their opponents.

Reuben. More than half drunk. Obviously too fond of his niece. Asshole to the waiter. Huge potential for trouble.

Wendy. Chronic bitch face. Jealous of Reuben, with good reason. Prone to talking loudly over anyone and everyone. Huge potential for escalating whatever Reuben decided to start.

Grandma Trudy. Narcissistic klepto. Had already tucked her silverware and napkin into her oversized purse and asked the confused waiter for more. Had skewered Bethany with more than one comment about her "trashy gangbanger" boyfriend. Needed a good kick up the bony ass, but would probably stay out of Reuben's way if he went postal.

The teenagers were non-issues. They were Reuben and Wendy's grandkids and would obviously rather be pretty much anywhere other than at the Olive Garden seeing their Great Aunt Trudy and distant cousin Bethany.

Trey ordered an iced tea when the waiter got around to him, and settled back with his hand firmly on the back of Bethany's chair.

"So, how long has this little…thing…been going on? I'd never have dated someone like that." Grandma Trudy looked like she'd smelled something bad as she asked the question. Her face resembled the backside of an alley cat.

Bethany smiled shyly over at Trey. "A couple months now. Trey's such a great guy."

"He's got an awful lot of tattoos," Reuben grunted over his "sample" glass of wine. He'd intentionally bumped the waiter's arm so his glass had gotten overfilled.

"I do," Trey said smoothly, presenting his fist to Reuben, knuckles first, only inches from his nose. "Want to check them out?"

Reuben blinked owlishly as he realized Trey's smooth reply was a threat.

"No, no, that's okay." Reuben rounded on the waiter, who'd stopped by with his notepad to take their order. "This sample tastes bad." He lifted his mostly empty glass of white. "What've you got in red?"

Trey's muscles twitched as he settled back in next to Bethany.

That poor waiter better keep those breadsticks coming. This was going to be a long lunch.

chapter

TWELVE

BETHANY WONDERED IF THE GREEN FLORAL CARPETING beneath her feet could swallow her up if she wished for it hard enough.

As glad as she was not to be alone with her terrible, loud, getting-drunker-by-the-second family, she couldn't help but be embarrassed that Trey was seeing all this and taking the brunt of the rude questions and comments about his, well, everything.

First Uncle Reuben had started on the tattoos, then Aunt Wendy on his beard stubble and shaggy hair. Then Grandmother on his clothes. So what if they were dark? So what if his leather jacket had scuff marks on it? And yeah, he was a big guy, but it was all muscle. Aunt Wendy's sniffling comment about big, hairy men was completely uncalled for.

When their entrees arrived, Bethany picked at her pasta, trying to let the conversation blow right over her. Beside her, Trey was munching on a breadstick instead of his own bowl of noodles and sauce. She wanted to ask him to make sure his food was okay, but she didn't want to draw attention to them again, since the discussion seemed to finally have veered away from Bethany's poor life decisions.

"...should have let me help you with that," Uncle Reuben was saying to his older sister. Grandmother was shooting daggers at him as he continued, completely oblivious. "At your age, you shouldn't be trying to do all that paperwork on your own."

"It's none of your business," Grandmother fired back as she speared a meatball with her fork. "I can handle my own affairs."

"But I've told you a million times, that's not the right investment for you. When your son died, I told you at the funeral that you should take that money and—"

Bethany's stomach dropped as if the penne she'd just swallowed was made of solid lead instead of wheat. "What did you say?"

Trey sat up straighter, as if the tension in Bethany's question had put him on alert.

God, she was glad he was there beside her. Even gladder when he reached beneath the table and put his broad hand over her cold one, squeezing slightly.

"It was life insurance money. Nothing that should have gone to you, you greedy little snot," Grandmother said, alternating her dirty looks between Bethany and Reuben. "I paid the premiums. It was my policy on my Marine."

Bethany didn't say anything further. Nothing surprised her anymore. Of course her grandmother had hoarded the money from her father's life insurance. The funeral he'd had had been so sparse, it had looked like he'd died penniless.

But a funeral wouldn't bring her father back. She'd given up being upset about her grandmother's decisions after Dad's death several years ago.

That didn't mean salt in the old wound didn't sting though.

"I've told you many times not to bring up my money matters in front of people," Grandmother said to Reuben with a glower. "My finances aren't to do with anybody else."

"They will be when Reuben puts you in a home," Aunt Wendy said with a gleeful little cackle. "He's just trying to make his job easier."

"What do you mean, a home? There ain't a thing wrong with me!"

"Now, Trudy, we both know you're getting on a bit," Reuben said, gesturing with his wineglass. A good bit sloshed out onto the front of his shirt. He frowned down at the stain before taking another swig and continuing. "I'm just looking out for your best interests. When you can't handle living on your own anymore, what do you think will happen?"

"I'm not going into any home!" Grandmother's voice pitched into a near-shriek as she stood and looked at her brother. "All my things are at my house. That's where I belong. And if I need help, I'll make Bethany move in with me. It's where she's supposed to have been all along."

Bethany's blood turned to ice in her veins, and instantly the promise she'd made felt like an iron shackle around her future. "No," she said, weakly at first and then stronger as she repeated it. "No. This is not happening. And it's not appropriate to talk about this in public."

"You're damn right it's not." Uncle Reuben slammed

his wineglass down so hard Bethany was afraid the stem would shatter. "I've got rights, and I'm not about to lose them to a girl who's sleeping with some kind of gangbanger. She's probably got all kinds of diseases now, and—"

"I'm going to give you about two seconds to shut your damn mouth before I shut it for you."

Four heads turned as if on swivels. Trey was smiling, but his expression wasn't cheery in the least. He was staring down Uncle Reuben like a big cat sizing up his prey.

"Bethany's off-limits. Talk all the shit you want to about the rest of your family, but keep your trap shut when it comes to her."

Bethany could do nothing but stare at Trey as Uncle Reuben's temper shot through the roof. Gratitude suffused her. She'd been silently praying for a fire in the kitchen or a meteor strike, anything to get them out of there. Apparently Trey was a mind reader.

"Who the hell do you think you are, talking to me like that?"

Aunt Wendy wouldn't sit back for it either. She jumped to her feet much quicker than Bethany had ever seen her move before. "My husband's got every right to talk however he wants! This is a free country!"

Grandmother, suddenly realizing that none of the attention was on her, jumped into the fray. "I can't believe you're acting like this in front of the family! You're embarrassing me, Bethany Ann Jernigan! I've never been so humiliated in my life!"

This was a scene Bethany had watched play out a billion times before. It was as if she were frozen in place, desperate to escape but held by the invisible shackles of an unlucky genetic link and the promise she'd made. God, she'd give anything to get out of this.

Trey stood too, pulling Bethany to her feet and grabbing the strap of her purse in his free hand. "We're not going to sit here and listen to you be like this. We're leaving."

"The hell you are! You'll sit down and act like a civilized person and not ruin my family dinner!" Grandmother reached for Bethany's arm, but Trey blocked her grip. Not to be outdone, Uncle Reuben decided that he'd be the one to pull his prodigal niece back into the fold where she belonged.

But because of his impaired depth perception—*thank you, alcohol*—he missed entirely, his balance falling victim to his ill-advised movement. Instead of Bethany, he grabbed the table and jerked.

Breadsticks and pasta went flying, glass breaking, wine spreading across the plush carpeting like floodwaters overtaking a flowered field. Bethany jumped back to avoid it puddling around her shoes.

Reuben stumbled toward them, red-faced and yelling, his fists held up as if he intended to start beating one or both of them.

"We're leaving," Trey said and dragged her out of the path of stampeding Reuben.

The waiter arrived then. "What's going on? What ha—"

His words were cut off midsentence, and Bethany turned just in time to see Reuben's wild swing connect with the waiter's midsection.

"Reuben!" Aunt Wendy screamed. Not to be outdone, Grandmother sank to the pasta-covered floor in a dead—presumably faked—faint.

Trey didn't stop. He shoved through the front doors

like the devil was on their heels. Bethany could have told him he didn't have to worry—Trudy was "passed out" in a pile of broken breadsticks and a river of wine.

It was true. They were leaving. She was getting out. For a moment she wondered if she was dreaming, as if mortification and a blow to the head had rendered her unconscious.

"Where's your car?"

Bethany nodded toward the neighboring lot. "I parked in front of the department store."

"No time," Trey said as blue lights lit up the distance. "Hop on my bike."

He passed Bethany his helmet as he cranked the engine. She locked her grip around his strong midsection, her heart in her throat as he left the lot at speed.

They passed the cop car as it peeled into the parking lot.

With his strong back against her cheek, Bethany held tight as the wind tore at her clothes and her hair where it streamed from beneath the helmet.

He'd saved her. Again. How could she ever repay him?

Trey would have found the whole situation hysterical except for two things—one, he'd been planning to take a bunch of those breadsticks home with him. And two?

That dick-for-brains had insulted Bethany.

The urge to deck the drunken asshole had been strong, but the need to get her away from the situation had won out. Good thing too. He'd had plenty of close calls with the law in the past, and he knew what happened if the cops started remembering you. It would be nothing good. No matter how innocent he'd been, he'd have a much harder time proving it than the belligerent asshole, drunk as he was.

Bethany's arms were locked around his middle as they moved into a more rural section of the county. Trey's temper eased a little as he sped down the road. The feel of the wind, the speed, the beautiful woman who'd leaned on him that day, her arms and legs still around him—how could he stay angry when he had that?

It was as if something in him had broken. No. Something in him had been broken, and it was healing, slowly but surely, with every minute he spent in her presence.

He didn't want to think about that too much. Distraction.

Maybe it was the intensity of the day, but this fake relationship was feeling all too real right now. Wouldn't it feel good to just keep pretending? He'd need to grab a second helmet if Bethany would be riding with him. He'd had short-lived relationships in the past, but none of those women had been on the back of his bike that often. But Bethany... Now that was a pleasant thought. She was thin and lean, but her grip was strong. He wouldn't take any chances with her. She needed some leathers too. The wind wasn't as cold as it had been, but at speed, those jeans and that sweater she wore would act like lace—all holes and no warmth.

He was insane to be thinking about having a future with her, but he'd never claimed to be wrapped too tight. After all, he had decided to pretend to be a goddamn wedding planner to impress his mommy.

"Where are we going?" Bethany shouted over the sound of the engine as they stopped at a red light.

"My place," he replied. "That okay?"

She nodded rather than yelling again, and he kicked off the pavement when the light turned green.

He hadn't really thought about his destination. He'd just automatically turned his bike toward home. Felt right, somehow, the idea of showing her his private hideaway.

Nobody but his brothers in the Shadows had been to his house. Hell, only Wolf and Jameson had been inside it. None of the women he'd spent time with had been invited.

After the childhood he'd had, Trey was much too protective of his private space to share it with just anyone.

As a foster kid, there wasn't much that he could call his own. He'd shared clothes, bedrooms, books, toys, everything. When he'd gotten attached to something, it was inevitably taken away. The idea of keeping his home private and sacred was ingrained, and the relief he'd felt at being able to keep the space safe had been worth a lot.

But Bethany he trusted. He wasn't sure why, or how, in such a short time. It might be because she'd revealed so much to him that morning.

Her family was obviously a huge source of discomfort for her. No wonder she stuck close to the Yelvertons. They were as different from her grandmother and company as night was from day. And though he knew there were things she hadn't told him, she'd showed him her vulnerability. Had trusted him with it.

How could he not do the same?

The wooded path that led to his house split in two, with the left branch leading to the bigger houses on the property, and the right branch heading toward the little house Trey called his own. The rumbling of the engine echoed off the trees as he slowly rolled toward home.

He could feel her body move as she looked around, and he smiled a little.

Was she worried he was dragging her out to the woods to take advantage of her? Or was she hoping for it?

Well, he couldn't deny that lying her down in a private bower wasn't tempting, but it'd be with her full support and on a much warmer day.

He cut the engine in front of his house, and the silence was loud around them.

"You live here?"

He lowered the kickstand. "Yup."

"I pictured something...different."

Trey snorted. "Sorry. Would you rather I hole up at the bar?"

"No, no, not what I meant. Sorry."

He reached beneath her chin and unbuckled his helmet. It was a little too big for her. He'd grab a spare from the house for her. "I'm just giving you a hard time. Come on."

Lacing his fingers through hers, he led her up the front porch steps.

"It's beautiful," she said as he unlocked the door. Her voice was soft as a flower petal. "So quiet and private."

He didn't say anything, just held open the door for her. And for some reason, his nerves stretched tight as she entered his private space.

It wasn't that he felt violated. In fact, quite the opposite. He was desperate for her to feel welcomed, to like what she saw.

What was wrong with him?

As she turned slowly, examining the room she'd

entered, he found himself standing stock-still, spine ramrod-straight, hardly breathing, his gaze trained on her.

She looked from the extra-long couch done in dark green to the cream-colored rug in front of the cold wood-burning fireplace. TV, game consoles, and DVDs lined the opposite wall. Just beyond was his kitchen, small, quaint, but neat. The hallway to the left led to the single bedroom and bathroom. And, straight ahead...

"Your view is gorgeous."

She walked toward the sliding glass doors, straight to his favorite spot on the whole property. And something inside him fell into place.

In his whole life, nobody had seemed to get him that way. Nobody loved the things he loved, nobody felt the way he did. But when he saw Bethany's eyes light up at the sight of the duck pond outside his deck, the weathered wood and rushes surrounding the little dock, the way her hand caressed the back of his chair as she sighed happily, he knew.

There was someone like him in the world. And she was it.

chapter

THIRTEEN

BETHANY HID HER NERVOUSNESS AS WELL AS SHE COULD BY staring out Trey's back door and into the beautiful scenery.

He really did live in a picturesque, secluded haven. The way the trees surrounded his little house, the light shining on the small pond a hundred feet from his back door, the simple, clean scent of the place…

She could quite happily spend a lot of time there.

Of course, that wasn't even mentioning the man who was standing behind her. She was keenly aware of the way he moved, even though her back was toward him.

He had surprised her at every turn, and it looked as though he intended to continue on that path.

Standing up for her against her family. Whisking her away from the turmoil before it got worse. Settling her on the back of his bike and showing her the homiest little cabin in the woods she'd ever seen.

His body heat leached into her from where he stood, just behind her left shoulder, and she fought the urge to lean into him.

This was dangerous territory. She'd promised herself that she'd treat him like a brother. And she'd been determined to do just that. But the charade in front of her family had given her a glimpse of what it might be like to be by his side in actuality, instead of playing pretend.

She liked it. No, more than liked it. She craved it, craved his touch, craved his caring, craved him.

"What's wrong?"

She started at his question. "What?"

He reached over and pressed a broad fingertip to her forehead. "You've got wrinkles here. Like you're worried."

She let her eyelids flutter closed as he gently rubbed his finger back and forth over her skin. His touch trailed along her eyebrow, down her cheek, along the edge of her jawbone.

Why did such a simple touch feel so good? So intimate? She felt it all the way down in the pit of her belly, which trembled with need with every sweep of his thumb.

"Bethany." His husky voice covered her, and she looked up at him.

He was staring deep into her eyes, his big body close, his hand the only contact between them, but it seared her all the way to the core.

"Let me kiss you."

It wasn't a question, but he clearly waited for an answer. She nodded, and he leaned down, and then his lips were on hers.

Last time had been hungry, hard, and fast. This—this was a quest. A journey, with each step paid loving attention.

First his lips took hers, gentle, sweetly asking rather than demanding. When she opened her mouth to his encouragement, his tongue first danced along the edge of her lip.

As if he were tasting her from the outside in, he took his time, exploring her lips, her tongue, the very edge of her teeth. She wound her arms around him, trying to get closer, deeper.

He obliged, his big, strong arms surrounding her, pulling her against his body. Pressing her against the door, his knee nudged her legs apart, and she moaned against his mouth as his thick, muscled thigh wedged against her core.

Her body was pounding, her pulse thready and hot inside her veins. She wanted, oh God, she wanted him.

He tore his mouth away just long enough to bury his face against her neck. With his fingers tangled in her hair, he pulled her head to the side, giving him greater access to the tender skin of her shoulder and neck. She gasped as his lips and teeth explored her sensitive column, his hands wandering down her sides to cup her ass.

His breath was hot, his kisses hungry, and she wanted every bit of this. Of him.

"More," he said and reached down to the hem of her sweater. She raised her arms willingly, and he tore both sweater and tank top off in one smooth motion.

His eyes darkened with hunger as he looked down at her lacy midnight-blue bra. She swallowed, wondering if she could be as demanding as him.

Her uncertainty lost the battle to the hunger that consumed her, the hunger that he'd driven into her. She reached for the hem of his shirt. He didn't wait for her to remove it. As soon as he realized what she wanted, he whipped the shirt over his head.

She paused, motionless, at the sight of him.

She'd known he was big—it was an impossible-to-miss fact. But somehow the image of him in clothing and the reality of his bare skin were worlds apart.

His muscles were so well defined, made even more impressive by the beautiful tattoo work that adorned his skin. Broad, strong shoulders tapered to a narrow waist, his arms hung loosely by his sides as he enjoyed her perusal.

"Do you like what you see?"

She nodded, breathless.

"Touch me."

Her fingers acted as if they had a mind of their own, spanning the space between them and landing on his left pec. The slight dusting of hair crinkled beneath her fingers as she let her hand trail downward over the flat masculine nipple to the slight dip in the center of his chest, and down, bumping lightly over his abs. God, she'd thought bodies like this only existed on airbrushed models in magazines.

But no. This was Trey. And he wanted her to touch him. The thought made her dizzy, and she swayed.

"Easy, Strong Girl," he said and wrapped his arms around her.

Bethany buried her face in his bare chest, hardly daring to believe this was happening to her.

It had been so long since she was with anyone, and even then, it had been a drunken fling that she'd later regretted. But somehow, with Trey, this felt like something much more.

"You're cold. Come with me."

She didn't bother to tell him that her shiver had less to do with the temperature than the magnitude of feeling he drew from her. She just let him lead her down the narrow hallway to his bedroom.

She'd surprised him, yet again. He wondered if he'd ever get used to the ways she changed, like quicksilver. So strong and determined one moment, so hesitant and questioning the next.

It made him proud as hell and then made him want to protect her. But the one constant that he could not deny was the fact that he wanted her. And by the way she'd looked him up and down, it was clear that she wanted him too.

He led her to his bedroom, her small, slender hand enveloped in his large, rough one. He wanted to hold her, take her to heaven, and then wrap her in his arms for the night.

He was insane. *This* was insane. He wasn't supposed to be doing this.

The bedroom door opened with a creak, and he let her precede him inside. He flicked on the bedside lamp, watching as she looked over the room.

It was a simple place, like the rest of his house. Plain bedding done in solid navy. Dark wooden furniture. A simple bedside lamp. It was a boring room, now that he thought about it.

"I like it," Bethany said, smiling shyly at him as she turned around. "It's very you."

He just shook his head. He didn't give a good damn about interior decorating at the moment. His body was throbbing with need, she was standing there in nothing but a bra and her jeans, and he was ready to show her just how crazy she'd been driving him over the past few weeks.

"Trey," she said, looking down at the floorboards. "I'm nervous."

He stepped close to her, wrapping his arms around her. "Don't be. I've got you."

"But what if…" She stopped and shook her head, her hair falling over her shoulder with the movement. He watched, mesmerized as the ends of one of those blond tresses caressed the soft swell of her breast.

God, he wanted her.

"I don't sleep with just anyone," she tried again, not looking him in the eyes. "It's important that you know that."

"Good to hear," he said, indulging his itchy fingertips by picking up that strand of golden hair and rubbing it across his lips before letting it fall behind her shoulder. "I'm not just anyone."

She reached up, standing on her toes as she kissed him with need akin to desperation. He lifted her off her feet as he met her, caress for caress, stroke for stroke. Her hunger stoked his own, the way her body undulated against him sending waves of need to curl around his cock.

His body throbbed for her as he walked her backward, settling her down on his bed. She looked up at him, eyes glinting, lips swollen, hair mussed.

It was a beautiful picture, but it would be much nicer if she was wearing less.

Well, there was the golden rule to consider.

He reached down and unfastened his jeans, sliding them down his thighs to pool on the floor. Stepping free of them, he was keenly aware of the fact that she was watching.

"Yours too," he said, nodding toward her clothing.

She stood and shimmied free of her own pants before tossing them aside. Her panties were lacy and blue, a perfect match to the bra he was determined to have her lose in mere moments.

Lingerie was beautiful, but in his mind it was solely a floor decoration.

Suiting action to thought, he reached behind her and unfastened the hooks of her bra. Slowly, reverently, he lowered the straps from one shoulder, and then the other.

"Let me see you," he said, dropping his hands.

This was up to her. He wouldn't take from her. He wanted to give, but it was up to her whether or not to accept it.

She turned her back, and the slim, pale expanse of her bare skin made him want to weep. Her waist was narrow, her hips almost boyishly slim. The scrap of blue lace fell to the floor while her back was still turned.

She reached behind her then, hooking her thumbs in the waistband of her panties. He didn't dare to breathe as she worked them over her hips, down her ass, to the floor.

Sweet Jesus in heaven.

Then, slowly, agonizingly so, she turned to face him.

His heart was in his throat. His body was straining as if his skin was so tight it was threatening to burst at any moment.

Her nipples were a dusky, dark pink, puckered sweetly at the tips. Her breasts were small, just a scant handful, but they were so, so perfect. There was a mole just below her belly button, a little mark that he couldn't wait to kiss. His eyes traveled lower.

God, he wanted to shove her back onto his bed and bury his face between her thighs.

She stepped forward and ran her fingers beneath the waistband of his black boxer-briefs. Stretching them forward, she brought them under his straining cock. Her lips parted as she knelt and worked them down his legs.

"You're big everywhere, huh?"

God, she said the sweetest things. But he was done with waiting.

The moment his underwear hit the floor, he reached down, scooped her up, and deposited her on his bed. She bounced with the movement, laughing with delight as he knelt on the bed beside her. He laughed for a moment too, the sheer joy of being beside her, seeing her mirth, taking her in, overwhelming him.

Then he leaned in to brush his mouth across her skin. He started with her collarbone, his kisses wild and unmeasured as he tasted her. She moaned in pleasure, her fingertips digging into his shoulders, her thighs spreading wide, the scent of her hunger causing his body to roar with need.

He could quite happily bury himself inside the glorious, dripping well of her, but he had to make sure she was ready first.

Kissing lower, he drew a peaked, pink nipple into his mouth and tugged.

"Trey!" She shouted his name, pulling at his hair as her back arched. He smiled against her breast, taking harder, deeper draws.

As he moved to her other breast, he splayed his hand over her flat belly, then lower, over the little nest of hair that covered her. Her gasp of delight fueled him on as he rubbed a finger over her clit.

She was slick, and hot, and sweet. So sweet. His

finger dipped inside her, only for a moment, then back out again, circling her clit and moving back down.

He repeated the circuit, over and over, suckling her nipples as his hand worked her. Up and down, over her tender flesh, his tongue flicking the bud of each nipple in turn, his thumb circling her clit before dipping slightly into the hot well of her.

"Trey," she gasped, her head thrashing against his pillows. "Please."

"Please what?"

"More!"

"More what?" He breached her deeper that time, his question blowing warm breath across her damp skin.

"More you."

Well, he wouldn't argue. He added a second finger inside her, stretching her inner walls slowly, gently. Her shuddering cry told him that was exactly what she'd wanted. Her body was needy, her core aching, and she needed him to fill it.

Rising up onto his knees, he gripped his cock with the hand that had been touching her. The warm honey of her body slicked his hand's way up and down the length of his cock. He indulged in a couple of quick pumps, leaning his head back at the feeling of Bethany's desire coating his length.

But they'd been teasing this thing between them out so long, and he wouldn't make her wait any longer.

He reached into the bedside table, glad he'd stowed some condoms there even though he'd never had a woman in his bedroom. It was the work of a moment to rip open the foil and roll the latex over his slick cock.

Bethany watched with an expression that could only

be termed ravenous. One hand covered her breast, fingers tweaking and teasing her nipple as she bit her lip and waited for him to come to her.

He poised himself between her thighs, his cock ready at her entrance.

Looking into her eyes, he asked one last time. "Are you ready?"

In answer, she reached up and pulled his head down to kiss her.

Then, with a deep, sure plunge, he was inside her.

Heat. Tight heat. Slick, tight heat. His mind was gone, lost in the feeling of Bethany surrounding him, Bethany holding him, Bethany's body welcoming him, gripping him, refusing to let him go.

And he was gone, lost in her. Pumping against her, their bodies straining, her cries soft against his chest, his arms straining with the effort of holding himself upright as his hips pistoned into her.

Nothing could have prepared him for this. He closed his eyes, intending to lose himself in the feelings, but then her hand cupped his cheek. Startled, he looked down into her eyes.

"Be here with me," she whispered, looking up at him with what could only be termed trust. "I've got you."

He hesitated for only a second, and then he gave himself to her. For once, he held nothing back, showing her the heart of him as they moved together. She held his gaze as they moved faster, Trey spiraling into passion he'd never imagined as her legs wrapped around his hips, her body matching his, stroke for delicious stroke.

"More," she cried, reaching down between their bodies to find her clit. "I want to feel you come, Trey, please."

She rubbed her clit as he sank to the hilt inside her, the fluttering muscles of her core squeezing him, milking him for all he could give. She shuddered and came, her hoarse scream of his name muffled against his chest. Her body strained against him, her hips trembling, sweat dotting her skin.

He wanted to last longer, wanted to give them hours of pleasure, but the squeeze of her body around his aching, heavy cock was undeniable. The ripples of her orgasm wrenched his from him, and he lost all control.

As the shudders racked his body, he looked down into her dazed blue eyes, shocked at the emotion cracking open within his chest.

"Beth," he said, his voice a husky rasp. "My Beth." And for this moment, it was true.

chapter

FOURTEEN

BETHANY WOKE WITH A START, DISORIENTED AS SHE stared up at a plain, white ceiling.

Where was her ceiling fan? She couldn't sleep without the slight breeze on her, the still air reminding her of the suffocating conditions at her grandmother's house. This wasn't her room.

A soft noise beside her drew her attention, and she let out a little gasp.

"Did you forget where you were for a minute?"

She smiled, shy suddenly as she looked up at him. "Yeah, I guess I did."

The sheet was up to her chest, and she was grateful for the little covering, even as she snuggled close to Trey's chest.

That had been...unexpected. Incredible, but entirely out of left field. Well, not entirely. After all, Trey had been the star of quite a few fantasies since she'd first clapped eyes on him a little over a month and a half ago. But he was supposed to be off-limits.

So much for that resolution.

Her body ached tenderly, sore in places that hadn't been used for far too long. Trey ran a long, strong finger up and down her arm, his big body taking up most of the space in the bed. She didn't feel crowded, though, which mostly had to do with the way he was curled protectively around her.

God, she could get used to this.

A question floated into her mind, and she slammed her eyes shut. No, she couldn't ask that. It was too clichéd.

"Yeah. It was good."

Thank Christ, Trey was a mind reader. She opened her eyes and gave him a tentative smile. "Yeah?"

"Mm-hmm," he growled, pulling her tighter into his arms. "Ready to do it again?"

She laughed. "In a little while. I'm not exactly used to that kind of activity."

"Stay near me, Strong Girl, and you'll definitely get used to it." He rolled on top of her, bracing his weight on his arms as she laughed and pushed at him.

But both of them went silent when her cell phone started ringing.

"Crap," Bethany said, scooching out from under Trey and dashing to the puddle of her jeans in the middle of the floor. "Crap, crap, crap."

Trey frowned a little as he sat up in bed, the sheet falling to his hips. She tried hard not to notice how sexy he looked with his nakedness and mussed hair as she yanked the phone from her pants pocket.

It was Mama Yelverton. With a quick *shhh* gesture to Trey, Bethany answered.

"Hey, Mama Yelverton."

"Bethany? Are you okay?" Mama Yelverton's voice was concerned.

"Oh yeah, I'm totally fine. Why? Is something wrong?"

"I just got a phone call from Trudy Jernigan. She said that she had been looking for you and couldn't find you."

Bethany rolled her eyes. Grandmother hadn't even bothered to call her. If she had, Bethany would have told her exactly where she was. "I'm so sorry she bothered you. No, everything's okay."

"She said you were with a stranger that she didn't trust. I know she's prone to exaggeration, but I thought I should call and make sure you were okay, just in case."

"No, I'm not with a stranger."

Trey snorted at that, and Bethany waved at him with a mock glare.

"All right then. As long as you know I'm here if you need me."

Bethany smiled down at her toes. "I know, Mama. Thank you."

"I love you, Bethy."

"I love you, too."

"Oh," Mama Yelverton's tone brightened, "I wanted to check with you. Have you heard from Trey about the invitations?"

Bethany winced. The invitations. She'd completely dropped the ball there. And Trey had wanted to work on them that afternoon. If she didn't cover for him, it would look like he was behind.

"Oh yeah," she said brightly. "He's got some mock-ups to go over with us whenever we're both free."

"Oh great! How about tomorrow afternoon?"

Bethany gulped, glancing around frantically for a

clock. Five p.m. Surely they had enough time to get something together. "Sure! That sounds good to me."

"I'll give Trey a call and confirm he can make it."

"No, no, don't trouble yourself. I'll contact him."

Mama Yelverton laughed, seeming not to notice the frantic note that had crept into Bethany's voice. "I did want an excuse to talk to him."

"Oh. Right. Okay." *Damn it*. Bethany tucked the phone into the crook of her shoulder and yanked on her panties, then her jeans. "I guess I'll see you guys tomorrow then."

"Great. See you tomorrow!"

As the call ended, Bethany sighed and zipped up her jeans. Movement from the bed caught the corner of her eye.

Trey was leaning back against the headboard, his arms crossed and pillowing the back of his head against the wood. His colorful tattoos stood out brightly against the dark sheet that barely covered his pelvis.

Bethany swallowed hard.

"Sure you want to get dressed already?"

Bethany just closed her eyes, shook her head, and bent down to scoop up his pants.

Trey frowned. "You got somewhere to be?"

"We both do." She shook her head as she tossed his now-ringing pants to him. "Mama Yelverton wants to talk to you."

She laughed a little as Trey scrambled for his phone. At least she wasn't the only one who was discombobulated by the interruption. He, however, played it much smoother than she had, easily conversing with his mother like he wasn't naked in a room that smelled like sex. With Bethany.

Oh God. She couldn't tell Sarah any of this.

Anxiety started churning in her belly as she finished dressing, the sound of Trey's half of the conversation ringing in her ears.

She'd never kept a secret like this from Sarah. They were best friends. Sisters, almost. They shared everything. But Sarah still wasn't sure how she felt about the whole Trey situation. How could Bethany complicate that by gushing about the fact that she'd had the best sex of her life with Trey? And that she hoped to do it again really, really soon?

Simple. She couldn't.

Glancing over her shoulder, she watched as Trey casually fastened his belt, the phone tucked between his cheek and shoulder. He was so unlike anyone she'd ever been with. He was all male bluster and control, with a chivalrous side she'd never expected.

Could she give that up for Sarah, if she was asked?

Bethany wasn't sure. And to be honest, it scared her not to know.

She walked into the living room, partly to give Trey some privacy to finish his conversation, and partly because she needed the distance to think. Her body was still humming from his touch, the faint pulses of her orgasm long since faded, but the pleasant tingling of the aftermath warming her blood. He'd been so careful of her pleasure, readying her body thoroughly, waiting for his pleasure until she'd reached orgasm.

Thoughtful. Caring. Strong. Everything she'd ever wanted and never gotten in a lover.

Bethany sank onto the leather couch in his living room, sighing a little to herself.

Of all men, why did it have to be him? She didn't

know anything about him, not really. Other than the fact he'd been separated from his family.

How had he grown up? What had caused him to be so tough, so strong? He couldn't have had an easy life.

She cradled her head in her hands. She didn't know anything about him, but she was dying to be with him physically again. That wasn't a fact that she enjoyed.

Trey killed the call as he came into the living room. Bethany straightened quickly. He didn't have to know she was all up in her head after what they'd shared. He might get the wrong idea, and she didn't want that.

"So, I guess we need some invitations for tomorrow afternoon."

Bethany stood and shouldered her purse. "Guess so. Sorry. Want to head to my apartment, and we can work on them? Maybe we can pick my car up on the way."

"No problem," Trey said and dropped a quick kiss on her forehead as he pulled his keys from his pocket.

As he led her out the front door of his little house in the woods, Bethany looked over her shoulder longingly.

She hoped she could come back here soon. But she wasn't sure how to do that without feeling guilty, like she was doing something she shouldn't.

And that sucked.

⚔

He couldn't remember the last time he'd felt this good. With Bethany on the back of the bike behind him, her legs and arms wrapped around him, the memory of sinking into her sweetness fresh in his mind, he found himself smiling for no reason other than her nearness.

It was damn strange, but he was enjoying it.

As the trees gave way to buildings, and traffic increased, he found himself resenting the fact that he'd be giving her up to her car in a moment.

He wanted to keep her there on his bike, close to him. Such a strange feeling.

"I'm over there." She pointed as he pulled into the lot. "Green Corolla."

He stopped next to the car she'd indicated and cut the engine.

She stepped off his bike, unbuckling the helmet strap. He tucked the spare in the saddlebag on the back of his bike.

"I guess I'll see you at my apartment," she said. Just then, her stomach rumbled, and her eyes widened as he laughed.

"We didn't really finish lunch, did we?"

"No, we didn't," she said, mock-glaring at his smirk. "I'll call in some delivery on the way. Chinese food?"

"My favorite," Trey said, balancing his bike. "I'll eat anything."

"Great," she said with a smile and a little wave, and climbed into her car.

He waited for her to crank up and make her phone call, then he pulled out behind her, following her the whole way to her apartment.

She drove well, handling her car like an extension of her body, maneuvering through the traffic with patience and confidence. It was good. Made his chest swell and his uncertainty ease just a little.

He frowned at himself as they stopped at a light. This protective feeling he had toward her was getting out of hand. Bethany was hot, and she was sweet, and he sure as hell wanted to have sex with her again, but he wasn't looking for anything more. Right?

Damn it. He hadn't exactly made that clear to her. But the idea of keeping her by his side was more appealing than it should be.

Trey shook his head and kicked off the pavement as the light turned green and the Corolla started rolling through the intersection.

Forget about all that complicated stuff. His motto for most of his life had been to enjoy the moment, because in the blink of an eye, everything could—and usually did—turn into ash. He'd enjoy this little piece of happy for as long as it was his.

He'd managed to cool his jets by the time they turned into the lot at Bethany's apartment complex. Of course, just as he cut his bike's engine, his cell rang.

He waved Bethany ahead of him, hanging back to take the call.

"Harding."

"Boss, it's Jameson. Look, we've got a problem."

Trey crossed his arms, his gaze following Bethany as she walked up the stairs. That little wiggle in her walk made him think of all sorts of carnal things he'd like to do to her.

"Vinnie just got off the phone with Lynn. He asked for a loan."

"You've got to be kidding me," Trey said, his attention snapping back to the conversation. "That low-life sonofabitch has the balls to ask Lynn for money?"

"He heard about her sister getting married. Said Ginger's new husband had to be rolling in it, so Vinnie deserved some of that child support back."

Adrenaline crashed through Trey's veins, his hand curling into a fist.

He'd thought Vinnie had gotten the message last time. That losing all his bankroll would be enough to show him Lynn had backup, and she and her family weren't to be screwed around with. But Vinnie was definitely stupider than he looked.

"Boss? What should we do?"

A vehicle pulled to a stop in front of the building, a little sign on the top announcing it as the Ming Garden Delivery. A tall, skinny kid with hair sticking up in eight directions got out of the car and mounted the steps two at a time to Bethany's apartment.

Trey couldn't leave now. Not only did he have a promise to keep to Mrs. Yelverton, but walking out on Bethany now would be like abandoning her. They'd just had sex. Things between them were tender, feelings were raw, new. His brothers had backup. Bethany? She only had him. And he wasn't about to leave her alone at that moment.

"Handle it."

"What, Boss?"

Trey walked toward the apartment building. "You and Wolf. Plan it out. Handle it. I'm in the middle of something tonight."

"But, Boss! You—"

"You heard me, Jameson. Keep it running tight. I'm counting on you."

Trey cut the call and passed the delivery kid on his way up the steps to Bethany's.

Yeah, he probably would regret shoving off his brothers for his girl. But at the moment, he had to make a decision. And right or wrong, he was choosing Bethany.

He only hoped he didn't regret it later.

"Everything okay?" Bethany met him at the door with a slightly concerned expression.

"Sure," Trey said smoothly, letting the door close behind him. "Just a little work thing that needed smoothing."

Her eyebrows knitted together slightly. "Wedding related, I guess?"

The question reminded him that she knew he was lying, and that he hadn't bothered—or rather, dared—to tell her the truth.

"Just business," he said shortly, tossing his jacket over the chair by the door. "Smells good."

He nodded toward the bar where she'd started spreading out the various takeout containers.

"Yeah, this place is good." She let it go, thankfully.

As they both grabbed plates and started eating, a silence fell between them. It was halfway comfortable and halfway filled with unanswered questions.

But Trey couldn't think of what to say to her. So he just ate, and prayed that she'd be satisfied with not knowing.

chapter

FIFTEEN

THE FOOD MIGHT HAVE BEEN DELICIOUS, BUT AS FAR as Bethany could tell, it might as well have been made from sawdust and Elmer's glue.

Trey was hiding something. A lot of somethings. And the fact that she'd slept with him even though he wasn't being honest with her was beginning to bother her a lot.

As she scraped the plates and set them in the sink to rinse them off, she glanced over her shoulder at him.

He was packing the leftovers back into their containers and stacking them neatly on the corner of her table. His face was serious, every motion slow and studied. Obviously preoccupied, he'd only said about ten words through the course of the meal.

She cut the tap and dried her hands. "So," she said, putting the dish towel back on the oven door handle, "should we take a look at these invites?"

"That's why I'm here," Trey said shortly. He filled up way too much of her small dining area, his presence almost overwhelming in its silence.

Damn it. She wasn't handling this well at all.

Instead of saying something else, and probably putting her foot in it, Bethany just headed to the spare bedroom where the die-cut machine and the paper supplies were still waiting from the other day.

Gathering everything they needed, she started to bring it back to the living room, but met him halfway.

"Let me carry that," he said, and before she could protest, he'd taken the machine and the bag of supplies straight out of her hands. "Where do you want it?"

"Kitchen table," she said, pointing. He set the things down and located an outlet for the die-cut machine.

"Okay," Bethany said, pulling paper and stamps and other assorted supplies they'd collected into neat piles on the table. "Let's do this."

Using the best of the ideas Trey had brought as a guide, Bethany began to assemble a wedding invitation with custom die-cut flowers and an elegant scalloped edge. Trey, who she'd been surprised to find out had beautiful handwriting, wrote out the information in several different styles for them to choose from.

They fell into a rhythm, asking each other for opinions and working steadily. It was good. Nice to feel some of the worry and strain drain away as she just enjoyed being beside his strong, quiet presence.

"I always enjoyed art," Bethany said, breaking a stretch of quiet that had been much more comfortable than what they'd experienced during dinner. "It's therapeutic for me. Even when I was a kid."

"I can see that," Trey said, looking up from where he'd been testing out a set of calligraphy pens Bethany had unearthed from a tote full of craft supplies.

"Yeah. When I was a kid, we moved around a bit. Well, a lot. So I was the new kid in every grade. It was hard, but I drew a lot and painted a lot, and that made me forget about how tough it was sometimes." Bethany kept her gaze trained on the delicate paper petals she was arranging on top of the layered card stock.

"Your dad was a Marine, right?"

Bethany's gaze flew to his, questioning.

He shrugged. "Your grandmother mentioned it."

"Oh." She looked down again. "Yeah. The military kept us moving. And kids being how they are, it wasn't exactly easy to make new friends every year or two."

Trey was silent for a moment. She shot a look over at him. His jaw was set, a dark wave of hair curling just at his temple, making her long to smooth it away.

"Yeah. I get that."

He didn't say anything else, and she sighed internally. She'd hoped—well, she'd hoped that her confession about her past would encourage him to open up to her. It appeared that she'd been wrong.

But maybe... He'd been kidnapped as a kid. And he'd just found the family who'd been searching for him. So now that he knew what kind of childhood he'd missed out on, was he having trouble dealing with what was instead of what could have been?

It made sense.

"I was kind of an ugly kid." She kept talking. If she wanted him to trust her, she had to show that she trusted him too. "Seriously. I was so thin that my dad constantly worried that there was something really wrong with me. There wasn't. I was healthy, just couldn't gain weight no matter what I tried. And I got made fun of for that. A lot."

She bit her lip, reaching for the next set of die-cut paper petals. "It's hard to be a teenager and still have to shop in children's sizes because everything's too big. And my skin was awful, my hair not any better. I just wished I—"

She hissed in a breath, jerking her hand away as blood welled on the tip of her index finger. "Damn it, paper cut."

"Let me," Trey said and grabbed a paper towel. His big hand cradled hers as he dabbed gently at the cut. She watched him as he moved, confidently, gently, as if he was taking care of something much more precious than a cut finger.

When the bleeding had stopped, he bent down and pressed a kiss on her palm. "You might have had it rough when you were a kid, but damn if you're not beautiful now."

His words took her aback for a minute. She was speechless, unable to do anything but watch him as he examined her little cut.

The miasma of feeling swamped her, confusing and overwhelming.

Beautiful? He thinks I'm beautiful?

"You don't mean that."

He stared straight into her eyes, his expression serious as a stone. "I do. I don't exaggerate, Beth. You're the most beautiful woman I've ever seen."

She searched his expression for any hint of untruth, but there was none. His gaze was naked, open, and for a moment, she actually believed what he'd said. That she was beautiful to him. Tilting her chin up to him, she waited.

He closed the distance between them in half a heartbeat, and he kissed her.

She clung to him, afraid that if she let him go, this dream would be over.

She'd never imagined this. It was too new, too exciting, too much. And she never, ever wanted it to end.

He leaned forward, standing, his big body crowding her against the back of her chair. She didn't care. She wanted more of him. Winding her arms around his neck, she leaned back, slanting her mouth open for him. He took advantage, his tongue delving deep.

Her blood sang in her veins, her heart pounding deep in her core as her hips lifted, needing to be nearer to him. It was as if it had been days rather than hours since she'd been with him.

He stirred that much hunger within her.

But before they went any further, his cell phone started a deep, insistent buzz in his pocket.

He tore away with a groan.

"God, Beth. I... Sorry. I've got to take this." He scowled with a dark expression that would have made her shiver if she wasn't sitting in that kitchen chair with her mouth swollen, her hair mussed, and her eyes bleary from his kiss.

"Harding," he said as he answered the call and strode from the kitchen into the living room.

The voice on the other end was deep, although Bethany couldn't make out any words they were saying. But Trey's response was crystal clear.

"Wolf, slow down. Who is it?" Trey fell quiet, and the deep voice started up again. Bethany looked down at the cut on her hand.

It was already closed up, a faint red line and the lingering sting of pain the only evidence it had happened.

Trey's voice floated to her ears again. "Jameson? God. Okay. I'm heading down there right now. Have Flash get the money and meet me."

Silence fell again, and Bethany looked over at the table. There were four invitations in various states of completion, and several more in bits and pieces strewn all over the oak top.

"Beth, I'm sorry," Trey said as he grabbed his jacket and shrugged into it. "I've got to go."

"What is it?" She stood, her nerves jangling. "Can I help?"

"Don't worry." He bent down and pressed a quick, fierce kiss to her lips. "I'll see you tomorrow."

And then he scooped up his helmet and walked out her front door, leaving her feeling like she'd just been kicked in the chest.

Heavy, hurting, and alone.

‑‑‑‑‑‑

Night had long since fallen by the time Trey made it to the county lockup. And the drive over hadn't done a damn thing to cool his temper.

He wasn't sure who he was pissed off at the most — Wolf for interrupting his kiss with Bethany, Jameson for getting arrested, or himself for blowing off his brothers to be with Bethany in the first place.

It was a toss-up of screwups, and the trifecta had definitely killed his good mood.

The red tape was thick, and even with the money Flash had brought, it still took a long time to get Jameson's bail posted. By the time they walked out of the jailhouse, it was past two in the morning.

Trey had sent Flash out to join the rest of the Shadows, and he alone escorted Jameson from the lockup.

"What the hell happened, man?"

Jameson darted a look Trey's way. The streetlight above them was flickering, the cold night air making their breath come out in white puffs. "You told me to handle Vinnie. I handled him."

Trey snorted. "You handled him right into your right fist in front of an undercover, you asshole. You know we don't do business in public. What were you thinking?"

Jameson stopped in front of the pickup Wolf had dropped off for them. Jameson's bike had been left at the club where they'd hunted Vinnie down, and Doc had picked up Trey's bike at his request.

"We tracked him down like you said. He was down at Cherry Ice, dealing. When he saw us, he tried to take off, so I grabbed him. I was walking him toward the exit to get some privacy for the shakedown when he said it."

Jameson's pacing was getting to Trey. It was almost like the man was fighting himself inside his own skin, the pain in the lines of his face clearly visible.

Trey planted his feet and crossed his arms as he looked at Jameson. He took a deep, steadying breath, hoping that his calm would rub off on the other man.

"What did he say?"

Jameson stopped, his face ashen as he looked at Trey. "He said he wished he'd killed those kids when he'd had the chance, because they were fucking up his life now."

Trey's stomach dropped to the pavement, and his insides went as cold as the surrounding air.

Jameson covered his face with his hands as he leaned against the pickup's front bumper.

"I lost it, Boss. I just… I thought about those little girls at Ginger's wedding, standing beside their mama, how happy they were, and then I thought about Cady. My girl. How I'd give anything—anything—for her to be alive. And that son of a bitch…" Jameson shoved off the pickup, bouncing it on its tires. "That son of a bitch is threatening those girls?"

Trey stepped forward. One step, then another, and then he wrapped his arm around Jameson.

"I know, brother," Trey said. "I know, and I'm sorry."

Silence fell. They stayed there for a long time as the anger and sadness tormented Jameson. Trey couldn't ever know the pain the man had gone through, but he'd made a promise to himself to be there for Jameson. And he'd let him down.

He'd let them all down.

And for what? The chance of reclaiming a past that could never be regained? The chance to be with a woman who was much too good for him and always would be?

He needed to get his head on right.

Jameson pulled himself together and stood up straight, looking Trey in the eye as he spoke. "I'm sorry, Boss. I let you down."

"No, J. I let you down tonight by not being there."

Trey grasped Jameson's hand and pulled him in for a back-pounding hug—an acknowledgment of fault, an unspoken promise to do better.

"Let's get out of here," Jameson said. He climbed into the passenger seat while Trey took the wheel.

With the engine of the Ford growling underneath them, they headed toward home. Jameson looked out the window, silent. Trey didn't bother him. If Jameson wanted to talk, he would. And Trey would listen. But if not, Trey would use the drive to think through some of the things he was mulling over.

He owed it to his mother to finish this wedding stuff. She'd spent his whole lifetime searching for him. She'd had someone precious taken away from her, and the only thing she'd gotten in return was his sorry ass. He wanted to give something to her to make her proud. And, like it or not, this wedding was it.

But Bethany—Beth. She'd stolen his wits and left him acting like a gobsmacked teenager with too much heart and not enough good sense. He had to balance things. And right now? He wasn't.

There were some decisions to be made there, some hard things to think about. Sooner or later, he'd have to face them.

But for now? He drove the pickup toward home, his brother in the seat beside him, nursing his heart's terminal wound.

Trey had to put his family first for the moment. The family he'd built with his own two hands.

The rest would have to wait till later.

chapter
SIXTEEN

DAWN CREPT OVER THE HORIZON, ITS SLOW GRAY fingers stretching up, then turning purple, then red, then orange as they lit the eastern sky.

Trey watched it all, the only sounds in his home his heartbeat and the hum of the refrigerator. Somewhere along the way he'd lost himself, and he knew exactly when that moment was.

When he'd heard his name. His given name, the one that he'd lost as a baby.

At that moment, he'd caught a glimpse of a future that might have been. He'd been blinded to his present by the wisps of a past that had never existed except maybe in some alternate universe.

But Samuel Yelverton was dead. He'd died in that car crash with his abductor. And though Trey Harding had the same eyes, the same hair, the same DNA, he was—and always would be—a different person.

The fiery orange ball hefted itself over the horizon, each second that ticked by giving Trey more clarity.

He'd neglected his business by chasing this dream. Jameson hadn't been ready to handle Vinnie. The only saving grace was that Vinnie had fled before he could be questioned by the undercover cop who'd witnessed the scuffle. There'd be no charges.

If Trey had been there… He scoffed to himself, resting his elbows on his knees as he leaned forward in the deck chair. If he'd been there, the best he could have done was yank his boy back and pound Vinnie into the ground himself.

But still. The rest of the Shadows trusted him. They leaned on him. And if he wasn't there, supporting them, anything that went sideways was directly his fault.

He stood, the chill of the morning long since having numbed his skin. He'd texted the need for a meeting first thing this morning. They'd be gathered at Wolf's, and he was going to confess.

He'd screwed up. They'd paid. And even though they hadn't complained, he was going to call it off.

As good a person as his mothe—Mrs. Yelverton—was, he would never be anything more to her than a stranger. And it was time he stopped pretending he could be.

His boots crunched on the gravel drive as he walked toward Wolf's. It was only a quarter of a mile, and the time alone was something he still needed.

Alone. He smiled to himself as he kicked a rock toward the tree line. It was his preferred state. At least, it had been before—

He stopped dead in the middle of the path, his chest giving an uncomfortable squeeze.

Beth.

If he gave up this wedding-business charade, what would she think? Say? Do? Would she still want to see him?

Even if she knew he was a lowlife, a common criminal?

The image of her came to his mind, as painful as it was beautiful.

Her pale-blond hair, her beautiful blue eyes. The way she dressed, so neat, so sleek. Her loyalty, her goodness, her strength and integrity.

She wasn't the kind of woman who could be his old lady. She was too good for that. And if he pulled the plug on this charade, his chance to be near her would be gone.

He resumed his walk, determination setting his jaw.

As wonderful as she was, Bethany had been a temporary distraction. Better to go ahead and rip off that Band-Aid than to prolong the inevitable. He'd become too soft, too attached. That had to stop now.

His footsteps were heavy on the steps to Wolf's front porch. As he stopped, his fist raised to knock, voices inside met his ears.

"…would just listen to me for a minute, I know what I'm talking about."

"Come on, Ace. You don't know anything more about this crap than any of us do."

"No, no, that's where you're wrong. I've been watching a documentary series about weddings, and now I know how brides think."

A snort came from someone, probably Wolf. "And what series is that?"

"*Say Yes to the Dress*."

A chorus of groans and curses followed, with some yelps that indicated Ace's smart-ass ways were earning him a few punches to the arm.

Trey rested his fist against the door, head hanging down.

Every time. Every goddamn time. Whenever he was ready to give up on everything for the good of the group, they'd rush right underneath him and hold him up.

"Boss?"

Wolf had opened the door, causing Trey's hand to fall. Trey just looked at him for a long, hard moment.

"Everybody's here."

"Wolf," Trey said, his voice even rougher than usual. "Step outside."

Wolf glanced over his shoulder, then let the front door close behind him. They were alone on Wolf's front porch, the painted white railings and dusky-gray boards surrounding them.

"I'm thinking about..." Trey coughed. "Sorry. I'm going to call off the wedding project."

Wolf's nostrils flared, the only indication of his surprise. "Why, Boss?"

Trey looked past Wolf, down toward the gravel path that led the way off their property, toward the highway. The road he'd take to her—Bethany.

God, he was going to miss her.

"Because I've put too much on you guys. Last night wouldn't have gone down the way it had if Jameson hadn't been on edge from the wedding."

Wolf shook his head, crossing his big arms over his chest.

"No way. You wouldn't have been able to stop him

from snapping when Vinnie said that. You know he's sensitive about kids."

Trey looked down at his second. "Whether or not I could have, my decision is made. I wanted you to know first."

The corners of Wolf's mouth turned down, difficult as they were to see with his majestic beard. "Of course it's your call, Boss. But they've really been enjoying all this."

Trey scoffed, but Wolf continued. "Really. It's given them something new to do. A challenge. Hell, I've enjoyed it myself. And honestly"—the volume of Wolf's voice lowered as he stepped closer—"I think it's been good for you too."

Trey bared his teeth. "Don't play armchair psychologist with me."

"As long as I've known you, you've never smiled the way you have the last few weeks. I've noticed it. We've all noticed it. And that's why we've thrown ourselves into this wedding crap. We care about you, Boss. And if this makes you happy, then that's what we want to do."

Trey shook his head. The burden of this… It was too much. Feeling was too much. He wished he could go back to before that investigator waltzed in and capsized his life.

But he couldn't wind back the clock, and he couldn't undo the damage. Especially those little dents in his heart that had been given by a certain girl with blond hair, blue eyes, and the sweetest smile he'd ever seen.

"My mind's made up. The wedding planning is over."

"Aw, come on, Boss! I was just getting good at it! Come on, I brought a freaking vision board!"

Trey started, then whirled on his heel. Ace was standing there in the open front door, an intense frown on his normally jovial face.

"Seriously."

"What the hell is a vision board?"

Ace grinned, then ducked into the house. Trey followed, Wolf at his heels.

"Look. See, fabric swatches, patterns… Look, I even did a mock-up of the cake."

"I told him that design wouldn't work," Doc interjected. "Look at the way those tiers are stacked. It'll never hold up under all that fondant."

"If you used some supports of some kind under that edge," Wolf pointed, "then it would probably have more structural integrity. Can't you have each layer stacked on cardboard?"

Doc scoffed as Ace nodded. Dean shook his head. "I don't like the colors."

Ace rounded on him. "What do you mean? It's white and pink! Chicks love pink!"

"Yeah, when they're seven. Grow the hell up, man. Grown women don't like pink."

A full-scale argument erupted, and all Trey could do was watch as eleven grown-ass, tatted-up biker dudes had a yelling match, complete with a few fists flying, over wedding colors.

"See?" Wolf crossed his arms, his grin flashing white through his beard. "They're having fun."

Trey just shook his head as the argument escalated, with Ace finally crying uncle.

"Let's put it to a vote," Dean yelled over the melee. "All those in favor of pink and white, say aye."

"Aye!" Ace's yell was hard to hear, since Rocco's boot was on his face.

"All opposed?"

The nays were so loud that Trey would have worried about the structural integrity of the room if anyone but Wolf had built it.

Trey smiled. Those roughneck assholes cared. And he wasn't going to take that from them at this point.

It was just another month or two. As long as he could balance things, it would be okay. He had to believe that.

Besides, he wasn't sure how long he could have kept away from Bethany. The need to see her again was almost a pain inside his belly.

"All right, boys."

The scuffle stopped at the sound of Trey's voice. He stepped in the middle of the group, settling himself on the couch. "Let's see the rest of your board so we can fix your fool ideas."

Ace grinned, Dean snorted, and the rest of the bikers settled themselves around the room, ready to give opinions whenever asked—and more often, whenever they weren't.

Trey couldn't have been more grateful for them. They'd kept him sane more often than not, and here they were, doing it again.

He was a lucky bastard; that was for sure.

Bewildered. That's how she'd felt all night long, from the moment he'd rushed out without a word of explanation, to the time her head had rested on her sleepless pillow, to the hours that had passed restlessly thereafter.

Bewildered as she'd finally given up and gone for an early-morning run, bewildered as she'd taken a long shower, bewildered as she'd eaten her breakfast. She was no closer to figuring out what had happened when Sarah, in town for the weekend, called her and invited her out to brunch.

Bethany had bundled up her feelings and shoved them into a box at the far back of her mind. Concealing things from Sarah wasn't easy. She was definitely one of the most intuitive people that Bethany had ever known. But she couldn't unpack all this on Sarah. Not when it involved her brother.

So she put on her makeup, dressed carefully, and headed downtown to the little restaurant that was one of Sarah's favorites.

"Hey, hey," Sarah said, giving Bethany a quick hug as they met at the front of the restaurant. "You look nice this morning."

"Thanks," Bethany said, resisting the urge to go into more detail. *Oh, I couldn't sleep because your brother sexed me up and ran last night. Oh, I wanted to look nice because I'm hoping to hook up with him again this afternoon.*

Damn it.

The host showed them to a little table in the corner, the scent of waffles and bacon hanging heavy in the air. "What can I get for you ladies?"

"Just coffee for me," Bethany said.

Sarah added her own order, and the server darted away.

"So I know I told you that I didn't want to have any responsibility for this whole wedding thing, and that totally hasn't changed," Sarah said, picking at the edge of her cloth napkin as she settled it on her lap. "But I've got to admit I'm curious. How's it going?"

Bethany fought the blush that threatened to climb up her cheeks when she thought of the "planning" she and Trey had been doing recently. "It's going really well."

"Mom doing okay? Not going too crazy?"

Bethany smiled. "I've managed to pull her back."

Sarah sighed with a smile. "Good. I would hate a three-ring circus. God, I'm so glad you're wrangling her for this. Especially with him helping too."

Sarah's expression fell with that, and Bethany's stomach flip-flopped.

"Are you still not sure what to think about Trey?"

Sarah shook her head. "It's hard. I mean, I want to take the time to get to know him, but I really don't have it. And I'm nervous, you know?"

Bethany gave the server a quick smile as their coffees landed in front of them. A quick gap in conversation gave her a chance to collect her thoughts as they gave their order.

Once the server had disappeared again, Bethany looked at her best friend and curled her fingers around the handle of her coffee cup.

"I've spent some time with him, you know. I think he's a really good guy."

"Really?" Relief filled Sarah's voice as she leaned toward Bethany. "Mom has raved about him, but honestly, I think he could be a serial killer and she'd find his good side, you know? Just because of who he is. But I trust your judgment. So, you think he's good?"

Bethany nodded. "He's kind. Protective. Rough around the edges, for sure. But underneath all that, he's actually really sweet."

Sarah gave a little smile. "You sound like you really like him."

Bethany shifted in her seat, the fake leather of the booth giving a squeak of protest at her movement. "What? No, I mean, he's nice. That's all."

Sarah hiked an eyebrow as she took a sip of her coffee. "Okay. Whatever you say. After everything's settled out with the wedding and graduation, I'm sure I'll be able to spend some time getting to know him. But for now, I'm glad you're getting along with him."

"Thanks," Bethany said quietly, taking a sip from the glass of water the server had dropped by their table.

A dreamy look came into Sarah's eyes, and she propped her cheek in her hand.

"What are you thinking about?" Bethany asked, glad to change the subject.

"I was just remembering when I first met Mark. He was so exciting. He took me mountain climbing, kayaking, caving. He just had all this intense energy, and being near him made me tingle all over, waiting for the next adventure. But all of that paled in comparison to how it felt when he kissed me."

Bethany smiled. The joy rolling off Sarah was contagious. "Do you still feel that way? Even after being with him all this time?"

Sarah nodded, looking down a little shyly. "I do. It's a little different now, more comfortable than exciting, but he's truly my other half. Being with him makes me happy. The distance is hard, but it's made us appreciate each other more. I feel like I'm more me when I'm with him, if that makes sense."

"It does," Bethany said without thinking. The server stopped by their table with their food, breaking off the conversation.

And it was then that Bethany realized she did understand what Sarah was saying. Because she'd felt it.

With Trey.

She'd never have been able to get it before him. The idea that someone else could complement her, give her the confidence to understand herself, to be the person that she really truly wanted to be. But with Trey...she was.

What was she going to do now?

The knowledge was exhilarating, exciting, and terrifying. It wasn't supposed to happen this way. Honestly, it could be infatuation, but somehow she didn't think so.

She was intensely aware of the fact that time was ticking away, each moment bringing her closer to him.

It was a scary—and wonderful—feeling. There was so much between them. And apart from him, it seemed like an impossibility that they could ever be together. But when she was in his arms? Things just felt—right.

As their brunch wound to a close, Sarah pinned Bethany with a scrutinizing look. "Hey, Bethy, you know you can tell me anything, right?"

Bethany's fork trembled a little in her hand as she set it down. "Of course I do."

"Good," Sarah said, wiping her fingers on her napkin. "As long as you know."

Bethany's phone buzzed in her pocket. Grateful for the distraction, she pulled it free.

A text from Mama Yelverton lit up the screen.

Can't wait to see you and Trey this afternoon. He told me that the invitations are gorgeous, and that you're responsible. Thank you, love! See you soon!

"What's that?"

"Your mom," Bethany said as she dropped her phone

into her purse. "She's all excited about the invitations. We're going over them this afternoon."

"Oh yeah?" Sarah propped her chin on her hands. "What do they look like?"

"Do you want to see?"

Her mouth fell open. "You have them with you?"

Bethany grinned. "I thought you didn't want to know anything."

"It's different if you've got them with you! Show me, show me!"

Bethany laughed as she pulled the folder from her over-sized purse and Sarah jumped into the seat beside her.

"Wow, Beth, these are gorgeous! I love each and every one of them. How are you going to pick?"

"We'll let your mom do that," Bethany said, the silky bow at the top of one invitation trailing over her finger. "These were our four favorites."

"Our?"

"Mine and Trey's," she admitted. "We worked on them together."

"Good," Sarah said softly, not raising her gaze from the four invitations spread on the table in front of them. "I'm glad. So, how did you make them?"

As Bethany told Sarah the process, her mind was churning.

Just a little while longer, and I'll see him again. Just a little while longer...

chapter
SEVENTEEN

As Trey walked into the Yelvertons' house, he was filled with a renewed sense of purpose. The Shadows had given him that. Their meeting had been much different than he'd expected, but he was buoyed by their enthusiasm for the project and determined to see it through to the end.

Whether or not it was good for him, it was good for them, and those guys needed it. So he'd stick it out. And hopefully at the end of this thing, he'd come out with his skin intact.

"Trey," Mrs. Yelverton greeted him warmly. She gripped his hand, stepping closer for a moment, and he wondered if she was about to hug him. He didn't move, and she put more distance between them.

He wasn't sure whether to be grateful or disappointed that she hadn't tried. How would it feel to be hugged by his mother? His real mother?

"Bethany's not here yet," she said, leading him into the kitchen. "It's just you and me for the moment, I'm afraid."

"No problem with that," he said carefully as he sank onto a barstool. She rummaged in a cabinet and pulled down some glasses. "Have you been doing well?"

"Just fine," she said brightly, pulling open the fridge. "Sweet tea?"

"Sure."

She poured him a glass, the ice inside clinking softly. As he sipped, he watched her.

Her movements were quick, efficient. They reminded him of himself, honestly. The way he liked to get things done without wasting time. Hell, she even stacked things in the cupboards the same way, he thought as she pulled out a plate for some cookies.

"You know," she said, leaning against the counter, "we've been so busy with the wedding planning that we haven't had a chance to talk much."

"I'm not an especially good conversationalist." He took a long sip of tea, discomfort prickling the back of his neck.

Conversation meant questions. And questions meant lies. And like it or not, he'd set himself up to lie to her over and over again. And he didn't like it. Not one bit. But the truth was worse. So he kept his trap shut.

"I'm not either, to tell you the truth." She handed him a cookie on a napkin. "Not really."

"You do all right," he said, and she laughed.

"I guess I do. It helps to have someone you're interested in to talk to."

"You're right there," he said, then looked at her.

That morning, he'd pulled his smartphone from the bedside table and done a Google search. The site he'd clicked on had made his throat close up, his chest curiously tight as he scrolled through photos, news items, and pictures of a downtown mission that had been built to honor him. The memory of the kid that had disappeared without a trace a long time ago.

Knowing that she'd done that—devoted her life to it—made him wish with all his being that he deserved it. That he could tell her how much it meant to him.

He cleared his throat. "I checked out the website for Sam's Place."

She paused. "You did?"

His nod was brief. "Yeah. Looks great. It's definitely the kind of place that would have been really helpful."

The "to me" was left unsaid. But she got it, because her smile was pained, and her eyes were suspiciously shiny as she responded. "Good. That's all I wanted."

The pang in his chest grew. He wished he was better at talking. At showing her what he felt. If he'd been able to, he'd have expressed just how honored he felt that she'd put so much of herself into a place that would help kids who were in his position. That her efforts had gone in such a positive direction. That even though every sign had pointed to his death, she'd not only believed enough to keep looking for him, but also extended the care and love and hope into a place that helped the disadvantaged, the lost, the broken.

But he couldn't formulate a sentence like that. Not out loud. So instead, he just picked up his tea. "This is good."

"I'm glad you like it," she whispered, and silence fell between them.

The sound of a door opening broke the quiet. He didn't turn his head. He didn't need to. He'd known who it would be.

"Hi. Sorry I'm late," Bethany said, her presence in

the room causing the whole place to feel brighter. "I had brunch with Sarah, and we lost track of time."

"Oh good. Did she come back with you? She didn't tell me her plans when she left this morning." Mrs. Yelverton pressed a kiss to Bethany's cheek as Trey tried not to look at her. God, it had only been hours, but the need to draw her into his arms was nearly painful.

That was impossible in front of Mrs. Yelverton. Bethany was almost her daughter. He'd keep his hands to himself out of respect for that.

But damn, it was hard.

"No, she went out shopping to blow off some steam. She's got a big project due this week, and she needed a little break."

"That's too bad." Mrs. Yelverton sighed as Bethany sank onto the stool next to Trey. "I'd hoped she'd be able to see the invitations at least."

"I showed her. She loved them." Bethany smiled at Trey, and he couldn't stop the squeezing feeling in his chest. "She said to tell you thank you."

"No problem," he rasped.

Mrs. Yelverton turned and busied herself pouring Bethany a glass of tea. In the split second of privacy, Trey reached beneath the counter and rubbed his palm along Bethany's leg.

Her bright smile and the spark in her eyes told him all he needed to know.

Damn, he'd missed that girl.

"Well, should we get started?" Bethany asked as she pulled a manila folder from her bag.

"Oh damn. I've left my glasses in the office. I'll be right back."

Mrs. Yelverton left the room, and they were alone.

He looked at Bethany for a long moment. How could he tell her what he was thinking? Feeling? How things were all mixed up and complicated, but when he was next to her...

"Hi," she said quietly, a small smile on her face.

"Hi," he said, reaching over to her. "I'm sorry for running out on you like that." He gripped her fingers in his own, raking his thumb over her knuckles.

"It was kind of sudden," she agreed. "I should probably be angry at you."

"Are you?" He lifted her hand to his mouth, his lips brushing across the back of her hand.

"I don't think you would have left if it wasn't really important."

"You're right. I wouldn't have."

"Then I'm not mad," she whispered.

Trey pulled her into his arms and kissed her. It was a sweet reunion at first, gentle and exploring. But Bethany opened her mouth to him, and as desire surged in his veins, he let his hands sweep down her back and passion spurred their kiss deeper. Bethany groaned softly against his mouth, and he wished he could scoop her into his arms, find the nearest bedroom, and press her into the soft covers.

Footsteps approached. Reluctantly, he pulled away, arms folded on the counter, sipping his tea as if nothing had happened.

Smiling to himself, he watched as Bethany blinked owlishly, trying to collect herself as Mrs. Yelverton walked back into the kitchen, glasses in hand.

"Bethany, are you all right, honey? You look a little pale."

"I'm just fine," she squeaked, and Trey bit the inside of his lip to keep from laughing. She kicked him beneath the counter. "Sorry. Fine. Here, you take my seat, and we can look over the invitations."

Behind Mrs. Yelverton's back, Trey shot a wink toward Bethany. She blushed.

This was going to be a long—and fun—afternoon.

The longest afternoon in Bethany's memory finally drew to a close. Mama Yelverton had been thrilled by the invitations, as well as the progression of other plans. They'd finalized colors—white, gray, and a brilliant turquoise—as well as the bakery, the photographer, and several other key decisions.

And every time Mama Yelverton's back was turned, Trey was there, reminding Bethany of what had been and promising her so much more to come.

She'd felt like a naughty teenager, sneaking off behind her mother's back as she prepared to leave.

"Let me get you those papers you needed for the venue," Mama Yelverton said and dashed off toward her office.

Trey was centimeters from her as soon as they were alone.

"You're driving me crazy," she whispered against his chest as he swept his broad hands down her back.

"That's the idea." He pressed his lips to her cheek in a sweet, gentle kiss. "My house or your apartment?"

She bit her lip as his big, hot body pressed into her. God. She wanted… She wanted to be with him again. Free. Complete. Comfortable.

At her apartment she'd be afraid of interruption

again. Every time she was there with him, it seemed like someone or something was always just behind. But at Trey's...they were safe. Alone. And she wanted the oasis of his home again—to understand him by being surrounded by things he owned and loved.

"Yours," she whispered, curling her fingers into the lapels of the leather jacket he'd donned just a moment ago.

"Good," he whispered, then stepped back.

Mama Yelverton appeared around the corner just then in a dizzying display of perfect timing.

"Here you go. I could have dropped them in the mail though."

"No need," Bethany said. "I'll drop them off tomorrow. Save you a stamp."

"Great," Mama Yelverton said with a smile. She looked from one of them to the other. "Well, this has been a lot of fun. What are you two kids up to tonight?"

Bethany fought to stifle her reaction. "Oh, nothing much. Think I'm cleaning out my linen closet."

Trey folded his arms over his chest. "Think I'll be doing a little rummaging of my own, actually."

Bethany nearly swallowed her tongue as Mama Yelverton shook her head.

"You two are much too wild for a Saturday night. Just let me know if I need to post bail."

Bethany laughed nervously. "No need."

She said her goodbyes, kissing Mama Yelverton's cheek, and excused herself. As she walked toward the garage door, she glanced over her shoulder.

Trey's body language was so hard to read. It was as if he wanted to lean forward toward his mother and embrace her, but another, larger half of him was keeping him back.

Bethany shook her head as she closed the door behind her.

She cared about Mama Yelverton. She cared about Trey. But she couldn't iron out the relationship there. It was too new, too complicated, and much too fragile. He made it difficult to think when she was with him.

But that didn't stop her wanting to keep two of her favorite people happy.

She climbed into the driver's seat and waited, her keys swinging in the ignition.

What was the protocol here? Should she wait for him? She'd been to his place once before, but she hadn't exactly memorized the way. It had been too difficult to see around his broad back as his motorcycle tore down the highway.

She shouldn't have worried. Just a few minutes later, Trey was walking out the door.

She rolled down the window.

"Follow me," he said, his hand resting on the door.

She bit her lip for a moment, unsure. It was getting late. As much as she liked Trey, should she really do this? He lived off the beaten path a bit. Would it be hard to find her way home in the middle of the night, GPS notwithstanding?

"You don't have to do anything you're not comfortable with," he said as if reading her mind. "But I will tell you I've got a brand-new box of Pop Tarts. And I brew a mean cup of coffee."

She smiled. "Is that your subtle way of asking me to spend the night?"

"Sorry, was I too vague?"

She laughed at his mock offense. "No, I got it. We'll see."

He nodded, and then he strode off toward his bike.

In her rearview mirror, she watched as he swung his leg over the saddle and balanced his bike, cranking the engine.

She'd never thought about motorcycles much before, but there was something really sexy about the way he handled the shiny vehicle, the control, the balance, the smooth way he did it all. It reminded her of how his touch felt, and her stomach did a full somersault.

"Easy, Bethany," she said as she turned around and followed him down the long drive, past the falling-down Victorian, and onto the highway. "Keep your brain on the road."

At least until she got to his house. Then her brain could wander wherever it wanted.

Within reason.

As long as reason could last around Trey.

Which, in her experience, wasn't very long at all.

The moon was hanging low in the sky, fat and glowing as Trey pulled off the road and down the gravel drive toward his house, Bethany following. Her headlights bumped up and down as they coasted toward his house. She took in the surroundings, biting her lip as her nerves started an intense twitching beneath her skin.

Here she was again. In his territory. On his turf. Under his protection.

Would it be as good as last time? As intense?

There was only one way to find out, she told herself as she gripped the door handle after cutting the car's engine.

Trey was there, ready to grip her hand and close the door after her. "Welcome back," he said, a little smile playing around his mouth as he led her up the steps to his front porch.

"This is the most beautiful place," Bethany said, running a hand over the carved wood alongside his door. "Did you do this?"

"Wolf did," Trey said as he opened the door.

"Wolf. That's right. He's your friend...your coworker?"

"Both," Trey said, flicking on the lights. "He's my right hand."

Bethany smiled. "I know how that is. I feel like Sarah's mine, sometimes."

Trey turned to her, his deep-green eyes showing immeasurable depths. "Thank you," he said, gathering her into his arms.

"For what?" She melted into him, beyond happy to be in his embrace again.

"For being you. For making me comfortable. For everything you are. Thank you," he whispered into her hair.

And in that moment, Bethany was desperately afraid that she would never feel complete again without this man by her side.

The depth of the tide of feeling swept her away, and she closed her eyes to the thoughts...and simply let herself feel.

chapter

EIGHTEEN

IT WAS STRANGE, THE FEELING THAT WAS OVERTAKING him as Trey embraced Bethany. An odd mixture of longing and contentment, hunger and happiness.

He'd never experienced anything like it. If he could freeze a moment in time, he'd have been sorely tempted to keep that one forever.

He bent down and took her lips in a kiss.

It was odd, the feeling of completeness that she gave him. His hands brushed across her shoulders and up to tangle in the hair at the nape of her neck, tilting her head for him. Her eyes fluttered closed, her arms winding around his shoulders as his mouth possessed her. She opened her mouth for his kiss, completely giving herself up to him.

Bethany was so trusting, so pure, so completely unlike anyone he had ever been with. He didn't deserve someone like her. Didn't deserve any of the things that were happening to him. Not friends like the Shadows, not the family he'd just found, and sure as hell not someone like Bethany.

But that didn't matter now. All that mattered was that she was here in his arms, and he did not intend to waste a moment of it.

Together, they stumbled down the hall, clothes disappearing piece by piece as they made their way to his bedroom without ever losing contact. Their hands were everywhere, Bethany's touch just as greedy as his. His blood was on fire inside his veins, his body aching with the need to possess her. Once they were naked, he pressed her down onto his bed, his body imprisoning her in the most delicious way.

"I want you," she whispered.

"I know."

He bent down to kiss his way from her neck down to her collarbone. Her sharp intake of breath urged him on, teeth and lips possessing her.

The sound of his name was like a prayer on her lips. "I want more."

He kissed his way down her body, stopping at each breast to worship the peaked, pink nipple that begged for his attention. Her skin was hot all over, so soft and smooth against his rough touch. He was slower than he wanted, but was still fierce and passionate in each caress. She matched him, her delicate fingernails digging into his shoulders as he kissed his way down her belly.

With every movement, she showed him that she wanted this as much as he did. Inside his head, inside his heart, the cry of *We fit—she's the same* repeated over and over.

Her legs shifted together, her mouth open in a soundless cry as his lips brushed at the top of her mound.

"Please." She was begging now, her hips rising to plead for his intimate kiss. "Please."

He knelt between her legs, spreading her to his gaze.

She was beautiful. All pale-pink, shiny, wet flesh, her delicate inner folds seeming to beckon to him. He leaned forward and allowed his tongue to dance at the seam of her.

She bucked against him. "Trey!"

He grinned against her most sensitive skin. "Do you like that?"

"Oh God, yes. More, please."

He had never been one to disappoint a lady. "Yes, ma'am."

He sealed his mouth over her, his tongue discovering every hidden part of her. She tasted sweet, succulent, like a ripe fruit. He left no part of her unkissed, unloved. His tongue danced over her clit, his own body aching with the need to plunge into her secret depths.

Bethany thrashed and twisted on the bed, her head tossing wildly as he kept up his intimate torture. God, he could watch her like this all night. Torturing her in this way was so satisfying, and knowing he could bring her to the heights of desire fueled his own passion. But he wanted more. He knew she did too.

With one last loving lick, Trey raised his head. Bethany was panting, gasping, her beautiful blue eyes wide and dazed.

The bedside drawer slid open beneath his hand, and he retrieved a condom. With quick, deft movements, he rolled it on, keenly aware of her gaze on him the whole time.

"Can I touch you?"

He nearly lost control at the soft-voiced question.

"Please," he rasped and fisted his hands at his sides.

She reached out and cradled him in her hot, slender

palm. Trey bit the inside of his lip, the momentary flash of pain giving him control over the sensation of her touch.

She gripped him gently, fingers sliding up and down his latex-covered length. He was incredibly grateful she'd waited for him to put the condom on.

Bethany's touch on his bare cock would have made him embarrass himself.

She smiled a little as she rubbed her thumb over the aching head. "You're so hot and smooth and thick. I love the feel of you."

Trey couldn't wait any more. And she was ready.

He pressed her down into the pillows, and with one smooth movement, he sheathed himself within her.

She gasped, the sudden invasion making her shudder and wrap her legs around his hips. Her teeth grazed his shoulder as he began a smooth, even rhythm, plunging high and deep into her hot, slick, welcoming body.

God, this was good. She was good. With every stroke, they climbed higher and higher, her beaded nipples digging into his chest, her sharp nails scratching down his back as her thighs gripped his churning hips.

With a ragged groan, he pulled away. Her lips were swollen and parted as she breathed heavily, looking at him in question.

This was good. So, so good. But he wanted more.

"Turn over," he said with a gentle slap on her hip.

She grinned. Then did as he'd asked.

"Good Lord." He could hardly believe the beautiful sight that was Bethany on her knees before him. Her ass was shapely, leanly muscled, and her beautiful pink lips were visible just below the cleft of her cheeks.

It was a mental image he'd gladly carry with him for

the rest of his life. Bethany bent over, her legs parted for him.

He positioned himself behind her, then reaching below to tease her clit, he plunged home.

They both gasped, sensation rocking them as Bethany's body accommodated his penetration. Trey's cock was aching with the beautiful, sweet grip of her around him.

He began to move, Bethany with him, each of them striving for that elusive peak.

Trey's fingers kept up a rhythm on Bethany's clit, and as her movements became more frantic, and her inner walls signaled an imminent explosion, he lost his grip on his own orgasm.

"Oh my God," Bethany cried as her body shuddered. "Oh God."

Fireworks exploded behind Trey's eyes as the orgasm rocketed through his body.

He collapsed beside her, bringing her close into the shelter of his body. Turning her head to face him, he pressed his lips to hers for a brief moment.

And then she smiled at him, and everything was right in his world.

The most contented feeling he had ever had, the most wonderful person he could remember being with. He didn't want this to end, ever.

And that feeling terrified the hell out of him.

Her body was sore, her feelings raw and open as her heart pounded against her ribs like a caged bird.

Trey was curled around her, his cheek pressed to the

top of her head, one leg slung over hers, his arm around her waist. There was almost no part of her that wasn't touching him.

It was overwhelming. It was delicious. Her body and brain were almost overloaded with sensation, and all she could do was stare straight ahead and will everything to come back online when the sensors had recovered from overload.

Trey's chin nestled atop her shoulder, the bristle of his five-o'clock shadow rasping slightly. "Are you okay?"

She smiled a little at his question. He was so thoughtful, even though he'd just shagged the life out of her. "I'm not going to be able to move for a while."

He laughed a little, a deep rumbling sound that sent a shiver through her. "Then I guess I did my job right."

"Did you ever." She stretched, her ass pressing back against him with the movement.

"Keep that up and we'll have to think about round two."

She sighed. "As much as I'd love that, I should probably get home."

Her legs swung over the side of the bed, but his grip around her waist tightened. "You don't have to go."

She paused. "Are you sure you want me staying here all night?"

He rose on his elbow and looked down at her, his free hand brushing the hair from her cheek. "Stay with me." He paused, then resumed stroking her cheek. "I mean, I want you to stay with me."

Her thoughts were a whirlwind.

This felt like a much bigger decision than whether or not she'd wake up in her own bed in the morning. This felt like…a step. A move toward the future that she wouldn't necessarily be able to take back tomorrow. A turning point of sorts.

Which path should she take? The safe one that led back to her lonely apartment, or the one that led toward a man who was more question than answer, more darkness than light, more passion than security?

But even though she barely knew him in reality, something deep inside her understood that Trey was the kind of person she'd have chosen under any circumstances.

"I'll stay," she whispered, turning toward him in the bed and wrapping her arm around him as she nuzzled against his chest's soft mat of hair. "I'll stay with you tonight."

And she did.

At first she thought the noise of a car backfiring had woken her out of a deep slumber. But then the sound happened again, and her heart jumped as she realized it was a gunshot.

She rocketed out of bed, her body catching a quick chill as she finally remembered she was naked.

Trey was nowhere to be seen, but her clothes were laid out neatly on the chair in the corner. She grabbed them and pulled them on, wincing at the crack of gunshots that were way, way too close.

"Trey?" she called as she jammed her feet into her shoes. "Are you okay?"

No answer.

She walked down the hall, glad for the momentary silence that had fallen. At least, until she reached the kitchen. Then she heard shouting voices, one of which was Trey's.

She hurried to the door to see what was up.

Trey was standing barefoot on the deck, wearing sweatpants and a T-shirt as he yelled out into his yard. A huge guy with a shotgun was standing only twenty feet away.

"Holy crap," Bethany gasped, and whirled. She ran for the living room to find her phone.

Shaking fingers opened the dial pad, and she'd just typed the nine when a bellow of laughter met her ears.

Was that—Trey?

Bethany cleared the number from her phone and hesitantly walked back into the kitchen.

Sure enough, Trey's head was thrown back and he was laughing his ass off. The big guy with the gun was laughing too. Behind him were three other guys that she hadn't noticed before. One of them was holding an RC controller, and another had a big drone with a pink-and-white poster board attached to the bottom of it.

Bethany slid open the door a little, her adrenaline still racing.

"I don't give a damn if you break it, but why do you have to do it in my cock-sucking backyard?"

"I told you, Boss. You've got more clearance over the pond. Too many trees in our backyard."

"Why the hell do you want to shoot it anyway?"

The guy holding the controller shrugged. "I got a new one. Wolf wanted to do some target shooting, and I figured this would give me some practice at evasive maneuvers. Besides, we agreed that Ace's vision board needed some adjustments."

"I can't believe you don't appreciate my artistic genius. Do you know how hard it was to go into the store and get those glitter markers? The pink poster board? You guys have no appreciation for how hard I worked!"

Trey shook his head as Bethany slipped out the door. "Ace, you've totally lost it. Rocco, you've got a few screws loose. And Wolf, I'd expect you to act like an adult."

Wolf, she presumed, was the big, bearded one with the gun. "I never turn down the opportunity to break something, Boss. Especially Ace's balls."

"My heart, more like." Ace sniffed. "All the time I spent slaving away…"

Trey noticed her, and a smile broke out over his face as he reached for her hand.

"Hey, Beth."

"Hi," she said quietly, curling her fingers into his. "Do I need to call the cops? Or do you typically use gunshots as an alarm clock?"

Just like that, his face went thundercloud dark.

"You assholes woke up my old lady."

"Shut up," she said, nudging Trey.

Instantaneously, all four men froze like statues. The silence stretched out so long that Bethany shifted nervously.

Had she done something wrong?

"Old lady?" the one holding the drone said. "Boss, since when do you have an old lady?"

"Since now," Trey said, slinging his arm around Bethany's shoulders. "Boys, this is Bethany. She's the maid of honor for the Yelverton wedding. Say hello." Trey nodded at each of them in turn. "That's Wolf, Rocco, Ace, and Dean."

A chorus of muttered hellos reached her, and Bethany fought her blush.

"Hey," she said, wondering why she felt so awkward. These were clearly the same guys that had been helping at the bar wedding. Trey's coworkers, or friends, or whatever they were.

But all in all, the situation was uncomfortable, and she was glad when Trey waved goodbye to them, and she walked back into the house with him.

"What was that about?" Bethany asked as Trey started making coffee.

"Just assholes killing time." Trey poured water into the coffeepot. "Sorry they woke you up though."

She crept up behind him and wrapped her arms around his waist.

"It's okay. You should have woken me up this morning. I didn't need to sleep in."

He looked over his shoulder with an evil grin. "Yes, you did. I kept you up too late last night."

She smiled back. "You did, but I don't mind getting up early to be with you."

He brushed a kiss across her lips and poured her a cup of coffee.

She took it and sat down at the table while he made her breakfast.

Damn. If she wasn't careful, she could get used to this.

chapter

NINETEEN

EVERY DAY THAT PASSED LEFT BETHANY WANTING him more and being more confused by him.

Trey was definitely an enigma. He'd disappear, sometimes for days on end, and then reappear like nothing had happened. When she asked what was up, he'd just tell her not to worry about it.

It was definitely worrying.

But then they'd spend time together, whole days naked in bed exploring each other, and she'd forget about the questions, the worry, the wondering.

She was walking on a tightrope that couldn't take her weight, and it would eventually snap. She knew it, but she also couldn't bring herself to care.

She was the happiest she'd ever been in her life, with the exception of a couple of tiny details. One, the constant phone calls and voicemails from her grandmother, who was still insisting that Bethany's "boyfriend" was a criminal thug, or worse, and two…

"Can't believe you dragged me to this freaking dress

store." Sarah was grumbling as she swam her way through about twelve yards of white tulle. "I told you I didn't want to deal with any of this stuff!"

"You've got to try on wedding dresses. I can't do it for you. You'd end up with something that your boobs wouldn't fit inside."

Sarah shot her a glare as soon as her face emerged from the neckline of the wedding dress. "I can get married in jeans and a T-shirt."

"And break Mama Yelverton's heart? You're not that cruel. Now come on, turn around and let me zip you."

Sarah bitched and moaned as Bethany slid the zipper closed, but then she caught sight of her reflection in the mirror and suddenly the whining turned to oohs and aahs.

"Oh, Bethy, it's so beautiful," Sarah gasped as she smoothed the puffy skirt down at her hips. It was a beautiful design, fitted at the bodice and with lots of fluffy princess poof at the bottom. A short train swished out behind, the ideal finish to the perfect wedding dress.

As soon as Bethany had seen it, she'd known it would be perfect for Sarah. The memory of taking Ace dress shopping would be one she'd carry to her grave, but she had to admit, behind the flirtatious, teasing playboy act, he actually had nice taste.

"I'm so glad you like it," Bethany said, pride and happiness swelling within her as Sarah laughed and spun in front of the mirror. "Just needs a little alteration in the waist and the tuck-up for your train."

The fitting-room attendant took the dress and made notes about the alterations, and Sarah and Bethany left the shop together.

"Thanks so much for finding it," Sarah was saying as

they climbed into Bethany's car. "I can't believe how wonderful it is."

Bethany shrugged as she clicked on her seat belt. "It just screamed you, that's all."

Sarah happy-sighed. "Great, that's done. How about some lunch? My treat."

Bethany glanced at the clock. She'd promised to meet Trey for lunch, presuming that Sarah had other plans, but she couldn't exactly tell Sarah that.

"Um, sure. I just need to rearrange a meeting or two, if that's okay."

Sarah shook her head. "No, don't worry about it. I should probably get home to study anyway. Just thought you could use a break. I hardly hear from you at all these days. You seem to be so busy with the wedding."

Bethany tried to keep her wince under wraps, but damn Sarah's sharp eyes.

"Are you sure this isn't too much on you? I can get Mark's mom to help…"

"No, no, that's not it." The need to tell the truth was like a flaming-hot knife inside her chest, but the fear of upsetting Sarah was even stronger. "I'm enjoying it. Really. Just worried about the job search and everything."

Sarah hiked her brow in her friend's direction. "Do you need more money for helping with the wedding planning? I'll be happy to pay more—"

Bethany shook her head vehemently. "No, you've been way too generous already. I've barely touched my savings. But even with this temporary wedding job, I need to figure out what I'm going to do with my life once your wedding is over."

"Well, you should take some time to have fun too. There's a month left before the wedding, and from what Mom has told me, you guys are in really good shape. And besides, Trey should be doing some of this. Mom's paying him for that too."

The note of disapproval in Sarah's tone made Bethany's stomach tense. "Still not sure about the whole brother thing?"

"No. Sorry. It's just…" Sarah shook her head as the car pulled to a stop in front of her apartment. "Eh. I've avoided dealing with it. Like usual, Sarah's patented 'Ignore the problem till it goes away' technique." She reached for the door handle, then paused. "Hey. I've got an idea."

Uh-oh. Sarah's ideas were usually cause for worry.

"What is it?"

Sarah turned and looked at her with eyes that could only be termed puppy-dog. "What if we did a family dinner? With both of us, Mom, Mark, and Trey. To get to know everyone a little. I'd feel more comfortable with you there to run interference. What do you say?"

Bethany closed her eyes and tried to swallow, but damn if her mouth wasn't full of cotton wool. It was hard enough pretending in front of Mama Yelverton. How could she keep her feelings for Trey secret if Sarah was staring at her the whole time at dinner?

It wasn't possible. It was a terrible idea.

But of course she'd do it. She never left her best friend in the lurch. *Damn it*.

"Sure, if everyone else is okay with it," Bethany said weakly.

Sarah leaned across the seat and gave her a quick hug.

"You're the best, bestie. I'll get the dinner set up and talk with you soon, okay?"

"Okay."

Bethany smiled tightly and waved as Sarah disappeared down the walkway. As soon as she was out of sight, Bethany let her forehead thump against her steering wheel.

This was not going to be fun, in any sense of the word.

She was screwed.

The drive to the little diner where she and Trey were meeting took much longer than she'd have thought. Being alone with her brain while it screamed at her for the double life she was leading wasn't exactly her idea of a good time.

By the time she'd turned into the parking lot, her hands were clammy, her shoulders aching, and all she wanted to do was take a hot shower and a nap, in that order.

She had to talk to Trey though. Tell him her worries, and get on the same page. Hopefully, he'd be on board with keeping their…relationship…secret. Was that even the right word? They hadn't made promises to each other, but he'd kind of claimed her in front of his friends a few weeks ago. That was like declaring her his girlfriend, right? And she definitely wasn't seeing anyone else.

The engine cutting left her in too much silence, and the worries rushed in to fill the gap.

What if she thought they were exclusive and Trey didn't? She shook off the toxic notion the instant it crept into her frontal lobe. No way. Trey was loyal; she didn't doubt that. Even though he could probably have four or five women every night if he wanted to, she didn't think he was the kind of guy to sleep around like that.

But what do you really know about him? He hasn't even told you what he does for a living.

That poisonous voice inside her head popped up at the most inopportune times.

She climbed out of the car and walked toward the diner, shutting the voice out yet again.

Everything is fine. Everything is fine. Everything is fine. And if she kept repeating that, it had to be true.

Didn't it?

Trey was outside on his phone when Bethany's car pulled into the lot.

He smiled to himself, the happiness and peace sliding through him like it always did when he caught sight of her.

Her car was looking more yellow than green, pollen from the pines covering it in a thin layer of golden dust. He'd wash it for her, maybe tomorrow afternoon when it was supposed to be sunny and warmer.

He started toward her, intending to walk her to the door of the diner, but the expression on her face stopped him.

There were lines on her forehead, her eyebrows were knitted together, and the corners of her mouth were drawn down.

She closed her eyes, and it looked for a moment as if she was arguing with herself.

Guilt crept in, pore by pore, overtaking his previous happiness.

With every day that went by, he felt worse and worse about the charade he was keeping up in front of her. She knew he wasn't what he'd claimed to be, but he'd never once tried to tell her the truth. And why?

Fear. He was a cowardly asshole, and it was eating him from the inside out.

She opened her eyes and climbed out of the car. He strode across the walk to catch up with her.

"Hey," he said softly, and she turned.

Her expression lifted slightly at the sight of him. "Hi. You okay?"

He nodded, wrapping his arm around her waist. "Yeah. You?"

She nodded and leaned her head against his shoulder. "I'll be fine. Just up in my head about some stuff."

You know that, asshole. It's not like you haven't given her a ton of crap to be up in her head about.

Shaking off the conscience that wasn't taking no for an answer, Trey held open the door to the diner and let Bethany precede him into the restaurant.

They took a booth in the corner, Trey facing the rest of the place, Bethany opposite him. They made small talk for a few minutes, each of them ordering from the menu and sipping on tea and water, respectively.

As he did whenever he was with her like this, Trey wondered what her reaction would be if she knew. What would she think if she found out that he'd been keeping the Iron Shadows—and the fact that he was their leader—a secret from her?

Nothing good. Nothing at all good.

"I wanted to talk to you," Bethany said, unwrapping the halves of her BLT, the wrapper crinkling under her hands. "About something kind of important."

He tensed. "Okay."

It wasn't okay, but it also wasn't as if he had a choice.

"It's Sarah. You know she's my best friend. I haven't

told her about…" Bethany's voice trailed off, and she gestured between them. "About us, I guess I mean to say."

Trey nodded, a little relieved that the conversation hadn't gone where he'd thought it was going, namely to *Why are you still lying to me, you asshole?*

Bethany took a deep breath, setting her sandwich down as she continued. "I mean, we haven't really defined what it is we are to each other. And Sarah has some unresolved feelings when it comes to the family situation. I didn't want to complicate things any further by telling her."

Trey sank back in the booth. He didn't say anything, wondering if there was anything else she wanted to say.

He didn't have to wait long.

"Sarah wants to have a family dinner to get to know you, and she wants me to be there as a buffer, since I said you were nice. But it'll be hard to keep our involvement from her, she's so freaking sharp."

A worry crept in, one that snaked its way up his spine and curled back down into the pit of his stomach. "Are you ashamed of being seen with me?"

Bethany's eyes flew open wide, her reaction too genuine to be faked. "No! Of course not!"

He took a deep breath, inwardly chastising himself for doubting her. "You're basically part of that family. A bigger part than I am, for sure, even though the DNA says otherwise. I'm the stranger in the situation, so whatever you say goes. Tell me what you want, and I'll make it happen."

He reached across the table and took her hand in his. Her fingers were cold, so he squeezed them slightly, rubbing them to return the warmth.

Worry was plain in her gaze.

"First, I need to know. What…what do you think this

is? I mean, how would you term our relation…erm, our association?" she asked.

Well, to be quite honest, he hadn't thought about it. There was Trey, and there was Bethany, and they were good together. He wanted to be with her at every opportunity, and it seemed like she wanted the same.

Why did it need a name?

Because she'd asked for one. That's why.

Feeling like an awkward teenager, Trey rubbed the back of his neck. "I guess *relationship* is a good word. As far as I'm concerned, we're together. Does that sound right to you?"

It was like he'd plucked the moon from the sky and handed it to her. He'd never forget the smile that she gave him right then and there. "Wow. That's… Yeah. I feel that way too."

He smiled halfway, unsure what else to do. "Good."

For a moment they just held hands and looked at each other. He should have felt weak, mushy, overly emotional. But he didn't. He felt strong, as if he could run ten miles without losing his breath or lift a car one-handed for her.

Anything she wanted. He'd do anything. And it felt amazing.

"So, if we have a big family dinner, can we keep us under wraps? Just until Sarah comes to grips with everything that's happening, and the wedding is over."

His smile faltered.

When the wedding was over, he'd be fading out of their lives. Only barely connected by the occasional phone call or visit every few years. There was no way he could keep up that facade long-term.

But he couldn't ask Bethany to separate from the family she'd chosen, any more than he could leave the Shadows.

His formerly buoyant heart turned to stone in his chest, but he pinned a smile on his face anyway.

"Sure. We'll keep it quiet if that's what you want."

She gave a big sigh. "Thank you, Trey."

The food might as well have been made of cardboard, but he ate it anyway.

Had to keep up his strength to continue being such an asshole.

chapter

TWENTY

PUTTING ON A BURST OF SPEED, TREY LEANED TOWARD his handlebars, the wind rushing past him as his adrenaline pumped.

His target looked over his shoulder, pushing the twenty-odd-year-old Camaro faster.

A grim smile stretched Trey's face as he gained on the fleeing vehicle.

He knew the man's face now. There wasn't anywhere in either Wake or Durham counties that the guy could go without Trey being alerted to his presence. For the idiot who'd had the temerity to deal meth in the Shadows' territory, it was the end of the line.

The Camaro took a sudden hard right, and Trey was forced to swing wide to avoid eating the pavement. The momentary falter gave Flash and Wolf the chance to pull closer to the car than Trey.

He glanced in his mirrors. Rocco and Ace were there backing them up, their bikes roaring toward the fleeing vehicle just as determinedly as Trey's was.

Trey goosed the engine faster as Flash made a move. His Triumph Daytona swerved into the opposite lane, and he pulled even with the driver's door.

The leather over Trey's knuckles stretched tight as he gripped his handlebars hard.

Almost there now.

One—

Flash reached a hand toward the latch.

Two—

Wolf pulled even with the passenger door.

Three.

In a feat that was born of perfect timing and consummate skill, the passenger door to the Camaro pulled open. The driver screamed and flapped his free hand at Wolf, the distraction ideal for Flash to open the driver's door and grab the driver's arm.

The Camaro kept rolling as the dealer hit the pavement. Ace's fist rose in triumph as the Shadows' bikes circled the downed man.

Trey watched as the Camaro came to a sudden, crunching stop against a big, old pine.

One by one, the bike's engines cut. Trey's leg swung over the bike saddle, and his men echoed his movements.

Groaning and cursing, the dealer—who went by the questionable name of Rat—rose to his hands and knees.

They'd been lucky that Rocco had managed to wrestle Rat's piece away before the chase started. Trey didn't want to think about how this might have gone down if they'd had to dodge gunfire too.

With the toe of his boot, Trey nudged Rat none too gently. "Get up."

Weaving and whining, Rat pushed to his feet.

The road rash on his left arm was dotted with gravel and streaming blood. A good-sized gash above his eyebrow was dripping blood down his cheek. That little skid across the highway hadn't felt good.

What came next would feel worse.

"What do you want?" Rat spat on the blacktop, coming perilously close to hitting Wolf's boots. Trey's arm shot out, blocking his second from throttling the beady-eyed loser.

Wolf would get his chance, but Trey needed information first.

"I've got reason to believe you're dealing in my territory."

Rat's beady eyes darted around the circle. Even the smallest Shadow, Flash, had a good four inches and sixty-odd pounds on him. No way he could fight his way out of this.

"So?"

"So," Trey said, walking a slow circle around Rat, one that came closer with each revolution, "you must be new around here if you don't know that we've got this area on lockdown."

"I just moved here. From Greenville."

Ace snorted. "Bullshit. I've seen you at Sharky's, at Bolero's, at Cherry Ice. Your ugly face has been here at least a year, if not longer."

Trey stopped only an inch from Rat's face, using his height and size to intimidate the dealer. Rat shrank backward but bumped straight into Wolf. Pinned between two bigger, stronger men, Rat began to sing like a nightingale. "Okay, yeah. I've been here for a year."

"Are you cooking, or just dealing?"

"Just dealing," Rat said, eyes darting from Trey to Ace and Flash, who were just behind Trey's shoulders. "I don't have the setup to cook."

"Where are you getting your stash?"

Rat bit his lip. Trey's temper kicked into a higher gear. He wasn't going to like this answer, and he knew it.

"From out of state."

"Bullshit." Trey's hand shot out and gripped Rat by the throat. "Don't lie to me."

"Boss, car's coming," Rocco interrupted. "It's at the stop sign with its signal pointing this way."

Trey glared at Rat as if it was the dealer's fault they were about to be discovered.

"Wolf, move my bike." Trey tucked Rat's head beneath his arm in a neat headlock and dragged the smaller man into the bushes at the side of the road.

Rat gurgled, hands clawing at Trey's grip.

"Shut up."

Trey watched as the other men cleared the road just in time enough to see the old, white Buick trundle by. And then the flash of brake lights as the driver noticed the crunched and still-smoking Camaro.

"We're about to get lit up with blues," Wolf grunted to Trey. "That little old man pulled out his cell when he saw the POS."

Irritation rode Trey hard as he looked at the Camaro and then back to the dealer who'd given up struggling and was hanging from Trey's grip like a rag doll.

What to do, what to do?

"Get Doc on the phone," Trey said. "He should be nearby. Tell him we need a pickup, and fast. The rest of you get the hell out of here before the cops show."

Wolf pulled out his phone and began dialing as the others cranked their engines.

"I've got a warrant," Rat croaked as well as he could through Trey's grip. "I can't go to jail."

"You should have thought about that before you started selling shit in my house," Trey snarled as Wolf began speaking into his phone. "Now shut up so my brother can hear."

Wolf cut the call and walked back to Trey's side. "He'll be here in five."

Trey nodded. "Good. Take your bike and get out of here."

Wolf crossed his arms, his tattoos shifting over his muscles as he shook his head. "Not going to leave you."

"Did it sound like I was asking you a question?"

Wolf stepped closer to Trey, toe-to-toe. "No offense, Boss, but I'm staying here, and there's not a damn thing you can do about it."

He was right. Trey had his hands full with Rat, who, given half the chance, would be running straight into the next time zone. If Trey wanted to find out where Rat's supplier was, he'd have to put up with Wolf's insubordination.

"I won't forget this," Trey said, his stare drilling holes into Wolf.

"I'd expect nothing less, Boss."

A few minutes later, Doc's tricked-out F350 pulled to a stop on the side of the road. Doc and Wolf got the bikes into the truck bed while Trey wrestled Rat into the backseat.

"You're not turning me in to the cops?"

"You'll wish I was when you see what I've got planned if you don't give me the information I'm looking for."

Trey's gaze flew to the rearview mirror as sirens sounded in the distance. "Wolf! Doc! Get in here."

The doors slammed, the engine rumbled, and then they were rolling down the highway. Three blue-light specials passed them, heading back to the smoldering remnants of the Camaro with its more-than-likely stolen plates.

"Where to, Boss?" Doc looked at Trey in the rearview.

They weren't far from Ruby's, but Trey didn't want to bring this kind of scum onto their turf. He ticked off a few nearby places. It wouldn't take long to get to the abandoned airstrip from here... *Wait a second.*

"What time is it?"

Wolf turned his head slightly as he answered. "It's almost seven."

"Shit."

Wolf pivoted to get a better look at Trey, alarm in his dark gaze. "What's wrong?"

Trey's head thumped against the cushioned headrest. "I'm late for the goddamn family dinner."

There wasn't much Bethany could say in Trey's defense. The clock clearly showed it was nearing seven thirty. He'd promised to be there at six thirty. She'd texted him at seven, wondering where he was.

No response.

"I'm sure he's on the way," Bethany said lamely as Sarah and Mark sipped their drinks. Mama Yelverton was in the kitchen, doing what she could to keep the food warm and edible.

Sarah just shook her head sadly. "Sorry, Mark. I shouldn't have insisted you come tonight. Such a long drive for nothing."

Bethany had been pouring herself another glass of water, but she spilled a little over her hand. "Oh no, did Mark have plans?"

Mark shook his head. "It's no big deal. Some friends of mine put together a last-minute rafting trip. I told them I had a prior obligation."

Sarah crossed her arms, having set her wineglass down on the table. "If other people had told us *they'd* had prior obligations, then you could have gone."

Bethany winced inwardly as she dried off her hand.

Where was he? This was important. This was supposed to be Trey spending time with his family. Had something happened to him? She didn't want to think about that, but what was she supposed to think? He hadn't given her any indication of where he was. And he hadn't texted Mama Yelverton either. Surely he hadn't forgotten the get-together?

No, she knew he hadn't, because they'd texted each other last night about it.

Blowing a breath upward, she lifted her water glass to her lips.

"Well, I can't starve you kids any longer," Mama Yelverton said as she brought in a big dish of lasagna. "This is starting to get dried out, so go ahead and eat while it's still edible."

"I'm sorry, Mama," Sarah said. "I shouldn't have suggested we do this."

"No, don't you dare. I love having meals with my kids," Mama Yelverton said, pressing a kiss to Sarah's cheek and looking lovingly at both Bethany and Mark. "I just wish Trey had been able to make it."

Mark held out Sarah's chair for her as she sank down into it. She spread her napkin over her lap as she shot Bethany a look. "I'd heard that he was a pretty good guy. I guess that being on time isn't one of his good qualities."

A defense sprang to Bethany's lips, but she bit it back when she realized how hollow it would sound.

Damn it.

Her stomach was churning, worry having changed her earlier hunger into a swirling nausea that made her push her lasagna around her plate instead of eating it.

She checked her phone's screen over and over again. Still no replies from Trey.

Just then, the distant sound of an engine wrenched her gaze toward the windows that faced the front of the house. A smile spread across her face when she saw a single headlight turning into the drive.

"He's here," she said with a relieved sigh and tossed her napkin onto the table as she shoved her chair back. "Excuse me."

Darting from the room, she headed straight to the garage and opened the rolling door with a press of the button. Slowly, Trey's bike was revealed as he cut the engine and removed his helmet.

She ran down the stairs, stopping beside him. "Where were you? I texted you over an hour ago."

Trey ran a hand through his hair, leaving it mussed. "Got tied up taking care of some stuff. I need to get cleaned up before I see Sarah and Mrs. Yelverton. Can you get me into the house without seeing them?"

Bethany frowned. "What do you mean?"

And then she noticed that his leathers were torn over his left thigh. He removed his gloves, and his knuckles were scuffed up and bleeding. A cut on his temple was partially obscured by a lock of his hair, but blood had trickled down his cheek.

She covered her gasp with her hands. "Oh my God, Trey! Were you in a fight?"

"Can you get me into the house without them seeing me? I don't want them to know."

She grabbed his arm. "Come with me."

Worry gnawed at her spine like a dog with a rawhide bone as she let him into the laundry room. Holding a finger up to him, she glanced into the kitchen. It was clear.

"Follow me," she whispered and darted up the back stairs to the second floor. His sure footfalls sounded behind her as he walked with her.

"In here."

She led him into the small bathroom she'd shared with Sarah while they'd lived there in high school. The pale-blue walls and seashell decorations hadn't changed a bit. But the six-and-a-half-foot tattooed, banged-up biker was definitely an addition she hadn't foreseen.

"Here," she said, unearthing the first aid kit from beneath the sink as he began washing off his hands. "There's antibiotic ointment and bandages in here."

"Thank you," he said as he dabbed gauze on the worst cut.

Bethany tried not to think about where the wounds had come from. She really, really did.

"I'll grab some black tape, and you can cover that cut in your pants," Bethany said, and left the bathroom.

In the hallway, she covered her mouth with a trembling hand and stilled for a moment.

Trey was… He was something dark. Something she'd feared but hadn't let herself believe was true.

But he was so kind! So good to her! Surely he couldn't be a bad guy, right?

But he doesn't tell you the truth, her subconscious whispered insidiously. *If he doesn't have anything to hide, why won't he be honest with you?*

She hurried back down the stairs to the laundry room where Mama Yelverton kept a small toolbox.

"Bethany!"

She jumped, nearly dropping the tape she'd unearthed from the bright-yellow plastic box.

"Is everything okay?" Mama Yelverton was holding the empty salad bowl, her expression concerned.

"Oh yeah," Bethany said with a tight, nervous smile. "Trey just had a little rip in his pants. He wanted to get it covered up before Sarah saw him."

Mama Yelverton shook her head. "I wish he wouldn't ride that motorcycle. They're so dangerous."

Not half as dangerous as the rest of the stuff he probably gets up to.

Bethany thought it, but she didn't say it.

"Be back in a couple."

She ran back up the stairs. When she got to the bathroom, she knocked twice. "It's me."

Trey swung open the door, and she nearly swallowed her tongue.

He'd lowered his leathers and was attending to the gash on this thigh. But even though he was injured, the sight of him standing there in his form-fitting boxer briefs made hunger rocket through her body—and then sink like a stone with a nagging worry that was getting more and more common. She looked at his face, but he wouldn't meet her eyes. It was as if he knew that he'd screwed up majorly and couldn't face her judgment.

"Here," she said, thrusting the roll of black tape toward him. "This'll cover the rip."

"Thanks. Mind shutting the door?" He nodded toward the opening. "I don't figure anyone else wants to get an eyeful of this."

"Oh. Right." She shut the door behind her as he plastered a wide bandage over the cut.

Silence fell, and she leaned against the counter, just watching him patch himself up. His movements were deft. Practiced. Uneasiness snaked up and down her spine.

He'd done this before. And more than once.

What did he do? Really? And if it wasn't illegal, immoral, or just plain wrong, why wouldn't he tell her?

She marshaled her courage.

"Trey?"

He glanced up, questioning, the roll of tape in his hands as he worked on mending the rip in his leathers.

She cleared her throat and forced out the words.

"What happened to you tonight?"

chapter
TWENTY-ONE

HE'D BEEN DREADING THAT QUESTION, BUT HE'D KNOWN he couldn't avoid it forever.

He'd have to choose his words carefully. Bethany couldn't know the truth, but lying to her was becoming more and more difficult.

What to say? Possibilities ran through his mind. He smoothed the tape she'd given him over the rip in his leathers that had appeared courtesy of Rat. The dealer had been hiding a knife in his back pocket, and hadn't minded using it on Trey.

He'd been paid back handsomely for that little trick.

Trey had nearly broken his knuckles on the dealer's face, then Wolf had a turn. By the time they'd extracted as much information as they could out of Rat, four Shadows had gotten a good workout on the bastard.

He wouldn't be offering meth to anyone in the next four counties without some serious physical therapy.

"If we're in a relationship, you kind of owe me an explanation."

And there it was. Trey drew in a deep breath through his nostrils.

This was what he'd been afraid of. The label carried expectations that he'd known would be nearly impossible for him to live up to.

"I had a job to do."

There. That'd have to do. It wasn't a lie, but it didn't carry enough truth that she could be upset about it.

"What kind of job? Did a bachelor party get out of hand? A drunk mother-son dance that ended in a brawl? Trey, you don't tell me anything. How am I supposed to stick up for you if you shut me out all the time?"

His temper rose as he slammed the first aid kit shut.

"It's not your job to stick up for me. I know you get off on taking care of everybody around you, but I don't need that."

She drew back as if he'd hit her. "I don't get off on that. It's what you do when you care about someone."

"Well, I don't need it." He shoved the first aid kit back under the sink, his guilt chafing him and making him snappish. "So you take care of you. I'm doing fine."

If he hadn't have looked up right then, he'd probably have gotten away with the way he'd spoken to her. But he caught sight of her face right before she whirled and left the bathroom.

The naked pain on her face showed him exactly what flavor of bastard he'd been, and damn, was it bitter.

"Beth…"

But she was gone, disappeared down the hall like the devil himself had booted her from the room.

Trey snorted. In a way, it was like he had.

Moving slowly, he made his way down the back stairs,

his body's little aches reminding him of every move he'd made that night. Of course, they weren't anything to the way his chest ached in a hollow, throbbing way.

That had been all his fault.

"I'm sorry I'm late," he said to Mrs. Yelverton as he walked into the kitchen. She was there at the refrigerator, pulling some sort of pudding from a lower shelf. "I got tied up in some work."

"I understand," Mrs. Yelverton said, a tired smile on her face. "But Sarah's a little upset. I think she nerved herself up to do this."

As if he didn't feel like a big enough bastard already. Trey sighed and raked his hand through his hair. "I'll apologize to her."

"She and Mark are in the dining room." Mrs. Yelverton pulled a serving spoon from a large drawer in the corner. "Is Bethany okay?"

"She's fine. Had to make a phone call." He guessed that was as good an excuse as any. Mrs. Yelverton seemed to accept it without complaint.

The remnants of a large tray of lasagna were in the middle of the table, only a quarter of it missing. Two people sat on the opposite side of the table, the man's face right beside Sarah's cheek in a tender position.

Trey cleared his throat a little.

"Sarah."

The man jumped to his feet. "You must be Trey. I'm Mark, Sarah's fiancé. Sorry we haven't met before now... Seems like every time I'm home, we're busy."

Trey shook the other man's hand. Mark was much shorter and smaller than Trey, but with a tanned, wiry strength that showed he was no pushover.

Trey approved, especially with the way Mark stuck next to Sarah, his arm slung casually over her shoulders as if to say not to push too hard.

His sister—if he could think of her that way, which he still wasn't sure about—was looking away, discomfort written plainly across her features.

Trey sank down in the chair opposite her.

"Listen," he started, leaning toward her with his forearms on the table. "I'm really sorry I was late."

Sarah gave him a glance. "It's not a big deal to me. You should apologize to Mom though. She went through a lot of trouble to cook for us."

"I apologized to her, but I know I let you down too. It was wrong of me. I'm sorry."

He got the full force of her gaze then, her snapping green eyes reminding him so much of his own. "It was shitty of you not to even text to let us know you were coming. We thought you'd ditched us."

"You're right. It won't happen again."

Sarah leaned forward, mimicking his pose. "If I didn't want to have a good relationship with you, it wouldn't bother me at all. But this is important, and you need to treat it that way."

"You're completely right."

She slammed her hands down on the tabletop. "Stop being so freaking agreeable! Why won't you get mad back?"

"Because it's totally my fault, and I can admit when I'm in the wrong."

Her nostrils flared as she stared at him. One heartbeat passed, then two, and then she sank back into her chair as if the wind had completely been sucked from her sails. "Well. I guess if that's it then."

Trey smiled. "You're a lot like Mrs. Yelverton."

Sarah snorted. "Not hardly. She gets along with everyone. I pick fights."

"No, you've got the same spine. I can see it. The approach is different, but the goal's the same."

Sarah looked a little pleased at that. Mrs. Yelverton chose that moment to walk into the room with the dessert.

"Here, baby, I made your favorite chocolate éclair pudding for dessert. Trey, get some lasagna. If it's not warm enough, I can pop it into the microwave for you."

As the dessert started being passed around, and Trey helped himself to the now-tepid pasta dish, Bethany slunk into the room.

Her cheeks were overly pink, as if she'd either been yelling angrily into a pillow or choking back tears.

He hoped like hell it was the former. He couldn't take the idea that he might have made her cry.

"Sarah, I hear you're in pharmacy school." Trey grasped for an easy conversational thread to get his mind off his complete fuckup with Beth.

"Yeah," she said, tucking her hair behind her ear as she raised a spoonful of her dessert. "Just a few more weeks, and I'll officially be Dr. Yelverton."

Mark smiled beatifically at his fiancée. "She's amazing. She works so hard at school, and keeps me straight besides."

Sarah smiled over at him, and the love between them was nearly palpable. "You're not hard to keep straight. You're pretty well house-trained."

They laughed, and Trey chanced a glance at Bethany. Her smile didn't reach her eyes, and she'd been drawing circles in her tiny portion of pudding.

Damn it. He'd really screwed up there. And he wasn't sure how to fix it without risking her finding out everything.

He did the only thing he could. Pretended the problem wasn't a problem.

Later, he and Bethany could have it out. He was in damage-control mode with the Yelvertons at the moment. When there was a debt to be paid, he did what he could to settle it.

Much as he hated it, fixing things with Bethany had to wait until later.

If he could fix them at all.

The rest of dinner seemed interminable to Bethany. If she could have run away without both Mama Yelverton and Sarah peppering her with questions, she would have.

But even her silent presence would cause less consternation than her disappearance, so she stayed through dessert. She stayed through two cups of coffee. She stayed through Sarah opening another bottle of wine and Mama Yelverton suggesting they play a board game. But she finally mustered the courage to fish into her purse for her car keys when the clock showed it was nearing midnight.

"You're not leaving, are you, Bethany?"

Bethany pinned a smile on her face as she answered Mama Yelverton's question. "I've got an interview tomorrow, and I need to be up early."

"Oh really? You didn't tell me that." Sarah's cheeks were bright from the wine she'd consumed. "Where?"

Bethany was keenly aware of Trey's gaze when she answered. "It's a software company downtown. They've got customer service openings in some of their other branches."

Honestly? She'd seen the ad for a group interview but hadn't intended to go. She'd been looking for something in the area. But with the way things with Trey were going, and with Sarah getting married, she'd begun to think about moving.

Maybe leaving the area would be better for her in the long run.

"Wait, other branches? Like, not in Raleigh branches?"

She stood and shouldered the strap of her purse. "Don't worry. I probably won't get it anyway."

Trey stood. "It's getting late. I should probably head out too."

The party started breaking up as everyone began saying their goodbyes. Bethany chafed at the delay, but she couldn't just run out the door without causing questions. So she waited as Mama Yelverton packed up dessert for her to take home, then gave Sarah a hug at the door.

"I know something's up," Sarah whispered, causing Bethany's lungs to squeeze involuntarily. "I won't grill you about it, but I'm here if you need me."

Bethany just nodded. No way would she burden her best friend with this. Not when Sarah was inundated with graduation, wedding jitters, and the knowledge that a stranger had just unexpectedly joined her family.

In comparison, Bethany's problems were nonexistent.

Fortunately, Mark and Sarah were staying over, so Bethany was able to hurry to her car without her best friend's too-keen gaze on her. Unfortunately, Trey was hot on her heels.

"Beth."

"I need to get going," she said, pulling open the driver door. "I do need to get up early tomorrow."

"We need to talk."

"We'll have to do it some other time. Maybe when you're not tied up with 'business.'"

He winced. Good. Maybe he knew he'd been a jerk. That didn't change the fact that she wanted to run.

If she stayed, he'd just kiss her and make her forget that he'd lied to her. Again.

"Come home with me."

"Can't."

"Okay. Let me come to your apartment."

"No," she said and closed the door on him. She cranked the engine and turned on the headlights.

His bike glinted, its silvery reflection causing wavy white spots in her vision. Oh wait. No. Those were unshed tears.

"Damn it." She rubbed her eyes. This was stupid. She was acting like a pissed-off teenager. The silent treatment wouldn't solve anything between them. There was only one thing that could.

She sighed, then rolled down her window. He hadn't moved from that spot.

"Come back to my place. But just to talk."

He nodded solemnly as she rolled up the window and put her car into Reverse.

She cursed herself for being an idiot the whole drive back to her apartment.

What was she thinking? Why was she setting herself up for more disappointment? Sure, it was exciting to be with him, but shouldn't she be pursuing a relationship with someone safer? Someone more stable, who didn't have so much mysterious baggage?

She was a fool, and allowing herself to be drawn in even more by him just made her a bigger one.

Steeling her resolve, she cut the engine in the parking spot in front of her apartment. Trey's bike rumbled to a stop beside her.

She'd stay firm. She'd keep her composure and not allow her body to overrule her mind.

He needed to give her some answers if she was going to forgive him for the hurtful things he'd said to her.

Why was it a bad thing to take care of those she cared about? Easy. It wasn't. He had hurt her feelings intentionally.

Why?

She closed the car door behind her and locked it, not looking at him as she climbed the steps to her second-floor apartment.

It was easy to figure out why. He was pushing her away. Fine. She could understand that. But why was he pulling at the same time? Why had he begged her to come home with him after doing his best to keep her at arm's length?

Bethany set her jaw. He called her *Strong Girl*. Well, it was about time he understood just how right that nickname was.

Inside her apartment, his presence seemed to invade her very pores. Her body reacted, even though her mind was in complete turmoil.

"Sit down," she said, more a demand than an invitation. He didn't say a word, just sank down on the couch, fingers laced together.

Nervous energy coursed through her, and she had

to move. Pacing in front of the coffee table, questions swirled through her head.

This had to end. This not knowing who and what he was. And if it didn't...

Well, if it didn't, this relationship wasn't a relationship at all, and she'd have to walk away from him.

Her heart gave a squeeze that nearly took her breath away at the thought, and she closed her eyes, standing still.

One heartbeat. Two. Oxygen came back into her lungs, and she was prepared.

Whether or not it hurt now, that was better than falling in love with a liar. Which she was perilously close to.

"Trey," she said, turning to look at him. She was glad he was sitting down. At least with her standing, she was able to pretend he wasn't so much bigger and stronger than her. That he wasn't so physically imposing and incredibly delicious.

Don't... Do not think about him that way. This is too important for your libido to get in the way.

"If you're not honest with me, then I can't keep doing this."

He closed his eyes and took in a deep breath. His face twitched, his eyebrows narrowing for a moment as if he was having a silent argument with himself. But then his expression blanked, as if he'd made a decision. "I understand."

"Good." Her weight shifted from foot to foot, and she cleared her throat. "Where were you tonight, when you didn't answer my text?"

His deep, rough voice was emotionless. Measured. "I was out on Route 17."

"What were you doing there?" She had been out there a time or two. There was literally nothing out there except a few hog farms and some old run-down houses.

"Chasing down a criminal."

Her head tilted, her ears refusing to process the answer they'd just been given. "What?"

"I was chasing down a criminal," he repeated, hands still folded in his lap. His tone was matter-of-fact, easy.

A criminal... Bethany swallowed hard. Did that mean...

"What do you mean?"

Trey leaned forward. "You might want to sit down for this, Strong Girl. There are a few things you need to know."

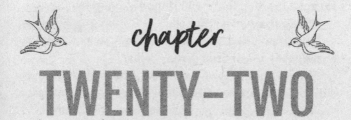

chapter
TWENTY-TWO

"My job has a lot of danger," he said, looking down at the floor. "I was trying to protect you from that by keeping you out of it."

Bethany had sunk down in the chair opposite him, and now she leaned toward him. "Thank you. I'm sorry I put you in the position of telling me."

He kept his gaze fixed on the floor as he answered. "No, it's my fault for not telling you ahead of time that my business would keep me away at odd times. It's not exactly...standard."

Bethany stood and walked over toward the window. Out in the distance, headlights twinkled, spaced far apart in the lateness of the night.

An undercover cop. No wonder he looked and dressed the way he did. She'd never have expected that of him, but now it seemed so obvious.

A sudden thought struck her, and she turned. "Is the wedding planner gig part of your cover?"

He shook his head. "No. That was a story I made up

on the spur of the moment. I couldn't tell Mrs. Yelverton the truth, and she'd just told me she'd basically started a shelter because of me. I wanted her to think I was something wholesome and upright." His fingers were laced together, knuckles almost white as they rested atop his bouncing knees. He looked at the floor as if he couldn't believe he was actually saying these things out loud. "If that wedding magazine hadn't been there, I might have come up with something believable."

Bethany sank onto the couch beside him. "No, Mama Yelverton believes it. She was completely overjoyed at the sight of those invitations. Couldn't stop talking about how artistic her son was."

Trey shifted as if uncomfortable with the praise.

"Hey." Bethany laid her hand on his arm, but he didn't look at her. "I'm right here."

He shot her a glance, but it fell quickly back to the floor. Tenderness filled her, and she combed his hair back behind his ear.

"It's okay. I'll keep your secret. And I'll help with the wedding stuff. But how long are you going to keep this up?"

Trey leaned back on the couch, propping his hands atop his head. "Just until after Sarah's wedding. I can't ask my men—my friends—to keep pretending longer than that."

Bethany's eyebrows rose slightly. "Your friends… Are they cops too?"

"Cops?" Trey moved to stand, but Bethany stopped him with a hand on his arm. She wanted him to know that she was there with him, that she wasn't blaming him for hiding the truth. After all, he was telling her now.

"It's okay," she said. "You can trust me."

"You've got... I mean, we're..." He raked a hand through his hair as if it would help him search for the right words.

"It makes sense that you'd be undercover cops," Bethany said encouragingly. "But don't worry. I promise I will keep your secret."

His mouth worked for a moment, and then the fight seeped out of him. He collapsed back against the couch. His eyes slid closed, and his Adam's apple bobbed as he swallowed. "Okay. I... Look, I really can't get into it. It's really complicated, and—"

She shook her head. "I get it. You probably weren't supposed to tell me any of that."

He didn't reply.

For a long moment, she just watched him. His chest rose and fell slowly, rhythmically. His tattoos highlighted the definition in his muscles, the position of his arms causing ripples and bulges that her fingertips itched to follow the contours of.

He didn't open his eyes. It was as if the weight of the truth was weighing him down, the act of confessing not lessening his burden.

She tucked her feet up onto the couch and laid her head against his chest. Her arms snaked around him, and she sighed happily as his arm fell around her shoulder.

Closer to him than she'd ever been, at least emotionally. The fact that he'd trusted her with the truth comforted her immensely, easing the sting of the way he'd pushed her away in the upstairs bathroom of Mama Yelverton's house.

"So when did you know you wanted to be a cop?"

"I don't want to talk about it."

Stung by his quick rebuff, she started to pull away, but he wrapped his arm around her.

"It's just not...not easy for me. To talk about the past."

"Right," Bethany said softly. "You'd mentioned. The foster homes."

"There are a lot of great foster families out there. But most of the ones that I landed in..." Trey shook his head. "There are a handful of people who are just in it for the so-called free government handout. They don't seem to care that the money's supposed to help them care for the kids they've been given."

"That's terrible."

Trey nodded. "There was one I liked. It's the first one I remember. The Kellys. They were the ones who got to name me, actually."

"I was wondering how you got your name."

A rueful smile escaped him. "I was the third foster kid they got. So, Trey. I'm not sure where the Harding came from. I always just guessed it was because my life had started out so difficult. Hard life for a Harding. The Kellys were great, but they moved out of state when I turned six, so I had to go to another home. The Greens. God, that one was rough. The next one wasn't much better, but I was only there six months. But—" He blew out a breath then, as if the memories were weighing him down. "Just suffice it to say I was relieved when I aged out of the system."

Bethany snuggled closer to him, relishing the steady thump of his heartbeat against her cheek. He'd been through so much...

"What did you do? When you got out, I mean."

"I was young, stupid, and really angry. I did a lot of things I'm not proud of."

"Like what?"

Trey was quiet for a long while, and Bethany began to wonder if she had pried too much. But before she could tell him she was sorry for asking too many questions, he spoke.

"Mostly fighting. Getting drunk, driving fast, searching for thrills in all the wrong places. Bouncing from town to town. When you're a dumb teenager, you can find plenty of trouble if you're looking. And I never stopped looking."

She placed her hand on his forearm, gently stroking the smooth skin, the outlines of his tattoos. "Is that how you ended up in North Carolina?"

"Yeah. I did a lot of driving. Worked a few shitty jobs, got enough money for a beat-up Yamaha bike, and then drove until I ran out of fuel. I walked to the nearest gas station, got jumped. When they figured out I only had seven bucks, they got pissed off and tried to beat me to death. That's how I met Wolf."

"He saved you?"

"In a way."

Trey went quiet again, and Bethany wondered how much of the story he was holding back. He was clearly putting himself on the line, sharing more than he ever had before, but there was so much she wanted to know about him. She stayed quiet, hoping the silence would be enough to draw him from his shell.

She just hoped he truly believed, deep down, that she was worthy of his truth. Of him.

H

Trey searched for the words, but they wouldn't come.

He'd been trying to figure out how to tell her that he wasn't a cop, but the moment had slid by, and right then it had been easier to let her believe the lie.

How he'd gotten onto the subject of meeting the guys and forming the Shadows, he wasn't sure. And finding a way to tell the story so that it fit the lie he'd unwittingly told her?

That was a whole new barrel of monkeys.

He decided the *Reader's Digest* version would have to do.

"Wolf ran a construction crew, and I asked for a job. He took one look at me, face still busted up from the beat-down I'd gotten, and hired me. He trusted me when I didn't look trustworthy at all. So I was determined to prove him right." Trey cleared his throat as his memory kicked into overdrive. Those early days seemed so far away now, eight years having flown by like mere minutes. "And when Wolf had some trouble of his own come up, I stepped in and defended him. A couple other guys eventually joined us."

Bethany's warm hand curled around his. "Wow. That's such a cool story. How did you guys leave construction and join the police force?"

Trey shifted in his seat. "Mind if we talk about that later? I'm kind of beat."

"Of course," she said, a slight frown on her face. "I'm sorry. Want to put on a movie or something?"

He nodded. As she reached for the remote and cued up an action flick he'd seen half a dozen times, Trey let his mind wander. Back to Wolf's run-ins with a rival biker gang, back to the time they'd met Lars and Rocco, the way the rest of them had eventually joined up.

As the sound of high-speed chases and witty quips emanated from the TV, Trey gave a wry smile. The rest had been history. His natural leadership qualities had emerged, together they'd formed the Shadows, and the family that Trey had always craved had come together like so much magic.

Yeah. His brothers. And now… He looked down at Bethany, whose breaths had become even and whose eyelids had fluttered closed. The movie wasn't even half over. He snagged the remote from her nerveless fingers and shut it off.

"Come on, Strong Girl," he said, scooping her into his arms as he stood. "You need to get to sleep."

He carried her down the hall as she wrapped her arms around his neck, her cheek snuggled on his shoulder. Gently depositing her in her bed, he looked down at the spill of golden hair on her pillow, the dusky lashes on her cheeks, the way her knees were drawn up, the curve of her hip.

She was so beautiful. So innocent. So damn *good*.

And he was…not.

He had to walk away. The bathroom offered a quick escape. Once the door had been shut behind him, he braced his hands on the countertop and hung his head.

He'd lied to her. Again. But this time it wasn't just a lie of omission. It wasn't just avoiding telling her anything. It was a bald-faced untruth, meant to deceive her.

But he couldn't tell her the truth, especially with what was about to go down. Bethany was the type of person who'd never so much as lifted a candy bar from a convenience store. What would she say if she knew that he routinely committed assault, theft, and assorted other jailable offenses? Especially since Rat had revealed that a nest of meth-dealing vipers was in their midst. They were just starting to uncover how deep this nightmare went.

Trey shook his head.

No. As bad as he felt about it, he'd done the right thing. Bethany needed to be kept as far from the Iron Shadows' business as possible. Their business was dangerous. The guys would understand the need to keep her away.

That didn't stop him from feeling like an asshole about it though.

He took off his watch, set it aside, and splashed some cold water on his face, hoping the chilly feeling would shock the cobwebs from his brain. He took his time about it. Once he was done, he left the bathroom. The soft sound of even breathing, with a little snore, made him smile. He made his way back to the bedroom.

Bethany had rolled onto her stomach and was holding the pillow in a near death grip of a hug. A strangely tender feeling spread through his chest. He reached to the bottom of the bed and pulled a blanket over her.

"Sleep well, my Beth," he said, turning out the light. He turned and left the bedroom, shutting the door with a soft click behind him.

He moved through her apartment, shutting lights off and checking windows to make sure they were locked. Yeah, she was on the second floor, but his woman needed to be safe. At the front door, he paused and looked back.

What he wouldn't give to stay here and snuggle into the bed next to her. What would it be like if his lie was the truth? If he could give himself completely to a woman like Bethany, to someone who would be there for him always?

He shook his head sadly and shut the door behind him, testing the lock.

That wasn't his lot. His die had been cast a long time ago, when his kidnapper had dumped him in that bathroom. He wasn't the kind of guy who could have that kind of life.

The need for survival had chewed him up and spat him out. The fact that Bethany was with him now was a delicious aberration.

It made him a bad guy, but he couldn't give up that now with her. It was the best thing that had ever happened to him, and he was greedy enough to make it last as long as it could.

Even if that meant lying to her to protect her from his reality. Even then. He'd be damned for his lies eventually, and hell was without her.

But the stolen taste of heaven with Bethany was worth it.

He mounted his bike and rode into the night, headed straight back to the airstrip.

He wasn't done with Rat yet.

chapter

TWENTY-THREE

When she woke up, Bethany wasn't entirely surprised to find herself alone. With a heavy sigh, she pushed the blankets back, the cool of the morning air kissing her skin.

Last night had been good. No, more than that. It had been incredible. The way Trey had shared his feelings with her, finally trusting her enough to know the truth, was a moment in her life she would treasure forever.

She wished he had been more comfortable with her though. Clearly, the admission had bothered him, and that was the one black mark on a most exquisite evening. But she'd show him, through word and deed, that she could be trusted with his secret. Being patient with him was paramount now.

Even though she was sure he'd gone, she did a quick walk-through of her apartment, noting that all the doors were locked. A quick glance out her front window showed that his bike was indeed gone.

The soft purple-gray dawn made her hum as she went

back to her bedroom and began to get ready for the day. As she picked out her clothes, she frowned.

Should she go to that interview? It had been such a big deal the night before, but today, she really wasn't interested in moving away from the area. Odd how something like a little argument, and then a kiss-and-make-up, could make her change her opinions about her future just like that.

She had just poured herself a cup of coffee, hair still wet from the shower, when there was a knock at the door.

Hardly daring to hope, she ran barefoot to the front door. Looking out the peephole, she sighed, a little disappointed.

"Well, if you're so sad to see me, I'll just leave." Sarah stuck her tongue out at Bethany as she walked through the door. "I brought you a bagel, but maybe you don't want it."

"Shut up." Bethany reached over and snatched the bakery bag from Sarah's hands. "It's just early. You know I don't do mornings well."

Sarah snorted. "You do all times of the day well. It's one of the reasons I hate you. Just kidding. Pass that blueberry one over. The cinnamon's yours."

Bethany did as Sarah asked and then poured her best friend a cup of coffee. It wasn't unusual for Sarah to drop by at all times of the day when she was in town, but Bethany's halfhearted hope that Trey might be at the door still held a little sting.

"So, what's on your agenda for the day?" Sarah licked cream cheese off her finger. "I'm avoiding a paper, so give me something fun to discuss."

"That interview is at nine this morning." Bethany looked at the clock on the stove. There was still time, but... "I'm just not sure whether I should go or not."

"Well, is it something you really want to do?"

Bethany thought about it. Customer service wasn't the most fun job in the world, but she was pretty good at it. On the other hand, that was the whole reason she had stayed at Hudson's as long as she had. While Sarah hiring her for the wedding had given her a small paycheck and something to fill the gap on her résumé, she couldn't stay unemployed forever. Maybe she was at a crossroads, and she could figure out what she really wanted to do with her life, instead of just taking a random job that she thought she could do.

"Maybe not. I guess. I don't know. I need more coffee."

Sarah laughed. "I knew there was something off about you last night. You were just all up in your head about this interview, weren't you?"

Bethany shifted in her seat a little, suddenly reminded of the way she had acted at the Yelvertons' last night. "I guess. Sorry about that. I know I was kind of rude."

"Bethy, you know I love you. And you're family, so you don't have to apologize for stuff like that. That's why I'm here. I just want to help you like you always help me."

Bethany smiled. "Thanks, Sarah. I can always count on you."

"You know it." Sarah pushed her chair back from the counter. "I'm going to use your little girl's room. Be right back."

Sarah walked down the hall, and Bethany held her coffee cup in both hands.

This was good. Today, instead of going to a job interview that she really wasn't all that jazzed about, she would start researching different career paths. She could find out what she was really passionate about doing, instead of just slogging through life as a customer-service rep when she wasn't all that into it.

Maybe she could do something like Trey, something exciting, dangerous. She had been having a lot of fun with Sarah's wedding. Maybe that was a job she could do.

Bethany sat up straighter, the idea really taking hold. Yeah. She was good at event planning. Sarah had nailed that right on the head. Bethany had turned Hudson's sales events into actual draws in the community. And she still had some connections... She could definitely leverage those into a wedding planning business. She glanced over at her laptop, ideas formulating quicker and quicker as she thought about it.

Trey might have come up with the idea, but she might just try to make it a reality. She smiled a little. What would he think if she did it?

The sound of the door opening met her ears, and Bethany glanced toward the hallway. Sarah sauntered back toward the kitchen, hands in her pockets, projecting a casual air.

"So, had any guys over recently?"

Bethany jumped. "What? No, why would you think that?"

Sarah just grinned and sank back down into her chair. "Oh, no reason. No reason at all. Definitely not anything in the bathroom."

The blood left Bethany's face as she stood. Oh God, she couldn't hide anything from Sarah. What was she going to do? Not only was Trey Sarah's brother, but now there was this other secret she was bound to keep.

God, this was so complicated.

"I'll be right back." Bethany dashed down the hall, desperate to see what Sarah was referring to.

Her hand covered her mouth. "Oh shit."

Bethany leaned weakly against the bathroom counter for a moment, the sight of Trey's watch clearly spelling out her lie. Yup, that was fairly irrefutable evidence that there had been a male in her apartment. That, or Bethany's style had changed pretty drastically.

And Sarah knew it.

Bethany grabbed the watch and stuffed it into her pocket while Sarah almost died laughing, nearly falling out of her seat in her mirth.

"Babe, you are the worst liar I have ever met. Come on, who is it? I'm dying to know."

Bethany thought hard. There had to be someone she could point to that wouldn't upset Sarah or make things more difficult for Trey.

"It's…a guy you don't know."

Sarah rolled her eyes. "Really?"

Bethany nodded. "Yeah. He's actually a good friend of Trey's. He introduced us."

"That's interesting." Sarah leaned forward, propping her chin on her hand. "What's his name?"

Bethany bit her lip. Trey's friends had weird names, but she couldn't remember all of them. Reaching desperately, she grabbed the first one that came to mind. "Wolf. His name is Wolf."

Sarah's mouth fell open. "Huh? Really? What kind of a name is Wolf?"

Bethany smiled weakly. "Um, it's a family name? I mean, yeah, it was his mother's maiden name. It's kind of a tradition in his family."

Sarah leaned back in her chair. "Well, get it, girl. I'm proud of you. Bring him around sometime when Mark and I are in town. We can do a double date."

Bethany laughed a little weakly. "Sure, I'll do that."

Thankful that the conversation was over, at least for now, Bethany drained her coffee. If Sarah didn't leave soon, she was going to need some alcohol, the fact that it was barely 8:00 a.m. notwithstanding.

She hoped that Sarah and Trey could get to know each other better soon, and Trey's undercover work would end so all this deception could stop.

Sarah was right. Lying really wasn't Bethany's strong suit.

Trey's morning was going even worse than Bethany's.

He leaned against the corrugated metal wall of the old airplane hangar, squinting against the brightness of the sun.

There had been yells and cursing from inside the building, but they'd gone quiet a few minutes ago. Any minute now, Wolf would come out to inform him of what progress had been made in their investigation.

Trey'd had to bow out at 4:00 a.m. Let someone else have a turn, because if he'd been left with the bastard, they'd be leaving him for the vultures this morning.

The rusted iron hinges squeaked as Wolf pushed open the door and moved onto the cinder block that served as a step.

"Boss," Wolf said as the door shut behind him.

Trey looked at him with an arched eyebrow.

"It's deeper than we thought."

Trey sank into a crouch, his mood dropping further and faster than his body. He'd suspected as much, but hearing Wolf confirm it sucked balls. "How deep?"

Wolf crossed his arms, looking out across the field toward the strip of woods that separated them from the highway. The sound of car engines was barely audible from this distance. "There are at least four other dealers, maybe more."

Trey's knuckles cracked. "That means there's a supplier too."

Wolf nodded solemnly.

"Who?"

"He's not giving that one up."

"Shit," Trey spat, shoving off from the wall. Long grass swished around his boots as he paced. His brain somersaulted with the numerous possibilities. Most of the big-time cookers had moved on when the Shadows had grown in numbers two years ago. They'd moved east, toward Greenville or the military base in Fayetteville. The odd entrepreneur had popped up every now and then, but the Shadows had always managed to convince them to move on before their network grew.

Until now. Whoever was working the area obviously knew who to look out for and had constructed his dealer network accordingly.

Damn it.

"What do you want to do with Rat?"

Trey stopped. He'd love to kill the lowlife, but he didn't want the blood on his hands. Letting the cops have him was another option, but Trey decided against that instantly.

If the police were looking into the same ring the Shadows were, there was a good chance they themselves would get busted for any number of things. No, they'd handle this one on their own. They'd let the cops take care of any cleanup after the fact, once the Shadows had ensured that none of these bastards would set foot on their territory again.

But the key was the supplier. That was the hinge point upon which everything hung. With the supplier named, they could take down the whole network.

"Let him go."

Wolf started. "What?"

Trey turned to his second. "Let him go, and have Flash and Jameson tail him. I want to know who he talks to, where he goes. Every bit of it."

Wolf nodded, his dark eyebrows knitted together.

Trey strode toward the bare dirt path where four bikes were parked. Body and soul were twitchy, uneasy. He didn't like this feeling. He wasn't used to it.

He'd trained himself to be cool, calm under pressure. His temper was a weapon to be used. But right now it felt as though he had a broken safety on a nine millimeter. And all he wanted was to gather his dearest close to him and protect them.

Faces and names flashed through his frontal lobe. Wolf. Jameson. Ace. Dean. Flash. Doc. Rocco. Hawk. Lars. Stone. Mac. The whole crew at Ruby's. Their families.

And then the ones he'd met so recently. The ones who'd changed his life from top to bottom. His mother. His sister. His soon-to-be brother-in-law.

And the last face, the one that stayed with him, asleep or awake, angry or afraid, alone or in a crowd, was hers.

Bethany.

Trey slung his leg over his bike, but he didn't crank the engine. Instead, he pulled his cell phone from his pocket.

It was after eleven. She'd said she had that interview early this morning. Surely she'd be done by now?

The need to talk to her overcame his good sense, and he swiped through his contact list before he allowed himself a second thought.

When the call went to voicemail, he gave a disappointed sigh before the beep.

"Hey. Just calling to wish you luck for your interview this morning. I…" He what? Rushing on without a second thought, he kept talking. "I hope it's going well. It *went* well. Talk to you soon."

He cut the call and let his hand, still holding the phone, fall beside his leg.

He was all shook up inside. He wanted her to do well. Of course he did. But if she got this job, then she could very well be moving away.

Wouldn't that make things simpler for you, his subconscious whispered. *If she just leaves, then she'll never find out you are a lying sack of crap.*

He cranked his engine and shoved the phone back into his pocket.

There were lies stacked on lies. Trouble over trouble. All to cover up the fact that he was who he was.

Not good enough for any of them.

Before he could pull away, Jameson exited the building and waved at him.

Trey cut the engine. "What is it?"

Jameson held out his phone, his expression thundercloud dark. "It's the floral supplier. They need a credit card to confirm the order."

Trey's situational awareness had whiplash. All he

could picture was meth dealers crushing up petals for some fancy new formulation.

"The flowers. For the wedding." Jameson nearly spat the word. He looked over his shoulder to where Flash was "helping" Rat leave the warehouse. Helping via boot to ass.

"Dammit," Trey said as realization dawned.

In the midst of all this drama, he'd forgotten the cock-sucking wedding.

"Hello?" He reached into his back pocket and pulled out his wallet.

As he held a polite, businesslike conversation with the floral warehouse on the other end of the phone line, he watched as Flash escorted Rat into the pickup. Rat's ugly face was even more pinched than usual and a little swollen from his "encouragement" to talk the night before.

All in all, he had gotten off easy.

"I'm sorry, what now?" Trey had missed that last part.

"I was just confirming your order. Three hundred peonies, one hundred orchids, and one hundred lilies. That'll be $1,249.99."

Trey's eyebrows hit the damn nape of his neck.

"For flowers?"

"Yes, sir."

Trey shook his head but rattled off his credit card number.

It wasn't like he couldn't afford it. Their regular under-the-table security gigs alone meant a comfortable life for all of them, especially with the way Lars invested their earnings. The numbers whiz had ensured they could live off their dividends for the next few years, even if they didn't pick up another paying gig. And Mrs. Yelverton had given Trey a healthy amount up front for wedding expenses and would reimburse him for the rest. But the incredible amount for such trivial things — fragile beautiful objects that would last for a matter of hours at most — seemed like a tremendous waste.

As he finished the call, he handed the phone back to Jameson.

"Should be good to go now," he said.

Jameson shook his head. "Seems stupid to be dicking around with this wedding stuff when we've got a nest of wasps right here in our territory."

"There's nothing else to do with the flowers until they get here the day before the ceremony. So stop your whining." Trey nodded toward the truck. "Once you drop him off, keep close. Let me know where he goes."

Jameson turned without another word, irritation plain in the set of his shoulders.

Trey watched him go.

He was tired of this tension. This drama. And in an instant, he knew where he wanted to be.

He cranked his engine and headed toward her place.

He'd wait for her, and then maybe they could celebrate her successful interview with lunch and an afternoon nap where they wouldn't sleep.

Tomorrow, she might move away. His lies could blow up in his face. But for today?

He'd take the comfort of her presence over the agony of worrying about the wedding, the Shadows, his new family, or the seventy-five other issues that competed for his attention.

He just didn't give a damn about anything but Bethany for the moment. She was the cure for his anxieties, and he'd get blind-drunk on her presence as long as he could.

chapter

TWENTY-FOUR

THE PHONE BUZZED IN BETHANY'S PURSE, AND SHE pulled it free just in time to see the name of the caller. Her pulse stuttered, her heart racing as she hastily pressed the power button to silence the ringer.

"Who's that?" Sarah was mounding spinach on her plate with tongs from the salad bar.

"Unknown caller." Bethany got busy with the cherry tomatoes, grabbing about six more than she'd intended. *Oh well*.

As she finished building her tomato-overburdened salad, her mind was whirling. He'd called. Why hadn't he texted? Had something gone wrong on the job? Was he hurt?

A thousand different possibilities charged through her brain as she took her plate back to the table she and Sarah were sharing in the corner of the restaurant.

"I'll be right back," Bethany said. "Restroom."

Alone in the stall, she listened to the voicemail. God, it was so good to hear him. Reassured, for the moment at least, she washed her hands and returned to the table.

"Thanks for grabbing lunch with me," Sarah said as she unwrapped her silverware. "Mark's back home, and I'm going to be spending the rest of my evening slaving in the library, so I really appreciate it."

"No problem," Bethany said, smiling. She'd call Trey back when lunch was over. Hopefully he wouldn't be busy with work... God, could she really have a boyfriend in such a dangerous job?

Boyfriend. She smiled down at her tomatoes. That was such a weird term to apply to Trey, but it was true.

"You must be thinking about Wolf again." Sarah's smug voice yanked Bethany back to the present.

"What? Oh yeah. Sorry. Tell me about this paper you're writing." Bethany took a big bite of her salad and crunched determinedly as Sarah began to talk about drug formulations and patient compliance and all sorts of things Bethany didn't really understand.

By the time lunch was over, she'd almost managed to forget what Trey had told her. Almost.

"Thanks again," Sarah said. She picked up the check despite Bethany's protests. "No, I got this. You just keep making my wedding beautiful." Sarah winked and waved as she walked toward the door. The server thanked Bethany for the tip, which she had had nothing to do with.

Oh well.

As Bethany walked into the bright spring day, she squinted against the brilliance of the early afternoon. And then a vibration started in her handbag.

Excitement surging, she reached blindly into the bag and swiped the screen to answer without even checking to see who it was.

"Trey?"

A derisive sniff sounded through the phone, and Bethany's heart sank as quickly as it had risen. "Still with that lowlife? I shouldn't be surprised. My Marine didn't have much taste in the opposite sex either."

Bethany bit the inside of her cheek at her grandmother's bitter tone. It hadn't exactly been Bethany's mother's choice to die in a training accident on the military base. Considering how her grandmother loved to idolize the military, Bethany would have thought she'd have loved a daughter-in-law who was in the service.

Not so much. The only blessing of her mother's death was that she'd been spared a lifetime dealing with Grandmother Trudy.

"What do you need, Grandmother?"

The wheedling tone replaced the bitterness as if it had never been there. "I have a doctor's appointment this afternoon, and they won't let me see him unless I pay my past-due balance."

"Why do you have a past-due balance?" Bethany marched quickly to her car, not wanting the curious stares of the restaurant patrons as they walked in and out of the building behind her.

"I had to have some tests run a few months ago. My secondary insurance policy lapsed, and Medicare only covers part of them."

"Tests? What kind of tests?" Bethany shut the car door behind her.

"A CAT scan and a biopsy."

Her heart went cold. "What for? How did they come back? Are you sick?"

A sharp note entered her grandmother's voice. "It's not your business, girlie. But I need to follow up with my doctor, and the office is being difficult about the money. Now will you help me out or not?"

Head thumping against the seat, Bethany stared toward the car's ceiling.

"How much?"

"Six hundred dollars."

Bethany sighed and shook her head. It was always like this. Her grandmother should have plenty of money. But she claimed she was always broke. And then when new items showed up at the house, she claimed to have gotten them for free or discounted heavily. There was always enough money for what she wanted, never enough for what she needed, so she appealed to the closest sucker.

Which was most often Bethany.

"Who's your doctor? I'll call and make a payment."

"That's not necessary, just give me the cash, and I'll take it with me to my appointment."

"Oh no. No, no, no. Not happening. Either you give me the office number and I call to make a payment, or that's the end of this conversation."

Sounding incredibly sour, her grandmother rattled off the phone number. Bethany cut the call with a weary sigh and dialed the doctor's office.

She knew exactly what would have happened if she hadn't stood her ground. Her grandmother would have pocketed at least half of that money for whatever piece of junk she had her eye on adding to her hoard and given just enough to the doctor's office to keep skating by.

"I'd like to make a payment, please," Bethany said when the receptionist answered the phone.

She rattled off her credit card number when prompted, and once the amount had been applied, she asked a question.

"That account belongs to my grandmother. She'd mentioned that she just had a biopsy. Is there any way you could let me know the results?"

The receptionist was polite but firm as steel. "I'm sorry, but that violates our privacy regulations. We aren't allowed to give out any information on our patients."

Bethany sighed. "I know. I'm sorry. She's just a really...difficult person."

A note of compassion entered the receptionist's voice. "I understand that. I wish I could help you."

"Thank you anyway." Bethany disconnected the call and closed her eyes.

God. The day had really gone off the rails. Lying to her best friend. Her grandmother squeezing more and more out of her, and then the bombshell that something might be really wrong with her.

Stress was eating her up inside, and there was only one place she wanted to be.

She picked up her phone and dialed. She pressed send on his number with no hesitation, just a desperate longing for the comfort and happiness that flooded her whenever she was in his presence.

He was the cure for everything wrong in her world, and at least when she was with him, she could pretend everything was perfect.

He answered on the third ring.

"Hello?"

She smiled, rubbing her thumb along the steering wheel. "Trey? Can I see you?"

His bike hugged the curves of the road as he made his way to her. The urge within him, the draw to see her, goosed his gas pedal even faster than usual.

Her call had come while he was stopped at a light, and he'd pulled over and cut the engine to talk to her. And he was glad. It sounded like she needed to be with him as much as he needed her.

Her building came into view, the lot mostly empty in the midafternoon. The other tenants were at their office jobs, enjoying the weather at the park, or doing whatever normal people did on a Wednesday afternoon.

But Bethany's car was in her spot. Apparently she'd pulled in only a few moments before, because she was climbing out of the driver's seat.

His chest warmed as he looked at her, his engine purring as he slowed enough to pull into the space beside her. *God.* Had there ever been another person he'd been as drawn to? As comfortable with? If things were different—

He stopped that thought in its tracks. Today wasn't about that. Today was about the opposite of that. Enjoying her company to the fullest.

"Trey," she said, waving as he cut the engine. Her smile was warm sunshine, her eyes sparkling with excitement to see him. As if he was someone special to her. Someone important.

Someone she wanted to hold on to.

He looked his fill, not bothering to turn as the ragged sound of a car engine sorely in need of a tune-up passed behind him. But Bethany's attention was grabbed, for sure. The color drained from her cheeks as she turned to watch the old Buick's progress as it pulled into the empty space beside her own car.

Trey followed her gaze. He didn't recognize the vehicle, but he'd seen the driver once before.

"Shit." He growled the word, swinging his leg over the bike saddle and crossing the two steps to Beth's side.

What did Grandma want now?

"Bethany," the woman said, leaving her vehicle. As she moved aside, Trey got a glimpse into the stained, yellowed interior. It looked like a bomb had hit a garage sale in there. Junk filled the backseat, the passenger side. Hell, there were even a line of little plastic hula girls along the front dashboard.

He shuddered.

"What is it?" Bethany stood stock-still, her hands fisted at her sides. "I paid your doctor bill. They'll see you."

"I need to talk to you." Grandma shot Trey a look. "Alone."

Trey reached over and wrapped a possessive arm around Bethany's shoulder. "We're a package deal. I'm not going anywhere unless she asks me to."

Bethany shot him a grateful look before turning her attention back to her grandmother. "Trey and I are together. What could you need to say to me that can't be said in front of him?"

Grandma glowered. "I don't particularly want to talk about my medical issues in front of a stranger."

Beth blanched. Trey was torn. As much as he wanted to protect Bethany from her toxic family, he knew he had to bow to her wishes there.

Bethany turned her wide blue eyes onto him. "Do you mind waiting a few minutes?"

He shook his head. "I'll be right here. Take as long as you need."

"Thank you." She reached up on her tiptoes and brushed a soft kiss against his cheek, a touch that seemed to sear down to his soul.

He closed his eyes and relished that sweet, simple touch.

How incredible that something with hardly more substance than a butterfly's wing could move his very soul.

He'd fight tigers for that woman. He'd climb mountains. He'd lie down in front of a train if she needed him to.

The thought should terrify him. But it didn't. It strengthened him. He felt as if he could run a marathon and then build her a house with his bare hands.

"I'll be back," she whispered. Then she and her grandmother mounted the steps to her apartment.

Trey sank down onto the curb beside his bike, glad for the L-shaped bend in the building that afforded him a good view of Bethany's door. Like one of those guardian dogs in Chinese folklore, he wouldn't budge unless she beckoned.

He laced his hands together, arms propped on his knees, looking at the door that separated her from him.

He hadn't expected this. Hadn't wanted it. But now that it was within his grasp, what was he going to do?

Keep near to her. That's all he could do. And when it ended—because it would—he'd be emptier and more alone than he ever had been before.

It was a thought that didn't bear thinking, so he emptied his mind and resumed his guard duty.

Time passed. The sunshine was warm, and the breeze was light, and the sound of a nearby bee was a calming, humming drone in his ears. It was the kind of afternoon that was inherently peaceful, the kind of time that made it easy to imagine lying back on the warm, green grass and closing his eyes.

But Trey's gaze didn't waver from Bethany's door. Which was how he was able to react so quickly.

A muffled shriek of pure rage rent the quiet afternoon air. Trey was on his feet before the door opened with a bang.

"It's mine!" The shriek contained words this time, and Bethany's grandmother was doing the screaming. "Let go!"

Bethany had something clutched to her chest, and she was trying to leave her apartment, but Grandma lunged at her, throwing her against the balcony railing.

"Ah!" Bethany cried out as Grandma clawed at her arm, trying to get at whatever Bethany held so tightly.

Trey was sprinting toward the steps, but Bethany's grip failed before he could mount them. She dropped it, both she and her grandmother grabbing for it as it fell.

A split-second decision made, Trey sidestepped and reached up.

He snatched the object before it could hit the ground. Opening his palm, he looked at it. A heart-shaped gold medal with a purple ribbon affixed at its top lay in his hand. He flipped it over.

FOR MILITARY MERIT. SSGT HUGH JERNIGAN, USMCR.

He looked up. Bethany was staring down at him, her eyes suspiciously bright, but her grandmother was already sprinting down the stairs toward him.

"Give that to me! It's mine!"

Trey raised the Purple Heart in his fisted hand, straight up into the air. Bethany's grandmother stretched for it, but there was no way she could ever reach it. "This isn't yours. You need to leave now."

"Give that to me! Thief! That's mine, it's my Marine, you don't have any claim to it!"

Bethany had arrived at the bottom of the stairs by then. Sidestepping Grandma, Trey reached over and grabbed Bethany's hand in his free one.

"Let's go," he said, striding toward his bike. Bethany hurried after him, climbing behind him and locking her arms around his waist. He jammed the medal in his pocket and cranked the engine.

"Come back here! I'll report this!" Grandmother was howling with rage, her face nearly purple as she grabbed for the bike's handlebars.

"Hang on," he yelled to Beth and kicked the bike into gear. Tires squealing, they peeled out of the lot.

Moving quickly, keeping an eye on his mirrors, Trey wound through the buildings of the apartment complex. Once he was certain they were out of sight of Grandma, he pulled over and freed the spare helmet from his saddlebag.

"Put that on so we can get out of here."

She didn't answer, just did as he asked. A heartbeat later, her arms were around him again, and they were off.

Trey's gaze was locked on the road ahead. The woman he wanted to protect more than anything was on his bike behind him. Her shuddering breaths indicated she was crying. Something incredibly precious to her was in his pocket, having narrowly escaped being stolen from her.

Cold rage suffused his limbs.

He'd be tempted to commit murder if anyone ever hurt Bethany like this again.

And it was then that he knew—

He loved her.

chapter

TWENTY-FIVE

THERE ON THE BACK OF TREY'S BIKE, COMFORTED BY the fact that no one could see her, Bethany gave way to her tears.

She was probably getting the back of his T-shirt wet. Gripping him tighter, she gave a shuddering sob.

Why did she still let that woman hurt her this way? When would she learn that her grandmother only ever cared about one person—herself?

But that promise shackled her to the woman. Her father had imprisoned her, and it wasn't like she could ask him to relinquish her from the deal.

Dad was gone. And he wouldn't ever be coming back.

The disastrous meeting with her grandmother had revealed plenty—and none of it good.

Bethany drew in a deep breath. It smelled like Trey: clean, lovely man. It smelled like safety, like excitement, like laughter and sunshine and protection and—

Her eyes flew open.

And love.

He hadn't hesitated. He'd caught her father's medal before it could hit the pavement. He'd kept it from her grandmother and whisked her away from the confrontation. He knew what she needed without her having to say it.

It had been coming for a while, but now, with what had just happened, she couldn't deny it.

She loved Trey Harding.

Squeezing him tighter, she pressed her cheek to his back, the strap of his motorcycle helmet biting into her skin with the pressure.

There, on the back of his bike, she could hold him with all the love in her heart. She could show her feelings without fear of repercussions. Because she was fairly certain if Trey knew that she loved him, he'd run scared.

She didn't want to be planning Sarah's wedding. She wanted to be planning her own. With him.

But Trey wasn't the marrying type. She was fairly certain that getting him to admit they were in a relationship was as far as he'd ever willingly go.

God. How hopeless.

All she could do was hang on and hope that he'd eventually feel about her the way she felt about him. And that maybe he could be the settling-down type later on.

She opened her eyes.

They'd been driving who the hell knew how long. The sun had sunk to the very edge of the horizon, a fat, orange ball flaring brightly before sinking behind the earth.

A sharp, familiar tang met her nostrils, and she lifted her head to smell again.

Was that—salt water?

"Trey, where are we?" She yelled the question to be heard over the whipping wind and the growling engine.

"You'll see," he said, rounding a curve and pointing.

A long bridge rose in front of them, spanning a large expanse of water. The tires vibrated with each thump over the bridge segments, and Bethany stared in wonder at the swirling waters of the sound below.

He'd driven her to the beach. They'd been on the road for three hours because he'd been bringing her here.

She rested her forehead against his back and resisted the urge to cry again.

How could she hide what he made her feel?

Fifteen minutes later, he pulled off the two-lane highway and onto a public beach access road. This late in the day, it was deserted.

The engine cut, and the sudden quiet was almost stunning.

Trey got off the bike, then turned around to help Bethany. It was then she realized that her legs were sore as all hell.

"Ow." She winced as she stood and stretched.

"Longest you've ever ridden, huh?"

She nodded as her fingers fumbled with the bike helmet strap. "I had no idea you were coming this far."

His eyes flashed darkly. "Is it a problem? I should probably have asked you first."

"No, it's fine." She set the helmet in the storage box he'd opened for it. He locked it and then laced his fingers through hers.

"Let's go for a walk before it gets too dark."

They crested the dune, and the sight of the churning, dark-gray waves nearly took her breath away.

It had been a long time since she'd made the trip down here to the Banks. In fact, it was one of the places that she felt closest to her father.

Bethany bit her lip as her feet sank into the shifting sand.

He'd loved it down here. They'd done a lot of fishing together as soon as he'd gotten stationed at Camp Lejeune. The tang of the salty air brought a host of bittersweet memories to the fore.

"Oh," Trey said, suddenly reminding her that he was beside her. "You want this back, I'm sure."

He reached into his pocket and withdrew her father's Purple Heart. She took it, curling her fingers around it. It was still warm from his body heat.

"I'll trade you," she said and pulled his wristwatch from her pocket. He'd forgotten that he'd left it in her bathroom, but he took it with a nod and slipped it back onto his arm.

"Thank you," she added, rubbing her thumb across the engraved letters of her father's name. "I can't tell you how much this means to me."

"I knew it had to be important to you. That's why I kept it away from her."

She shook her head. "I wasn't just talking about the medal. I mean, all of this. The way you've helped me. The way you've stepped up to be there for me, when there really wasn't anything in it for you."

She tucked her hair behind her ear, the ocean breeze playing havoc with her blond tresses. "I appreciate it all. I appreciate you."

She looked up into his eyes as he stepped forward, cupping her cheek in his hand.

"Bethany, I would do that a hundred times for you. I would do so much more."

He tilted his head down slowly, inexorably, and she let her eyelids flutter closed. Feeling suffused her, heat and light and warmth and love filling her full, then overflowing.

Was this what it meant to be in love?

His lips captured hers, his arms surrounding her and pinning her close to the warmth of his body. His shoulders were so broad and strong as she gripped them, opening her mouth for his kiss.

Trey possessed her, touched her, kissed her like their lives depended on it.

And in that moment, for her, they did. If she didn't have him, she couldn't live. Not happily.

Having known the joy of his touch, life without him would be empty and not worth living.

Heaven help her if she had to try to be without him ever again.

A sudden gust of wind blew her hair around them, and Trey pulled her even closer. Their bodies were aligned, legs and hips and chests and mouths. Hands and arms. Skin to skin.

Heart to heart. At least she hoped.

Slowly, lingeringly, he broke their kiss. In the dim twilight, he looked into her eyes.

"Come on, Strong Girl. Let me walk you down the beach. You need to stretch your legs after that long ride."

She wanted to protest. She wanted to kiss him some more. She wanted him to lay her down in the sand and be with her.

She laced her fingers through his and let him take care of her.

"Okay," she said with a smile.

For now, with her tall, burly, tattooed protector beside her, this was enough.

He was enough.

⁓Ht⁓

Trey walked with Bethany along the beach until the moon was reflected in the crashing waves.

He wasn't sure what he'd been thinking when he nosed his bike eastward.

No, he knew.

They'd both needed a place away from the chaos of their present. Away from Bethany's nightmare thief of a grandmother, away from the drama and danger of the Shadows' territorial dispute, away from the planning and stress of the impending wedding.

There, on the shadowy coast, were only him, and her.

Her hand was slender and cool in his, and he squeezed it slightly, trying to warm it in his grip. She gave a little shiver.

"I'm sorry. You're cold."

"A little," she said, wrapping her arm through his and tucking herself closer into his side. "The wind coming off the ocean is cool."

"Let's get out of here," he said and led her back to the small sand-covered parking lot. His bike was the only vehicle there.

He handed her the spare helmet and grabbed his. She looked a little wan as she buckled the strap beneath her chin.

"I don't know if I can stand another three hours on the back of the bike tonight."

"We can get a hotel and go back tomorrow."

"I'll split the cost," Bethany said as he mounted his bike. He reached out a hand to help her on.

"I've got it. I brought you out here, so it's my treat."

He cranked the engine, cutting off any argument she may have given him, and nosed his bike onto the highway.

The road was dotted with hotels and rentals. It was just a matter of finding one with a vacancy. And, this early in the season, that wasn't too difficult.

The Days Inn was clean, nearby, and thankfully had a room with a king-size bed available.

Bethany didn't say a word, but he'd noticed the wry little smile she gave at his request of the front desk clerk.

What? He wasn't about to spend a night in a hotel crowded into one of those double beds if he didn't have to. No matter what beds were available, he'd be in hers, guaranteed.

He'd thought she'd been about to take him down in the dunes earlier. The least he could do was provide her a comfortable bed if she was going to jump his bones.

And he sure as hell hoped she would jump his bones.

They made their way to the elevator and ascended to the third floor.

Trey's phone buzzed in his pocket. He handed the room key to Bethany. "Check it out. I need to take this real quick."

She nodded and went ahead to the room. Trey kept walking toward the window at the end of the hallway as he answered the call.

"Harding."

"I've got some names," Jameson said.

"Hit me." Trey crossed his arms as Jameson gave his list.

Trey frowned as Jameson finished. "That's it?"

"That's where he went today. Once he left us, he went straight to Hampton's. I think that's where he's getting his stash. If Hampton's not cooking, I'm sure he's distributing."

"Hampton doesn't have the brains to cook."

"Lars and Rocco are going to take over tailing Rat. He's holed up at the Morningside apartment complex right now, so we're going to tag them in."

Trey sighed. "Okay. Good work."

"I want to go after Hampton."

Trey's eyebrows lowered. "No, not on your own."

Jameson's sigh was irritated. "Boss, Rat doesn't know anything. It's obvious he's low on the totem pole. But Hampton—"

"Jameson, I didn't stutter. Leave Hampton the hell alone for now. Go home and get some sleep. I'll check in tomorrow."

"Boss—"

But Trey had already pressed the end-call button.

He frowned as he rubbed his hand over the stubble on his chin. None of them were big time. They were all penny-ante dealers, people who had been caught in the Shadows' territory before, usually just dealing weed or X. A few times they'd been caught with something harder, and they'd gotten the rough side of Trey's men. He'd thought they'd shrink away like garbage usually did when confronted with a bigger threat.

Someone had to be backing them up. Someone concerning. Otherwise why would these pissants come back for more punishment from the Shadows?

Hampton... Trey knew Hampton. He spent his time

at Cherry Ice, trying to get into every stripper's G-string, and getting pissed when they turned him down. He liked to flash his bankroll, and he'd been pally with a few other small-time dealers, like Rat, Tombstone, and Vinnie. But Hampton didn't have any big connections, not that Trey knew of.

This was getting more complicated.

A door opening down the hallway broke into his thoughts, and he looked toward the sound.

A couple of teenagers were giggling on their way to the elevator.

And only two doors down from him, Bethany was waiting for him.

Making a decision, he shoved his phone in his pocket and made his way toward her.

There was nothing he could do about the problem right now. Tomorrow, once he'd gotten Bethany back where she belonged—and made sure that psycho grandma didn't have a key to Bethany's apartment—he'd go after Hampton himself and figure out what was going on.

But tonight? Tonight he was going to hold her and make her forget the tears she'd shed on the way here.

He could do that much for the woman he loved.

She answered his knock as if she'd been waiting by the handle. "Is everything okay?"

"Yeah," he lied, drawing her into his arms. Closing his eyes, he rested his cheek on top of her silky blond hair.

God, was there a feeling as good as this? As holding her in his arms, feeling her melt into him, knowing that there was no one in the world who was as good for him as her?

If there was, he didn't want to know. For him, this was perfection.

"You know," she said, pulling back just enough that she could look up into his eyes, "I don't have any pajamas."

"Hmm," he growled suggestively, "that is a problem."

"You don't have any either," she pointed out.

"That's true. I don't."

"We'll probably get cold."

"Probably."

"I might catch pneumonia."

"Could be," he said, reaching down for the hem of her shirt.

"You'd have to nurse me back to health."

"Might be difficult if we're both naked," he said, pulling her shirt over her head.

"It'll take some special, intensive care."

"Yeah?" He pushed the button of her slacks through the slit and lowered the zipper.

"I get the feeling that you might be a little distracted."

She was smiling down at him as he knelt at eye level to her silky pink panties.

"What makes you say that?" He hooked his thumbs beneath the elastic at the top.

She laughed as he lowered her panties and scooped her into his arms in quick, successive movements. In two strides, he had her on the bed, where she'd pulled the covers back earlier.

"Don't worry. I'll give you a good reason to stay well," he said, grinning down at her as he pressed her into the mattress.

"I never doubted it," she whispered, and he lowered his head to kiss her.

chapter

TWENTY-SIX

HIS BELT BUCKLE WAS COOL, A LITTLE CHILLY KISS against her skin. And then the heel of her hand brushed against the growing bulge beneath his leathers, and Trey bucked.

"Beth, you're playing with fire."

"I know," she said, slipping the tail of his belt free from the buckle. "I know because I'm getting hot."

He laughed a little at her line, but the mirth quickly turned into a sexy moan as her fingers seized the catch of his zipper.

The soft rasp of it seemed loud in the quiet of the room, accompanying breathing that was becoming rougher with each passing second.

Lifting his hips for her, Trey watched as she pulled his leathers down his legs. His gaze was heavy on her as she bit her lip and reached for the waistband of his boxer briefs.

Her breath caught as she revealed his hard, proud length. His cock stood rigid, his sac pushed close to the base by the elastic waistband of his underwear.

A rush of heat and moisture flooded her core, and she slipped from the bed to kneel in front of him.

"Trey," she said, rubbing her hands up and down the strong muscles of his thighs, careful to avoid the bandaged cut on his left one, "I want to taste you."

He closed his eyes for a second, then nodded.

Feeling like a siren temptress, she reached forward and wrapped her fingers around his length. Hot, silky, smooth, he felt so good, so right against her palm. Moisture sprang to the tip, the flared head becoming shiny as she gently stroked his cock.

This was heaven. Being with him, showing him with every move how she felt about him...

It was all she'd ever wanted.

His body tensed and relaxed, hips rolling slightly with each movement she made. Watching him was pure delight. It was almost as if he were her marionette, and her every movement was connected to his body. If she moved faster, he reacted more. But even her slow movements drew delicious moans and deep growls from him.

She licked her lips as she bent forward until her breath was blowing across the damp head of him.

"Beth," he growled, lifting his hips slightly. His cock's head brushed her lower lip, and he cursed. "I want to fuck your mouth."

"Keep still," she chastised him, squeezing gently around the base of his shaft with one hand and sweeping her other thumb over the slick, plumlike head. "This is on my time."

His heat was intense in her mouth, across her tongue, as the sweet tangy taste of his precum hit her taste buds. His silky, velvety skin felt amazing on her lips as she drew him deep, then let him pop free of her mouth.

His hardness glistened with the moisture her mouth had left behind, and she blew a soft breath across it. He shivered.

God, she loved how he made her feel. Powerful. Strong. Able to affect him as deeply as he affected her.

Her body was throbbing with need, but she wasn't finished tasting him.

Over and over she drew him deep into her mouth, the flared head smoothing over her tongue to bump the back of her throat. His girth made her gag once or twice, the involuntary movements contorting her muscles around him.

His hips flexed with her movements, thrusting in time. He grew harder inside her mouth, tangling one hand into her hair as her head bobbed up and down on his erection.

Bethany closed her eyes and swallowed him as deeply as she could.

"Fuck," he said, and his cock jerked inside her mouth. "I can't... Beth, stop."

She lifted her head, licking her lips as she looked at him.

"I need you," he said, reaching down and lifting her against him. "Right now, I need to be inside that beautiful body of yours."

He reached into his pants pocket and withdrew a condom from his wallet.

Thank Christ he'd come prepared.

His hands trembled as he put that condom on faster than he ever had before. His blood was roaring behind his ears, his skin hot and prickling and so incredibly alive with the need to possess her.

This was more than sex. Somehow, this was a marking. A declaration. A union of more than bodies.

She'd taken his soul, even if she didn't know it. It belonged to her.

She lay back on the bed, spreading her thighs wide, eyes hungry as she reached down and parted her core for him.

The sight of her naked, glistening pink folds almost made him come. He closed his eyes against the deliciously tempting sight and fell to the bed.

Bracing his weight above her, he looked down at her wide, hungry eyes. "Are you ready?"

He didn't know what the hell he would do if her answer was no.

He didn't have to worry.

"Take me, please," she whispered.

Surging forward, he sheathed himself to the hilt.

She cried out, her head thrashing against the pillows as he started pounding into her immediately.

Over and over, he plunged into her depths. The hot, slick channel gripped him and eased his way, pulling him deeper, farther inside her.

The way her muscles spasmed around him, gripping the aching, sensitive head of his cock, the way her sweet, white teeth sank into his shoulder, the way her clean-scented blond hair tickled his nose as he buried his head in her pillow…

This was too much. Beth was too much. She'd sucked him good, so good. It made him want to bury his face in her beautiful body again, to let his tongue find all her secret folds, to taste that sweet, womanly tang that was all Beth, only his Beth.

"God, Trey!" Her voice was half breath, half cry. Their

bodies smacked together, the sweet, wet sounds of their movements driving them harder, faster toward that peak.

"Please," she begged, fingertips digging into his back. "Please, I need to come, please…"

He looked into her eyes, wide, wild, so blue the sight made him ache. There was so much written there, so many feelings and thoughts, and he wanted to know every one of them.

This was enough. It had to be enough.

"Come on, Strong Girl," he said, then reached between them to find her clit.

At the first touch of his fingers on that sensitive nub of flesh, she arched her back, shuddering cries ripping through her, inner muscles spasming around his aching hardness sheathed deep inside her.

He lost control, the hot spurts of his orgasm finally escaping into the welcoming grip of her body. Trembling with the effort of keeping himself still as the waves overtook Bethany, Trey could only breathe as his own climax ripped through him.

Her skin was damp now, as was his, and he braced himself on his forearms, never losing the connection with her gaze.

There was so much more than sex there. So many moments condensed into one, the culmination of the past and the promise of the future coalesced into this moment.

Together. That's all he needed. To be together with her.

Waking up in Trey's arms was the most wonderful way Bethany could imagine spending a morning.

"Hmmm," he groaned, his chest rumbling deeply

against her ear. She smiled, nuzzling the sprinkling of hair that covered his pec.

"Morning," she said, her bare leg sliding between his.

"Morning." He wrapped his arm around her hip and gave her ass a squeeze.

Her body was achy, sore. Delicious memories assailed her as she rubbed her palm up and down his back.

He'd been ravenous and tender, sweet and fierce in turn, and she'd loved it. He'd left no part of her body unexplored, and she'd been overjoyed to return the favor.

Never had anyone taken her the way Trey did, and never had anyone given himself to her the way Trey had.

Last night had been more than sex—it was a communion of souls that she was convinced she could only experience with him. With this man.

"I love you," she whispered soundlessly into the skin of his chest, secure in the knowledge that he couldn't hear her. But she had to say it, silent though it was.

She closed her eyes and held him tight. She never, ever wanted to let him go.

Trey. She loved this man.

He had only started to stir to wakefulness when her phone started buzzing on the bedside table. She was completely content to ignore it, but Trey reached for it.

"It's Mrs. Yelverton," he said, handing her the phone.

She frowned and swiped the answer key. It was still kind of early for a phone call from Mama Yelverton.

"Hello?"

"Oh, Bethany, we've got a problem." Mama Yelverton, normally such a calm, confident woman, sounded completely unglued.

"What's going on?" Bethany sat bolt upright, the covers falling to her waist.

"The farmhouse we booked for the wedding burned down. There was an event last night, and some drunken guest set the place on fire with a cigarette. The whole place went up. The wedding is in three weeks, and we don't have a venue."

Bethany plastered her hand over her eyes. *Oh God*.

"It's okay. Don't panic," she told Mama Yelverton.

Trey looked at her, a furrow between his brows at her words, but she waved him away.

"But the invitations have gone out! We'll have to contact everyone, sign a new contract, and everywhere will be triple-booked because of the time of year!"

"It's okay. I'll work on it today."

"I'll call Trey as soon as it's ten. I didn't want to bother him so early. I don't know what time he gets up."

Bethany looked beside her to where Trey had just stood up from the bed. He stretched, giving her a beautiful view of his muscular back and ass, covered with a generous number of tattoos.

"I'll contact Trey, and we'll make a plan. Don't worry. Everything will be okay."

Mama Yelverton didn't sound convinced, but she allowed Bethany to end the call anyway.

Trey exited the bathroom, frowning. "Is everything okay?"

She crossed the room and held him for a long moment without saying anything.

His hand cupped the back of her head, the other sweeping down her back.

She didn't want to leave this room. This little haven

of peace they'd found in the midst of all the turmoil. It felt like leaving the Banks and heading back to Raleigh would pull them apart when she'd only just managed to get this close to him.

"Beth?"

She sighed and looked up at him. "Reality calls."

Beth's voice was remarkably calm as she relayed the latest wedding disaster to Trey, but there was a clear sense of panic in the way she rushed around the room getting dressed.

He wished like hell he really was who he'd said he was. Someone who knew what to do with the wedding. Someone who could fix everything for Bethany so she wouldn't have to worry.

But he wasn't. He'd lied. And now he had to juggle who he'd said he was with who he really was—the head of a biker gang who was about to go to all-out war with a circle of drug dealers.

He frowned as he walked down the hall after Bethany, a weight on his shoulders that pressed harder with every step toward home.

The night before had been amazing—wrapped up in Bethany's arms like nothing could touch them.

But in the cold, harsh light of the morning, he saw how precious, fragile, and brief those moments had been.

Even all the love in his heart for her couldn't stop their reality—that they were so, so different.

"Are you okay?"

He stopped in mid-motion, his motorcycle helmet held between his hands. Bethany had already put hers on, and as she stood beside his motorcycle, her shaded eyes held unspoken worry.

He forced a smile onto his face. "I'm fine. Just thinking about what to do about the venue."

Bethany sighed as he buckled the strap on his helmet. "I don't know. That farmhouse was perfect. It was exactly the kind of place Sarah wanted. She'd be miserable with a church wedding, but where are we going to find another place big enough on this short notice?"

Trey started to answer, but his cell buzzed in his pocket. He pulled it free and looked down at the screen.

The text was from Wolf.

Where are you? We've got trouble.

"Damn it," Trey said under his breath as he unlocked the screen to tap out a reply.

"Everything okay?" Bethany asked.

"Fine," he said shortly as he typed.

I'm out of town. Be back in a few hours. What's going on?

Wolf hit him back in a matter of moments.

Jameson's missing. He didn't come back home after tailing Rat. Not answering texts. I'm thinking he might have gone after Hampton.

Trey gripped the phone so tightly that his knuckles cracked around it.

He'd told Jameson to wait. Why couldn't that idiot have listened? Thinking quickly, he replied.

Get everyone who's free to start looking for him. Do not confront anybody without contacting me first. If Jameson's in the tank, leave him there till I get back.

With the text sent, Trey shoved his phone back in his pocket. His thoughts awhirl, he slung his leg over the bike and cranked the engine.

Suddenly, slender arms wrapped around his middle as a warm, soft weight settled on the bike saddle behind him.

His tension eased as he closed his eyes and leaned back into her just a little.

"We'll get it figured out," Bethany said, her voice soft in his ear. "Don't worry."

If she only knew… He wished things were as simple as needing a new place for Sarah's wedding.

It was way more screwed up than that.

"Yeah. It'll be fine."

She pressed a kiss to the back of his shoulder as he walked the bike out of the parking space and headed toward the exit.

Things were nowhere near that simple. And since there weren't three Treys to handle the three facets of his current life—the biker Trey, the wedding Trey, and the Trey who wanted to do nothing but crawl into bed beside Bethany and stay there forever—he'd have to figure out how to juggle it all.

The ocean breeze grabbed at them as he sped toward home, spurring his desperate fear that his grip on everything wouldn't be sufficient to keep things from breaking.

His mind was so wrapped up in all the things competing for his attention that he drove home on autopilot. Time passed, but it did so without his attention.

The only thing that kept pulling him back into the moment was the sure grip around his midsection. The tiny adjustments she made, the way she sat up and stretched when they stopped at a light. The warm circle of her arms around his waist when they resumed their journey.

God, he'd fallen so hard, and he had no clue what to do with that.

As trees gave way to more and more homes and businesses, there was no escaping the reality that their little escape was over. Once they hit the Raleigh city limits, he steeled his resolve and nosed his bike toward Bethany's apartment.

With any luck, Grandma would leave Beth alone.

He put his bike in the same parking spot beside Beth's car that they'd peeled out of yesterday. It seemed like ages ago now.

The quiet around them was deafening when Trey finally cut his bike's engine.

"God," Beth said, sitting back on the saddle and pulling the helmet from her head. She ran her hands along the crown of her hair, shaking it out as she bent to the side. "After the last two days, I'm not sure I can walk straight for a while."

Trey smiled wryly. "Take a hot shower. It'll help ease your sore muscles."

Bethany climbed off the bike, then turned to look at him. Trey hadn't moved.

"Are you not coming in?"

Trey shook his head. "No, I've got to do some things."

Bethany frowned slightly. "Is it work? Or are you trying to find somewhere else for the wedding?"

He'd have to try to do both.

"Don't worry about my work. It's fine. I'll scout out some places today and get back with you."

"Are you sure? If your job needs you—"

Trey nodded, shifting his weight on the bike. "Yeah, no worries. I can handle it."

"Okay," she said, a note of doubt in her voice.

"C'mere."

She leaned over, taking his outstretched hand, and he pulled her close. Brushing a fierce, possessive kiss over her lips, Trey tried to channel all his feelings through that brief, commanding touch.

She swayed as he let go.

"It'll be all right, Strong Girl," he said and cranked his bike's engine.

As he pulled away, he looked at her in his mirror.

Her eyes were wide and a little sad, her arms wrapped tightly over her middle as she watched him go.

He couldn't shake the feeling that the heights they'd ascended last night were the end of something—something that had only just begun.

Shaking off the melancholy, he steeled his resolve and headed toward Ruby's.

He had to find his brother. The idea that Jameson had gone off half-cocked was bothering him. After that last incident with Vinnie, Trey didn't trust Jameson's judgment.

For some reason, Cady's death was hanging heavier than usual around him lately. And a wounded animal was the most dangerous kind.

In the early afternoon, Ruby's was fairly deserted. But Trey found who he needed only moments after walking through the door.

"Hey, Trey," Ginger said with a smile. One of Lynn's kids was sitting at the table in the corner, coloring. Trey waved at the little girl, who smiled shyly at him. "What can I do for you?"

"Have you seen Jameson since last night?"

Ginger's smile faltered a little. "You haven't talked to Wolf?"

"He texted me this morning." Trey reached for his

pocket. The screen showed several missed calls and texts. He hadn't even noticed.

Ginger bit her lip as Trey looked up at her.

"What is it?"

"It's not good."

chapter

TWENTY-SEVEN

BETHANY STOOD LOOKING AFTER TREY'S BIKE LONG after the sight and sound of it had disappeared into the early-afternoon sunshine.

Something had changed for him this morning. From the moment they'd left that hotel at the Outer Banks, he'd been preoccupied, darkly silent.

Bethany turned and walked up the stairs to her apartment.

No, he'd been quiet and thoughtful as they'd checked out of the hotel, but the tension hadn't really tightened his shoulders until he'd gotten that text message this morning.

Bethany frowned as she flipped through her keys for the one that unlocked the door to her apartment. Who had texted him? And what had they said that made him so clearly disturbed?

Her ruminations ground to a halt the moment she opened the door to her apartment.

She clapped a hand over her mouth, and her eyes flew wide with complete surprise.

"What...what have you done?" She whispered the words through her hand to a woman who wasn't there.

Her apartment was a shambles.

Bethany's shoes crunched on broken glass as she walked into her living room.

She'd been robbed, but she knew exactly who the culprit had been.

Her TV and laptop were still there. But all her books had been dumped on the floor, knickknacks and houseplants scattered like a tornado had ripped through her living area.

And the bottom shelf, the one that held her photo albums...

"Damn you," Bethany bit out as she scooped up the torn-up remnants of an album.

The vast majority of it was gone. The only things that were left were photos Bethany had taken of some school friends, some landscapes, and the trip to the zoo she and her dad had taken when they first moved to Raleigh.

Every picture that her father was in had been ripped straight from the album.

Her heart sinking, Bethany stood and half-sprinted toward her bedroom.

The framed photos of her father that had sat atop her dresser were gone.

"Why?"

The word came out half choked as she sank down on her bed. She remembered now, the way she'd run out of the apartment to get away from her grandmother—the fight over Dad's Purple Heart.

Clearly, she'd left the door unlocked, and as Trey had whisked her away with the precious medal, her grandmother had taken her rage and revenge where she could.

"You can't take him away from me," Bethany whispered, reaching into her pocket for the Purple Heart. Her hand shook as she traced the engraved lines of her father's name. "He's my father, and no matter how jealous you are, you can't have my memories of him."

She let the tears fall then. For the loss of her father, which still hurt. For the violation of her home, a raw, gaping wound with the ragged edges evident all around her. For the distance between her and the man she'd just realized she loved.

And for the anxiety and uncertainty that permeated the air around her.

A few moments later, she wiped her cheeks and pulled out her cell.

As much as she'd love to press charges against her grandmother, the promise she'd made her father prevented her from going that far.

But she couldn't stay here any longer. Not with the way her grandmother kept violating her privacy.

In order to protect herself, and her memories of her father, she had to move—and she had to do it now. She was only a few weeks from her yearly renewal, anyway. That made the decision easy.

With the call to the landlord taken care of, Bethany started packing.

She'd been at it for a couple of hours when her cell phone rang.

"Hello?"

"Oh, Bethany. How is the venue search going?" Mama Yelverton still sounded stressed, but there was a note of hope in her voice.

Memories took Bethany in a rush. She hadn't heard

anything about the venues from Trey, and she hadn't done any work on it herself, too caught up in her own family drama.

"Fine! It's totally going fine. We've got a couple possibilities," Bethany said in a rush. Her phone was tucked in the hollow of her shoulder as she finished shoving clothes into her suitcase. "We were going to call you when we had some ideas finalized."

"Oh good. I've just been so worried, and there's an issue at Sam's Place that I've been tied up with all day, so I haven't been able to do any looking myself. I should have known that you and Trey would have it all taken care of."

Bethany winced. "Sure, don't you worry about it. I'll call you in a little while when I've got some firmer details."

"Sounds good. Want to come over for dinner? I was going to get some Chinese food, and Sarah's hiding out upstairs studying."

"Maybe, yeah," Bethany said, eyeing the mound of stuff in the corner. "I actually might need a place to stay for a few days, if you don't mind."

"Oh really?" The note of surprise in Mama Yelverton's voice was gone as quickly as it had come. "Say no more. Your room is always ready and waiting for you, no matter what. If I can help in any other way—"

"No, no, everything's fine. I'll see you in a couple hours," Bethany said with a relieved smile. "You're the best, Mama Y. Love you."

"I love you too, Bethany. See you soon."

Bethany cut the call, a mixture of relief and guilt suffusing her limbs.

Damn it. She had to figure out something about the wedding before she showed her face at the Yelvertons' tonight. Sarah's board exam was coming up, and the last thing she needed was to know that her wedding plans had slid off the rails into oncoming traffic.

"Let's see if Trey's had any better luck," Bethany said to herself as she swiped through her contacts to find him.

She carried some boxes to the living room as she listened to the ring on the other end of the line. Fortunately, the liquor store on the corner had been getting rid of a bunch of boxes. She'd darted down there and loaded up her car with them as soon as she'd hung up with the landlord.

On her second trip with arms loaded, Trey's voicemail kicked in.

Bethany sighed and set her boxes down. Grabbing the phone from the crook of her shoulder, she tapped out a text.

Just talked to Mama Y. She wants to know how the venue search is going. Had any luck?

She waited a moment, but when he didn't hit her right back, she grabbed her laptop, skirting the pile of broken glass she'd swept into the corner.

It wasn't fair to expect Trey to do all this when he had an important job to be doing at the same time. She'd spend a little while on the phone trying to get an alternate venue and hopefully keep Trey's cover.

But her shoulders and jaw were curiously tight as she typed into the search box.

It would have been nice to know what Trey had done so she could make sure they weren't covering the same territory. He had promised to work on the venue today.

"Don't be stupid, Bethany. He's an undercover cop. He might be in the middle of something dangerous."

Small comfort that was really no comfort at all.

Bethany bent her head down and got to work.

"Hello? Is this the Wharton Rose Gardens? I've got some questions about your wedding services…"

Trey's pulse had been thundering in his ears from the moment Ginger's story had started.

As he'd strode from Ruby's toward his bike, his phone was in his hand, and Wolf picked up nearly instantly.

"Where?"

"Duke. ER. I'm here with him now. Dean's got Lars and Rocco, and they're looking for Hampton."

"Tell them to back off," Trey barked as he slung his leg over his bike. "Hampton's off-limits until I figure out what the hell is going on."

An uncharacteristic note of anger crept into Wolf's normally even tone. "Boss, you've been MIA since we let Rat go. If you really wanted to know what was going on, then why'd you leave us?"

"I—I…" Wolf was right. But that only made Trey angrier—angrier at himself, at the choices he'd made, at Jameson for ignoring his orders last night and landing himself in the hospital.

"Don't anybody move, and that's an order."

Trey cut the call and roared out of the lot, not even bothering with the helmet.

He needed to get to his brother, even if it had been Jameson's fault that he'd landed in the ER.

Trey wound through the traffic in downtown Durham, a cold knot sitting in the pit of his stomach. Parking was a nightmare, but Trey didn't give a damn. His bike fit neatly between a concrete pillar and the wall of the parking deck.

The tunnel beneath the street was unbearably long,

and claustrophobia started to press in on Trey long before it opened up to a bank of elevators.

He followed the signs that led to the emergency department, urgency chasing him every step of the way.

"I'm looking for Jameson Mott's room," he said to the woman at the desk. As she typed into her computer, Trey looked over his shoulder.

The chairs held all manner of humanity in various states of boredom, sickness, and distress. Young, old, rich, poor, health was a great equalizer, and that was clear in the population of the lobby.

If only one of his men didn't number among them. If only he'd been there to prevent Jameson from making such a stupid decision.

But the road to hell was paved with if-onlys, and building a thoroughfare was a job he didn't have time for today.

"Room 22." The receptionist handed him a visitor tag with the number scrawled on it in Sharpie. "I'll buzz you through."

"Thanks," Trey said, sticking the neon tag on the dark fabric of his shirt and walking through the slow-moving double doors into the chaos of the emergency department.

It was an odd atmosphere, both still and full of movement simultaneously. The little rooms were quiet and full of noise by turns.

Trey concentrated on finding the right room, making a couple of wrong turns on the trip. But eventually he came to a small exam room with the door only halfway closed.

He knocked, then pushed it open.

Wolf was seated by the bedside, a dark expression in his eyes. He nodded at Trey, much more coldly than usual.

Wolf would have to get over it. Trey couldn't take back the last twenty-four hours, and he probably wouldn't even if he could. The stolen moments with Bethany had numbered among the best of his life. But they'd had such a high cost.

Trey looked at the hospital bed, and his throat started to close up.

"Damn." The word was unnaturally rough, even considering Trey's usually gravelly tone.

But the curse was appropriate. Jameson looked like hell.

Trey could understand Ginger's initial panic. The fear and anxiety in her words made much more sense now than when she'd recounted how she'd come across Jameson that morning.

As Jameson lay in that hospital bed, his dark, angry bruises stood out in stark contrast to the white sheets. But his knuckles were bloody and scraped, as if he'd gotten in a few licks of his own before he'd been overcome.

But the worst thing was the way his arm was bent unnaturally in the center. Cushioned on all sides by pillows, it was clearly a break that hadn't been fixed yet.

"Jameson." Trey stepped to the bedside. "Can you hear me, man?"

Jameson's eyes fluttered open, as much as they could through the swelling in his face.

"Who did this to you?"

Jameson turned his head toward Trey, clearing his throat. "Hampton had a crew with him."

Rage flooded Trey's chest, a low, threatening tide that wanted to overtake his senses. He kept it tightly leashed. For now.

"Did you catch him cooking?"

"No," Jameson whispered, trying to adjust his position. He cried out as he jostled his arm, and Trey pushed him gently back into the bed.

"Stay put, my man."

Wolf stood, moving just behind Trey. "He told me some of what happened."

Jameson closed his eyes, a pain-filled, ragged breath leaving him as he relaxed against the pillows.

Poor bastard.

Trey turned his attention to Wolf. "What'd he say?"

Wolf crossed his arms over his broad chest. "He caught Hampton out in southern Wake County. He was meeting a bunch of dealers and doling out product. Jameson waited till they'd dispersed and then tailed Hampton. He'd gotten as far as Apex when Hampton saw him and turned on him. Got a few good licks in before Hampton's buddies got there."

The idea that Hampton might be hurting too was a little balm to Trey's soul, but just a little.

"Did he get any more leads?"

Wolf nodded. "He followed Hampton to an abandoned convenience mart. Jameson said it looked like someone might have been cooking there recently, but they'd moved on."

Shit. So close.

"So they beat the hell out of him and dropped him at Ruby's as a warning."

Wolf nodded at Trey's summary. "Yeah. Pretty damn ballsy for small-time dealers. They're too brave."

"They know something we don't," Trey said, his spine locking into a cold, steel column.

He looked down at his brother.

He'd let him down. He'd let them all down.

It stopped now.

Closing his eyes, Trey brought the thought of Bethany to the forefront of his memory. The way she smiled at him. The way she'd held his hand as they walked beside the surf last night. The way her body took him in, so warm, so welcoming, so perfect.

That wasn't the life he'd chosen. Way back then, he'd known that he couldn't rely on anyone but the Shadows.

And they relied on him just as much. He'd let them down, and Jameson had paid the price.

Trey's phone vibrated in his pocket, and he looked at the screen.

Bethany.

Once before, he'd promised them that he'd be there for them. This time, he wouldn't break that promise. No matter what. His decision made, he declined the call.

The text message that came next was even easier to ignore than the phone call. He'd already sat down beside Wolf at Jameson's hospital bedside and started to lay out plans for revenge.

This had to end, and nobody but Trey could ensure that.

Even if it meant letting her down, he had to do it.

He'd made a vow, and he had to keep it. No matter how much it hurt him.

And her.

chapter

TWENTY–EIGHT

THE LIGHT WAS GETTING LOW BY THE TIME BETHANY drove down the long, winding path that led to the Yelvertons' house.

Mentally exhausted, emotionally drained, Bethany gripped the steering wheel hard as she passed the empty, staring windows of the neglected Victorian.

There was too much to do. Too many feelings and worries and anxieties. She longed to be able to lean on Trey, to have him reassure her that things would be okay.

But he hadn't called her back. And he hadn't answered any of her texts. Presuming he was tied up with his work, she'd stopped after the third one.

He'd get back to her when he could.

She cut her engine and opened the garage door. Box by box, she emptied her trunk and backseat into an unoccupied corner.

Dusting her hands off on her jeans, she leaned against the pile to catch her breath.

Another couple of carloads should do it for boxes,

but she'd have to get a moving van for her furniture. Renting a storage building for the moment was probably a wise move—she didn't want to monopolize Mama Yelverton's garage while she found another place to live.

Bethany shook her head as she shut her trunk.

It sickened her that her grandmother had managed to chase her out of her apartment. It seemed like she was getting worse, not better.

Glancing up at the twilight sky, Bethany blew out a heavy breath.

"What do I do, Dad? How long does this promise last? Is there any way out?"

There wasn't any answer, even in the pale, cloud-covered moon.

She hadn't expected one. But it would have been nice to have her guilt at running away absolved. Even if she changed her number and cut contact with the woman completely, she'd still feel like she was letting her father down.

It was a terrible situation, and she didn't know the way out.

The sound of a shout from inside wrenched her attention, and Bethany hustled toward the house.

Uh-oh. She yanked open the door. It seemed like while she'd been up in her head about her grandmother, things had been spiraling out of control.

"It's insane! I can't believe this. What kind of idiots don't have their fire extinguishers inspected?"

Bethany rounded the corner to catch sight of Sarah pacing angrily around the kitchen. Mama Yelverton was in the midst of unpacking takeout boxes from the Chinese restaurant they liked.

"Honey, I know. I'm upset too. But we'll find somewhere else."

"But the wedding's in three freaking weeks! You've sent out invitations, you've done all this work…" Sarah turned, and then she noticed Bethany standing there. "Bethy! Oh God, I'm glad to see you. Mom just told me about the disaster."

In damage-control mode, Bethany moved next to Sarah and grabbed her best friend by the hands. "Hey. Listen. It's going to be fine. Don't you worry about it at all."

"Exactly," Mama Yelverton said, pulling plates down from the cabinet. "Bethany and Trey have been working on another venue all day, haven't you?"

"Of course," Bethany lied, turning to put her purse down. "Trey's been at it nonstop."

"Oh good," Sarah said, and the relief in her voice was enough to make Bethany wince. "Have you got somewhere else?"

"Well…" Bethany stopped. What should she do? Tell them the truth? That Bethany had called six places over the past two hours, and none of them had space? Or should she lie?

God, where was Trey when she needed him?

"Let's get settled at the table, and then Bethany can tell us all about it."

"Yeah," Bethany said, more grateful to Mama Yelverton than she could say. She grabbed a carton of noodles and another of steamed vegetables, and hustled them to the table.

As she moved, she thought. She had to come up with a good, believable story. Maybe telling them she and Trey had another good lead was the best idea. That way she could just say it fell through when Trey found another place.

Bethany frowned as she set glasses on the table.

That was, presuming Trey actually *had* found another place. But he'd promised he would. And she trusted him.

But then again, he did have a big, important job that was incredibly unpredictable.

Sighing, Bethany sat down. She just wasn't sure which way to go. Pulling her cell phone from her pocket, she checked her texts again.

Zero unread.

Where the hell was he?

"We had an incident at Sam's Place this morning," Mama Yelverton said with a sigh as she sat down in her usual spot. Sarah was helping herself to some broccoli as she answered.

"What happened?"

"Do you remember Vincent? He came in and out for a while, then he got into drugs and didn't really stick around."

"Oh yeah," Sarah said, wrinkling her nose. "I didn't care for that guy. He picked on the younger guys a lot. Kinda creepy too."

Mama Yelverton nodded. "I'd hoped he would stop using. We offered him counseling several times, but he always refused. Well, he came by this morning, pretending to need help, but he caused a big ruckus."

"What happened?" Bethany stopped, her chopsticks halfway to her mouth.

"He picked a fight with Lester in the kitchen. Lester caught him stealing some of the oddest things."

"Like what?" Sarah asked, her mouth full.

Mama Yelverton paused, looking down at her fork

thoughtfully. "Coffee filters, matchbooks, a couple of first aid kits. Some of the Pyrex dishes. Just a weird assortment of stuff." Mama Yelverton shook her head sadly. "I called the police, but he'd already left by the time they got there. They said he might be manufacturing drugs. I sure hope not."

Bethany frowned. "They'll call the police if he comes back, right?"

"Oh yes. Lester was really angry about it." Mama Yelverton tucked her hair behind her ear. "I just hope he gets his life straightened out. He is one of those people who seem to attract trouble and like it."

Bethany sighed. Attracting trouble was a problem she had at the moment, but thankfully of a much different sort.

"So that was a great call to get after the one about the farmhouse burning down," Mama Yelverton said, determinedly shaking off her melancholy. She smiled over at Bethany. "So, you've got some better news for us?"

"Well... First, I brought some boxes over. I need to stay here for a while."

"Wait, what?" Sarah put down her glass of water, a drop of condensation rolling over her thumb. "Is something wrong with your apartment?"

As much as she hated to complain, Bethany told them an abbreviated version of the story about her grandmother's home invasion, leaving out the part about Trey whisking her away for the night. Both Sarah and Mama Yelverton were horrified.

"That miserable old bitch." Sarah spat the words.

"Sarah," her mother chided without venom. She looked as if she agreed with Sarah, actually. "Of course you can stay here."

Sarah sighed. "With all this going on, I feel bad about asking the two of you to do all this wedding planning. You've both got so much happening. Maybe I should take it over."

"No!" Mama Yelverton reached over and grabbed Sarah's hand. "Don't you worry about it at all. Your test is coming up next week, and you need to study hard. Besides, your brother is handling it." Mama Yelverton smiled.

Bethany wished she could sink into the floor when Mama Yelverton turned that sunny expression on her.

"So, what are you looking at for the secondary venue? I haven't had a chance to chase down any myself today, so I'm so grateful that you and Trey were on top of it."

Bethany coughed, covering her mouth with her napkin.

"Sorry," she croaked, grabbing her glass. "I need to get some more water."

Dashing from the dining room, she headed into the kitchen and yanked on the tap. Glancing over her shoulder, she dialed Trey's number again.

Where the hell was he? She was drowning in lies, and he was her only hope.

Without him, she was so screwed.

As much as Bethany would have liked to remain in the kitchen for the next six hours, or until Trey got in contact with her, whichever happened first, she realized that wasn't feasible.

With a heavy sigh, she shoved her phone in her pocket, stuck her glass under the running tap, and shut off the water.

Pinning a benign expression on her face, she composed herself and headed back to the dining room.

"Sorry, something went down the wrong pipe," she said with a sheepish smile as she set down her glass and slipped into her seat. "Got caught in my throat."

"You okay?" Sarah hiked an eyebrow in her direction.

Bethany nodded. "Totally fine."

"You do look a little pale," Mama Yelverton observed. "Are you sure?"

"Totally. Anyway, what were we talking about? Your test, Sarah?"

"No, you were about to let us know where the wedding's going to be." Sarah didn't even pretend to play Bethany's game.

Damn it.

She had to do better than this, or Sarah would see through it all.

"Trey's got a lead on a place," Bethany said slowly, formulating her ideas as she spoke. They needed somewhere quiet. Outdoors, ideally. Large enough to hold the two hundred or so guests that would show.

"Really? Where?" Mama Yelverton leaned forward.

As the mental image popped into Bethany's brain, she knew she shouldn't. It was a really, really bad idea. But the most beautiful place she'd seen recently was also someone's private retreat. His home.

And there might have been a tiny bit of anger inside her that prompted her to use it to help her out of this jam. After all, she wouldn't be in it if he'd done what he said.

So, it was with a dose of self-righteous anger and an inescapable hint of guilt that she said, "A beautiful privately owned property right on the edge of Durham County. It's got a pond, plenty of wooded areas for shade, a nice drive…"

As she went on to describe Trey's property, a spear of longing went through her.

He should be there. With her. With his family. But he wasn't, and he'd left her to bear this all on her own.

It wasn't fair. Not when she loved him so much.

"That sounds lovely," Mama Yelverton said when Bethany fell silent. "And you're sure it's available?"

"I'm negotiating with the owner."

Sarah frowned down at her plate. "Shouldn't Trey be doing that? He's being paid for all this too. And it's his business, supposedly. He's the wedding planner Mom insisted on hiring without any references other than a DNA test that could have been faked. He must be really terrible at it if Bethany's having to handle all this on her own."

"I'm not—" Bethany protested, but Mama Yelverton cut her off.

"Sarah Josephine Yelverton, what horrible things to say. That is enough. I know you're stressed because of the wedding and school, but that is no reason to run down your brother's—"

"My brother? Bullshit. He's not my brother." Sarah had shoved her chair back and was standing with both palms splayed, braced on the table as her words poured out of her like magma from an angry volcano. "He hasn't made any effort to get to know you. Or me. Or even Bethany."

Bethany blanched, but no one was looking at her, thankfully.

Sarah continued, a runaway train going downhill. "I haven't seen him do anything to earn your trust. From my perspective, you and Bethany have done more for this wedding than him! Wedding planner? My ass. He looks more like a drug dealer or a gangbanger."

"Sarah!" Bethany's body had gone cold, numb.

Tears were streaming down Sarah's cheeks now. "You've been tied in knots all day with this venue crap on top of your terrible grandmother wrecking your home, and have you even heard from him? Well, have you?"

Mama Yelverton's silence was damning.

"I just don't understand. Why would you let this stranger into our lives without a second thought? Right when I'm taking the biggest step of my life, and I need my momma, you're running right toward him instead. I—I…"

Sarah ran out of steam then, but it might have been because Mama Yelverton had rounded the table and taken her grown-up daughter into her arms.

"Sarah, baby, I'm not leaving you. I swear. I would never hurt you on purpose."

As Mama Yelverton held her, a hand stroking Sarah's long, blond hair and her sobs muffled against her mother's shoulder, Bethany backed from the room, silent tears tracking down her cheeks.

She left the house by the back door, not bothering to turn on the lights. In the pale gold streaming from the living-room windows, she sank down on the wooden steps and stared up into the night sky.

"Daddy," she whispered, missing him in the face of the family blowup inside. "What do I do?"

Her head rested lightly on the handrail beside her, and she sniffed, dashing moisture away from her cheeks.

She hadn't known that Sarah was still so touchy about Trey. Hadn't seen it. But it made sense. Sarah was a very decisive person, and emotions sometimes confused her. She obviously hadn't had a chance to deal with the feelings that having to share her mother with someone other than Bethany was stirring inside her. Bethany joining the family had been Sarah's choice, Sarah's suggestion. Trey? He wasn't.

If only... Bethany sighed as the night wind stirred around her, rustling the plants in the bed beside the deck. If only Trey's job didn't put him in the position of lying to them. If only she'd been able to be honest about their relationship, maybe they'd have spent more time with Sarah. If only...

Bethany cradled her knees and put her head down.

"Trey, where are you? I need you. I love you."

But her whisper carried no weight, and her questions went unanswered.

For as long as she was with him, she was deathly afraid she'd carry this burden.

Thing was, she didn't know how to go without it.

"Hey. Sorry."

Bethany looked up. Sarah was standing on the deck, two glasses of wine in her hands. She took the one Sarah offered and scooted over to give her space to sit down.

"Sorry I kind of lost it in there."

Bethany shook her head, the sip of wine warming her from the inside out. "You're under a lot of pressure. It's totally understandable."

"I don't want you to think I don't appreciate the job you're doing. I totally do. You're amazing at this." Sarah sighed. "I just don't understand Trey."

Bethany looked over at her best friend, just waiting.

"He's not what I imagined my brother would be, if he'd lived. I guess I had this white knight of a perfect intellectual jock in my head. You know, the kind who would beat up anybody who was rude to me, while teasing me mercilessly himself."

"But he is protective like that," Bethany said, the memory of him whisking her away from her family moving her to speak. "He's loyal to a fault, and—"

"I guess you have had some time to get to know him, since you're dating his friend," Sarah said, and Bethany shut up quickly. Sarah sighed. "I'm just feeling emotional. Everything's changing for me. I'm getting out of school. I'm getting married. If it all falls apart, you, and Mom, and home are my safety nets. And it felt like all that was changing too."

"C'mere." Bethany reached over and wrapped an arm around Sarah's shoulders. "I'm not changing."

"But you're looking at jobs far away." Sarah sniffed. "After graduation, and when Mark's degree is finished, we'll be moving back here. How am I supposed to live here without you?"

"I'm not going anywhere right now," Bethany said, inwardly praying it'd be the truth for a long time. If things with Trey fell apart, she wasn't sure how she could stand to be in the same area as him. But for now…

"Your mom will always be there for you. And once things calm down, and you give Trey a chance, I know you'll see the good in him."

Sarah sighed. "You're probably right." She straightened and looked back over her shoulder. "I really upset Mom, I think. I need to go make sure she's okay."

"Go for it," Bethany said with a smile. "Thanks for the drink."

"Anytime," Sarah said as she stood. "And Bethy?"

"Yeah?"

Sarah turned. "Thanks for being someone I can always count on. I love you, girlie."

"Love you too," Bethany said. Sarah walked away.

Swallowing hard, Bethany pulled her phone from her pocket. The screen glowed in the blackness.

It was late. No missed calls. Zero text messages.

Another glance up into the night sky didn't give her any further clarity.

Where was he? Was he safe?

Did he worry about her the way she worried about him?

Her heart ached with the need to know, and the powerlessness she felt was a sore that wouldn't heal.

All she could do was trust him, and wait.

But how long? She wished she knew.

chapter

TWENTY-NINE

A WEEK LATER

TREY SQUINTED INTO THE DARKNESS OF THE SINGLE-wide trailer's living room, having just stepped in from the bright spring sunshine. The door had been hanging open on drunken hinges, so he hadn't waited for an invitation.

Not that one would have been forthcoming anyway.

"Who the hell are you?"

The voice came from a broken-down La-Z-Boy in the corner. As Trey's vision adjusted, he recognized the speaker.

Justina, a former dancer at Cherry Ice, was seated in the corner and smoking a J. In contrast to what she'd worn on the job, she was dressed in ratty sweatpants and a stained T-shirt.

"It's Trey Harding."

She stubbed out the blunt and stood, rolling her hips suggestively as she walked over to him. "Why are you here, baby? I don't lay for pay anymore, but I might just be willing to do you for free."

Trey stepped back to avoid the brush of her hand across the front of his jeans. "No thanks, Justina. I need some information."

She rolled her eyes. "Since I stopped dancing, all anybody wants to do is talk to me. I still got it, you know."

Trey gave her a cursory glance, and he had to admit that she did. Any other time, he might have been tempted to take her up on the offer. Justina's dark skin accentuated a plethora of curves that seemed designed to fit a man's caress.

But the only person he wanted to touch was completely off-limits forever. The voicemail he'd left her four days ago was proof of that.

He'd thanked his lucky stars she hadn't answered the phone. No way could he have said what he needed to directly to her.

Bethany, it's Trey. Look. I'm sorry. I… My job is getting too complicated. I didn't mean to ghost you, but the situation is tougher than I'd thought. I'm going to have to end this… Us, I mean. It's not because of you. I just want to keep you safe.

He'd had to stop to clear his throat, which had gone curiously thick. *Anyway. I'm sorry. I… I'm so damn sorry.*

And he'd ended the call, feeling like the biggest coward in the world.

The way he'd broken up with her was criminal, but the Shadows needed him.

If he was going to prevent anyone else getting hurt during this mission, he had to take charge of it himself.

"I need to know who's giving Hampton his orders."

Justina's previously sultry expression fell, and she turned and walked toward the tiny kitchen area. Her bare feet padded against the linoleum, making a soft slapping sound.

"Why do you think I know that?"

Trey followed her, his hands in his pockets. "Because Rocco saw you out at Georgie's the other day. Hampton and Georgie are tight, but you and Georgie are tighter."

Justina shot him a dark glance as she poured herself a glass of water. "Georgie's my brother. I don't agree with everything he does, but I protect my own."

"I understand that," Trey said smoothly, "and I'm not trying to put you in an awkward position. But Hampton's moving meth through this area again."

Justina's shoulders tensed instantly, and he knew why.

"You're still clean, right?"

Her terse nod belied the tremble in her hand.

"It's hard as hell, isn't it? Why don't you let me help by getting that crap out of here. Hampton is the head dealer, that much I'm pretty sure of. But I need to know who's cooking. I want to cut it off. For you, and for all the rest of the people that finally have a chance because that shit's out of their lives."

"I didn't know," Justina whispered, her wide brown gaze turned back on Trey. "I swear, I didn't. I wouldn't have let them into the warehouse if I did."

"The warehouse?"

She nodded. "Hampton told Georgie that he came across a trailer full of stuff from a department store. Purses, jewelry, perfume, high-end merchandise. He wanted somewhere to go through it to prep it for sale. So I gave Georgie the keys to the warehouse behind Cherry Ice. It's empty back there, just old broken furniture and props that the owner didn't throw away. I swiped the keys a long time ago, before I quit."

A tear rolled down Justina's cheek. "I wouldn't have given it to him if I'd thought...if I'd known—"

"Hey," Trey said and gripped her arm. "I'm going to fix this. And you can help."

"Tell me how." Justina swiped her cheeks, and the tilt of her chin was defiant. "Tell me how to fix this. That shit almost took my life, and I don't want it anywhere near here."

"Find out from Georgie who Hampton's been hanging around lately. As much as you can without tipping him off. I'm going to get my crew together, and we're going to check out that warehouse."

Justina followed him to the front door. "I'll do what I need to. But you be careful. Hampton's got a mean streak a mile wide."

"Good thing mine's two miles wide," Trey said with a dark grin and strode out into the light again.

As he swung his leg over his bike, his mind whirled as his helmet settled into place.

They were prepping for something big. But what? Why did Hampton need that much space? That old warehouse had been used to sell tobacco many years ago. What kind of operation was he planning that would possibly need that kind of space?

Trey didn't know. But he was going to gather his men together to figure it out.

Leaning low over his handlebars, he took the curves

of the back roads toward home at a much higher rate of speed than was probably wise. But the velocity felt good. The sting of the wind on his exposed skin felt good. The sharp bite reminded him he was alive—

Even if he was a rat bastard for leaving her.

As if on cue, once he'd made the turn onto the gravel drive that led to his property, his cell phone started to ring in his pocket.

He pulled over to the side of the path and looked at the screen.

Bethany.

Again.

His finger hovered over the answer-call button for a half second.

He wanted to talk to her. The longing was so bad it was almost a physical pain, shredding the inside of his chest like a chain saw without an operator.

He hated what he'd done to her—to them. Promising her so much, and then bailing with a piss-poor excuse for an explanation. But every time he thought about going back to the way things were, he remembered the other promises he'd made.

The ones to his brothers.

Seeing Jameson in that hospital bed had reminded him that he was the one who'd effectively put him there. That he alone was responsible for leading these men and keeping them and what they treasured safe.

Bethany had been fine before him, and she'd be fine after him.

And his family—he winced and swallowed. Not his family. The Yelvertons. Their questions had been answered, mostly. But like it or not, Samuel Yelverton had really died when that nurse had whisked him away in the middle of the night.

Trey Harding was not Samuel Yelverton, and he never could be. It was time to stop pretending.

The phone fell silent in his hand, voicemail having kicked in after so many rings. He shoved it into his pocket and drove the rest of the way down the path.

When the trees opened up, his stomach sank as he took in the view of a familiar green Corolla and the beautiful fall of blond hair that the driver was pushing back over her shoulder.

His chest suddenly cracked open inside, the most hideous mixture of love and longing and sheer magnetic draw shoving him toward her.

But he couldn't... He couldn't.

"Hey," she said, climbing out of the driver's seat. "I've been trying to call you."

"I know," he said, cutting the engine. He did his best not to look at her as he climbed off the bike. "What do you need?"

The hurt and confusion was clear in her tone. "Well, first of all I think I deserve an explanation for that sudden breakup. Also, in about fourteen days there's a wedding, and we still don't have a venue. Unless you've found somewhere..."

Her voice trailed off. He didn't answer.

His footfalls were heavy on the porch steps as he climbed. She was right behind him. He closed his eyes for a moment as the fresh, clean scent of her blew past on a momentary breeze.

He wanted—no, he needed—to draw her into his arms. To apologize for all this, to fix it for her.

But he couldn't.

"I'm sorry," he said without turning, his hand on the knob of his front door. "I can't do this anymore. Not with you, not with the Yelvertons. I can't handle it."

"I don't buy it. Sorry, I need more information than that. You can't just leave me a voicemail, and it's over. Besides, your mom, and your sister—"

"Sorry," he repeated and shut the door between them.

Closing his eyes, he leaned against the portal.

The pain was eating him up from the inside out. His heart was on the other side of that door.

But his loyalty to the Shadows wouldn't let him go. He'd given them his word before he'd given it to her.

If he were a different man, he'd step away from it all to be with her. But like it or not, he was Trey Harding. And Trey Harding was a man who wasn't meant for the softness that Bethany Jernigan provided.

As much as it was killing him to admit that.

It was over. The dream was dead.

And he was the one holding the smoking gun.

"You've got to be kidding me."

She said it to the closed door in front of her, but it was mostly directed to the man who'd just shut it in her face.

Bethany's temper surged within her, a good dose of fear cresting the wave.

"Trey!" Her fist connected with the door, more a pound than a knock. "Open up and talk to me! You can't just disappear like this!"

But there was no answer from the other side.

Turning, she slumped against the door. *What now?*

When she'd set off for his place that afternoon, she'd been full of determination and righteous anger. He'd been dodging her for a week, that single voicemail the only indication he wasn't dead in a ditch somewhere. She'd been worried sick. But now that she'd seen him, seen the empty, cold look in his beautiful eyes as he'd turned away from her, she didn't know what to do.

"I love you, you idiot." She said it aloud, but there was nobody there to hear her words.

Setting her jaw, she stood and faced the door once again.

"I love you, Trey! You can't just walk away from me. It's not fair." Her voice was strained, but she didn't care. "It's not even about the wedding anymore. Not the wedding, not Sarah, not your mother. It's about you and me. And I need you."

Silence. Thick, heavy, silence.

The pain grew so big that it threatened to swallow her. But she wouldn't crumble. She wouldn't give in.

She was too angry for that.

"Fine. You don't have to love me back. But your family… You can't turn your back on them. And I will prove it to you or die trying."

Glaring at his door, she turned on her heel and stalked toward her car.

The windows of his house were blank, empty as she climbed into her car. He wasn't there watching her. Had he even heard her shout? She had no way to know. The engine rumbled to life, and she slowly drove away from his house, away from him.

Semper fi. Always faithful. The words echoed in her head as she left him.

There was too much of her father in her for her to give up now.

Tears clogged Trey's throat, a thousand knives lodged in his windpipe as he tried to breathe.

God. Why had she said that? Why had she told him the truth?

He could have pretended to be indifferent to her. He could have told himself that her infatuation with him had waned the moment he'd walked away from her.

But then she'd gone and told him the one thing he'd never heard from anyone's lips.

Ever.

I love you.

He didn't deserve it. He didn't deserve her. His soul was stained, dirty. Had she sullied herself by giving her heart to him?

Stumbling away from the front door, he looked out the window of his living room.

A faint cloud of dust hung over the gravel drive, empty except for his bike and his old pickup, as if she'd just passed over it.

She was gone.

As if drunk, he staggered down the hallway and into the bathroom. Without waiting for the water to warm up, he stripped and stepped into the shower.

Clean. He had to fix this. He wasn't clean enough for her, wasn't good enough for her love. He had to get cleaner, scrub the stain and sin and ugliness away.

But no matter how hard he washed, he couldn't scrub away Trey and reveal Samuel.

Tilting his head toward the spray, he shivered as the soap ran down his naked body.

He couldn't stop this. Couldn't change it.

But he could use it.

The cold suffused his limbs, filling his chest with an icy numbness that he embraced. And when he shut off the water and stepped out, it was with purpose.

Deftly toweling himself off, he stepped into his bedroom.

Boxer briefs. Leathers. A plain, black short-sleeved shirt, leaving the tattoos on his arms exposed. The damp ends of his hair left wet circles on the shoulders of his shirt.

He didn't give a good damn.

Stopping by the code-operated safe in his hall closet, he armed himself for the showdown.

A knife in the sheath at the back of his belt. Two handguns. Another smaller knife secreted in the top of his boot. He wouldn't leave anything to chance. There was a good possibility that he would put himself in the position of getting harmed, or even killed.

And honestly? That was okay by him. If he died in defense of the Shadows? It'd be a good way to go out.

"Wolf," he said into his cell phone as he walked to the other house. "I need everyone."

"No problem, Boss. We're all here."

Trey hiked up his eyebrow in surprise as he rounded the bend and took in the sight of a plethora of bikes clustered around the other house. "How'd you know I'd want to see everyone?"

"I didn't. We're working. Come on in, the door's open."

Wolf cut the call, and Trey stared at the phone for a moment before resuming his walk to Wolf's house.

Why the hell were they already together?

The easy chitchat and laughter that met his ears when he neared the front door would have sounded welcoming at any other time.

But now? With the ice still running through his veins, the cold need for violence still humming inside him?

It just pissed him off.

He shoved open the door.

At one point, he'd thought that nothing this band of bastards could do would surprise him. He'd watched them in all manner of odd scenarios throughout the years. From pranks that any teenager would have been proud to pull off, to drinking competitions culminating in wild escapades, to motorcycle tricks à la Evel Knievel.

But this? This was a whole new circle of hell.

"No, no, that's way too much essential oil." Ace was chiding Dean as the other man was hunkered over the stove, stirring something. "That's going to smell like a Tropicana factory butt-fucked a Bath and Body Works."

"Get lost, asswipe. I'm working on the wax. It's trial and error. Go harass Lars with his burlap bows some more. These last ones are hopeless." Dean pointed at a row of mason jars on the table where Lars was affixing brown fabric bows around the necks. The row at the end looked like little, drunk Doctor Whos.

Rocco, Flash, and Doc were pouring wax into jars and tying strings to little skewers, suspending them to form candlewicks. Jameson, his arm in a cast, was glowering at the rest of them from the corner.

"What the hell is going on here?"

Trey's roar barely registered on the Yankee Candle assembly line.

"Wedding favors," Wolf said casually as he hefted another box of mason jars onto the table beside Lars. "We realized that we hadn't done any yet."

Ace grinned. "My idea. I had a girl that was really into Pinterest. Downloaded the app so I could impress her. Found some cool shit. Apparently, handmade and rustic are 'in.'" He made air quotes.

Hands fisted at his sides, Trey stared at the sight in front of him.

No.

No.

Everything was different.

He'd screwed up. He'd screwed up so much.

The numbness inside him dissipated, the temporary bandage on the wound of his heart ripping in two, the pain spilling out and turning into rage.

"Get this shit out of here," Trey snarled, surging toward the table. He gripped the edge, sending jars crashing to the floor. He'd have flipped it if Wolf hadn't grabbed his arms and spun him away.

"Boss!"

"That's it. This is over. Drop this wedding bull, and don't think about it again. Suit up and get what you need. We're moving on Hampton tonight."

Eleven stunned gazes were trained on him, but Trey didn't give a damn.

"Fine with me," Jameson grunted, standing.

"Your ass is staying home. You need to heal up."

"But what about my candles?" Ace glowered at Trey,

his jaw set as he crossed his arms over his chest. "This beeswax is expensive, and it takes time—"

"Fuck your beeswax! It's over. We're not doing this wedding anymore."

Without another word, Trey stalked from the house. A heavy set of footfalls was close behind him. *Goddamn it*. Wolf. He wanted to turn around and deck the man, but he'd done enough.

He'd done more than enough.

"Boss."

Trey kept walking. He'd get to his house and get on his bike. If the rest of the Shadows knew what was good for them, they'd be armed and waiting for him when he got back there.

"Boss!"

Trey ran through the coming scenario. Going downtown during daylight was the best choice. They could hide out and watch whoever was coming and going from the warehouse. They'd split into three groups, one coming through the front door, another two flanking behind the warehouse to enter—

"Trey!"

At the sound of his name in that angry bellow, Trey finally stopped. He turned and faced the bearded, glowering giant who was his second-in-command. "What?"

"What the actual hell is wrong with you?" Wolf snarled the words, sounding angrier than Trey had ever heard him. "You got some kind of stick up your ass, that's fine. But why are you hauling off and making piss-poor, split-second decisions? It's not like you."

"Like me? Like who? Who am I? Do you know me? Do you really?" Trey stalked right up to Wolf, going nose to nose with him. "Maybe it's exactly like me. Maybe you've been wrong all along. Think about that."

"I know you. You're not the kind of person who would go off half-cocked like this." Wolf's tone eased a little, hard as nails but with half the volume. "You're not the kind of man that backs out of his obligations like this. You made a promise to do this wedding, didn't you?"

"That's none of your business." Trey shoved past him to continue on his way to his house.

"You made it my business when you dragged the Shadows into it!"

Wolf's yell echoed through the woods, an angry bellow that settled its full weight of guilt on Trey's shoulders.

"I know," Trey whispered. "I know."

"Then let us finish it."

"I can't. It's too… I can't." Rough as concrete, Trey's voice cracked. "We need to get Hampton taken care of. Then…then we'll discuss what to do about that."

"I can't convince you to take your time on this?"

Trey's phone chirped in his pocket with a new text message.

Justine.

G sed H's been w Vinnie lots n that he will b @ warehouse 2nite. IDK if that's who u r looking 4. GL.

Vinnie. That son of a bitch.

Trey looked up at Wolf, adrenaline surging through his veins.

"We're taking care of business tonight. Get ready. We roll out within the hour."

chapter

THIRTY

"What's this all about?" Sarah asked as she entered Mama Yelverton's living room.

Bethany had been there for a good two hours already. Her tension heightened, she'd kept Mama Yelverton's questions at bay as long as possible. But now that Sarah was there, she was going to lay it all out.

"Sit down," Bethany said, gesturing to the couch. Both Mama and Sarah sat, looking at her curiously.

"What's going on?" Mama's expression was concerned.

"I need to talk to you both." Bethany drew in a breath, hoping the extra oxygen would calm her vibrating nerves. "It's about Trey."

Sarah blanched slightly, but Mama showed no emotion. "Go on."

Bethany had decided this was the best decision. So she had to go through with it. God, this was scary. Wiping her damp palms on her jeans, she straightened her spine and said it.

"I'm in love with him."

Sarah's hand clapped over her mouth, but Mama laughed delightedly. "I knew it! I caught those looks that passed between the two of you. Oh, Bethy, I'm so happy for you."

Sarah sputtered a little. "But I thought you were dating his friend. The one with the weird name."

"All his friends have weird names. But no." Bethany shifted her weight to her other foot. "I lied to you because I was worried it would make you upset. And with your school winding down and the wedding, I wanted to keep as much stress off you as possible."

Sarah looked down at her hands. "I can understand that, but I wish you'd trusted me."

"Oh, Sarah." Bethany rushed to her side, sinking beside her on the couch. "I trust you completely. I do. I just was worried about you. Things have been so crazy lately—"

Sarah's smile sent a wave of relief through Bethany. "It's okay. I know your heart was in the right place."

"So, where is Trey? I haven't seen him or heard from him in days. Has he been working on the venue problem?"

Mama's innocent question sent Bethany spiraling right back into the depths of worry.

"That's the other thing I need to tell you. He's... Well, he's not a wedding planner."

"I knew it!" Sarah jumped off the couch. "I knew he wasn't!"

"Sarah," Mama chided her.

Beth continued. "He's an undercover cop. That's why he couldn't tell you what his job was. I promised I'd keep his secret, so you can't tell anyone. I wouldn't have told you now, but he's abandoning us, so I didn't feel I had a choice."

Mama Yelverton frowned. "An undercover..." She shook her head. "Of course we'll keep quiet. But where is he?"

"That's the thing. He's feeling guilty for lying to you." Bethany turned to Sarah. "To you both. He doesn't feel like he's good enough for this family."

Sarah snorted. "Well, that's total crap. I know I haven't exactly given him a ton of reasons to feel welcome, but is he really going to give up on Mom that easily?"

"Not if I can help it." Bethany pulled her phone free of her pocket and held it aloft. "If you guys agree, I'd like to arrange to meet up with him tonight so we all can gang up on him a little. Tell him that he does belong, that his past doesn't affect how we see him, and that we all want a relationship with him." Bethany's chin fell, and she stared down at her toes. "Even if he doesn't love me back, I don't want his relationship with the two of you to end because of that."

Mama nodded, and Sarah backed her up. "We'll do it. But do you think he'll agree to see us?"

Bethany looked down at her phone. "There's only one way to know."

The late-afternoon light spilled over the concrete and metal surfaces that surrounded them downtown. Trey shifted his position, the chipping paint of the back wall of Cherry Ice falling to the pavement below.

"Boss."

Trey looked over. Doc was jogging toward him, a

serious expression on his dark features. "Lars just texted. A big, black Escalade just pulled up behind the warehouse."

Trey nodded. "Okay. Keep watch here. I'll circle and get a better look."

Doc nodded and pulled his ball cap low over his features as he took Trey's position.

Reaching into his pocket, Trey pulled his phone free. He tapped out a text to Wolf.

Doc is watching CI's door. I'm rounding 2 back of warehouse 2 check out new arrival.

The answer hit him back right away.

K. Side door still clear.

Trey broke into a jog, phone still in hand. He was crossing the street when the sound of screeching tires met his ears.

"Shit!"

He dove for the curb, barely escaping a collision with a faded-black Ford with heavily tinted windows.

The horn blared, the driver waving an angry middle finger out the window as the car continued down the street without slowing. It disappeared around the corner, not bothering to stop for the light.

Trey brushed his hands off on his leathers. Bits of gravel had ground into the meat of his palms. But where had his phone landed?

Glancing over his shoulder, he spotted it in the middle of the road. But before he could retrieve it, the sound of voices approaching had him diving for cover again, this time behind the dumpster in the alley between the warehouse and the empty storefront that sat beside it.

Trey peered out from the gap between the dumpster and the wall.

There were four of them. Hampton, Rat, someone Trey didn't recognize, and Vinnie.

Trey's hands curled into fists.

They crossed the street, heading toward the warehouse and Trey's hiding place. He held his breath as Vinnie stopped in the middle of the road.

He crouched down and scooped up Trey's phone. Trey bit back an irritated growl as Vinnie looked it over, then pocketed the phone.

The group continued to the front door of the warehouse, disappearing inside, still talking and laughing.

Trey waited, one heartbeat, two, three, before moving. He hustled to the back of the warehouse where Lars, Flash, and Dean were stationed.

He'd have to get a phone off one of them. It had been an unbelievably stupid mistake to lose his. And now it was in the hands of the enemy.

A mirthless grin spread across Trey's cheeks as he flattened against the wall, looking carefully before moving behind the building.

It didn't matter. He'd have his phone back in a matter of hours.

And Vinnie would be sorry he'd ever crossed the Shadows, and Trey in particular.

Bethany's hands didn't tremble a bit as she composed the text to Trey, even though her insides were nearly vibrating from the stress.

This had to work. He couldn't just walk out of their lives. Hers—well, she couldn't deny that she was praying he'd give them another chance. But if nothing else, he couldn't walk away from the family that had just found him after all these years.

They needed him, and he needed them.

She read over what she'd written.

Trey, I know what you said. But I'm not ready to give up on you, on us. And your family needs you too. Your mom, your sister, and I would like to come see you tonight and talk things through.

She bit her lip, debating for a second.

Should she add it? She'd said it out loud, but she had no way to know if he'd heard it. And if he hadn't? Well, she didn't want her admission of her feelings to come via text.

Selfishly, she wanted to see his face when she told him again.

Text me back, please.

"And, sent." She looked over at Mama Yelverton and Sarah, who had been talking in low voices while she texted. When she spoke, they looked over at her.

"So what if he says no?"

Bethany looked down at the phone in her hands. "He won't."

Sarah didn't look convinced, but Mama Yelverton's eyes were clear and bright as she nodded.

"Whatever it takes."

When her phone vibrated in her hand, so suddenly and unexpectedly, Bethany jumped. She had to swipe the screen three times before it would unlock.

632 Industrial Drive. C u there.

Hope flared to life in her heart as she read the text again.

It was brief, but it was an opening. A chance to lay out their case to him.

Bethany memorized the address, then shoved the phone in her pocket.

"I'll drive," she said with a smile. "Let's go get him."

Bethany's phone GPS took her to an area of downtown that she wasn't overly familiar with. She had been through there a time or two, when she and Sarah had gone club hopping downtown, but they had never stopped. The seedy strip joint wasn't exactly their scene, and the warehouse just across the street behind definitely gave her a big case of the heebie-jeebies.

"Are you sure this is the place?" In the passenger seat beside her, Sarah leaned forward and looked out the window as Bethany parallel parked. "This kind of makes me wish I had brought my pepper spray with me."

"Yeah." Bethany cut the engine and pointed at the number spray-painted above the warehouse's ratty-looking door. "There it is, 632 Industrial Drive. It really is a weird place for him to want to meet though."

Her stomach was tense, butterflies bouncing around the cold knot that had settled in the center. But she had to do this. No matter how scared she was, this was their chance to get Trey back. Not just for her, but for him and for the Yelvertons. For everything they had done for her.

If she did nothing else to help heal the wounds that Trey's disappearance had left, it wouldn't even come close to repaying the debt she owed them. But she had to try.

"Well, I guess we go inside." Mama Yelverton pushed open the backseat door and stepped out. Bethany and Sarah followed suit. Bethany pressed the door lock on her key fob three times, just in case.

Their footsteps made echoing sounds in the long afternoon shadows as they walked across the street. With each step, Bethany's confidence wavered.

The text had been so short, so terse. Was he angry? Was that why he just wanted to meet them fast and get it over with? Was he going to take one look at them and tell them to get lost for good?

Suck it up, Beth. He doesn't call you Strong Girl for nothing.

She curled her hands into fists at her sides and steeled her resolve. They would talk things out, and it would be okay. It had to be.

At the door, Bethany hesitated before knocking.

"Maybe we should go." Sarah was looking around nervously. "I just don't like this at all."

"This is a really odd place for Trey to want to meet. Maybe we should take a second to think about it." Even Mama Yelverton was nodding.

Bethany paused, weighing their options. Her instincts were definitely screaming at her to take notice, but the longing in her heart for Trey was blinding her to good sense. A hand on her arm stopped her just before she knocked.

"Come on. We'll invite him over to the house and try to get him to see reason." Sarah pulled her back toward the car. "Let's go."

"But—" Before Bethany could get out a protest, the door to the warehouse flew open.

Mama Yelverton, who hadn't stepped back as quickly as Sarah and Bethany had, was the first to be grabbed. She yelled in surprise, then quickly recovered, pinning a strained smile on her face.

"Vincent. Oh my goodness, you startled me. Why are you here? Are you friends with Trey?" Mama Yelverton's tone was thin, high. Bethany and Sarah hesitated, only a step off the curb.

The man she had called Vincent—a pale, wire-thin man with a greasy ponytail and a gold tooth—grinned. Bethany disliked him on sight, the grip he had on Mama Yelverton's arm cementing the opinion instantly.

"Well, lookee here what we got." He ran a finger down Mama Yelverton's cheek. Beside her, Bethany could have sworn she heard Sarah growl. "I didn't expect all this. I just figured I'd get Mr. Boss Man's girl, and here's an old friend too. Come on in the house, get comfortable."

"Bethany. Run," Sarah whispered hastily, then yanked her away from the door.

Bethany hesitated, reaching for Mama Yelverton, but just then Vincent's backup appeared.

"Not so fast." Two more men had appeared behind Vincent. Bethany started to run, but she wasn't fast enough. One of them grabbed her with a vicious grip around her forearm, causing a burning, twisting pain that took her breath away.

With one last pained look over her shoulder, Sarah took off at a dead run. Her footsteps pounded down the alleyway, and Bethany watched helplessly as another two thugs gave chase.

Sarah was fast, but would she be fast enough to get away and call someone for help?

Bethany could only pray.

"Don't worry, they won't hurt her too bad." Vincent laughed as he dragged Mama Yelverton through the doors.

Bethany's arm screamed in pain as the man holding her cranked it high behind her back. She stumbled as he shoved her forward into the darkness of the warehouse.

It took a long, scary moment for her eyes to adjust. Blinking furiously, she peered into the blackness.

The warehouse was musty, the floor caked with dust and dirt. Concrete columns dotted the place, doing an imitation of holding the shabby roof up. Tables and chairs were stacked along one wall, looking like a restaurant of some type had closed down and the items had been dumped there to decay. Boxes and bags containing she didn't know what lined the back of the place.

A stack of chairs leaned drunkenly against the back wall, several of them having been pulled down to accommodate about eight more men sitting around, smoking, and looking curiously at the newcomers.

Bethany's blood ran cold.

She knew now with almost complete certainty that Trey had not been the one to respond to her text message.

Sarah had been right. They should've kept on driving and not stopped.

She had led them straight into a trap, and she had no one to blame but herself.

chapter

THIRTY-ONE

TREY HAD SEEN SOME BAD THINGS IN HIS LIFETIME. Seen friends hurt, seen people turn their backs on him, watched the train wreck of drugs and alcohol destroy lives.

But he'd never been as terrified as when he saw Vinnie's thugs grab Bethany and his mother and drag them into that warehouse.

He surged to his feet, almost rounding the dumpster before his brain kicked in.

Don't be stupid. You can't do this on your own.

Rapid, desperate footfalls pounded down the alleyway where he still hid, just out of sight of the front door. A mirthless grin spread across his face, and he waited.

One.

Two.

On three, he stepped out from behind the dumpster and grabbed Sarah, spinning her around behind him and facing her pursuers.

Two of Vinnie's meathead pals had ground to a sudden halt when they saw that their prey wasn't alone.

"Trey!" Sarah's breathless voice was surprised, shrill.

"Stay back," he warned her, holding an arm out behind him to keep her there.

"No worries there," she said dryly, crouching down and scooping up a double handful of gravel from the ground beneath them.

If he'd had the time, he'd have been impressed at her forethought to grab something to defend herself with, small though it was. But he was too busy sizing up the competition and making a game plan.

"Who the hell do you think you are?" the bigger one spat, an ugly sneer curling his upper lip.

"I'm her brother, and I'm going to fuck you up," Trey said, and then he lunged.

Fists flew, grunts and explosions of pain being traded among the three. Trey roared as one of them pulled a knife and got in a shallow slash on his upper thigh before he kicked the thug away.

A solid elbow to the temple took out the bigger one, who dropped like a sack of wet sand to the pavement.

Rising to his feet in a loose, easy crouch, Trey reached back to the sheath on his belt and freed his knife. The shorter one's blade was stained with Trey's blood, and that made him less inclined to take it easy on the bastard.

"Trey! Look out!"

The shriek came from behind him, and he ducked on instinct. A shower of gravel shot above his head, deflecting the lunge from a guy who had crept up undetected.

Yelling, the man fell backward, rubbing furiously at his eye. Sarah had good aim, apparently.

Time to end this.

With a quick movement, Trey knocked the knife

from the small guy's hand. A love tap to the skull put him on the pavement beside his friend.

Standing over the one Sarah's well-timed throw had incapacitated, Trey looked over his shoulder at his sister.

"Good aim."

Sarah shrugged. "I played a lot of softball when I was young."

Just to make sure their new friend stayed down, Trey gave him a well-placed kick to the ribs. Then he grabbed Sarah's hand, and together they hurried around to the back of the warehouse.

"Is this where your police backup is?"

Trey groaned. "Did Bethany tell you that?"

Sarah nodded. "She had to. You were threatening to walk out on us, like a moron. Why'd you hide something like that?"

"It's complicated, and not exactly…" Trey ran an irritated hand through his hair. "We don't have time for this. Listen. I'm going to get Bethany and Mom out of this. But you're going to have to trust me. Things aren't what you might have heard, but there's no time."

Sarah stared at him, long and hard.

"Just tell me one thing. Do you love them?"

"I swear to you, Sarah, I do."

And he did. Not just Bethany, who'd rocked his world and made him believe he could truly be happy, but Mrs. Yelverton. His mother. The woman who'd moved heaven and earth to bring her son home.

Mom.

"I'll do anything to keep them safe."

She looked deep into his eyes. "Okay. You get this

one chance. But if it goes wrong, understand that I might never forgive you."

"I wouldn't ask you to."

When they got to the dark corner of the neighboring building where five of the Shadows were gathered, surprised looks greeted them.

"Boss! I've been waiting to hear from you."

Trey nudged Sarah forward. "Vinnie's got my cell, and he used it to lure Beth and my mom and sister here. Sarah's okay, but I need one of you to get her away from here. Stone?"

The short, stocky guy stood and nodded. "I'll be happy to."

"Trey," Sarah said.

"Yeah?"

"Keep them safe." She gripped his hand so hard her knuckles cracked.

"I swear to you I will."

Stone escorted Sarah away, and Trey looked at his brothers.

His family. And they'd help him rescue his other family.

He wasn't sure what star he'd been born under, but it was turning out a lot luckier than he'd ever anticipated it would be.

"Here's what we're going to do," he said.

When Bethany had first met Mama Yelverton, she'd been an introverted twelve-year-old with an acne problem who was convinced that the only person she could count on was her father.

But then she'd met Sarah. Funny, fierce, brave Sarah,

who'd basically declared without any warning that she and Bethany would be best friends. And when she'd brought Bethany home to her very first sleepover?

Bethany had never imagined there could be someone like Mama Yelverton. So caring, so strong, so loving to people not even in her own family.

So, the presence of the closest person she'd had to a real mother helped her tremendously as Vincent and his friends shoved them into the back corner of the warehouse and tied them to a couple of half-broken chairs.

"Your boyfriend should be here soon," Vincent said, smiling as he watched his underlings wind duct tape around Bethany's and Mama Yelverton's wrists. "I've been waiting for this."

"What do you want with him?" Bethany asked angrily as she jerked ineffectively at her bonds. Her skin burned in protest.

"Vincent, this isn't the path you want to take," Mama Yelverton said gently, not moving against the bindings. "You'd been doing so well. And you can again. A mistake doesn't have to cost you your future. You can stop this now. Let us go, and I'll do whatever I can to help you."

Vincent lunged forward so fast Bethany almost missed it. The loud crack of his hand across Mama Yelverton's face made Bethany cry out in impotent shock and anger.

"Shut up! You know, people like you don't know shit about what it's like to be someone like me. Now keep your mouth shut before I shut it for you. Actually…" He reached over and grabbed the roll of tape.

"No!" Bethany cried out as he slapped the length over Mama Yelverton's mouth.

A tear ran over the silvery fabric, and she hung her head.

"I don't understand," Bethany said, anger pitching her voice low. "Did Trey arrest you at some point? Is that why you want revenge?"

Vincent barked a laugh. "Arrest me? What, like he's some kind of cop?"

Bethany bit her lip. She'd really stepped in it now. Trey was working undercover, and she'd just tried to blow it.

"No, I didn't arrest him. But if he doesn't let you go, they might have to lock me up for manslaughter."

"Trey!" She'd never been happier to see him in her life.

There, striding through the doorway, was Trey. Behind him walked the big, black-clad, tattooed men who'd helped him with the wedding she'd seen. His friends. His...fellow cops?

But none of them had badges. She couldn't help but see the guns tucked into waistbands, the baseball bats a couple of them held, the eager way they sized up the competition...

"About time you showed up," Vincent said, drawing himself up to his full height. He was a good six inches shorter than Trey, but that didn't stop him from sidling up in front of the bigger man as if he were his equal.

"You've been cooking in my territory," Trey said, looking down his nose at the other man. Vincent's friends had gathered around behind him.

Trey's gang was outnumbered by at least four men. A shiver ran through Bethany.

"I've done what I had to do to keep my business afloat."

"And I'll do what I have to do to keep that shit out of my house," Trey countered. "Let them go so we can settle this."

"As if I'd hand you my best bargaining chip. Now, let's make a deal. I'll let your girlfriend and your *mother*"—he sneered the word—"go, if you agree to keep your biker assholes away from my dealers. You're interfering in my business, and I can't have that."

"No."

Vincent trembled with rage. "What do you mean, no?"

Trey hiked up an eyebrow. "Did I stutter? I said no."

"I'm just giving the people what they want."

"And so am I. There are plenty of other places to peddle your poison. Move on, or face the consequences."

Vincent bared his teeth. "You think you're such hot shit. You walk around like you own everything around here. I'm not the only one who's sick of you."

"Boss, I'm tired of conversation," Wolf said, his dark eyes positively glinting. "Can we take care of business now?"

Trey grinned, a dark, evil expression that both scared and thrilled Bethany. "Do it."

Fists were flying, knives flashing, grunts and curses and angry yells filling the air like a cloud of violent dust.

Bethany struggled against her bonds, but they held tight. But in the chaos, a large man with a dark complexion and a ball cap pulled low over his eyes appeared at their side.

She started to call out in fear, but he clapped a hand over her mouth.

"I'm with Trey," he said, and she nodded. Working quickly, he slashed the duct tape that held her wrists together. Bending down, he freed her ankles. "You both need to get out of here before the cops come in to cause trouble. We won't be able to protect you then."

He handed Bethany the knife, handle first, and melted back into the fight.

The cops? Trouble? But weren't they on the same side?

Adrenaline surging, Bethany searched for Trey in the fray.

There he was. Moving as fast as lightning, as swift and sure in his strikes as a jungle cat. He attacked and withdrew, dancing on his feet as his opponents rushed him.

She cried out when she saw him take a heavy fist to the ribs.

Mama Yelverton let out a muffled sound beside her, yanking her back to the present.

Trey's friend was right. She had to get them out of there.

Bethany bent down and removed the duct tape from Mama Yelverton's ankles as fast as she could. Behind her, the battle raged on.

She pulled the tape from Mama Yelverton's mouth, wincing in sympathy at the red streak where the tape had affected her skin.

"Hurry," Mama Yelverton urged in a low voice. "They're losing."

Heart in her throat, Bethany looked over her shoulder.

Trey's Shadows were outnumbered, and all she could see were Vincent's cronies and their flying fists. But were they—the Shadows—holding back?

She didn't understand. Didn't have the time.

Slamming her eyes shut, she turned and cut and yanked the tape free from Mama Yelverton's wrists.

Trey could take care of himself for now. She had to get Mama Yelverton out of there. And then... And then...

She'd figure out what to do.

"Let's go," she said, and Mama Yelverton stood, wincing as circulation returned to her feet.

As quickly as they could, they dashed to the door.

With one last glance over her shoulder, Bethany wished Trey luck.

He had to last through this. Whoever—and whatever—he was. It didn't matter. She didn't know what she'd do without him.

chapter

THIRTY-TWO

FROM HIS POSITION ON THE FLOOR, TREY WATCHED AS Bethany and his mother left the warehouse. The door shut behind them. At Trey's nod, Mac slipped out too.

He had a call to make.

One.

Two.

Three.

"Now!" Trey roared as he surged upward. At his call, Wolf, Flash, Doc, and Lars—who had all been on the floor playing possum too—gave their respective assailants hell.

Knowing that his precious ones were safe gave Trey the strength to push through the pain of his wounds and make Vinnie and his men pay.

He fought his way through flying fists and angry kicks to his target—

Vinnie.

"Screw this," the drug dealer was saying and turning tail to run for the door. Once he'd realized that the

Shadows wouldn't go down easily, he wasn't interested anymore.

"Not so fast," Trey said, his arm going around Vinnie's neck. "I need information from you."

"Fuck off," Vinnie said, clawing at Trey's arm.

"You said that you weren't the only one who was coming for us. Who else?"

Vinnie's teeth sank into Trey's arm. With a curse, he shoved the bastard away.

Straight into a concrete column.

Knocked cold, Vinnie slumped to the floor.

"Boss! We've got company," Rocco yelled into the warehouse. They could just make out the sounds of sirens in the distance. Mac had done his job well.

"Let's go," Trey said. He knelt down and removed his phone from Vinnie's pocket and beat feet for the door. The rest of the Shadows scattered.

Outside, Trey looked over to where Bethany's car had been parked. It was gone, thank God.

He slung his leg over his bike and peeled away. Behind him, the rest of the Shadows fell in line.

It was over. They were going home. And now… And now…

He wasn't sure what. There might not be a home to go back to.

Because without her, his former existence felt empty.

They pulled off the road at Ruby's and took stock of their injuries. Minor cuts, scrapes, and bruises marred the crew, nothing too serious. Stone had reported back after dropping Sarah at the Yelverton place. The police scanner was abuzz with the news of the big bust that had taken place downtown. A large amount of meth had been taken into custody, along with Vinnie, Hampton, and most of the network of dealers.

It was a clean sweep. So why did Trey still feel so awful?

"You off to see her?"

Trey looked up at Wolf's question. He'd been heading for the door when his second-in-command had stopped him.

"Yeah."

Wolf nodded. "She's a good woman."

"Too good for me."

"Probably. Doesn't mean she doesn't want you too."

Trey cleared his throat. "I'm going to apologize for dragging her into that shit and lying to her, then I'm out of her life for good."

Wolf hiked a brow at him and gave a cryptic smile. "Good luck with that."

Without bothering to reply, Trey headed out the door into the late-spring night.

The weather was warm, ideal for riding his bike into the darkness, but he couldn't enjoy it. Not really. Not with his future in such doubt.

By the time his tires touched the drive that led to the Yelvertons' house, to her, he'd convinced himself that it was a waste of time. She'd never forgive him for leading her into that danger. And his mother, and his sister...

Trey winced as he cut the engine in their driveway.

He was exactly the kind of person he didn't want any of them around. But he didn't know any other way to be.

"Better get this over with," he muttered to himself.

Hefting himself off his bike, he walked quickly to the front door before he could change his mind.

Before he could knock, the door was flung open.

"Trey." His name left his mother's lips on a choked sob, and suddenly he was in her arms.

Too surprised to move for a moment, he swayed a little. She clung to him, desperate devotion in every shuddering breath she took.

He closed his eyes and hugged her back.

His mother. Not Mrs. Yelverton anymore. This was his mother.

"I'm sorry," he whispered to the top of her head. "I'm so sorry."

"Hush," she said, wiping her eyes. "I'm just relieved you're okay." She ran her hands down his arms and gripped his palms. "Come in."

Holding his mother's hand, he walked into the living room.

And there, with a carefully blank expression on her face, stood Bethany.

His heart.

The love of his life.

She raised her arms to him, and he crossed the room at a dead run.

Cradling her close, he didn't realize he was speaking until long moments later. "I'm sorry. I love you. I'm sorry. I love you. I'm sorry."

Over and over, the words left his lips. He'd wanted to say so much to her, but when it came down to it, the only important things to convey were the depth of his regret and the breadth of his love for her.

"I love you too," she whispered and then kissed him.

With all the feeling inside him, he returned the gesture. Deep, passionate, with every bit of the longing and fear he'd felt in the last few days, he kissed her.

It wasn't enough. He could kiss her like that all day, every day, and it wouldn't be enough.

He was desperately in love with her, and if she'd let him, he planned to spend the rest of his life trying to show her.

When she finally pulled away, she wiped at her tears. "I love you, but there's so much. So many things, the lies…"

"I know," he said, the hole in his chest aching as if he'd been shot point-blank. "I know." But then he noticed someone else in the room.

"Hey," Sarah said, looking a little hesitant.

"Hey," he said back, his arm around Bethany's shoulders. There'd be time to explain himself to her. If she'd forgive him? Who knew.

"So, you're not a wedding planner."

Trey shook his head. "No, I'm not."

"And you're not a cop."

He glanced down at Bethany guiltily before answering. "No, not a cop either."

"So, what exactly are you?"

He swallowed hard. "Maybe we all should sit down."

So they did, and he told them. About the Shadows and the jobs they did, the way they skirted the law. And through it all, he watched for Bethany's reactions.

She was clearly surprised, but there was no hatred or disgust on her face. And through it all, she never let go of his hand.

He was grateful for that. Maybe there was hope.

"Wow." Sarah sat back against the cushions of the couch once he'd finished. "That's... Wow."

"I'm sorry I lied to you. To you all." Trey rubbed a thumb over the *n* tattooed on his knuckle.

"Trey, I have to tell you the truth." His mother looked over at him with a slightly guilty expression. "I knew you weren't a wedding planner."

His mouth fell open. "What?"

She laughed a little. "It was obvious, honey. But you were so determined to pull it off that I wanted to give you the chance. And call your bluff a little. But up until about a week ago, you were really pulling it off. I've been impressed."

Trey looked at the floor, the memory of his disappearing act chafing. "Yeah. Sorry about that. I hope I haven't wrecked things."

"Not at all." His mother laughed. "I haven't had this much excitement in a long time."

"Or hopefully ever again," Sarah muttered. She stood and walked over to her mother. "Come on, you've still got sticky stuff on your wrists from that tape. I've got some baby oil upstairs that will take it off."

"We'll be upstairs if you need us," his mother said with a smile at him and Bethany, and allowed Sarah to lead her upstairs.

Alone, Trey looked at the woman beside him. "Do you think you can forgive me for being such a lying bastard?"

"I don't know." She looked at the back door. "Want to take a walk?"

"Sure," he said, lacing his fingers through hers. Anything she wanted. "Let's go."

His mother's backyard was a beautifully landscaped private garden, complete with a paved path and a tiny koi pond in the corner. Hand in hand, he and Bethany wandered through the late-spring blooms, the stars twinkling brightly overhead.

"Why did you do it?" Her voice was barely above a whisper.

"Lie to you?" He took a deep, steadying breath. "Because it was easier than letting you know the truth. Because I was afraid that if I told you I was in a biker gang instead of a police squad, that you'd run away. And since you're the best damn thing that ever happened to me, I couldn't face that idea."

She sank down onto the bench beside the koi pond. Behind her, a flowering dogwood's petals rippled softly in the breeze. He sat down beside her, wishing like hell he knew what to say to make this all better.

"You hurt me," she said, no trace of malice in her words.

He didn't think she could have said anything that would have made him feel worse than that.

"I'd do anything to take it back," he said honestly, squeezing her hand. "I know you've got no reason to forgive me. But I swear, I would do anything to make it up to you."

She gave him a small smile, and hope leapt in his heart.

"I believe you. And I want to move forward. I've spent too long trying to heal old wounds. I have to give myself permission to move on. To be happy."

A tear ran down her cheek, and Trey put his arm around her shoulders. Tucking her close to his side, he waited, silently lending her his strength.

"My father made me promise to take care of my grandmother. Before he died. And that woman has put me through hell. But now?" She looked up at Trey. "I know what to do now. My uncle's moving her in with him. And he'll take care of her, for the money that'll be there after she dies if nothing else." She gave a sad laugh. "In a way, they're perfect for each other. And my promise to Dad will be finished. I don't think he meant to chain me to her for life."

"If he was anything like you," Trey said, holding her close, "he'd have moved heaven and earth to see you happy."

Bethany laid her head on his shoulder. "I think so. And I want to be with you. I'm choosing you. If you promise me one thing."

"Anything."

Her hand brushed his cheek as she turned him to face her.

"Never lie to me again. And promise you'll never leave me. I can deal with a lot of things, like you being the head of a biker gang, but the one thing I can't deal with is being without you."

"I swear," he said and bent down to kiss her. "I love you, Bethany Jernigan," Trey murmured against her mouth.

"And I love you, Trey Harding. No matter what. I love you."

They spent a long night at the Yelverton home, talking, laughing, apologizing, getting to know one another. It was one of the happiest nights in Trey's memory.

The next morning, while he was with Bethany,

Sarah, and his mother in the kitchen, preparing a Food Network–worthy breakfast, Trey's cell phone buzzed.

Sarah, sitting at the counter beside him, stopped peeling mid-orange.

"Who's that? The mafia?" She winked as if to make sure he knew she was joking.

"No, it's the FBI. They want to hire me." He swiped the answer-call button. "What is it, Ace?"

"Hey, Boss," he said, sounding a little jittery. "Listen. I know you're probably busy, and you're going to kick my ass for asking this, but… I mean, since it's so close, and we've done all this work…"

"The wedding job is back on."

Ace's whoop was so loud it made Sarah jump beside him.

"Really? You mean it?"

Trey laughed. "I do." He covered the speaker and addressed his mother. "Hey, Mom, you still want the rest of the bikers to help with this wedding?"

Mom grinned. "Of course."

"What?" Sarah squawked. Bethany giggled.

Trey moved his hand and spoke into the phone again. "Gather up the rest of the asylum, and you guys meet us here." He rattled off the address.

For the next half hour, there was a huge amount of cooking, laughing, and a good dose of sheer panic from Sarah once she'd figured out that it was true—a biker gang was actually planning her wedding. But when the guys arrived, it was as if they had always been part of the family.

Mom cooed over Ace's new vision board, done in more proper colors of gray and turquoise this time.

Bethany and Doc worked in the kitchen, perfecting ideas for the wedding food. Wolf, Dean, and Sarah talked about the platform and archway for the end of the aisle.

And Trey? He watched them all, wondering how he'd gotten so lucky to have a family like this.

It must have been some lucky star shining that night when he'd been born.

When Doc was called to another part of the house, Trey slipped into the kitchen behind Bethany, who was looking on her phone for wedding recipes.

"Hey," he said, wrapping his arms around her.

"Hi," she said, looking up at him with a smile.

"Listen, I know I've apologized for the lying, but I wanted you to know I'm sorry again for leaving you with the venue problem. I feel really bad about that."

"Well," she said, turning in his arms, her cheeks pinkening suspiciously, "you actually can make up for that."

"Really? I'll do anything," he said, bending down to brush her lips with his.

"You can let us use your house."

"*What?*"

chapter

THIRTY-THREE

"Oh God, I can't find my veil. Bethy! Bethy!"

Laughing, Bethany ran into the room.

"Sarah, relax. It's right here. It was a little crumpled on one side so I was steaming it. Here."

Sarah obediently bent down so Bethany could affix the veil to the cascade of golden curls that tumbled down her back.

"There." Bethany stepped to the side to admire her work. "You're perfect."

Sarah's smile was brilliant. "It's all thanks to you. I can't imagine having pulled this off without you. And Mom. And even Trey." She laughed, picking up the bouquet of orchids and peonies that Hawk had dropped off earlier. "God, is it really time?"

Bethany nodded, picking up her own bouquet. "It is."

Together, they walked down the hall of Trey's house, out onto the deck, and down the stairs. The crowd was visible through the windows, seated in front of the beautiful custom arch that Wolf and the other Shadows had built beside the picturesque pond.

The flowers, the music, all of it was straight out of a fairy-tale wedding. A surge of pride filled Bethany's chest as she took it all in.

They'd done that. She, and Trey, and Mama Yelverton, and the rest of the Shadows. After several disasters and lots of false starts, they'd ended up with a beautiful ceremony.

"Let's get you married," she said to Sarah, pressing a kiss to her friend's cheek before walking down the aisle. Her turquoise maid-of-honor dress swished around her knees, the delicate color offset by the pink and white in the stems of the flowers she held.

Smiling, she walked sedately down the aisle, accompanied by the string quartet's classical music. But she didn't look at the beautiful decorations or the smiling crowd.

Instead, she only had eyes for the man in the front row, seated on the bride's side, right next to Mama Yelverton.

Trey.

He looked immaculately handsome in a well-fitting suit, at odds with his usual gruff biker style. But damn if it didn't do it for her. Her stomach fluttered at the thought of taking it off him later.

God, he was amazing. And he was all hers.

He gave her a wink, and she blushed, stopping at the front of the crowd and taking her position next to the custom platform Wolf and the others had constructed for the bride, groom, and officiant.

The ceremony went beautifully, and there were more than a few tears when Sarah and Mark exchanged their vows. The reception was perfect with food and wine and music and laughter in the rooms of the big house that Wolf and some of the other bikers shared, Trey's place being too small for the after-ceremony party.

A perfect send-off for her best friend, and as Sarah and Mark got ready to leave, Bethany pressed an envelope into her bestie's hand.

"What's this?"

"A little something from Trey and me," Bethany said with a smile. "Don't open it until you get to the hotel."

Sarah shook her head. "You've done too much."

"Not as much as you've done for me." A little choked up, Bethany gave Sarah a quick hug. "Now get going, or your new hubby will come looking for you!"

With a wave, Sarah was gone.

Back in the much-emptier living room, where the music had stopped and only a few stragglers were finishing their drinks, Bethany sank down into the empty chair beside Trey.

"Go okay?" He pressed a kiss to her cheek as he asked the question softly.

"Yup. She didn't suspect a thing."

Trey grinned. "Good."

"You're kind of proud of yourself, aren't you?"

"Why shouldn't I be? She's always dreamed about hiking in the Alps, according to Mom. She wouldn't have taken a gift like that trip directly from me, so how was I supposed to get it to her otherwise?"

Bethany shook her head. "You're too good."

"Not good enough for you." He nuzzled her ear, and she trembled.

"Jeez, are you guys ever going to get a room?" Ace threw a mint at them, which Trey deflected with a glare.

"Watch it, asswipe."

Just then, Mama Yelverton came toward them, an exhausted smile on her face. Trey jumped up and dragged a chair from a nearby table, and she gratefully settled into it.

"Thank you," she said as Trey sank back down beside Bethany. "I'm exhausted."

"It was a beautiful ceremony," Bethany said, patting Mama Yelverton's hand. "You should be proud."

"You and Trey and the Shadows pulled it off. I barely did anything."

Bethany looked down at her hands. "Actually, it's led me to a discovery. I want to do this." She gestured around them. "The organizing, the planning, helping people create their dream weddings. I think I finally know what I want to do when I grow up." She grinned at her surrogate mother. "I want to be a wedding planner."

An odd, mischievous light climbed into Mama Yelverton's eyes, and she leaned forward. "As a matter of fact, that gives me a brilliant idea. Come on. There's something I want to discuss with you."

"Uh-oh," Trey said. "Why is this making me nervous?"

"I've got a proposition for you. For all of you," Mama Yelverton said, nodding at the rest of the Shadows who were scattered around the hall. "May I?"

At Trey's nod, Wolf gathered the rest of the Shadows around the table. Bethany laced her fingers through Trey's and shot him a questioning glance. He just shrugged.

"Now," Mama Yelverton said, templing her fingers as she looked at each of them in turn, "I know that the Iron Knot wasn't exactly a business in the beginning, but you have to admit that this was a beautiful wedding."

"Fucking amazing," Doc said, and everyone else laughed and agreed.

"The favors were perfect," Ace said, patting the mason jar candle in front of him. "Everybody commented on them."

"Exactly so." Mama Yelverton smiled over at Bethany. "Considering the soul-searching that Beth has been doing lately, and the way this came together, I think that this could be a lucrative business for all of you."

Silence fell, broken a minute later by a slight cough.

"You mean, like, permanent?" Dean's eyebrows had climbed halfway to his hairline. "Like, weddings all the time?"

Mama Yelverton nodded. "I do. Let me explain. You had everything taken care of. Bethany nailed the concept. Trey delegated, organized, and negotiated. You all performed your roles perfectly. The only spanner in the works was the venue, correct?"

Bethany nodded, conscious of Trey's position change in the seat beside her. He was leaning forward, as if listening harder to his mother's words.

"Do you remember that Victorian house that's in the woods before you get to my place? That beautiful home that's run-down?"

Trey nodded.

"The man that lived there has finally agreed to sell it to me. I close on it next weekend."

"That's a gorgeous place," Wolf grunted. "It'd take a lot of work to fix it up though."

"I know. But when I look at the work you did here, I know that you and the Shadows could take it on. Here's what I propose. The Iron Shadows become the Iron Knot

Wedding Planning Venue and Service. You fix up that house and host weddings there, and I'll provide any start-up capital you need for a stake in the business. On one condition."

Bethany couldn't believe her ears.

"Name it," Trey said.

Mama Yelverton smiled. "That you hire people from Sam's Place whenever possible. Servers, bartenders, setup work, whatever you can."

Trey looked around at the table, and Bethany followed his gaze.

One by one, the Shadows were nodding. Only a couple still looked nonplussed, but eventually they gave sharp nods to indicate their agreement.

Trey squeezed Bethany's hand.

"Strong Girl? What do you think? This is your dream. Would you mind if a bunch of obstinate assholes joined you?"

Bethany laughed. "We'd be amazing. Let's do it."

"Mom? You've got yourself a deal." Trey shook his mother's hand, Ace whooped, and Dean socked his friend on the shoulder.

Conversations broke out—Wolf talking through the upcoming renovation, Ace yelling at Dean for his supposed abuse, and Doc outlining recipes for the next reception. Flash picked up Mama Yelverton and spun her in a circle.

Bethany laughed, but out of the corner of her eye, she watched Jameson exit the room.

He'd been one of the holdouts. She hoped he was okay.

"Beth."

She looked up at Trey, beyond overjoyed that this man was hers.

"Yes?"

"Come with me."

He led her to a set of sliding glass doors at the far end of the room, then slid them open. A small deck looked over the lawn, just a short walk away from the place Sarah and Mark had promised to love each other forever.

Trey held both her hands and looked down into her eyes.

"Bethany, I love you."

"I love you too…" she started, but Trey shook his head.

"Let me get this out. It's important." Trey cleared his throat. "I love you. We got off to such a rocky start, but I know I want to spend the rest of my life with you."

"Oh, Trey," she said, her voice trembling a little. "I feel the same way."

"I don't deserve you yet. But I swear to you, I want to. And I will. When I'm better, when I've given you some time to see that I truly am devoted to you, that I can come close to being what you need, I will drop to one knee and propose."

She cupped his cheek, smiling brightly up at him.

"I can't wait," she whispered.

"Neither can I," he admitted, and then he swept her into his arms.

No matter who he was, she belonged to him, and he belonged to her. They belonged together. And they always would.

Forever.

Acknowledgments

Writing a book sometimes feels like a solitary endeavor, but if it was up to me alone? It would never get done. So, these are the people that spur me on, give me encouragement, and otherwise force me to write the darn book!

My husband, Scotty. My big sister, Heather. Mom, Dad. My brother Jason. My besties, Stephanie and Denise. My incredible agent Nicole. And lastly, the best editor in the universe, Mary. This team is how I am ever able to do anything, and I'm so grateful to you all.

About the Author

Regina Cole, writer, wife, mom of twins, potter, cook, and professional procrastinator, loves sharing make-believe with readers. She's an unapologetic romantic and Korean drama addict, and is proud to bait her own hooks and take her own fish off the line, thank you very much. Her greatest ambition is to make a vase that her kids could hide in. Powered by mini-marshmallows, she and her wonderful family live in eastern North Carolina. Find her online at reginacole.net.

If you liked *To Have and to Harley*,
then be sure to read on for a look at
Bad Reputation by Stefanie London!

To: Wes Evans
From: Sadie Marshall
Subject: You're famous…well, part of you is

Wes,

I'm sure you're not enough of a douchebag to have a Google Alert set up for your own name (or if you are, no judgment. Okay…a little judgment), so you may not have seen this. But your junk is famous! No, that's not a typo.

I'm not the kind of woman to have a one-night stand, but after I saw a picture of him on holiday in Bora Bora with that Victoria's Secret model, Nadja Vasiliev, I HAD to know if it was real. And I can tell you, ladies, that bulge is not a product of Photoshop.

Let's just say that most guys are garden snakes. If you're lucky, you might get a king snake. But Wes is an anaconda…and he knows how to use it.

Oh. My. God.

I don't even know what to say. There's this app that allows New York women to rate men they've dated or something crazy like that. I was checking it out for a friend *cough-it-was-totally-me-cough* and I found you on there. Your reviews were enlightening, my friend. Maybe I should rescind my previous request that we never get in each other's pants. Because apparently, you've been hiding a predator in there.

Here's the link: badbachelors.com/reviews/
Wes-Evans/

Happy reading.
Sadie out.

Chapter 1

"Does size really matter? I think you know the answer to that."

—NoPicklesPlease

SOMETHING WASN'T RIGHT. EITHER IT WAS TOO LONG OR too…thick. Remi Drysdale tilted her head and stared. "I don't think it's going to fit."

"They all say that." The man in front of her flashed a brilliant smile, which was enhanced by yesterday's five o'clock shadow. Remi rolled her eyes. She was used to cocky guys talking a big game. But if online dating had taught her anything, it was that men grossly overestimated themselves.

Noting her unimpressed expression, he added, "It'll fit. Trust me."

"I don't know about that." She leaned forward, narrowing her eyes. "I'm assuming you've done this before."

His smile slipped. "Of *course* I've done this before."

Suddenly he didn't look so confident. Remi stepped forward and touched his arm, using her sweetest smile to keep him from leaving the job unfinished. "We don't want to damage anything. Just…go easy. Slow and steady, all right?"

"You wait and see. It'll slide right in and fit like a glove."

"If you say so."

She stepped back as the man and his partner carried the long piece of wood across the barre studio and set it in the glossy, black brackets they'd installed moments before. The barre fit...barely. The rounded edge was a hairbreadth from the wall, and her boss had insisted that the studio's fresh paint job remain scratch-free.

"See." He winked. "Told you."

"You were cutting it close." She inspected the barre, running her hand along the smoothly polished surface. "But I stand corrected."

"We'll bring the other one in along with the portable units," he said. "Then I'll need someone to sign. If your boss isn't here, it'll have to be you. I've got another delivery to make right after this."

Remi nodded. "I'll call her again."

She waited for the men to leave before her lips split into a wide grin. She punctuated her excitement with a pirouette, the rubber soles of her Converse sneakers squeaking against the polished floor.

The studio was *perfect*. Formerly an accounting office, it had been so run-down it could have been used for the set of a zombie apocalypse movie. But Remi's boss, Mish, had replaced the windows and flooring, painted the walls, and installed floor-to-ceiling mirrors on two sides—behind the barre and along the front of the room, where the instructors would stand. The mirrors made the room look enormous and gave the space a bright, airy feel.

Best of all, this new studio was a scant ten-minute walk from Remi's Park Slope apartment, which would mean no more getting up at the butt crack of dawn to haul ass to the Upper East Side.

Remi pulled her phone out of her bag and swiped her thumb across the screen. She was about to hit the Call button when Mish burst into the studio.

"Sorry, sorry, sorry!"

Remi laughed. "I know you're Canadian, but three sorrys seems a bit much. Even for you."

"Shut it, Aussie." Mish pulled a hair tie off her wrist and attempted to tame her mane of wild, blond frizz into a ponytail. "This looks amazing."

"It really does. The guys are bringing in the second barre now, and then they've got the portable ones too. Where were you thinking of putting those?"

"Probably in the storage room. I don't know how full the classes are going to be until we open, so we may not need them until business picks up."

Mish had opened Allongé Barre Fitness with a single tiny studio on the Upper East Side. When Remi started working there four years ago, she'd only taught two classes per week. But over the years she and Mish had grown close and Remi's schedule had expanded. Now Mish was about to open her third studio—the first in Brooklyn—and Remi was going to be the main instructor.

A quiet voice niggled in the back of her mind like a tiny pinprick in her skull. Not big enough to cause any real pain, but she felt it nonetheless.

This isn't what you're supposed to be doing...

Shoving the feeling aside, Remi wrapped her arms around Mish and squeezed. "I can't believe you're opening studio number three. I'm *so* proud of you."

"I couldn't do it without you," she said. "Seriously. Owning a small business is tough, and I feel so much more confident knowing you have my back."

"Always. This is going to be a huge success, I know it."

The men returned with the second barre and installed it a foot below the first one. Remi could already see her little students in here—the parents and kids' classes were her favorite. She loved the wide-eyed wonder of children learning something new, the way they tackled things without the fear of embarrassment or failure that inhibited her older students.

Sure, this wasn't *real* ballet. Perhaps that was why it suited her.

"We're going to set up the rack for the hand weights here." Mish pointed to the back corner of the studio. "And the yoga mats can be rolled up and put into containers. They get too messy when they're stacked in a pile."

"Agreed."

Mish walked over to the deliverymen and apologized for being late. She directed them out to the studio's reception area, leaving Remi alone.

This place was exactly what she'd yearned for as a young girl—a bright space with a long barre. A room rife with possibility. The floor waiting for the strike of her *frappé*, the graceful *whoosh* of her toes as they left the floor in a *grand battement*. The soundless landing of a perfect *pas de chat*. And the mirror was there to watch it all. To soak in her excitement and creativity and the little thrill she got whenever the wind rushed through her ponytail, fluttering the ribbon holding it in place, as she turned and turned and turned.

"Remi?"

She jumped at the sound of Mish's voice, startled by the sudden intrusion on her thoughts. "All done?"

"Yes." Mish shot her a rueful smile. "Thanks so much for coming here last minute to meet the delivery guys. You totally saved me."

"No worries." Remi hitched her bag higher up on her shoulder. "Hopefully the kitten doesn't have any more stomach troubles."

"Who knows? That's what I get for taking in strays, eh?" She shook her head. "We've got an appointment with the vet later today to get him checked out."

"You've got a good heart."

"And a deep disrespect for my carpet."

Remi laughed and checked her watch. "I've got to run. I promised Darcy I'd meet her for coffee this afternoon, and I want to walk, seeing as it's so lovely out."

"Go." Mish made a shooing motion. "I'll call you tomorrow so we can review the timetable."

Remi waved as she headed out of the studio. It was a perfect early fall day—sunny and pleasant but with a hint of crispness to the air—cool enough for a jacket if you felt so inclined. After a long, sticky summer, Remi craved this kind of weather. Not to mention fall was beautiful in New York—all those golden-amber and rich-red tones. They hardly got any of that back in Australia. Too many native evergreens.

"Speaking of home," she muttered to herself as she turned onto Flatbush Avenue. She was due to Skype with her parents soon.

They would be arriving back from their "retreat" any day now. For most couples their age a relaxing getaway probably included a cruise or a resort. Even touristy holidays seeing the sights of another country At the very least, there'd be a caravan trip of some kind—or, what the heck did they call them here? Winnebagos? Motor homes?

Anyhow, her parents weren't like most couples their age. No siree.

For Opal and Dan Drysdale, a vacation was not complete without some kind of enlightenment. In this case, it was a tantric couple's retreat in Nimben, a.k.a. the hippie capital of Australia.

Her parents were taking sex workshops.

Remi cringed. Undoubtedly, her mother would want to tell her all about it too. And, as usual, she'd have to listen to Opal complaining that Remi had turned into one of those "conservative, middle-class prudes" who got all squeamish about sex. Remi *wasn't* squeamish about sex. Not even a little bit. She happened to quite enjoy the occasional roll in the hay with a hot guy. In fact, she'd *very* much enjoyed her sexy weekend with the hottie from Texas who had asked her to strut around his hotel room wearing only a pair of pink-rhinestone-studded cowgirl boots. No, she was definitely *not* a prude.

But she didn't want to hear about her parents doing it. Ever.

Remi pulled out her phone and set a reminder to check in with her folks that weekend. They might be New Age–this and grass fed–that, but Opal and Dan still expected to talk to her once a month. *That* was where they clung to tradition.

Half an hour later, Remi turned onto Schermerhorn Street. For some reason, every time she headed to Darcy's new place in DUMBO, she'd take this detour.

The street itself wasn't particularly interesting. At this time of year, it was clogged with the "prewinter" construction rush, which meant walking under scaffolding and dodging traffic cones.

But there was one thing that always drew her down this street.

"Excuse me." A small woman with inky hair pulled into a tight bun gracefully stepped around Remi. She wore a pair of black leggings that ended at the bottom of her calf, exposing a few inches of pink tights above the top of her high-top sneakers.

She was one of a dozen people streaming in and out of the Brooklyn Ballet building. Mostly women, but a few young men as well. All with that strong yet willowy figure ballet dancers were known for.

Their movements were fluid, making everything seem perfectly choreographed, from the gentle wrist flick of a wave to how they darted across the street between traffic. Even something as simple as bending down to tie a shoelace embodied an otherworldly grace.

After she'd soaked it in, Remi hurried down the street, sliding her headphones over her ears to drown out the city.

Wes Evans was used to women checking him out. He exercised often and presented well, always living by his father's advice that he should dress like he was about to meet someone important. In New York City, a meeting like that could take place anywhere—riding in an elevator, sitting in the back of a cab, or lining up to order a coffee.

After a stint as a guest judge on *Dance Idol*, his face

had garnered even more attention. Fans of the show wanted to gush over their front-runner picks, and wannabe performers tried to make an impression in the hopes he might remember them the next time he held an audition.

But this…this was different.

"What can I get you?" The barista devoured him with her eyes, the smooth dart of her tongue leaving behind a glossy sheen on her pink lips.

"Cold brew." He pulled his wallet out of the back pocket of his jeans. "Black."

She tilted her head slightly. Behind a set of thick-framed glasses, her gaze roamed down his body, lingering south of his belt. "Size?"

"Grande."

She reached for a clear plastic cup, sticking the cap of her Sharpie into her mouth and pulling the pen out with a pop. Another barista passed behind her, also checking him out. "I heard he was more of a Venti," she said in a not-so-quiet whisper.

The first barista mushed her full lips together as though trying not to laugh while she marked the cup. "It's Wes, right?"

"Yeah."

He wanted to ask how she knew his name, but frankly, he wasn't about to subject himself to more assessment. He felt like a piece of steak being wheeled around on a cart at one of those fancy restaurants, just waiting for people to comment on his shape and size.

"Can I get you anything else?" she asked.

"No thanks." He handed over a ten-dollar bill and walked away before she had time to count his change.

He was ready to be done with today. And the quicker he got his caffeine fix, the better. Perhaps he should have chosen a place a little less public for this meeting. But when Sadie, his best friend and now business associate, had forwarded him the email about the Bad Bachelors website earlier that morning, he hadn't taken it too seriously. The second he'd stepped out of his Upper East Side apartment though, he'd realized that Sadie wasn't the only one using this tabloid cesspool of a website.

The barista placed his cold brew on the counter and winked at him. She'd written her phone number on his cup.

"Wes!" Sadie waved at him from a table in the back corner of the café. Her hair was cropped close on one side and left longer on the other, the blue and purple strands curving down around her jaw. "Or should I say, Mr. Anaconda?"

"Don't start," he said, dropping into the seat across from her. "I'm beginning to wonder if the human race suddenly developed X-ray vision with the way everyone is looking at me."

"I doubt they need it. Someone did a digital recreation over that picture of you and...what was her name? The Russian chick. Natasha? Natalia?"

"Nadja."

"That's it." Sadie snapped her fingers. "Anyway, it's floating around online. They Photoshopped it to show what was going on underneath your board shorts, and I have to say—"

"You *really* don't."

Sadie grinned and waded her straw through a mound

of whipped cream sitting on top of some caramel-mocha monstrosity. "You've been keeping things from me."

"I thought we had an agreement."

Wes and Sadie had been friends as long as anyone could remember. They'd grown up as neighbors in one of the most exclusive apartment buildings in Manhattan, traded lunches on the playground, and, after a disaster of a kiss around the time they were eighteen, had promptly agreed that they would always and forever be friends. Nothing more.

"We do. But that was *before* I knew you were packing more than the average salami." She couldn't keep a straight face and burst out laughing. "Ew. No, I can't even joke about it without feeling dirty."

"Gee, thanks."

"Nothing personal. Besides, you're going to have every other woman in this goddamn city chasing after you now. You don't need my attention too."

"Excellent." He clapped his hands. "Can we cut the locker room bullshit and get back to work, then?"

"No need to get snippy." Sadie looked too damn smug for her own good.

Wes opened the spreadsheet that had their production budget outlined to the very last detail, with a total that would make most people's eyes pop. Broadway productions were expensive. Even those classified as "Off-Off-Broadway," which were held in small theaters that seated fewer than a hundred people, cost a pretty penny. In this case, many of those involved were taking part for next to nothing, hoping the show would break out. But the theater still needed to be paid for, costumes needed to be created, and sets needed to be designed.

All of which required deep pockets.

"I got a final figure from the Attic," Wes said. "It's more than we budgeted for, but we can manage it. I'll push the investors harder, and I have wiggle room with my own funds."

"You're already pouring so much of your own money into this." Sadie frowned.

She didn't often show her stress, but Wes knew her too well not to detect the hint of concern in her voice. It wasn't exactly unwarranted. He *was* putting everything into this crazy idea.

Out of Bounds was his brainchild, a dance production with no separation between stage and seating. The cast was part of the audience and the audience part of the show. It was the antithesis of the world he'd grown up in, one fortified with rules and posture and tradition. With his big-picture view and Sadie's talent for turning his vague descriptions into something living and breathing, he *knew* they had something special. All they had to do was back themselves long enough to give the rest of New York a chance to agree.

"I can manage a bit more," he said. "I want this to work."

Sadie bit her lip and nodded. "I do too, but I'm worried you'll get cleaned out if this fails."

"It won't fail."

Even as he said the words, the stats danced in his head. Successful Broadway productions were in the minority, with less than 25 percent turning a profit. And those were the ones with big advertising budgets. Breakouts like *Hamilton* were rare, and most productions ended up in a financial graveyard littered with the bones of failed dreams.

Fact was, the numbers were against them. They were more likely to crash and burn and end up with bank accounts drier than the Sahara.

"Besides," he added, "I have the city's best choreographer working for me."

Sadie snorted. "Flattery won't get you anywhere, Wes. But I hope you're right. I burned a hell of a bridge leaving your parents' company to do this with you."

"You and me both," he muttered.

Out of Bounds was either going to make or break his future, and Wes wasn't the kind of guy who backed down from a challenge.

"Now all we need to do is secure the funding and find our perfect ballerina," he said with a grin. "No sweat at all."

BAD BACHELOR

First in the Bad Bachelors series
from *USA Today* bestseller Stefanie London

If one more person mentions Bad Bachelors to Reed McMahon, someone's gonna get hurt. Reed is known as an "image fixer," but his womanizing ways have caught up with him. What he needs is a PR miracle of his own.

When Reed strolls into Darcy Greer's workplace offering to help save the struggling library, she isn't buying it. But as she reluctantly works with Reed, she realizes there's more to a man than his reputation. Maybe, just maybe Bad Bachelor #1 is THE one for her.

"Sizzling, sexy, and so much fun!"

—Sarah Morgan, *USA Today* bestselling author of *Moonlight Over Manhattan*

For more Stefanie London, visit:
sourcebooks.com